D1012840

Moon Burning

"If you like medieval historicals and paranormals, then you can't go wrong with this series."
—*The Book Reading Gals*

"Should not be missed." —*Romance Reviews Today*

"A sizzling story . . . Fast-paced and intriguing."
—*Joyfully Reviewed*

"*Moon Burning* doesn't disappoint. Ms. Monroe is an incredible author." —*TwoLips Reviews*

Moon Craving

"[A] sexy, stay-up-all-night read." —*RT Book Reviews*

"A book that will grab you right from the beginning."
—*Romance Reviews Today*

"Ms. Monroe captivates the readers with her spine-tingling explosive action and highly intense, sensual love story."
—*Fallen Angel Reviews*

"Impossible to put down." —*Rites of Romance*

"A passionate and wonderful book. Don't miss it."
—*Joyfully Reviewed*

Moon Awakening

"Simply awesome . . . Stunningly sexy and emotionally riveting . . . Easily one of the best paranormals I've ever read!" —*Joyfully Reviewed*

"A sensual, humorous story with intriguing and entrancing characters . . . Outstanding . . . I'm looking forward to future stories."   —*Fresh Fiction*

PRAISE FOR LUCY MONROE AND HER NOVELS

"Lucy Monroe is one of my favorite indulgences."
        —Christine Feehan, #1 *New York Times* bestselling author

"A Lucy Monroe book is a treat not to be missed."
        —Lora Leigh, #1 *New York Times* bestselling author

"[A] wicked and wonderful temptation . . . Give yourself a treat and read this book. Lucy Monroe will capture your heart."   —Susan Wiggs, *New York Times* bestselling author

"Lucy Monroe's romances sizzle!"
        —JoAnn Ross, *New York Times* bestselling author

"If you enjoy Linda Howard, Diana Palmer and Elizabeth Lowell, then I think you'd really love Lucy's work."
        —Lori Foster, *New York Times* bestselling author

"Monroe brings a fresh voice to historical romance."
        —Stef Ann Holm, national bestselling author

"A fresh new voice in romance."   —Debbie Macomber

"An intense, compelling read from page one to the very end. With her powerful voice and vision, Lucy packs emotion into every scene."   —Jane Porter, bestselling author

"Lucy has written a wonderful, full-blooded hero and a beautiful, warm heroine."
        —Maggie Cox, *USA Today* bestselling author

"A charming tale . . . The delightful characters jump off the page!"   —Theresa Scott, bestselling author

Warrior's Moon

A CHILDREN OF THE MOON NOVEL

Lucy Monroe

BERKLEY SENSATION, NEW YORK

THE BERKLEY PUBLISHING GROUP
Published by the Penguin Group
Penguin Group (USA) Inc.
375 Hudson Street, New York, New York 10014, USA

USA I Canada I UK I Ireland I Australia I New Zealand I India I South Africa I China

Penguin Books Ltd., Registered Offices: 80 Strand, London WC2R 0RL, England
For more information about the Penguin Group, visit penguin.com.

WARRIOR'S MOON

A Berkley Sensation Book / published by arrangement with the author

Berkley Sensation Books are published by The Berkley Publishing Group.
BERKLEY SENSATION® is a registered trademark of Penguin Group (USA) Inc.
The "B" design is a trademark of Penguin Group (USA) Inc.

For information, address: The Berkley Publishing Group,
a division of Penguin Group (USA) Inc.,
375 Hudson Street, New York, New York 10014.

ISBN: 978-0-425-25442-4

PUBLISHING HISTORY
Berkley Sensation mass-market paperback edition / July 2013

PRINTED IN THE UNITED STATES OF AMERICA

10 9 8 7 6 5 4 3 2 1

Cover art by Gregg Gullbronson.
Cover design by George Long.
Interior text design by Laura K. Corless.

ALWAYS LEARNING   PEARSON

For Patty and Curtis, dear friends and family by marriage. Curtis, your music has helped me write hundreds of pages, and Patty, your appreciation for my stories and characters always touches my heart. Much love to you both.

THE BEGINNING

Millennia ago, God created a race of people so fierce even their women were feared in battle. These people were warlike in every way, refusing to submit to the rule of any but their own . . . no matter how large the forces sent to subdue them.

Their enemies said they fought like animals. Their vanquished foe said nothing, for they were dead.

They were considered a primitive and barbaric people because they marred their skin with tattoos of blue ink. The designs were simple: a beast depicted in unadorned outline over their hearts. The leaders were marked with more elaborate bands around their arms. Mates were marked to show their bond.

And still, their enemies were never able to discover the meanings of any of the blue-tinted tattoos.

Some surmised they were symbols of the tribe's warlike nature and in that they would be partially right. For the beasts represented a part of themselves these fierce and independent people kept secret at the pain of death. It was a secret they had kept for the centuries of their existence while most migrated across the European landscape to settle in the inhospitable north of Scotland.

Their Roman enemies called them Picts, a name accepted by the other peoples of their land and lands south . . . they called themselves the Chrechte.

Their animal-like affinity for fighting and conquest came from a part of their nature their fully human counterparts did not enjoy. For these fierce people were shape-changers.

The bluish tattoos on their skin were markings given as a right of passage when they made their first shift. Some men had control of that change. Some did not, subject to the power of the full moon until participating in the sacred act of sex. The females of all the races both experienced their first shift into animal form and gained control thereafter with the coming of their first menses.

Some shifted into wolves, others big cats of prey and yet others into the larger birds—the eagle, hawk or raven.

The one thing all Chrechte shared in common was that they did not reproduce as quickly or prolifically as their fully human brothers and sisters. Although they were a formidable race and their cunning enhanced by an understanding of nature most humans could not possess, they were not foolhardy and were not ruled by their animal natures.

One warrior could kill a hundred of his foe, but should she or he die before having offspring, the death would lead to an inevitable shrinking of the race. Some Pictish clans and those recognized by other names in other parts of the world had already died out rather than submit to what they considered the inferior but multitudinous humans around them.

The Faol of Scotland's Highlands were too smart to face the end of their race rather than blend. These wolf shifters saw the way of the future. In the ninth century AD, Keneth MacAlpin ascended to the Scottish throne. He was of Faol descent through his mother; nevertheless, his human nature had dominated.

He was not capable of "the change," but that did not stop him from laying claim to the Pictish throne (as it was called then) as well. In order to guarantee his kingship, he betrayed his Faol brethren at a dinner, killing all of the remaining royals of their people—and forever entrenched a distrust of humans by their Chrechte counterparts.

Despite this distrust but bitterly aware of the cost of MacAlpin's betrayal, the Faol of the Chrechte realized that they could die out fighting an ever increasing and encroaching race of humanity, or they could join the Celtic clans.

They joined.

As far as the rest of the world knew, what had been considered the Pictish people was no more.

Because it was not in their nature to be ruled by any but their own, within two generations, the Celtic clans that had assimilated the Chrechte were ruled by shape-changing clan chiefs who shared their natures with wolves. Though most of the fully human among them did not know it, a sparse few were trusted with the secrets of their kinsmen. Those that did, were aware that to betray the code of silence meant certain and immediate death.

Stories of other shifter races, the Éan and Paindeal, were told around the campfire, or to the little ones before bed. Since the wolves had not seen a shifter except their own in generations, however, they began to believe the other races only a myth.

But myths did not take to the sky on black wings glinting an iridescent blue under the sun. Myths did not live as ghosts in the forest, but breathing air just as any other man or animal. The Éan were no myth, they were birds with abilities beyond that of merely changing their shape.

Many could be forgiven for believing tales of their prince nothing more than legend. For who had heard of a man shifting not only into the form of a raven, but that of the mystic dragon from ancient tales as well?

If the dragon were real, then were the *conriocht* as well? Those whispered about Faol that had defended the race in ancient times, able to shift not only into a wolf, but the fearsome beast: the werewolf.

Chapter 1

To abandon one's sacred mate is to abandon one's very
soul.

—CHRECHTE SACRED LAW, FROM THE ORAL TRADITIONS

Sinclair Holding, Highlands of Scotland
1150 AD, Reign of Dabid mac Mail Choluim, King of Scots

"Mummy, they're giants!"

It wasn't her son's excited shout that sent a shard of pain
spiking through Shona's head, but the sight of soldiers
wearing the Sinclair colors approaching at speed on horses
every bit as oversized as they were.

And not a one of them was smiling in welcome, either.

The headache had arrived with the large brown wolf,
which had paced them for the better part of the morning.
Only, the pounding in her head hadn't left when the
beast did.

Terrified the animal would attack, she'd ridden tense in
her saddle with a dagger to the ready. It had maintained its
distance, however, finally running off just before the noon
sun cast its shadow.

Her mind and senses already stretched to the point of
exhaustion with what had come before this journey, the

appearance of the wolf had pushed Shona that much nearer collapse.

But she would not give up. Her children's lives and those of two loyal friends depended on Shona maintaining both sanity and composure.

So, she had taken her daughter back onto her horse from where little Marjory had taken turns riding with Shona's companions, Audrey and her twin brother, Thomas. And then Shona had continued on as if the wolf had not scared her out of her wits.

Shona had hoped her luck would hold, as it had miraculously for nearly two sennights of their mad dash north, but it was not to be.

They'd reached Sinclair land late the night before, managing somehow to both evade anyone her stepson may have sent after them and avoid the inhabitants of the clan territories she and her small band had passed through.

Until now.

She had no trouble understanding how her five-year-old son had mistaken the approaching soldiers for giants. Like some of the men from her former clan, these Highlanders would easily stand a head taller, and half again as wide, as any knight who had sworn allegiance to her dead husband.

Considering the horror she'd run from, Shona could wish that these imposing men were of the clan she'd come north to seek refuge with. They were more than capable of protecting her small band, but she had no friends or family among the Sinclairs.

And they weren't likely to take kindly to what they would perceive as an Englishwoman trespassing without leave on their land. She could but hope the laird would approve safe passage through his lands, if only to get rid of her and her companions.

She *had* to make her way to Balmoral Island.

It was the only chance they had at safety, her one hope to preserve her son's life and her own virtue. Or what was left of it.

There, at least, she had family. Though the relation was somewhat distant and she'd no doubts her arrival would come as something of a shock. She could but pray it was not a wholly unwelcome one.

"They're not giants, sweeting, merely warriors of the clan that makes these lands their home." Shona tried to infuse confidence in her tone, while her own mind raced with warnings and worries.

"Really?" Eadan asked, eyes the same gentian blue of his father's filled with awe.

"These are Highland warriors?" Audrey asked before Shona had the chance to affirm her assertion to her son. "They're huge."

"'Tis the way of the Highlands, I suppose." And among the clans that bordered the Highlands as well, like the one in which she'd grown up.

Audrey gave her twin brother a sideways look. "Perhaps you've got more growing to do, but I don't think you'll reach their stature, even so."

Thomas looked chagrined. "You don't know that."

Shona couldn't imagine why they were speculating at all. Thomas was English, just like his sister, children of a lesser baron whose holding bordered her dead husband's on the west and lay only a few miles from land claimed by Scotland's king.

Audrey and Thomas no longer had a home to return to—not since their eldest brother had taken over the barony.

Shona's sleeping daughter stirred in her arms. "Mama, is there giants?"

At three, Marjory was as different as night from day from her five-year-old brother. Petite like Shona, with matching green eyes and red curls, she was quiet-spoken (which was not so much like her mother at all).

Marjory adored the older brother who was big for his age and confident to the point of brashness. So like his father it made Shona's heart ache, though she'd never let them see it.

"They're the laird's guards come to greet us," she claimed, her voice maintaining a shocking steadiness despite the blatant lie.

One look from her two adult companions left her in no doubt they weren't fooled by her words. But neither of her children were frightened and that was what mattered.

Shona simply had to believe that the Sinclair was a better man than some that had been in her life. His reputation as a fierce but fair leader even as far south as England had led to her choice to travel on his lands instead of taking a more circuitous route to her final destination.

They rode for another ten minutes before meeting up with the Sinclair warriors.

Shona halted her horse and the rest of her party followed suit.

"Who are you and what are you doing on our land?" Though the big warrior's words were abrupt and his demeanor nothing less than fierce, Shona felt no fear.

Something about the man speaking made her think he would not hurt them. Perhaps it was the flash of concern in his eyes when he looked at her children. The Sinclair soldier would have been devastatingly handsome but for the garish scar on his cheek, but Shona felt no draw to him.

She had only ever wanted one man in her life, despite having been married to another. And that had not changed. Nor did she believe it ever would. She did not lament her lack of interest in the opposite sex, however.

They could not be trusted and she was better off keeping what was left of her heart for her children and her children alone.

"I am Shona, Lady Heronshire, seeking safe passage through your laird's lands to visit my family on Balmoral Island." The words were formal, but she spoke them in flawless Gaelic . . . her native tongue.

"Did you get that scar in a fight?" Eadan asked in Gaelic before the warrior had an opportunity to reply to Shona's words.

Audrey gasped, but Shona just sighed. Her son had no cork for the things that came out of his mouth.

The fierce warrior's attention moved to her five-year-old and he studied Eadan closely for several long moments, Shona growing increasingly nervous with each passing one. Why such an interest in her son?

Surprise flared briefly in his gray gaze before it narrowed in inexplicable speculation. "I did. Do you ride as protector of your mother?"

Shona didn't understand the man's reaction to her son, unless it was to the fact that such a small *English* child spoke Gaelic so well. She'd spoken to both her children in her native tongue since their births and they each communicated equally well in Gaelic and English.

Just as she did.

Her son mayhap even better than she did. His grasp of English exceeded her own, despite her years living in that country.

Eadan puffed up his little boy chest and did his best to frown like the warriors in front of them. "I do."

"You sound like a Scot, lad, but you dress like a Sassenach."

"What's a sassy patch?" Marjory whispered from her perch in Shona's lap.

"An Englishman," the big warrior answered, with a barely there smile for her daughter's interesting pronunciation of the word, proving he'd heard the quietly uttered question.

"Oh." Pop, Marjory's thumb went into her mouth. It was a habit Shona and Audrey had worked hard to break her of, but the little girl still sucked her thumb when she was overly tired or nervous.

After two weeks of grueling travel and coming upon men who looked more like giants than soldiers, the tot was no doubt both. Shona sighed again.

This brought the big man's attention back to her. "I am Niall, second-in-command to the Sinclair laird. My men and I will accompany you to the keep."

"Thank you." What Shona really wanted to say was *thank you but no*.

She'd rather head directly for the island. She was tired of traveling and she wasn't going to feel safe until she'd gotten the Balmoral laird's promise of protection for her and her small band.

To refuse the hospitality of the other laird, however, would not only be considered rude, but she'd no doubt they would end up traveling to the keep no matter what she might say on the matter.

She'd learned long ago that some things were beyond her control.

The keep was a fortress, far superior to that of the MacLeod holding where she'd grown up and even more formidable than that of her deceased husband. The high wall surrounding the laird's home and guard towers was stone, though the buildings within were crafted mostly from wood.

The keep itself was on top of a motte, the manmade hill only accessible by a narrow path she just knew Niall was going to tell her they could not take their horses on. Even from this distance, the keep looked big enough to easily accommodate fifty or more in the great hall. The imposing nature of the holding made her wish her family was of the Sinclair clan. She could do naught but hope the Balmorals lived equally as secure.

The bailey was busy with warriors and clanspeople alike, many of whom seemed interested in the new arrivals. And slightly suspicious, if the frowns she and her companion were receiving were anything to go by, but the overt hostility she might have expected toward those garbed as the English was surprisingly absent.

Niall stopped his horse, and the warriors with him followed suit. Shona guided her tired mare to a halt, so fatigued herself she was not absolutely sure she would make it off the horse without sending both herself and Marjory tumbling.

"Should we dismount then?" Audrey asked, her tone showing no more enthusiasm for the prospect than Shona felt.

Shona opened her mouth to answer, only to lose any hope she had of speaking as her gaze fell upon a warrior standing near the open area in front of the blacksmith's. The man, who was easily as tall and as broad as Niall, wore her former clan's colors with no shirt beneath the MacLeod plaid to give him any hint of civility.

His back to them, his lack of interest in the English strangers was more than obvious.

But she could not claim the same apathy.

Not when every inch of his arrogant stance was as familiar to her as the mane on her mare's head after a sennight spent in the saddle.

His black hair was a little longer than it had been six years ago, the blue tattoos covering his left shoulder and arm were a new addition, and his muscles bulged more, but she had absolutely no doubt about the identity of the MacLeod soldier standing so confidently among the Sinclairs.

Caelis. Her beloved. *Her betrayer.*

Even the sound of his name in her own thinking made her heart beat faster and her hands tighten into fists.

Deceiver, screamed that voice in her mind that had never gone fully silent though she'd been forced to marry another man. *Mine*, cried the heart that had learned that neither love nor a lover could be trusted at this man's feet.

She'd given him her love and her innocence.

He had repaid those gifts with false promises and, ultimately, repudiation.

She'd thought never to see him again, been certain that even her return to Scotland would not cause their paths to cross.

After all, she hadn't gone home to her former clan and she'd been careful to avoid their lands in the journey northward. She'd no desire to come in contact with her former laird and even less her former swain.

How cruel of fate to dictate differently. To ensure that despite the habit her former clansmen had of keeping strictly to themselves, this man would be in this place the one day she would ever spend in the Sinclair keep.

The head of Shona's mare jerked against her tightened hold on the reins and she felt gratitude that they were no longer moving. Holding the reins like that was one guaranteed way to get tossed from even a loyal horse's back.

Marjory slept on, oblivious to the near-miss, their new surroundings and to the cataclysm happening inside her mother.

As if Caelis could feel the weight of Shona's regard, he turned. Slowly and with no evidence of curiosity, his gentian gaze slid over her, his expression dismissive as he took in her English clothing.

She could tell the moment he recognized her, though, the very second he realized she was not just an Englishwoman, but a woman from his past.

He went rigid, his eyes widening with a shock so complete it would have been amusing if she were not so devastated at his appearance in her already turbulent life.

He went as if to take a step and stumbled.

How odd. He was a sure-footed man. Perhaps one of the other warriors had tripped him? Men played games with each other like that.

Even as the nonsensical thoughts floated through her mind, fear screamed through her body. Caelis could not see Eadan. Her son could never know the man who had denied his very existence and rejected the woman he had professed to love.

They needed to leave. *Now. The laird of the Sinclairs would simply have to do without the pleasure of making their acquaintance.*

That thought alone gave her the strength to break her gaze from Caelis as she jerked her head around, searching frantically for Eadan.

He was already on the ground, his hand held in Niall's

giant paw, a smaller man standing quite near to the huge warrior, talking to them both with an engaging smile.

Shona wanted to scream at them to *please* put her son back on his horse and then get out of her way. But no words left her lips. She could neither move, nor speak, her panic freezing her as stiff as death.

Even as the need to escape continued to tear through her, she knew it to be hopeless.

Even if she could make herself move, to cry out for Niall's assistance in getting her son back on his horse, she and her companions would not be allowed to leave the Sinclair holding without seeing the laird. It had already been decided.

And as had happened too often in her past, Shona knew she was subject to the whims of men who held authority over her. This time, it was only by her trespass on his land, but that would not matter to the Sinclair laird.

He was a man with power.

He would demand to be obeyed.

'Twas the way of things.

Hopelessness washed over Shona near to drowning her.

The boy was out of Caelis's line of sight, but that gave Shona little comfort.

The warrior was bound to see her child soon and when he did? He would know the truth, no matter how much he might like to deny it.

But what he would do with that truth, she could not guess at. Nothing good for her. She'd discovered in the past six years that men rarely made choices to benefit women.

But most particularly her.

Caelis had only been the first man in a long list in her life to exhibit this truth.

"*Shona . . .*"

She looked down and saw that both Audrey and Thomas were there, standing beside Shona's mare. Audrey's hands were upraised to take Marjory so Shona could dismount.

When had they gotten off their horses?

"Are you all right?" Thomas asked, his tone clearly worried. Both he and Audrey wore matching expressions of concern. "We've said your name *three* times."

"I . . . no . . ." she answered with honesty before she thought to control her tongue.

"What is it?" Suddenly Niall was there, having moved very quickly. "Lady Heronshire, do you need help dismounting?"

He reached up as well. "Give me the babe."

Dropping the horse's reins, Shona wrapped her arms around her daughter in a reflexive move of protection.

"Do not touch her." The snarl came from behind Niall and then Caelis was there, shoving the other warrior away from Shona's horse.

Niall spun on the other man, knocking him back and shouting. "The hell!"

"She's mine," Caelis growled, his voice so animal-like the words were barely discernible.

"Calm yourself," Niall snapped, sounding less angry for some reason, though he didn't back away. "The Englishwoman—"

"She is *not* English."

"Do ye see how she is dressed? She is a lady, Caelis. Stop and think."

But Caelis appeared beyond reason, his aggression not lessening one iota. And Shona did not understand it. In no scenario of this moment she might ever have imagined would she have considered him laying claim to her . . . or was it her daughter?

None of this made any sense.

Marjory chose that moment to awaken, squirming to sit up. "Mama! Want down."

Caelis jerked as if pierced by an arrow, his gaze landing on the little girl in Shona's arms. Some great emotion twisted his features, and then his blue eyes, so like their son's, locked with hers, the accusation in them unmistakable.

She stared back, defiant, furious like she had not been since the night he told her it was over.

All the fear she'd felt over the past months, the anger she'd experienced at the perfidy of men since his betrayal six years ago, followed by treachery of others—her own dear father included—bolstered that fury so that if it were possible, she would have burned him to ash with her gaze.

His head snapped back, surprise again showing on his handsome features, this time mixed with confusion.

If possible, his surprise made her even more livid. Did he think she had forgotten the way he had used and discarded her? Did he think she would no longer hold it against him?

More the fool him, if so.

She would never forget. She spent each day with a living reminder.

And what Caelis had to be *confused* about she did not know. Did he think that just because he didn't want her that no other man would ever want to wed her?

Arrogant blackguard.

"Mummy?" Eadan's worried voice rose from where he stood beside Niall.

She needed to tell her son all was well, but could not look away from Caelis's face as he got his first look of the son they had made.

The child he had told her would never happen.

She'd been naïve and believed him. She would never make that mistake again.

Chapter 2

A Faol's strength means little in the face of his mate's wrath.

—LACHLAN OF THE BALMORAL

The warrior fainted.

With a great resounding *thud* as his big, over-muscled body hit the dirt.

Caelis had taken one look at their son, his blue eyes widening in recognition that had quickly turned to horror and then he'd sunk to the ground like a stone.

Several people, Sinclairs and Shona's friends alike, made sounds with varying degrees of shock and volume.

Her own heart in her throat, though why she should be concerned for the blackguard she did not know, Shona paid none of them any heed until her son spoke. "Is he dead then, like my lord?"

The fact that her former husband had insisted on the formal address from the boy all but he and Shona considered his son never seemed so absurd and yet appropriate as it did in that moment when Eadan stood staring at the unconscious body of the father who shared his blood.

Niall shook his head and turned away from the other big

soldier, as if a warrior collapsing was of little notice. "Nay, laddie. He's alive, just taking a wee nap."

"On the ground?" Eadan asked, blinking up at Niall uncertainly.

"Aye."

"He fainted," said the smaller man who had been talking to her son and Niall earlier, a certain amount of glee in his tone.

"Like a damsel in the stories Audrey tells us?"

Niall snorted a laugh. "Aye, just like that."

"Audrey?" the redheaded smaller man asked. "Not your mother?"

"Mum doesn't ever tell stories where the damsel faints or needs rescuing. In all her stories, the knights and princesses fight side by side. My lord said they were nonsense, but Marjory and I like them," Eadan said with staunch loyalty.

"As you should," Niall said with a pat to her son's head. "Let Guaire take you and the others to the keep."

"What about Mum?" Eadan gave her a worried frown, hanging back.

She couldn't even dredge a smile of comfort for him, but she did manage to say, "Go with Master Guaire, sweeting," through a very tight throat.

"Here," Niall raised his arms. "Give me the girl."

"My name is Marjory," her daughter decided to inform the giant man.

"Aye, lass, so I heard and a fine name it is. Will you come to me?"

Marjory turned her face into Shona's chest, her shy nature asserting itself.

Thomas stepped forward. "Come, little dumpling, Uncle Thomas will carry you."

Marjory shook her head, not looking away from the cocoon of safety she'd created for herself.

Shona would have laughed if she had it in her to do so. Her daughter's stubborn shyness was all too familiar.

"How will your mama get down from the horse if you don't let go of her?" Audrey wheedled.

But to no avail.

"We'll stay here. It's comfortable," Marjory claimed in a voice muffled by Shona's body.

"Marjory, don't you want to meet the laird?" Thomas asked.

It was exactly the wrong thing to say because Marjory grabbed Shona all the tighter and exclaimed her very clear denial.

Caelis groaned and shifted on the ground. Shockingly, it was that action that caused Marjory to release her tight grip on her mother's waist and turn to see the big man sit up in the dirt.

"You felled down." Marjory's observation was met with a confused nod. "I takes naps, but Eadan doesn't. Big boys don't take naps."

Marjory spoke in a mixture of English and Gaelic, which Shona was used to interpreting. The perplexed look on Caelis's face said he wasn't. She knew he'd learned rudimentary English like she had among their clan, so she wasn't surprised when his confusion eventually cleared.

"I don't normally nap, princess."

"I'm not a princess."

Shona was so shocked by his kindness to her daughter that she gasped.

He flicked a glance at her, but it didn't linger.

"Are you sure? You look like one." Caelis stood, dusting himself off and ignoring the curious stares of the Sinclairs around them. He appeared wholly unaffected by having fainted in front of a bailey full of people.

Six years ago, he would not have been so sanguine about revealing any weakness to others.

"My papa was a baron."

"He isn't one any longer?" Caelis asked.

"He's dead. Brother is baron now, but I don't think he likes Eadan and me."

Out of the mouths of babes.

This time when Caelis looked at Shona, his regard stayed with her. "You are a widow?"

"Yes."

"Good."

"That is hardly a civilized response to learning a woman's husband has died," she remonstrated.

Though she could not claim to feel grief over Henry's demise, the fact that she'd been left alone in the world—*again*—without even the baron's marginal protection, was hardly cause for rejoicing.

"I am not a civilized man."

He would get no argument from her in that regard. There had been a time that the wild side to his nature appealed to her very much. No longer. "Still, I cannot fathom why you should think my present circumstances *good* ones."

She'd thrown off one yoke only to find herself at the risk of falling prey to another, far more onerous one.

Caelis shrugged. "It is good I do not have to kill him."

Shona gasped, unable to fathom him expressing such a sentiment. "You cannot say such things in front of my children."

Regret flared in Caelis's eyes, but his jaw set in stubborn lines she remembered too well for her own comfort. "Please pardon me for speaking so in front of you, princess."

Marjory giggled.

"What about me?" Eadan demanded.

"You are a big boy, five summers are you not?" Caelis asked.

Eadan nodded without his usual questions of how the man could know this.

"Warrior talk will not upset you," Caelis said with certainty.

Eadan puffed up at the implied praise and nodded solemnly. "Sometimes a man must do what needs doing."

Caelis flicked a glance at her. "That is a clan warrior's saying."

"My grandfather told me."

"Where is your grandfather now?"

Eadan's eyes filled with grief. "The horse kicked him and he died."

"What horse?"

"Mine."

"It was not your horse, sweeting. It was only the horse an idiot man put you on." Shona hated the guilt her son struggled with over his adored grandfather's demise. She told Caelis, "Eadan's older brother put him on an untried horse. Percival claimed he did not realize the horse was so temperamental. My father died saving my son."

"Not a brother." Caelis's tone brooked no argument.

Shona was saved from a reply by her son's. "No, Lord Percival is a bad man. I do not want him for a brother. Mummy said I did not have to claim him if I do not want to now that we are in Scotland."

"Good."

Eadan nodded. "Aye."

Oh, good Lord above, give her strength. She was not going to survive this meeting with her heart or her sanity intact.

The boy and man were so alike.

"Shona . . ." Audrey's prompt reminded Shona that she still had yet to get off her horse.

She looked down at Marjory. The child seemed less reticent about her surroundings. "Will you let Audrey take you, now?" she asked.

Marjory's thumb popped into her mouth and she shook her head.

Caelis looked them over and then looked down at her son. "Your sister does not want to come down."

"She's shy of strangers."

"I see."

"If I were bigger, she'd come to me."

Caelis nodded with serious mien. "Perhaps if I lift you to her?"

Eadan considered this before nodding. "She'll come to me," he said with certainty.

Caelis picked the boy up, deep emotion covering his

features as his son put his arm around the big warrior's neck for stability. Shona wanted to shout at him, to tell him that he, too, was a very stupid man.

If he felt the connection so deeply, than why deny even the possibility of a child? Why tell her that they could not marry?

Caelis leaned down and inhaled a long breath against Eadan's neck, his big body going rigid for several seconds in response to her son's scent. He used to do that to Shona, and the memories evoked by seeing him do it to her son were no longer welcome ones.

"Caelis," she said sharply.

He lifted his gaze, the gentian eyes filled with such deep grief even she could not deny this moment was truly profound for him. "Aye?" His voice came out strained, as if even that single word came at only great effort.

She shook her head, her own throat too tight to speak.

"We're getting Marjory," Eadan reminded the big man, clearly at ease in his father's arms.

Caelis nodded, the movement jerky. "Aye, that we are." He approached the mare, his hold on Eadan secure.

Shona's son put his arms out to his little sister. He didn't say anything, just looked at Marjory expectantly.

And her tiny arms stretched out to him. She did not seem to notice the huge warrior supporting them both as she was taken off the horse. Caelis set the children down together beside Niall and Guaire, rather than Audrey or Thomas.

Shona found that telling. He trusted the Scottish warrior, even of a different clan, over the English he did not know. Which meant that he had some measure of trust for Niall, a Sinclair. Which was odd, but not as strange as the fact that Caelis was here on Sinclair lands at all.

His travels were the least of Shona's concerns at the moment. What did matter was that Caelis cared if her children were protected.

That was more concern than he had shown for her six years ago.

Guaire dropped to his haunches so he was eye level with Eadan and started talking gently to the children.

Shona sighed, letting her rigid muscles relax. Pain shot through her lower back, up her spine and into her shoulders. She could not stifle her groan of agony, though she tried.

Getting off the mare was going to be more than tricky; it was going to be impossible. She might as well just tip sideways and fall into the dust like Caelis.

Before she had a chance to work up any worry over it, big hands closed around her waist and she was lifted to the ground.

Caelis did not release her, however, once her feet were on the dirt. He held her, his face a study of emotions she no longer knew how to name with this man.

"You must release me."

"Nay."

"It is unseemly." Not to mention entirely dangerous to her hard fought composure.

The emotional calm she wore like a façade to protect those depending on her was already beginning to crack at the edges under the strain the past months had put on it.

Caelis made a sound of disgust. "You are not an Englishwoman to worry about such, no matter what garb you wear."

"Had I worried about the like as a younger woman, many of my hardest choices would not have been forced on me." She pressed against his chest to push him away, knowing the additional touch was risky.

And indeed, her hands wanted to stay pressed against hot skin over strong muscle and a plaid worn to softness. She could not give in to such weakness and forced her hands to drop to her sides again when her attempt had no effect on the big man.

Instead, Caelis reacted to her attempt to free herself by pulling her closer. "I can explain."

"Explain?" At first she could not comprehend what he could be talking about.

And then it came to her. He thought he could *explain* six years ago? There was no explanation for that kind of betrayal.

She shook her head vehemently, her emotion threatening to overwhelm the calm she clung to. "Nothing you say could ever undo what you have done, what I have had to endure these past six years."

A spasm of regret crossed his face, but it was quickly followed by the obstinacy she'd once found comforting. "You will still listen to what I have to say."

"I'll do that," she said with bite. "Exactly when the Highland clans bow to England's king."

She could not imagine in her worst nightmares that day coming and neither could Caelis, she knew.

He scowled when he got her meaning. *"Mo toilichte,"* he whispered as if the words themselves had the power to heal the breach between them. "There were things you did not know, could *not* know then."

"I'm no more your *happiness*, than you are *my* warrior." She shook her head, trying again to step away. *"Please.* Let me go."

Perhaps he realized the cost to her to plead with him, or mayhap he simply decided he had held her long enough, but hands so large they covered her shoulders completely dropped and she was able to step away.

"Whatever talking you seek to do will have to wait until the English lady has spoken to our laird." Niall's tone left no room for argument.

Surprisingly, Caelis did not make one. He simply nodded. "I will accompany you to the keep."

The reminder that their discussion had been overheard by others, many of whom could not fail to note the resemblance between Caelis and his near–mirror image son, brought the heat of embarrassment crawling up Shona's neck. She should be used to it by now, but the sting of humiliation still pricked deeply.

Caelis looked down at her, dark brows drawn down over his blue gaze. "Are you well?"

To answer truthfully was not a luxury Shona could afford, so she merely nodded and indicated they should begin their trek to the keep.

Niall did exactly that, leading them all onto the narrow path, her son's hand still firmly held in his big warrior's paw. So tired and stiff from day after day of riding that her limbs did not want to work, Shona trudged behind.

Shona stumbled. Her exhaustion—mixed with the near dreamlike state of the fact she'd come face-to-face with Caelis again after six years and all that had come between—making her clumsy.

Audrey took one hand, giving Shona a reassuring smile, and Thomas offered his arm.

The growl from behind them should have made the young Englishman drop his proffered arm. It certainly sent chills down Shona's spine.

But Thomas just scowled over her shoulder at the big warrior who had taken up position behind them. "I know what you are, and you forfeited your rights to her. I will offer my friend assistance and if she will take it, I *will* give it to her."

Shona felt a prick of humiliation to realize her friends did indeed realize *this* man was the father to her eldest child, not the man she had called husband for a little over five years.

She thought Thomas's wording odd, saying *what* instead of *who* to Caelis, but she did not mention it. Would prefer not to acknowledge the mortifying truth at all.

Mayhap he considered Caelis every bit the monster the baron's son was. For six years, Shona had certainly believed that—or at least convinced herself she did.

Regardless of her weakness and past indiscretions, Thomas's youthful eagerness and firm loyalty touched her.

"Thank you, Thomas." She reached for his arm.

But Caelis's hand was there, his body pushing the younger man aside just as he'd done to Niall earlier. "He will not thank *you* if I have to challenge him over rights."

Thomas blanched. For the second time in mere minutes,

Shona was filled with fury by this man. "You'll do no such thing! You have no rights to me. You repudiated them when you abandoned me six years ago."

"'Twas your family that left the clan, not me."

She stopped, pulling poor Audrey to a halt beside her so Shona could glare up at the man. "Do not even *attempt* to pretend it was the other way around. I listened to your lies once, but they will never dictate my life again."

He winced as if her words had wounded, though she knew it was not possible. "Make no mistake: whatever my errors in the past, I will challenge this young one if he tries again to come between me and my mate."

He spoke of her like an animal, and she wished they were. Animals did not abandon those they chose as mates, but this very human man had undeniably deserted her.

If Caelis had cared at all, he would not have disavowed Shona before her own father.

Choking emotion surged up inside her at the memory and she felt the burn of tears at the back of her eyes. She blinked furiously, adamant they would not fall.

Caelis swore, looking pained, if she could believe it.

She wouldn't. "I'm not your mate. I'm not your wife. I'm not even your former betrothed." The banns had never been called. "I am *nothing* to you."

Without another word, he took her hand and slid a far too gentle hand for a man who kept threatening others around her waist. She was too tired to continue fighting his help.

He took so much of her weight she was barely walking as they continued up the path.

After several steps in silence, he said quietly, "In that, Shona, you are very wrong. You are not only the mother of my child, you are *mine*. And I will convince you of that truth. In time."

"I will never be yours again!" Where the energy or will to shout came from, she could not say, but her voice carried with it all the desperation and conviction she felt in that moment.

Marjory turned back to look at Shona from where she walked hand in hand with Guaire. "Why are you yelling at the nice man, Mummy?"

Nice man? Had her daughter lost her mind? Marjory didn't like strangers and now she'd decided Caelis, the man who said he would have killed her father if he wasn't already dead, was a *nice man*.

Perhaps Shona's sanity wasn't as intact as she'd convinced herself. Mayhap this was all some truly bizarre nightmare and she would wake soon.

She could but hope.

Chapter 3

Sacred mating supersedes all claims among the Chrechte, including that of pack leader, *celi di* and parental
authority.
— CHRECHTE SACRED LAW, FROM THE ORAL TRADITIONS

Considering the grandeur of the keep's size and
strength of defense, the actual keep itself was rather sparse.
None of the ostentation Shona's dead husband, the Baron
of Heronshire, had been so fond of in evidence at all.

The great hall *could* easily accommodate a large gath-
ering of the clan, but the silk wall hangings so common in
an English baron's home to denote his wealth and stature
were conspicuously absent. No superfluous pieces of furniture graced the cavernous room, either.

The long tables and benches that served the laird and
his warriors were plain wood; no special carvings, even on
his chair.

Though there was no doubt where the laird and his lady
sat, for those two were the only actual chairs at the tables
in the hall. There was a grouping of other chairs near the
main fireplace, though, which had cushions in the clan's
colors. She had no doubt, however, that the cushions were
for comfort rather than show.

The lovely blond woman had a parchment of accounts

in front of her that Guaire frowned at upon entrance. "I thought we were going to go over those together, Lady Abigail."

"I'd hoped to save you some time, Guaire."

The man looked pained and Niall laughed. "You know he'll feel the need to go over them himself regardless."

The Lady Abigail smiled, mischief glinting in her light brown eyes. "You think so?"

"You do like to tease, my lady," Guaire said with some exasperation.

"Mama, you shouldn't tease," a young boy said from beside the laird. "You get ever so *disappointed* when I tease Drost."

"That is because you have not yet learned when not to push so far that your brother resorts to tears or violence, Brian," Abigail said with a musical laugh.

Shona had heard rumors that the Sinclair lady was afflicted with deafness, but this woman appeared to hear as well as the next person.

"I don't like him to tease me even if he learns that," the boy who must be Drost said from the other side of his father.

Brian seemed keenly interested in the sword his father was sharpening, while his brother, who looked too much like him not to be his twin, carefully drew with charcoal on a clay tablet.

Eadan marched up to the table and pointed to himself. "I am Eadan. You are Drost." He pointed to the boy handing his father a cloth for wiping the oil from his sword's blade. "And you are Brian." He pointed at the other child. "I heard you say so."

Her son was so intelligent, Shona often marveled at how quickly he grasped the world around him.

Both boys looked impressed. Drost observed neutrally, "You aren't wearing clan colors."

"Your clothes are funny," Brian added with a clear opinion.

Abigail gasped and looked ready to jump in, but Eadan didn't give her the chance.

"They're English," he said with a shrug.

Brian frowned. "We don't like the English."

This time, Abigail jumped to her feet and spun to face her son, a fierce expression on her face. "*I* am English."

"You *used* to be English," the laird, who had remained silent thus far, inserted. "However." He fixed his son with a stare that would have intimidated Shona *now*, much less when she'd been a small child. "You know very well we do not hate *all* the English."

Abigail's huff of offense just made her husband shrug, as if to say that was the best she could hope for. It was clearly an old argument.

"You'll like me, and my sister," Eadan said with false bravado, pulling Marjory to his side.

The tremble of worry in Eadan's voice made Shona want to wrap him in her arms to take that fear away, and Marjory, too. Who stood with wide eyes and thumb tucked firmly between her teeth.

But Shona knew this was only the beginning of what they might face in their flight to safety.

The Highlanders were not known for their kind disposition to the English.

Taking a fortifying breath, she curtsied to the laird and his lady. "I am Lady Shona, widow to the second Baron of Heronshire. This is my companion and friend Audrey and her brother, Thomas."

She deliberately left their father's name unspoken as neither wished to acknowledge a man who had sold them into service though his own wealth clearly precluded the need to do so.

She indicated her children. "My son has seen fit to introduce himself, and this is my daughter, Marjory."

Shona straightened, doing her best to hide both fatigue and trepidation, unsurprised when Caelis pulled her back to his side.

He had kept hold of Shona through the trek up the path and into the great hall. He'd managed to maintain his nearness even as they approached the Sinclair laird, clearly intent on giving every sort of wrong impression.

Before either the laird or his lady could reply, Niall said to Eadan with far more assurance than her son had shown, "Of course they will like you, laddie. You're a good Scottish boy at heart."

Shona didn't begrudge the Highland warrior his lack of manners, not when it had been in aid of comforting her child.

"I am?" Eadan asked.

The laird had been looking with thoughtful interest at her son. The Sinclair's gaze slid to Caelis, then back to Eadan again. When the light of understanding dawned, Shona could not miss it.

Again, she felt the heat of embarrassment steal into her cheeks. She had never thought to be faced with Caelis again, much less have their past exposed so inexorably to anyone who cared to look at him in the same vicinity as his son.

"You are, just as your mother is a fine Scottish lass," Guaire answered for Niall.

Shona sent him a look of gratitude, which he replied to with a warm smile. No condemnation there; not like in her own parents' eyes until first her mother had breathed her last breath two years past, and then Shona's father so recently.

Neither had ever forgiven Shona for shaming them the way she'd done. At least they had not taken their unhappiness with her out on Eadan. His grandparents had loved him well.

Though both had made it clear they thought the baron's willingness to raise Eadan as his own son fully compensated for any deficiencies he showed as a father.

Eadan nodded, as if settling something inside his head as he often did. "That's all right then. I'm Scottish. We can be friends."

"You don't speak like the English," Drost said in the

language of his mother's people, perhaps to prove that like Eadan . . . he could.

"Mum says me and Marjory must speak both the language of the Gael and Angle. My lord did not like it, but even when he beat Mum, she would not stop talking to us in the way of her people."

Caelis growled, his anger pulsing around them like thunder in the sky. "He beat you?"

"It is of no consequence." Her husband had not been the worst of men, but neither had he been the best.

He'd only struck her a few times, and had always been kinder after. Not that he ever apologized.

But then, he hadn't thought he was in the wrong.

"It is a good thing your mother has returned to the Highlands then. No one will be allowed to beat her here." The laird's voice carried absolute authority.

"And me?" Eadan asked with a frown and a telling glance down at his sister. "Will anyone be allowed to beat me?"

"The baron beat you?" Niall asked, his tone even, but the expression in his eyes chilling.

Eadan looked away. "One time, but Mum screamed at him. She said she'd gut him in his sleep if he did it again. I wasn't supposed to hear. They thought I was sleeping on my stomach, on account of my back and butt hurt too much. But I couldn't sleep. I was crying quiet like."

"And he did not take the switch to you again?" Guaire prompted.

Shona just wanted the earth to open and swallow her whole. If the cost to keep her son safe was her pride, she would gladly pay it, but that did not mean each strip at the flesh of her spirit did not hurt.

"No. He blustered some. Said she could not speak to him that way, but he never done it again. He threatened once, but I told him my real father was a giant warrior and he would come and kill my lord dead. He believed me."

"Your *real* father?" Laird Sinclair asked carefully.

Suddenly Eadan went silent, sending a stricken look to his mother.

She stared at him, completely at a loss as to what to say. She'd never told Eadan that Henry wasn't his father, though she'd been tempted a time or two.

Even Henry's odious son, Percival, had not known that Eadan was not his blood kin. He might have guessed as Eadan grew older and the only resemblance between him and the baron had been the dark color of hair the older man was reputed to have when he was younger.

Caelis finally released her.

She refused to acknowledge the abandonment that washed over her, but in that moment she felt more vulnerable than she had since leaving Scotland pregnant by a man who had categorically rejected her.

Audrey stepped forward to slide her arm around Shona's waist. "All will be well, dear friend."

Shona simply shook her head. How could it possibly? The greatest fear she had not even prepared herself to feel now stared her in the face with the ferocity of a ravening beast.

In her desperation to save her son's life, Shona now risked losing him to the father who had denied even the chance of his conception.

The same man who even now dropped to one knee in front of *their* son. "No one will be angry at you for the truth, do you *ken* me, Eadan?"

The boy nodded.

"You said *real* father. Why is that?"

"*You* know," Eadan said in a fierce whisper they all heard.

Cold chills washed over Shona as her breath turned shallow. Her son knew Caelis was his father? How could he?

It was impossible. Not only untenable to believe her son knew Henry had not been his father, but that Eadan would have somehow divined that Caelis *was*, thoroughly flummoxed her.

"Aye. I do know," Caelis said, exhibiting none of the disbelief plaguing Shona, wonder and warm affection shining in his blue eyes. "And my heart rejoices in this knowledge, but I am needing you to tell me how you came to know of it."

"Oh. Do you like me, then? You think I'm a fine Scottish laddie?"

The broken sound that came out of Shona made Caelis tense, but he did not turn away from their son. "I do," he promised with absolute solemnity.

"You want a little boy. In the dreams you cry for me, wishing I was with you."

"Dreams?"

"The real dreams. The ones that come true."

"Do you have other *real* dreams?" Caelis asked.

Eadan looked to Shona, asking for permission to speak. She nodded her head. She knew about the real dreams. Or thought she did, but he'd only ever told her about two. And Shona had always wondered if the dreams had been more wishful thinking and imagination on her son's part than anything else.

She'd always considered his dream about her daughter and the pond fortuitous, not prophetic.

Clearly her son had not shared all with her. Mayhap her initial disbelief had shown through and that was why?

"I dreamed my lord would die and he did. I dreamed Marjory would fall into the pond and hit her head. Mum saved her from drownded."

"Drown*ing*," Shona automatically corrected.

Eadan nodded and repeated obediently, "Drowning."

"Oh, Heavens, he's another Ciara. Did you know Caelis was of the royal blood?" Abigail demanded of her husband.

He didn't reply, but with a furtive glance at Shona, Abigail subsided just as if he had.

Shona had no idea who Ciara was, or what Abigail meant by Caelis being of royal blood. Any other time, she would have demanded answers, insisted on understanding, but she was barely able to maintain her composure as it was.

Exhaustion beat at her more relentlessly than her husband had ever done, mention of her son's "gifts" bringing additional worry Shona simply could not take in at the moment.

"I did dream of you," Eadan said to Caelis. "Lots. 'Specially since we left the barony. I knew we'd meet you here."

Shona gasped. That was a bit of information she would have liked to be privy to. Though would she have believed her son, or thought him guilty of wishful thinking again? This time with an uncanny similarity between reality and his dreams?

"I am very pleased you dreamed of me," Caelis told their son. "I am even more pleased you have come to the Highlands so we can be a family again."

Shona's knees would have buckled if Audrey had not held her up. Shona had her own dreams, but they had *not* been prophetic and she'd known without any doubt that they could *never* come true.

For him to stand there and talk like everything had been decided without a word from her . . . it was too much. Once again, a man she could not trust sought to take her choices. How would she fight him? Law and tradition stood firmly on Caelis's side.

Shona felt the waters closing over her head as air became more and more difficult to draw into her lungs.

"You have to love Marjory, too." Eadan had no trouble making demands of his own. It was not the first time she'd seen similarities between father and son. "She's your daughter like I'm your son. My dreams said so."

"Naturally."

Her son accepted Caelis's easy agreement with a firm nod of approval, but Shona could not be so trusting. Even if he told the truth, she desperately did not want to link her life to this man's after the way he'd hurt her so deeply six years ago.

Then, incredibly, Shona's overly shy daughter, who would hide in her mother's skirts at the first sign of a stranger, released her brother's hand and moved over to

Caelis. Marjory put her hands out to the big warrior as if to be picked up.

Though his focus was so intent on Eadan that Shona could not believe Caelis had seen the gesture, he turned and took the wee girl into his big arms without hesitation or pause.

The world grew black around the edges, but Shona would not give into the blessed solace of unconsciousness. She inhaled more deeply, clutching at Audrey, pleading silently with the other woman for help.

Audrey, true friend that she was, strengthened her hold and asked Lady Abigail if they could not have a goblet of watered wine.

Abigail's attention shifted from the spectacle of Shona's children clinging to the man they'd met only that day. When her eyes landed on Shona, they widened and concern filled her gaze. "Of course."

Caelis turned then, as if somehow attuned to Shona's distress. He stood with Marjory in his arms.

Shona lifted her hand in a staying motion and spoke through barely moving lips. "Do not come near."

The hand not holding her daughter fisted at his side, his expression hardening. "Shona . . ."

"Nay." It was Thomas speaking, surprisingly enough. He shifted so his body was a physical barrier between Shona and Caelis. "You have wrought this with your actions. I do not know how our Shona came to be in the predicament she is, but you've done her grave damages in the past, breaking sacred law and dishonoring your own nature. The boy standing by your side is testament to it."

Incredibly, Caelis made no effort to deny it. In fact, he nodded, his jaw hewn from rock, torment she neither understood nor wanted to see swimming in his gentian gaze.

Thomas's own visage was harsher than Shona had ever seen it. "She has told you to stay away. You will stay away."

"Are you her protector then?" Caelis asked in a dangerous voice.

"I am her *friend*."

Audrey added, "A truer one than you have been. Thomas and I were there the few times the baron's temper overcame his sense. My brother taught the boy you seek to claim for your own to sit his first horse. Like me, he helped nurse both Eadan and Marjory through the fevers of babyhood when neither the baron, nor his son, nor even the snooty servants they employed were willing to lift a finger in aid."

Caelis dropped his head, then lifted it to meet Thomas's stare. "I am in your debt."

"Aye, you are, but more important, you are in Shona's."

Caelis nodded, his gaze slipping back to her. The yearning she saw there had to be a trick of the light.

He was the one who had told her love meant nothing between the two of them. That the marriage he'd promised those nights they had shared their passion would not come to pass.

Not content with that, Caelis had made an official declaration of lack of intent, telling both her mother and father that he would no longer be courting her.

They had accepted his rejection without comment or argument, telling Shona that it was for the best. They had not known she carried his child then. She had not known it, either.

She'd had a feeling and taken Caelis aside to express her worries, but he'd adamantly denied any possibility that she could have his child in her womb. He'd gone so far as to say that if she were with child, it must be another man's by-blow.

Sick at heart from the memories and unable to stomach the sight of him one more moment, she turned away.

He made a sound like denial and plea all rolled into one, but she ignored it. Just as he had ignored her begging and desperate words of love six years ago.

"Mummy?" Eadan's little boy hand tugged at hers.

She looked down at her son, always so beautiful to her regardless of the memories his visage kept alive. "Yes, sweeting?"

"You are sad."

"No." She was not lying.

It was so much more than sadness. Despair fought for control, but she would not give in. She was stronger than that.

"I can smell it," Eadan chided.

He was always saying things like that.

She squeezed his hand. "I am well."

"You are tired," Audrey corrected. "Too exhausted by worry and travel for this discussion."

Thankfully, the goblet of watered wine arrived then, delivered by a smiling young woman who looked like the princess Caelis had called Marjory.

"Drink, it will help," she said in tones that soothed. "I am Ciara, oldest daughter of Talorc and Abigail."

She was too close in age to Abigail not to be adopted, but Shona had enough manners not to remark on it. "Thank you."

She hadn't the wherewithal for further pleasantries.

"You are most welcome. Mother is quite excited to have an Englishwoman visiting who can share news of her former homeland."

"No news of England is always good in my eyes," the laird opined.

Ciara laughed. "Watch yourself, Father, or one extra guest room will be in use tonight, I am sure. And I do not think it will be one with a comfortable bed."

Surprisingly, everyone laughed at that, rather than taking offense, even the laird himself.

The banter went on around Shona, but she paid it no heed. Drinking the watered wine in small sips, she was proud that she did not require Audrey's assistance to bring the wooden goblet to her lips.

At some point, everyone had stopped talking. And now they all looked at her, an air of expectation indicating someone had asked her something they expected her to answer.

"I'm sorry?" Shona looked to Audrey to tell her what had been missed.

But the Englishwoman simply shook her head.

"Further talking will wait. It is clear that Lady Heron-shire needs her rest. If you will allow your children to keep mine company until the latemeal is served, you can find rest in your guest chamber, my lady," Abigail said with perfect manners and in clearly native English.

Shona wanted to accept without caveat, but she did not know these people, no matter what she thought she knew *of* them. There was also Caelis to consider and his undeniable desire to now claim Eadan as his son.

Could Shona trust the Sinclairs to stop him from leaving the keep with the boy?

"Do not worry, I will stay with them," Thomas offered. "Brian and Drost are bound to like the game of sticks I taught Eadan this past winter."

"We like games very much," Drost agreed, so obviously trying to comfort the adult woman falling to pieces in his father's great hall, Shona wanted to cry.

She managed a very forced smile instead. "Thank you."

"I will go with you," Audrey said, proving her friend's staunch support and ability to see correctly that Shona had reached the very end of her tether.

After she slept, she would again be strong, but right now, Shona had naught left to give to the circumstances so overwhelming her.

"I would have your word," she said to Niall, falling back on instincts when reason was too difficult to employ. "You will not allow Caelis to take *my* son. Eadan and Marjory will be safe under the protection of you and Thomas."

The young man's loyalty had no equal in that room, but he was an untried youth of nineteen. No true match for the hardened warrior Caelis had become.

"I would not," Caelis claimed, trying to make it sound like a promise.

But his promises were long past being trusted by her. So, Shona ignored him, demanding with the fierceness of her expression that Niall give her *his* vow.

The scarred warrior nodded. "Aye. You have my word."

"Let us pray it has more value than the last time a Scotsman gave me his pledge."

Niall placed his fist over his heart and bowed his head to her. "On my honor and that of my clan, I will keep those you hold dear safe."

A small and genuine smile touched her lips at that promise. He was assuring her he would keep Thomas safe as well and she was grateful to the point of tears. A weak and foolish reaction to be sure, but she *was* tired.

With a nod of acknowledgment, she turned away before anyone could see the evidence of her emotions.

Eadan, Marjory, Thomas and Audrey were all that was dear left to Shona in the entire world.

She would not only die to protect them but kill as well. And so that blackguard Percival, new Baron of Heronshire, would discover if he had the impudence and stupidity to pursue her and her own into the Highlands of Scotland.

Chapter 4

There is no colder bed than the one without your mate.
—Barr of the Donegal

Caelis watched his sacred mate leaving the great hall, his wolf howling with the need to follow the petite female form, his body itching with the desire to shift.

But like he'd done so many times in the past six years, Caelis forced his beast to heel.

Their beautiful mate wanted nothing of them.

Shona's scent used to be the most delectable of fragrances to both him and his wolf, though she'd never met the beast. All wild heather and summer rain, he would sit outside her parent's hut in his wolf form, inhaling it for hours.

Now the acrid scent of bitterness came off her in waves when he was near.

'Twas no easy thing to accept, that change in his mate's regard, no matter that his own actions had brought it on.

He'd survived the last six years holding her promises of eternal love inside where none could see, question or condemn. He'd known he didn't deserve her love after letting her down as he had, but he'd been without choices.

Though she did not know it, he'd taken the blame on himself. He hadn't wanted to add to her resentment of their laird, realizing too late what a mistake that had been. Not least because when her parents decided to move away from the clan, showing no hesitation, Shona had gone with them.

Caelis had never considered she might leave their people, *or him*. He'd thought he would have time to change his alpha's mind about the mating, to make up to Shona the hurt he'd caused her.

Caelis had believed in their future even as he told her they had none. Her father's leaving the clan had been an unforeseen circumstance. The fact that Shona went with him had shocked Caelis to the core. She had a life among her clan, friends if no family left.

The clan was her family. It was what they'd been taught since infancy.

And Caelis had believed her love stronger than even his alpha's will.

There was no love in her pretty green eyes *now* when they fell on Caelis. At worst they swam with pain filled fury, at best with distrust so sharp it cut him to the core of his soul.

Not even the briefest flicker of joy had shown in the emerald depths since he'd first spied her in the courtyard, none of the relief or happiness *he* felt at this chance reunion. She did not share his delight that they had made a child together.

She would deny Eadan's paternity if she could. Caelis had seen it in her eyes, but the boy looked too much like Caelis to be mistaken for anything but his own.

In Shona, Caelis could sense only resentment toward him.

While it might be well-earned, he hated it—almost as much as he had loathed every moment of their time apart.

He had spent six years craving nothing more than to be reunited with her. She had spent those same years despising him completely.

Even when he'd believed his laird that she was *not* his

true mate and the later lies (when word had come of her death, which he'd later come to question but could never be certain about), Caelis had never stopped aching for her.

Not one day had gone by in six years that he had not wished to have the mate of his heart by his side.

But 'twas clear she'd rather be in the presence of a diseased rat than him.

She trusted the two *English* wolves and even Niall more than she did Caelis.

Shona worried that he would take their son away. His promise to the contrary had had no impact on her at all. She denigrated his vows as of having less value than the border treaties signed by an English king.

But he was not the only one who had broken promises.

She had sworn she would never stop loving him and that she would always belong to him.

Mayhap he had no reason or right to expect her to keep such a promise, but he and his wolf shared a sense of betrayal that would not simply be shaken away.

'Twas clear that Shona did not understand Caelis's determination to make them all a family, either.

His duty to his people would prevent them being together for a time. But now that he knew where she was, that she was indeed his true mate, nothing would keep them apart permanently.

Caelis had begun to doubt his laird's claim that Uven alone could identify a pack member's true mate within a year of Shona leaving their clan. Caelis's wolf had grown increasingly difficult to control after she left and only Caelis's dedication to his pack and his duty kept him among the MacLeod instead of chasing after her.

But Caelis had believed Uven, laird of the MacLeod and pack alpha, to be a great man. Caelis had accepted the other man's words as truth when they'd been nothing more than vicious lies.

It had been hard to admit he was so wrong about the other man and too easy to doubt himself after the laird told him Shona had died.

His wolf was not so easily swayed, though it submitted to the more powerful (at that time) alpha wolf without question.

Still, the beast longed for the woman that was no longer in their life. The longing never abated and the wolf refused the touch of any other female, no matter how lovely the Faol Uven had paraded before him. Despite Caelis having believed for a time that Shona was dead, he wouldn't even try to mate another.

He'd only begun to doubt that lie in the last year, when he'd started to question far more about his laird than his clear predisposition toward Chrechte-only matings.

That stupid, prejudiced man had cost Caelis five years of his son's life. Even if duty did not dictate Caelis returning to the clan and challenging Uven for leadership, knowledge of what the man's lies had cost him personally would make the challenge necessary.

"Nice man," Marjory said for the second time that day, patting Caelis face. "No be sad."

He smiled at the wee one. "All will be well, *mo breagha*."

She giggled. "I'm not beautiful."

"You look just like your mama." Though Marjory's curly red hair was more a halo of fine baby curls and her mother's fell in long ringlets down her back. "You are beautiful indeed."

"My dreams say we are a family," Eadan said from near his hip. "But I do not think Mum wants to be one."

Caelis dropped to his haunches, careful to keep Marjory secure in his arms, and met his son's blue gaze. "We will have to convince her then, won't we, my son?"

His voice nearly broke on the word *son*, but he was a warrior and he would not show such weakness. Bad enough he'd fainted down in the bailey like a woman at court.

"We can try," Eadan said doubtfully. "Mum doesn't change her mind easy."

"I remember that about her." Though her stubborn tendencies hadn't often shown with him, he saw them in the way she related to others all too frequently.

"She didn't want to be with Percy. We runned away instead. I don't like Percy, either."

"Who is Percy?" Niall asked.

"My not-brother."

"Percival." Shona had mentioned him, Caelis remembered. "The new baron?"

Eadan nodded. "He has a wife but no children. He wanted Mum to be his lemon and give him children. But she wouldn't let him have us."

"*Lehman*, he wanted to make her his *lehman*." Percival would have made Shona, his former stepmother, his mistress with all the responsibilities and none of the privileges of his wife.

It was monstrous and disgusting, and no more than he expected of an English baron, though he'd never tell Abigail that.

Fury filled Caelis, but he did his best not to let it bleed through his countenance and scare the children.

"In my dreams, men turn into wolves sometimes but women never turn into lemons."

He didn't correct his son's pronunciation, but he did wonder at it.

"What is a lemon?" Niall asked, however.

Eadan's brow furrowed like he was surprised by the question. "It's a yellow fruit. Sour. Mum read to me about it from a book written by one of the priests in Italy. My lord was ever so fond of the writings of the Church."

"I see." Caelis made no attempt to hide his smile. "Percy isn't turning your mother into his *lemon*, or anything else."

Eadan nodded in complete agreement. "Mum won't let him."

"Neither will I."

"Good. Mum isn't as big as she thinks she is."

Niall laughed. "She seems plenty big to me."

"Mama is tiny but strong," Eadan replied staunchly. "I'll be taller 'n her soon enough. She always says so."

"Aye." Emotion threatened to choke Caelis.

This child standing before him with blue eyes the same

gentian shade and oval shape as his own was *his* son. The fruit of sacred passion he had shared with his true mate.

Because only a true mate could become pregnant by a Chrechte when she was human.

All his former laird's arguments against the mating shattered in the face of that truth. Not only had she given birth, but his son's enhanced ability to smell indicated that he would go through the change into wolf form when he reached age.

Caelis shuddered to think what would have happened to his son if he had shifted without a pack to protect him. But then, he had a pack.

An *English* one.

He looked to Thomas, who was already teaching a game with sticks to the Sinclair's twin sons. Their baby daughter slept above stairs this time in the afternoon.

Caelis carried Marjory to where Thomas and the children played on the floor of the great hall nearby. He set the girl down and she immediately grabbed for her brother's hand. Eadan took it, as if he was used to doing so and led her to the others.

Caelis lowered himself to the floor beside Thomas. "Teach me this game," he demanded.

The young wolf merely nodded and explained the rules. They'd played for a bit, even getting the wee Marjory to participate, when Caelis asked, "How came you to be such close friends to my mate?"

"Her father sought us out. I do not know how he knew of our true nature, or that of our mother, but the steward was well aware and wanted us nearby in case Eadan made the transition."

"What of your own family?"

"My father is a minor baron and wanted nothing of us, offspring from his *lehman*."

"Does he know she is Chrechte?"

Grief twisted Thomas's youthful features. "No. He never knew and now she is gone."

"I am sorry." Caelis had lost his own parents, only

to learn recently it had been at the hands of the very man who had insinuated himself into Caelis's life as a second father.

Uven had played mentor and parent to Caelis, all the while guilty of the most heinous betrayals.

"She loved us, but fate picked poorly in her true mate," Thomas continued in a quiet voice as he directed the children's play. "Our father is a hard man with no love in his heart for those he uses so cruelly."

"How did she die?"

"Fever. She was pregnant again, but too old to carry mayhap. Anyway, she and the babe died. That was five years ago. Father took a fee from the Baron of Heronshire for us to come into his household as personal companion and servant to his lady wife."

"The ways of the English are beyond my ken," Caelis said with disgust.

"It was Shona's father who instigated the transaction. As I said, he wanted us to be near if his grandson made the change."

"Eadan will," Caelis and Talorc, laird of the Sinclairs, said in unison.

The others had remained in the great hall, watching the children play, remaining quiet amongst themselves, though Caelis did not doubt Abigail and Talorc had conversed across their mate bond.

Ciara nodded her agreement. "His wolf is already strong in him."

"Shona is still ignorant of the Chrechte's existence," Caelis observed.

"She is." Thomas didn't sound happy about that. "There was no pack nearby, but our mother taught us that we could not share our secret unless there was dire need."

"Mating constitutes dire need, in case you are wondering," Abigail said with more sting than she usually spoke, and a look of old censure at her husband.

"Aye. Though how you could not realize she was your true mate when it is clear you shared in the physical bonds of love . . ." Talorc let the criticism trail off, but there was no doubting his disapproval.

"My laird told me she wasn't and I didn't believe her when she told me she thought she was pregnant. I asked Uven and he said that it wasn't possible. That Shona could not be my true mate; as my alpha, he would know if she was. I knew matings between humans and Chrechte were rare, but I had hoped so fervently. I was very angry I had to let her go; I wasn't thinking clearly at the time."

The admission was hard to make.

Ciara frowned. "Unless he had the gift, an alpha has no more hope of divining one's mate than any other member of the pack."

"I know that. Now." It would have been a great benefit to have known this truth of their heritage six years ago.

There were too many things Uven of the MacLeod had kept from his people in his quest to control the clan and the pack so completely.

"You made one hell of a mistake," Niall observed without rancor but without pity either.

"I did." But Shona would forgive him once she understood.

His sweet mate's forgiving nature was every bit as ingrained in her as her stubbornness.

He turned his attention toward getting to know his children while the woman he and his wolf ached to claim slept upstairs.

Shona woke to the absolute dark of the wee hours on a moonless night.

It had been so long since she had slept well and deeply, comfortable in a bed she knew would not be disturbed.

She wasn't sure why she knew this bed was an absolutely safe one, but she did, in that place in her brain not too influenced by waking. So why the urge to get up?

The next question her brain always conjured upon waking answered the first.

The sensation of something not being *right* pushed her into full wakefulness when her body wanted to settle back into sleep.

Where were her children? She remembered coming to the guest room in the Sinclair keep for a much-needed nap, but that had to have been hours ago.

She must have slept through the evening meal, her children's bedtime and into the night. Though Shona could not be sure of how late it was without seeing the stars position in the sky, how refreshed she felt indicated she'd slept away all of the afternoon and a good deal of the night.

She reached out to feel around for the edge of the bed and realized two things at once. The first was that she was in the center and the second that Audrey was no longer in the room.

This concerned her nearly as much as not knowing where her children were. Though Audrey was no fool, at nineteen she had a less jaundiced view of the world than Shona.

This made her vulnerable to those who might deceive and use her, as Shona had been six years ago.

With increasingly urgent moves, Shona used her hands to find her way around the room. On a shelf that jutted out from the wall near the head of the bed, fingers encountered a candle and flint for striking. 'Twas an unexpected extravagance, but she quickly made use of it and lit the candle.

The glow from the single candle dispelled the darkness, though the corners of the room remained in shadow. Shona spied a dark shape that she assumed was clothing Audrey had pulled for her from the small bundle of possessions taken on the flight from Heronshire barony. She grabbed the fabric, only to realize that Audrey had pulled out Shona's green velvet dress.

Shaking her head at Audrey's silliness, Shona donned the garment free of dust and the detritus of travel, unlike the dress she'd arrived in. It took precious time to secure the sleeves, but running about the keep in nothing but her shift was not an option.

Especially after the last months at the barony, when the most innocent of gestures had been taken as invitations she'd never had any intention of offering.

She didn't take the time to brush or pull her hair back. Neither did she search for her shoes.

Shona needed to find her children and hoped she would not wake the entire keep doing it. But if that was what it took, wake them she would.

She rushed out the door and nearly tripped over Caelis's form. He was sitting directly in front of her door, looking around as if trying to figure out where the danger was coming from. His big body rippled with muscle, even in his low position on the floor.

"What are you doing outside my room?" she demanded in a whisper, wishing she had not noticed anything appealing about his physical appearance.

He stood with the fluid grace she'd worked hard to forget. "What are you doing rushing around in the wee hours of the morning?" he asked instead of replying.

"Looking for my children."

"They are sleeping in the room beside yours. Your champions are in there as well, guarding the lad's and lass's sleep." Caelis's disgruntled tone implied he wasn't as pleased about that as Shona was.

Her own heart, which had been beating near out of her chest, settled into a more normal rhythm. "Which one?"

He indicated a door to the right with an incline of his head in that direction.

She immediately headed toward it, but Caelis's arm shot out, his hand closing over her wrist. "Where are you going?"

"To see them." She spoke slowly as if to a not very bright child.

"You will wake them."

She didn't intend to, but 'twas not her greatest consideration at the moment. "I will be quiet."

"Eadan will hear you." The certainty in Caelis's tone implied he somehow already knew about their son's acute ability to detect sound.

"Nevertheless, I will see them."

"Why? I have told you they are resting with your friends. Do you not trust Thomas and Audrey to watch over the children?"

"Of course I do, but I only have your word that Eadan and Marjory are behind that door, safe and sleeping peacefully."

Caelis's head snapped back as if she'd slapped him with all the fury she'd wanted to six years ago. Back then, she'd been too much in love to do him harm, despite his betrayal.

Now, she would not hesitate.

"You do not trust my word?" he asked with shock too real to be feigned.

She was hit by her own sense of unreality. "You *expect* me to?"

"Aye."

"Then you are a bigger fool than I was six years ago."

"I have told you there were reasons for what happened between us." And he sounded like he fully expected her to listen to him list them.

"What happened was that you made promises that had no more substance than the morning mist." And no amount of explaining could change that.

"I meant my words to you when I spoke them."

That was supposed to matter to her? She jerked her wrist from his hold. "But not later."

He'd broken his vows and she'd ended up married to an old man whose touch had near to driven her insane. If she had not had her children, Shona would not have survived the last years.

She was sure of it.

She moved away, intent on finding Eadan and Marjory. He did not try to stop her again.

She pushed against the door, but it did not give. If Caelis were indeed telling the truth, then Audrey or Thomas must have dropped the bar into place on the other side. She appreciated her friends' dedication to safety, but Shona would not return to the guest room without confirming her children's well-being.

She knocked softly on the door, knowing the siblings slept more lightly than even her son.

Only a few seconds passed before the door swung inward, revealing Thomas's sleepy countenance.

"You wish to see the little ones," he guessed.

She nodded.

Thomas stepped back and Shona moved into the room. The candle she carried casting a soft glow over the space, revealing the bedding on the floor where Thomas had obviously been resting. Beyond that was a bed similar to the one Shona had been sleeping in, but this one was a lot more crowded with Audrey in the middle and Eadan and Marjory on either side of her.

Audrey's eyes were open, but she did not move. Obviously not wanting to disturb the children, she sent Shona a small smile of reassurance. Eadan shifted, making a soft noise, but he didn't wake, proving just how exhausting the past sennights had been for him.

Shona did not speak, but simply sent a questioning glance to Audrey. The blond woman gave an infinitesimal nod, telling Shona all was well.

Thomas patted her on the shoulder. "We will waken you in the morning when they rise, if you are still sleeping."

He spoke quietly, his mouth very near her ear.

She nodded, sending them both a grateful smile before going back into the hall. Caelis stood there, glowering at Thomas as Shona pulled the door closed behind her.

She turned to face the man she was quickly coming to view as her nemesis. "I cannot imagine what you find so objectionable about young Thomas, but he will grow into a fine warrior with great honor one day. You will stop glaring at him so."

"He is already a man."

"He is but nineteen." Which admittedly was three years past the generally acknowledged advent into manhood, but

Thomas was still so *young*. Despite his own experiences to the contrary, he saw the world through eyes that believed in man's goodness and inherent honor.

"He is almost a child." Though she knew he would not thank her for saying so.

"He is too familiar with you."

"He is my friend."

Caelis appeared unmoved. "So he claimed earlier."

Chapter 5

The Chrechte are stronger than humans but not superior to them. They are brethren as the Faol are brethren to the Paindeal and the Éan.

—CAHIR TRADITIONS

The tone of Caelis's voice implied he was no happier about her friendship with Thomas than he was about the youth's supposed *familiarity* with her.

Shona gave a mental shrug. Caelis's feelings were of little import to her. "It is true."

She considered Audrey and Thomas the siblings her parents had never been blessed to provide her. Shona had never looked on them as servants as her husband and the rest of the household did.

"Does every male *friend* you have whisper words into your ears as a lover would do?"

"You are daft. Thomas is no more lover-like than . . . than a *fish*. He and Audrey are my dearest friends." Shona's only true friends, if she wanted to be honest about it.

Shona had allowed none but those two to breach the walls she'd built around her heart after this man's betrayal and her parents' rejection because of it. She'd felt the twins' helplessness in the face of their fates being chosen for them by an uncaring father because it was so like her own.

Her father had cared, but he'd been equally certain he knew what was best, and forcing her into marriage with the baron had been at the top of that list.

"I owe them both a debt of honor for watching over you and the children."

He'd said something like that before. It made no more sense to her now than it had earlier.

But she would make no attempt to disabuse him of the notion. If he felt some obligation to Audrey and Thomas, perhaps he would be more apt to help them find safety, if not Shona herself.

"I am going back to bed." She turned to retrace her steps to her room.

"You are still tired?" he asked, keeping pace with her.

"No." In fact, she was not, but she wasn't about to wander the passageways of the sleeping keep, either.

"Then perhaps we can talk?" Caelis asked, sounding less demanding than she'd ever heard him.

Shona stopped at her door, looking up at the only male visage that had ever stirred desire in her.

Even now, after everything, her need for him was a low rumble in her belly. She'd been sure that part of her was dead, but one day in his company and she knew it was not. She wanted him as much as she ever had, but she would *not* have him.

Forcing the visceral need aside, she asked with no small amount of unbelief, "You wish to discuss the issues between us *now*, in the wee hours?"

"Aye."

"'Tis hardly appropriate behavior." She shook her head. Not to deny him, but in wonder at his audacity.

"I do not concern myself with what is proper."

"You never did." But she'd thought he had the honor to make improper behavior right.

He had not.

"There was a time when you would have laughed at this English sense of propriety you seek to hide behind now."

"I learned why proper behavior has its place." As protection from what had happened to her, for one thing.

"Please, Shona. Hear me out."

Honestly? She felt no inclination to do so, but she needed information on what Caelis planned to do now that he'd discovered he had a son. If he'd denied Eadan, all would be so simple. She would have gone to Balmoral Island as planned and thrown herself on the mercy of family relations—however tenuous.

But now Shona feared losing her son to his father as much as her flight from England had been spurred by her terror of losing Eadan to Percival's evil machinations.

"You will not take my son from me," she promised Caelis as she pushed the door to her chamber open.

"That is not my intention."

She turned to face him, still on the threshold, not letting him into the room. "You mocked me once with words that did not match your actions; this time I will not be so easily fooled."

"Let me explain," Caelis said again, more plea than demand.

It was so unusual to hear the strong warrior speak thus, she found herself nodding and stepping back to allow him into the bedchamber.

There was a low boxlike chest against one wall and Shona used it to sit on, ignoring the very existence of the bed and hoping Caelis would do so as well.

She would have gone to the great hall, but she wanted someone to overhear her shame even less than she desired to be caught in a compromising position with Caelis.

"I find it odd you were sleeping outside my door," she said as Caelis paced the room but did not start this grand explanation he had alluded to.

"I was not sleeping."

"What were you doing then?"

"Guarding you." Caelis stopped in front of her. "Fighting my need to come inside."

She almost laughed. "You would have me believe that after you tossed me aside six years ago, your passions for me burn so bright they keep you up at night on vigil outside my room?"

'Twas ludicrous. If he'd been as afflicted by desire for her as she was him, he never would have repudiated her.

"Aye."

"I am not that naïve." Did he think he had to lie to her to gain access to his son?

Why did he even want Eadan now, when Caelis had been so quick before to reject even the possibility she was pregnant?

Her thoughts whirled in her head like the most complicated court dance.

"Just stubborn." He sighed, running his hand over his face. "I do not remember you being so stubborn *with me*."

Because she'd *wanted* to give into him and that was her own shame to bear. At least he'd known her truly enough to realize it was in her nature to be obdurate with others.

When she didn't dignify his words with a reply, he sighed again, looking quite put out. "I have been without physical comfort for six years. You married another."

"First, I have absolutely no reason to believe you. And I don't," she inserted for good measure. "Second, you cannot call what transpired between the baron and myself *comfort*."

Not when the old man's very touch made Shona's skin crawl and he'd used her as the whore her mother had called her upon discovering Shona was with child with no suitor, much less husband, in sight.

"I do not want to hear about it," Caelis said with deep feeling.

She had no intention of telling him anything about her life that he did not absolutely need to know. "Rest assured, you will not."

"Marjory is his."

Shona gave a single jerk of her head in acknowledgment.

"Eadan is mine."

This time Shona merely stared, refusing to agree with or deny the statement.

"You would deny it?" Caelis accused, though she'd done no such thing.

"You were the one who told me that if I were pregnant then it would have to be by some other man." Her fingers curled around the edges of the chest, the grip so hard she could feel her heartbeat in them. "Do you not remember?"

"I was angry at having to let you go. I took that fury out on you." Guilt washed over his chiseled features. "I did not mean it. I was under orders to cease my attentions to you. I knew those words would push you away as nothing else would. Your loyalty and determination were too strong to give in otherwise."

She did not know what he meant by orders to cease his attentions, though she could guess, but Caelis had been right about his methods. "You succeeded spectacularly in your efforts. I would have been content to live the rest of my days without seeing you again."

Because she had wished so strongly for that claim to be reality, it came out with all the conviction her heart lacked.

The candle's glow was not bright, but it illuminated enough of his handsome face to reveal the pain that crossed it and settled in his gentian gaze. "To my great regret."

"I do not believe you." Was it a lie if she wanted it to be true?

Again, he seemed surprised . . . even hurt . . . by her lack of faith in him.

"Our laird denied my request to mate you." There was a ring of sincerity to his tone she could not ignore.

More important, the words rang true with the actions of the laird of her former clan. Uven was not a kind, or even just, man. He had his favorites among the clanspeople and they could expect his support and beneficence. Everyone else had had to sacrifice for the treasured few.

Uven's own daughter often suffered at his hand, not that Caelis had ever believed it. While they'd had a near-idyllic courtship before Caelis rejected her, the one area they never agreed on was the true nature of their laird.

Her lack of loyalty, as he called it, used to infuriate her then beloved warrior to no end.

Because, unlike her family, Caelis had never been shown the ugly side of the MacLeod laird.

"You are one of his favored," she reminded Caelis.

"I *was.*"

She didn't ask what had happened to change that. The very fact he was among the Sinclairs rather than their former clan spoke of a great breach between laird and vassal. And she did remember her former laird's true ways. Nothing he did would have surprised her.

But some things were less likely than others. "You want me to believe that our laird refused one of his favored?"

"He did not think us a good match. He was adamant that you were not my mate."

There was that word again, as if they were animals, but it didn't matter what Caelis called it. Mate, wife or even beloved, none of the titles fit her place in his life. They never had, no matter how much she had once wished to believe otherwise.

"He did not think I was good enough for you." She'd not understood why the laird had such antipathy toward some of his clan, but the fact could not be denied.

He'd believed Shona's family beneath his notice and replacing her father as seneschal had only been one of many slights against them.

Caelis did not deny her interpretation of events.

She sighed. "And this is your grand explanation?"

Caelis jerked, his eyes widening and then going narrow as if her reaction surprised him. "I had no choice but to deny you."

"You had a choice. You could have left the clan when we did."

"The laird would never have given permission for me to leave."

"And yet here you are." Living among another clan but still wearing the colors of the MacLeod.

Perhaps the breach was not as great as she'd first thought. In truth, there might not be any breach at all, no matter what Caelis claimed.

The sense of despondency that gave her made no sense and she chose to ignore it.

"It is complicated." And he was clearly reluctant to share the nature of that *complication*.

"You are welcome to spare me the details."

Again it appeared as if she'd surprised him. "You used to be so curious."

"The one thing I want to know about you, Caelis—the *only* thing that matters to me any longer—is if you are going to try to rob me of my son."

"I will not."

She wanted to believe him, for her own sake. Wanted to feel relief at the hard promise. Not only could she *not* trust his promises, however, she didn't believe it could be that simple.

Caelis had already verbally claimed Eadan. To walk away now would be to impugn his warrior's honor. He would not do that for her sake, or even their son's. Of that, she had no doubts.

"Then you have no objection to us traveling on to Balmoral Island as soon as the Sinclair laird gives us his leave to do so?" She didn't believe it, but she needed to push Caelis into revealing his plans.

"Why Balmoral Island?"

"I have family there."

"I did not know that."

She shrugged. Confidences that they had, or *had not* shared six years ago had no importance today.

"Who is it?"

"My great-grandmother came from the island. Her sister also married and had children. The last I had heard, some still lived from that generation as well as those of my own."

"You do not know?"

"There has been no direct contact between the two branches of the family in many years, but I am certain my Balmoral kin will welcome my children and me into their clan." At least, she hoped with great fervency.

Everything she had learned of her grandmother's clan of origin pointed to a people who put great store by family and loyalty. A clan she could depend on to keep her and her children safe from a greedy Englishman's desires.

"The Balmoral clan is a good one. I have spent the last year training with a special group of their soldiers."

That at least explained what he was doing away from MacLeod lands. Though the fact her former laird had sent one of his soldiers to train under another did not meet with overweening arrogance she remembered.

"What are you doing here then?" She knew the Balmoral and Sinclairs were allies, and Caelis staying in the keep on his way southward made sense, but he was more of a long-term guest here.

That seemed clear enough.

"More training with the Sinclairs."

Things must have changed a great deal since she left her clan behind. "I see."

He waited for her next question with a patience she did not remember from their past.

"So your plans are to return to the MacLeod clan?" she asked with undisguised hope.

Caelis's expression turned very serious. "Aye."

"You will not take my son from me."

"I told you, I have no intention of separating mother from child."

"But?" She knew there was a caveat. Why did he have to pretend there was not?

"I cannot live among the Balmoral. I have obligations to my people. I have to return to the MacLeod."

"What has that to do with me, or my children, for that matter?"

"*Our* children," he emphasized, finally revealing his

true colors. "If I am not living among the Balmoral, naturally you and the children will not be, either."

"I will not go back to that clan." Her former laird had not been a good man, no matter what Caelis might think.

"Not immediately, no, but once I have discharged my duty, you and our children will join me."

She laughed then, the sound bordering on hysterical. The man was completely daft. "You speak as if we have promises between us, plans to be together as a family. We have none."

Her voice rose and the hysteria edged closer. She forced air in and out of her lungs as she pushed away the overwhelming sense of panic.

"We *will* have the future we dreamed of six years ago." He dropped to his knees in front of her, his big hands engulfing her own. "I am no longer willing to live without my true mate for the sake of a corrupt alpha."

"You are not making any sense, Caelis."

"You belong to me. 'Tis simple as that."

He could not truly believe that?

"Oh, no. It is not simple at all. I *do not* belong to you." Though her heart called her a liar. "Mayhap I did all those years ago, but not now. Never again."

"Never is a long time, lass."

"And sometimes not long enough." When it came to seeing Percival, new Baron of Heronshire, again, never would be too short.

She'd thought the same about Caelis, but the heart that had gone dormant when she left Scotland began to flutter again. True that flutter brought naught but pain now.

And yet a very tiny part of her was glad not to be so dead inside. She'd felt emotion for her children, but it was a different place in her heart that had been sleeping these past years.

A place that at one time had given her both her greatest joy and most devastating sorrow.

"I will change your mind." He promised. "We are meant to be together."

"I used to believe that." She'd been certain to the very depths of her soul that she and this man had a glorious future together.

A love story to write with their hearts and their bodies so profound, their children's grandchildren would tell it to their babes. Losing her faith in the future had hurt almost as much as losing him.

"Believe it again."

"No." She'd been hurt enough by this man and by her own dreams.

Neither would ever be given free rein in her heart again.

His impossibly blue gaze bored into hers. "Some things in life, we have no choice about."

"You mean like six years ago?" she asked sweetly.

An expression of relief (no doubt that she'd *finally* understood) came over his features. "Exactly like six years ago."

"Then you are a very ineffectual man, Caelis of the MacLeod. Six years ago, you had a choice indeed."

"I told you—"

"That our laird denied us the right to marry in the clan," she interrupted. "But what does that signify? Only that your love for his regard far exceeded any small feelings you might have had for me. You denied me. *You denied our son.* All on the say-so of a despot worse than the man I am currently running from. Do not you claim you had no choice. You had a very real choice, Caelis, and you made it!"

"You do not understand."

"You think not? I know this. Had the choice been mine six years ago, I would have run from the clan, abandoned my family and followed you across the waters if need be for us to be together. You wouldn't even leave with me to another clan."

"I could not!" His bellow was louder than hers, but she was not impressed.

"Then I say again, Caelis, you were a very ineffectual man. And I believed you a warrior at heart."

"I am. How dare you doubt my fighting spirit!"

"How dare *you* claim one when you never fought for the right to be with me!" He surged to his feet, towering above her, his rage a palpable force around them.

She was not impressed.

"I thought he wanted only what was best for me. As you said, I was one of his favored ones. He claimed that as my alpha he could tell you were not my true mate. How was I supposed to know he lied?"

"You wanted to believe him. You wanted to believe that some in the clan were more important, superior to others. You wanted to be one of those *superior* beings." She put all the derision she felt into that word, letting Caelis know just how *un*superior she considered a man who could abandon her as he had done.

His face contorted as if holding something of great import back. Finally, he said, "I was."

"I would say that I am sorry you lost your place, but I am not. The longer you held favor with that man, the more of your humanity you would have given up to him."

"You do not know how true your words are," Caelis said, his tone subdued, his face cast in shadows so she could not read his expression.

She had no answer for him. He had chosen, no matter that he claimed there had been none, and he had done so poorly.

He sat on the edge of her bed, leaving his scent behind, though she would not tell him so. She'd always been sensitive to it, reveling in his nearness even when she could not see him.

He looked down at the floor, as if it might have the answers he sought. "There are things I did not tell you then. Things you will have to know now."

"You sound very mysterious."

He nodded, his expression sober. "It is a great mystery, a secret the humans who are privileged to know must keep at the pain of death."

"You say *humans* like you think yourself something

greater than." Was this truly the man she had loved so dearly?

His sense of superiority and excessive vanity might even rival Percival's.

"Not better than—I understand that now—but not the same either." Caelis's expression pleaded with her for understanding.

But once again, his words were more confusion than explanation.

"Will you ever start making sense?" she demanded with asperity. "No matter what your exalted laird would have you believe, you are *not* some superior being."

"I am Chrechte," Caelis blurted out with exasperation, jumping to his feet and turning away as if frustrated with her obdurate behavior.

Really? If he persisted in trying to unite them as a family, he would soon learn that she was capable of far more obstinacy than this.

And the whole Chrechte mystique? Not so mysterious after all. Everyone in the clan knew about the band of warriors that considered themselves elite among the soldiers.

She rolled her eyes. "So I heard on more than one occasion six years ago from you and others. You considered your skills as a warrior something to set you apart."

He spun back to face her, his expression growing increasingly astonished as she continued speaking.

"My skills as a warrior *are* above those of other men, Chrechte as well," he declared with affront.

"And I am an English lady with claim to title and little else. Do you know how it has set me apart?" she asked scathingly. "Not one wee bit. I am still a mother, a friend, a woman with less say in my life than the steward who ran my dead husband's estates."

"You ignore everything you do not wish to hear," he accused, his frustration obviously mounting.

She glared at him, her own ire rising to match his. "If you want me to *hear* you, may I suggest you try talking sense rather than the ravings of arrogant idiocy."

"I am no idiot!"

"Well, you're certainly not a lord of logic, either."

"I am a shape-changer," he practically yelled. "Chrechte means I share my nature with an animal. Mine is a wolf."

Her heart nearly stopped in her chest. She'd called him daft, but she hadn't meant it. Had not truly believed he had lost his ability to think and behave rationally.

His talk now made her cold with dread.

"Stop this nonsense. Please, Caelis, do not show yourself truly insane," she pleaded with him.

He simply shook his head and then removed his plaid with an economy of movement. He made no move to come closer to her, but she jumped off the chest anyway, sidling toward the door and escape.

"No. Caelis. I will not take you to my bed."

"Aye. You will, but not right now."

She shook her head, her heart beating so fast in her chest that it hurt.

He lifted his head, sniffing at the air and then looked with concern at her. "You have nothing to fear, Shona. Not ever from me."

"You have hurt me more than any other," she baldly disagreed.

That was one lie she simply could not let stand.

"Let me show you why."

What did he expect her to do? Give him permission? She just wanted out of the room, but before she could make her move for the unbarred door, a flash of light shown around Caelis.

Then, where he had stood was now a large dark-haired wolf.

Chapter 6

One must have grave reason for revealing the knowledge of the Chrechte's true nature to a human. For to betray that knowledge carelessly is to invite certain death.

— CHRECHTE ORAL TRADITIONS

Shona blinked slowly.

Perhaps it was *she* who had lost her grasp on reality, but when she opened her eyes again, the wolf still stood there.

She backed toward the wall, fear mixed with disbelief making her stomach roil. When her shoulders encountered the hard ungiving barrier, she whimpered.

The wolf whined, tilting his head to one side as if trying to tell her she had nothing to worry about.

"Caelis?" she asked in a voice that trembled. And then immediately began to berate herself for doing so. "No, he is not a wolf. He cannot be. My eyes are deceiving me."

The wolf stalked across the room, crowding close to her.

Her entire body shook with the terror and confusion gripping her. "No, stay away."

The wolf stopped, letting out a short bark that sounded so much like Caelis when he was exasperated with her, she gasped.

"Caelis?" she asked again.

The wolf's head nodded up and down.

"But how? This is not possible." She knew it was not.

No matter how her eyes deceived her, men did not transform themselves into wolves.

A more practical woman than most, Shona did not believe in faeries, or magic, or any such. How could she accept the evidence of her eyes?

The wolf moved closer, sniffing the air, a happy-sounding rumble coming from his chest.

"Don't . . . don't come any closer."

The wolf whined again, moving back and then forward again, as if it could not help itself.

"What?" she demanded. "What do you want?"

He took a step closer and she remembered how the stable master had told her to behave with the dogs on her dead husband's estates.

Shona put her hand out, her arm trembling.

The wolf stretched forward, first sniffing at her hand and then licking it.

"Oh." It was not so terrible, though it was strange to have a wild animal that could tear her apart with its claws and teeth so gently caressing her hand with its snout.

The beast came closer so that she was crowded against the wall and pressed its body to her.

She stared down at him. "I am not going anywhere. You do not need to sit on me."

But the animal ignored her words, rubbing against her with its sides, nuzzling at her with its snout.

"You're very affectionate, aren't you?" she asked, not remembering the estate dogs being quite so friendly.

Then she remembered this wolf was supposed to be Caelis and she had another reason altogether to resent his nearness.

"Caelis, if that is indeed you in there, you must step back."

He barked his denial and she had no doubts that was exactly what it had been, either, climbing her so his forepaws rested on her shoulders and he could rub her neck with his snout.

She giggled, the sound shocking her as much as the sensation of being tickled.

He licked her again, growling against her throat in a way that should have frightened her, but it did not.

One thing was certain, while she still feared Caelis the man because of his power to harm her and destroy her happiness, she did not fear his wolf.

At all.

"You are very sweet like this."

The wolf chuffed, as if he found her sentiment immensely funny and she found herself smiling at him.

The light flashed and then Caelis the man was again there, naked and far too close. "Your smile is still as beautiful and bright as the sun."

That very same smile slid from her face more rapidly than water going over the falls into her favorite loch.

A small scream escaped her throat, but she pressed her hand over her mouth to keep other sounds inside. She could not afford to alert her friends or her children to her distress.

Caelis had turned into a wolf. Might well do so again. While she'd never doubted her own security, others might not be safe around him. Especially Thomas.

She shoved him from her. "Get away."

At first, he did not move, but she shoved again. Harder.

He stumbled back a step. "You are frightened of the wolf."

"No. I don't want your naked body so near," she stated without apology.

He didn't fight her, moving back quickly, his expression unreadable. But the intensity of his regard was unsettling.

She hugged herself. "You need to put your plaid back on."

He laughed, the sound harsh, almost bitter, and he turned away. Not to get his clothing, but to drop to the floor.

He knelt there for several seconds, breathing deeply.

"Did it hurt you?" she asked in a halting voice. "Changing into a wolf?"

"Do not speak," he rasped out.

She closed her mouth, once again not understanding. *Why couldn't she speak?*

"My control over my wolf is precarious," he answered as if she had spoken aloud.

"Is it always like this after you shift between forms?" she asked and then regretted doing so when an animalistic sound came from his mouth. Did the wolf wish to return to his animal form?

Mayhap he did not like living as a man.

Caelis's muscles corded with some great effort. "No. But I have not claimed my true mate in six years and she stands alluringly before me in a bedchamber. What do you think my wolf wants to do?"

This was about sex? "Control yourself, like you didn't six years ago," she answered immediately and with some bite.

He leapt to his feet, his naked body turning to face her all in one smooth movement.

There was ample evidence that he was indeed very aroused. Whether it was by her or by shifting, or would have happened with any woman in a similar circumstance, she could not know.

"You think I did not control myself six years ago?" he demanded, his expression stark, his tone feral.

"No," she replied starkly and then added, "Had you, I would not have become pregnant."

"And do you regret that? *Can* you regret our son?"

"Of course not." And how unfair of him to ask. Caelis had not been the one to live with the consequences of pregnancy outside of wedlock. "I love my children with my whole heart, but having our son the way I did came with great cost, not the least of which was the regard of my parents for the rest of their lives."

"They were angry with you?"

"Do not jest. You know full well how furious they would have been. They were disappointed in me and disgusted by the shame I had brought on our family name. My mother called me a whore and never forgave me. My father, either, though he was less vocal in his criticisms."

Horror washed over Caelis's features, though whatever he was feeling had no apparent effect on his arousal. "They loved you so much."

"And that made my betrayal of them that much greater."

"You did not betray them."

"I did. You know well a woman is to save her innocence for the marriage bed."

"It doesn't always happen."

"Nay, but you were not there to make it right, were you? You and your laird had judged me and found me wanting as a mate for the beast, is that it?"

"Not me."

"Just the laird, but you went along."

"I did. To my own shame."

"You do not know what shame is until you have had your husband treat you like a dockside whore on your wedding night."

Caelis looked sick. "I am sorry."

Three little words. They shouldn't have mattered, and in the great expanse of life probably didn't, but in that moment they healed wounds still bleeding in her heart.

"I am sorry I left you, but I cannot be sorry I claimed you. I wanted you from the moment your body showed itself to be fully a woman. I waited a full year to make you mine." And then he'd let her go.

Did he expect her to cheer his supposed restraint? "You should have waited forever since you had no intention of marrying me after."

"It was not my intentions that were at fault."

She might begin to believe that. *Might.* "Merely your dedication to keeping your vows to me," she mocked.

"Do not provoke me." He growled, the sound just like a wolf.

"Or what? You'll lose control?" Heavens above, what was she doing? Did she want to see his beast come out?

Mayhap, she did.

"Yes," he ground out, stalking closer, his once again

fully tumescent sex testimony to the veracity of his passions at least.

Though again she had to remind herself there was nothing to say that he would not physically desire *any* woman after shifting from his wolf form. It was a very primitive action and there was nothing more primal than sex.

He towered above her, the beast in his eyes so clear she wondered how she'd ever been able to miss it. "My wolf would claim you, *mo toilichte.*"

"Your wolf and you are the same, are you not?" It had certainly seemed so when the beast stood before her.

The wolf had shown the understanding of a man.

"We are."

"Then *you* want to claim me."

"Aye." He closed his eyes, his head tilted back, his tone so guttural it was barely more than a whisper. "I crave you as no other."

"Me? Or any woman's form?"

His head jerked down, blue eyes snapping open and filled with rage-fueled desire. The sound that came from his throat was not human. He had not liked that question at all. It was as if she was casting aspersions on some intrinsic element to his nature, or maybe even something deeper.

"*You.* My sacred mate. I have told you, I can have no other. Six years . . ." His neck muscles corded, he let his words trail off.

Had he said that, or merely claimed he had not had *comfort* in all that time? "What do you mean?"

"As Faol—a wolf shifter. I mean—once I have had sex with my sacred mate, I *cannot* do so with another."

"Explain the *cannot.*"

Something seemed to snap inside him and he grabbed her hand, pressing it to his hard flesh.

Her fingers curled around the erection of their own volition, squeezing before she was even aware of what she was doing.

He groaned, the sound both pained and filled with ecstasy. "*This* does not happen."

"This?" she asked as she squeezed again, this time quite deliberately.

"Yes. I become aroused for none but my true mate. *Six years . . .*" he said again, his voice pained. Caelis's eyes slid shut again, his head tipping back. "Only you, Shona."

The urge to touch him in ways that would push that pleasure over the cliff grew with each second she held that velvet-soft hardness in her hand.

She *should* release him, push him away. Her brain insisted on it. But once again, instinct was taking over reason and her body refused to obey the dictates of her brain.

"I am your sacred mate?" she asked, trying to understand what that really meant.

"Yes."

"Why?"

He cupped each side of her neck, his thumbs rubbing the underside of her chin and leaned down so their foreheads touched. "Only Providence knows, but the sacred bond is a gift few among the Chrechte find."

"Then how could you throw me away?"

"I was convinced of a lie." She could not deny the pain in his voice.

But she could not let it dictate her responses either. "You let yourself believe a lie," she corrected.

The sound he made was one of an animal in pain. "Aye."

She nodded, their foreheads brushing. She'd needed to hear him admit it. Even if he did not take full responsibility for their separation, Caelis needed to acknowledge his role in it.

She would never forget.

"Believing your laird's claim . . ." She would not call that man *her* laird. "That I was not the one, you were willing to push me away on the hope you had a sacred mate."

"No. Maybe." He lifted her head so their gazes met, so close she could see herself in his pupils. "I expected him to realize his error."

"You believed I was your sacred mate?" she asked.

"No, but I didn't think I would find mine. Uven made it clear that even if I could not, he expected me to catch another wolf with child. I hoped he would change his mind about that."

"Or maybe you thought you could get another woman pregnant and leave her?" Shona asked, her own pain too close to the surface.

"No. If you believe nothing else about me, believe that I would not have let you go had I allowed myself to accept the possibility of a child. And there was no other woman I would have given my seed to. Chrechte or human."

Could she accept his words as truth?

No deception shadowed his blue eyes made dark by the candlelight; but then, she'd seen no deception there six years before either.

"You want to believe."

She could not deny it.

"Then believe," he said, his tone cajoling and demanding at once.

Desire that had nothing to do with the words between them coursed through her, heating her blood as even he had never done before. 'Twas as if the six years apart had only increased her body's need for him.

It should have been the opposite. After so long, even residual passion's spark should have gone out.

But the flame burning inside her was hotter than the sun and demanded to be assuaged.

"You want me," he said, his tone laced with wonder and undeniable joy.

"I—"

"Do not deny it." He sniffed the air, another feral noise sounding from deep in his throat. "I can smell it. I can taste it on the air."

"Your wolf senses . . ." Suddenly her son's enhanced abilities made sense. "Eadan—"

"Is like me, though he will not shift for the first time until he is of age."

"No. I would know if my son was more than human."
Though memory after memory flashed through her mind,
reminding her of oddities she'd dismissed over and over again.

Simply because what they pointed to had made absolutely no sense.

Her son shared his nature with a wolf.

"How? When you knew nothing of our existence?"

"He is my son."

"And mine."

What would have happened if her son had shifted without Shona or him being aware of werewolves? "The dreams."

They had prepared her son when no parent had been around to do so.

"Told him of his true nature, yes."

"It's incomprehensible."

"Is it truly?"

After she'd witnessed Caelis's transformation? No, but this was her son. "He'll be stronger."

"And faster."

"Safer."

"Aye." Though he'd met his fair share of humans among both the Balmoral and Sinclair clans that were strong enough.

"This thing between us, it's because of our son." It had to be.

Otherwise, how could she want Caelis so much? They had not even kissed.

"Nay. Rather, he exists because of the bond between us."

A bond that was like a living thing. It was as if Caelis's naked body drew hers with inexorable power she could not deny.

Mesmerized by the sight of his sex hard for her and pulsing with power, once again her hand moved without thought. Her fingers slid against the hardened flesh they were curled around. The tender skin warmed her own, evoking memories much more pleasant than those found in her marriage bed.

"It hurt to have my husband touch me, every caress making my skin crawl and burn most unpleasantly. Was that because I am your mate?" She looked up, wanting to see the truth in his eyes.

Caelis met the look, his expression far too pleased for the words she'd spoken. "I do not know. We had no human-wolf pairings in the clan, and I know little of Abigail and Talorc's mating."

She yanked her hand from him, moving away and staring at Caelis in shock. "The Sinclair laird is a shape-changer like you?"

"He is."

"And Abigail . . ." Caelis's words played over again in her head. "She is human, like me?"

"Yes. Their children are the first evidence I have seen to prove that humans and wolves could be sacred mates."

"Eadan is further proof?"

"He is *all* the proof between us."

She nodded, accepting that at least as truth. "There is much I still do not understand."

He put his big warm hands against her face, peering down at her with such hunger, there could be no question that whatever beset her body affected his as well. "Later, I will answer every question."

"I—"

"Please, Shona, *mo toilichte*. Give me this gift and I will never allow you to regret it again."

The words were so similar to the ones he'd spoken six years ago that she nearly let a bitter laugh tumble from her lips.

The hunger for his touch was stronger now though. She'd thought it near impossible to resist back then. And ultimately, she'd given in to it.

In this moment though? She had no hope to deny the potent need controlling her.

It should be easy now. She no longer loved him. He was not the center of her world, as he'd been to her younger self. To deny him should have been the simplest of things, but Shona did not find it so.

Everything inside her wanted to give herself to this

man, though he'd proven himself unworthy of the gift. It had to be part of being *mated* to a Chrechte.

Would her own body betray her because of it?

The answer seemed to be yes as she swayed toward the giant warrior who shared his nature with a beast.

Caelis's head dipped and his lips pressed reverently to hers. Despite the undeniable hunger raging between them, the caress of his mouth was gentle. Not tentative, but not demanding, either.

The sensation was both so familiar and so far removed from what Shona knew in her present life that she found herself incapable of responding to the kiss in any way. She did not open her lips to give him entrance to her mouth, nor did she repudiate him.

Paralyzed by conflicting emotions, she allowed him to kiss her, his own passions and desires fully in evidence. They called to her, insisting she acknowledge them as well as her own physical need.

He pulled her close, wrapping her in his strong embrace and lifting so their mouths might align more easily.

She remembered how he used to do this, compensating for the great difference in their heights. The way he made her feel both safe and cosseted as he used his strength to protect her and increase her enjoyment of their moments together.

Her husband had never made any accommodations for Shona, though his sexual needs had not been overly onerous. Just very unpleasant.

Henry had not treated her with the tender care or even respect Caelis had. She'd learned to be grateful for the sporadic sexual appetites of an old man.

Caelis growled and broke the kiss. "You will think only of me."

She did not question how he'd known she was thinking of Henry. It did not matter. She had no more desire to dwell on her life in England with the baron than to return to do Percival's bidding.

"Make me." If the order came out sounding more like a plea, neither she nor Caelis remarked on it.

With another primitive, animalistic sound, he kissed her again, this time unquestioningly demanding entrance to her mouth with his tongue. She gave it, letting him wash away unhappy memories and revive good ones.

He tasted like he'd had at least one draught of *usquebagh* before taking up his sentry duty outside her door. Mixed with his own natural flavor, 'twas a heady combination.

The kiss fulfilled one hunger while fueling another. The craving that had beset her so deeply to have his touch became less acute, though it did not disappear, while the need to have him inside her grew.

Caelis's hand roamed over her body, pulling at her dress as if the English clothing annoyed him.

She helped him undress her, her instincts and desires in full control now.

At the first touch of his hand on her naked flesh, she cried out with the satisfaction of a long abandoned need. Her body had craved him the entire time they had been apart, though she only now realized it. She was certain she would have continued to do so until the end of her days, even if she had never seen him again.

No other man's touch would have satisfied, or even come close to pleasing her.

At least now, she understood why. He'd done this to her with the wolf mating thing.

Hands that had once known her body better than any other, learned her anew, big fingers so gentle the caresses brought tears of emotion to her eyes.

And not sadness.

Only he could do this to her. And she let him. They tumbled to the bed, her body trembling with the need to be claimed by his, his strong warrior's muscles tense with the need to claim.

They touched one another as lovers who had never parted, with sure hands and knowing caresses meant to evoke further passions. He teased her nipples, sending pleasure throughout her body, making her ache and writhe even while her own fingers caressed bulging muscles and traced battle scars.

Her heart cried out in possession, *mine*, with each pass of her hand over his body. She neither denied nor acknowledged that heart's cry, but made no effort to hold back on her desire to touch either.

Neither did she try to stop him when his hand delved between her legs to touch her intimately, pushing the pleasure to a higher, almost unbearable level.

But when she spread her thighs for him, he did not enter her.

Instead, Caelis arranged their bodies so that when he pressed down with his pelvis, his shaft rubbed between her swollen folds, his manhood trapped between their bodies so penetration could not occur. This position also ensured that the hard flesh rubbed back and forth over the sweet spot so filled with pleasure for her.

She arched upward, uncontrollable sounds of pleasure spilling from her.

His kisses grew voracious, his movements hard and demanding. Ecstasy spiraled tighter and tighter until it exploded with starbursts inside her.

He climaxed, too, his shout muffled against her lips, his seed marking her stomach with his primordial scent.

She did not know how, but she sensed that his wolf was very happy with that achievement.

The contented growl that sounded in his chest as he reached down to lazily rub the creamy substance into her skin indicated that the beast was indeed pleased.

"I cannot believe I let you do that," she said with more honesty than anger.

"It was inevitable."

Perhaps, if all his claims were true, it had been. Shona didn't feel particularly comforted by that fact, but neither did she feel as if she had betrayed herself completely.

It was a sign of her constant inner conflict with this man that it seemed as if for every thought or feeling she had, an opposite one rose up to meet it.

Chapter 7

The proof of a warrior's strength is in the contentment
of his mate and children.

—ÉAN ORAL TRADITIONS

Caelis gave her a look, his brown gaze filled to over-
flowing with satisfaction. "You smell like me."

His gratification was more than a little annoying. He
wasn't beset by conflict like she was. It was apparent that to
him, all was quite simple.

But it wasn't just typical warrior arrogance.

"Your wolf likes that." Again, she did not understand
how she knew, but she had not doubts on the matter.

"Aye, but do not be mistaken . . . the man is just as content to have every wolf in this clan know you have been
marked as mine."

"They'll be able to tell?" she asked, heat at the thought
filling her cheeks and spreading over her chest. *"They'll
smell you on me?"*

It was a most disconcerting, not to mention embarrassing, thought. How many wolves were there? If the laird
was a shape-changer like Caelis, how many others were as
well?

"Aye."

"Do not sound so pleased about it."

"I cannot help it. You are mine, Shona, and should always have been with me. I have lived without you for too long. For a time, I even believed you were dead."

"What? Why?" She could not imagine how much worse the last years would have been had she believed Caelis dead.

"Why do you think? Our laird told me you had been killed by a wild boar. I carried great guilt along with my grief until I began to realize perhaps that had been a lie along with so many other things Uven told me."

"He is not *my* laird."

"No, he is not."

She was glad of the easy agreement, but it was not enough. "I am English now."

"No, you are not."

"I am." No matter how he would stubbornly refuse to admit it.

"Are you not here seeking a life in Scotland for you and your children?"

"Yes."

"Because at heart, you are a fine Scottish lass." His smile was irresistible.

But still she said, so there could be no confusion, "I'll not wear the MacLeod colors again."

"Not now. But later."

"Never."

"Never is—"

"A long time. So you've said."

"Best you remember that." He was smiling again.

She responded with some bite, "Best you remember that I am not so easily gotten around."

He looked between their naked bodies with significance.

"Your wolf can take credit for this, I think."

"My wolf is me."

"The one part of you I just might trust."

He jerked a little and then stared down at her. "You trust my beast?"

"Yes. I don't know why, but I do."

"You do not trust me—the man—though?" he asked carefully.

"No." She made no effort to soften the effect of her denial. He had betrayed her most thoroughly.

"Yet you allowed me to touch you."

"I told you, blame your wolf. There is some kind of magic in this mating thing and my body is not my own."

The glow of satisfaction around him dimmed. "You truly believe this?"

"Absolutely." And he'd best not try to deny it. "Give me another explanation for a craving I cannot stand against for the touch of the very man who has betrayed me so cruelly."

Caelis looked down at her with shock, as if her words were beyond his ken. But surely he knew the truth of it more certainly than she. He had lived with knowledge of his wolf his whole life. She'd just found out about it.

Finally, his mouth opened and a very ugly word came, but nothing else.

She frowned up at him. "What is the matter?"

"You must ask when you have just told me you still hold my actions against me in such a grievous way? That you allowed me to touch you only because you could not help yourself?"

What did he expect? Protestations of love as she used to give him? "Did you think pleasure could erase the past?"

The expression on his warrior's features said he'd believed exactly that. Men! They uprooted a woman's life, made changes over which she had no control and then expected a thank-you at the end of it. Her father had been the same.

"Have you forgotten your anger *at Uven* for lying to you now that we have once again shared passion?" she asked, wondering if Caelis would let himself understand.

"Nay! I am more furious with that liar than I was before. What you and I have just shared only shows what he took from us *both* with his lies. He robbed me of my sacred mate, of my son."

As Caelis had allowed the man to rob her. She did not say it, having earlier made her point on that issue.

Instead, she reiterated, "So, the pleasure did not negate the pain?"

Sighing, Caelis shook his head. "You are saying you do not forgive me, either."

"No." Though maybe she was beginning to.

He frowned, his overt satisfaction all but gone. "I see."

Perhaps he did. Mayhap he even realized that only time would prove him more worthy of her trust than she now held him.

"You have grown into a hard woman, Shona."

"Circumstances have forced me to draw on strengths I did not know I had." Though the strength to resist him clearly was not among them.

He nodded. "When you realized you were indeed pregnant, why did you not send word?"

"You assume I had some way of doing so. I did not, but even if I had, I *would* not have. You had already told me you would consider my child someone else's by-blow."

"I did not mean it. You had to know that. You were untouched the first time we shared our bodies."

"I did not know it. You said it after rejecting me; why would I believe you would want me even if you knew of the babe?"

"I am not a man who would abandon my child."

"Tell yourself whatever you like, but you already had."

He stared at her, his expression clearly showing how foreign he found the concept of her words, but then great sadness came over his features. "You are right."

She knew she was. So, why did seeing his grief hurt her as it did?

He turned and moved as if to leave the bed.

Her hand moved out to touch him before she could snatch it back. "Where are you going?"

"Back to the hall." His massive shoulders hunched. "I have no place in your bed."

"You are already in my bed."

He merely shrugged, but he did not stand.

"I do not want you to go."

"That cannot be true."

"It is."

His head turned so he looked at her over his shoulder. "Because of my wolf. Because we are mates."

"Maybe. I would like to think so. It paints me a stronger woman, but all I know of a certainty is that when I am with you, I have peace I have not had these past six years."

"Even with all the anger you have toward me?" he asked with disbelief.

His reaction was understandable. She found her own desires and behavior very confusing indeed. "Prove yourself trustworthy to me."

"How?"

"Begin by not leaving my bed now that you have gotten what you wanted from me."

"You think one moment of passion is all I want from you?" he asked, this time the disbelief huge in his tone and demeanor. "I have gone six years without you. We could spend until the next new moon in this bed and I would not have gotten all I wanted of your body."

And suddenly, the desire was rolling off him again in hot waves that reached out and covered her. Inexplicably, but not surprisingly, her own rose to match it.

This time, their coupling was no less hungry than the last. In fact, his body moved against hers with greater urgency, though he still refused to enter her. And a part of her was grateful for it.

She did not want another pregnancy outside the bonds of matrimony. The last had cost her dearly.

Though as he'd pushed her to admit to him, she would never truly regret it.

When their passions had been spent, Caelis lowered himself to lie by her side. "Tell me about Percival wanting to make you his *lehman*."

"The disgusting degenerate. He's not content to *tup* half the serving wenches and his own poor wife, but he wanted to make me his official mistress, thereby making my children by his father at risk for being considered natural, rather than legitimate."

"Is that the way it works in England then?"

"In England it is no more common, or acceptable, for a man to take his father's wife as his *lehman* than in the Highlands."

"But he would have done it regardless?"

"He's too arrogant to care if others approve of his behavior." She worried her lower lip, deciding if she wanted to tell Caelis everything. "You are committed to claiming Eadan?"

"Aye, and Marjory too."

Could she trust him to be father to both her children? Again, only time would tell, but Shona had to take the first step forward. Whether she liked it or not. Trusted him, or didn't.

She took a deep breath and let it out. "Percival tried to kill Eadan, on more than one occasion. He always denied his intentions, but the accidents were no accidents at all. Percival wanted no competitor for his father's barony."

"But as the eldest, he was the acknowledged heir." Caelis sounded confused.

"Yes, but if Percival could not provide offspring—and thus far he has not, though his marriage is older than mine to his father—the king would naturally name Eadan's eldest son the heir to the title. Percival's pride would not allow it."

"He would rather there be no heir to the barony?"

"Oh, yes. In that case, the king would appoint an heir who would likely come from the monarch's own extended relations."

"Percival sounds like a very vain, manipulative man."

"He is, and cunning and determined."

"You think he would come after you here?"

"I do not know."

"If he comes, I will kill him."

"He is an English baron; it would be considered an act of war." Not that she would miss the man's existence on this earth.

"If England's king is foolish enough to go to war over such a worm, then he deserves the losses he will suffer at our hands."

Shona shook her head. "Stubborn man."

"We are well matched then."

Audrey quietly pushed open the door to Shona's bedchamber, disturbed to find it not barred from the inside. Thus far, the Sinclairs had shown themselves hospitable and unlikely to harm, but they were still a clan of strangers.

Except that man who wore different colors and was so obviously Eadan's father. There was no doubt that Shona had known *that* man very well at some point in the past. And though perhaps it should not, that fact had quite shocked Audrey.

She had always known the baron wasn't blood relative to her dear friend's first child, but she'd never guessed the father was a Highland warrior.

It was testament to Audrey's agitated thinking that the scents of the Highland Chrechte and that of unmistakable passion did not become apparent to her until Audrey's gaze fell on the bed occupied by one more person than it should have been.

The wolf was awake, staring at her with dark, unfathomable eyes, his hold on Audrey's dearest friend too proprietary to be mistaken. The air of protection was no less certain.

"How? What?" she stuttered out, her shock so complete, she nearly lost her breath.

Shona woke in that moment, her eyes widening at the sight of Audrey and then in horror as realization of her circumstances dawned. "Audrey! I . . . It's . . ."

Audrey shook her head. "Come, we will bathe before the rest of the keep is up and sniffing around."

Whatever explanations Shona wished to make, she could do so later. When she was no longer embroiled in an undeniably and hopelessly compromising position.

Audrey's heart ached for her friend even as her brain spun with ways to help the baroness.

Shona nodded her head vigorously while the wolf frowned his displeasure.

Though Audrey had hoped the Faol warrior would wait to make his claim, she was not entirely surprised he had moved to establish his place in Shona's life so quickly.

According to Audrey's dear departed mother, the mating bond for a Chrechte was so strong as to be undeniable. Otherwise her mum had said, *she* would never would have allowed herself to become a married man's *lehman*.

Her position as such had gone against the teaching of their race, or so Audrey's mother had insisted. She'd shared little enough of them with her children. Both Audrey and Thomas were almost wholly ignorant of their people's ways.

Audrey's current stupefaction lay in the fact *Shona* had welcomed this man . . . *any* man, really . . . into her bed. A human, she was not driven by the instincts of an animal sharing her nature toward their mate.

At least, that was what Audrey had always believed. She'd never noted her father being particularly weak with longing toward her mother or abundant in caring toward the children the English Chrechte had born him.

"Water can be brought to your chamber," Caelis said grumpily to Shona, ignoring Audrey altogether.

"Nay," Audrey immediately denied, refusing to be intimidated by the huge Chrechte. She would protect Shona's reputation even if the baroness was not currently up to the task herself. "My mistress will have a bath in the loch."

Shona could wash off the scent of this man's seed at the very least. Though it was unlikely she would be able to remove it entirely.

The humans would be unaware of Shona's nighttime visitor, but the wolves would know Caelis had staked some sort of claim.

Audrey smiled at Shona, trying to give the other woman a message of her own unwavering support. "Lady Abigail told me of one nearby that is used by the clanswomen."

She was not worried about finding the loch. Her wolf's senses would lead Audrey to the water easily enough.

"You aren't bathing outside these walls with naught but this Englishwoman to guard you," Caelis pronounced.

Though the wolf had not left his mark on Shona's neck, his air of possession was as strong as if he had.

Shona shrugged, doing her best to hide her discomfort at climbing from the bed as naked as the day she'd come into this world, but climb from it she did and Audrey could have cheered. "Then you may accompany us as our protector."

Audrey frowned. She was not sure that was a good idea at all.

The warrior opened his mouth to argue and then shut it again without uttering a word. Maybe he realized what an easy victory he had just won from the stubborn Shona.

Audrey was not so sanguine. "We traveled all the way from England without need of your guard. Your presence is hardly needed for our morning constitutional in the Sinclair's loch."

"You would risk your lady's safety?" he asked, addressing Audrey for the first time.

"There is no risk."

"You are naïve if you believe that."

She'd been accused of such more than once. It never made her smile. "I am not so naïve as to believe *you* have her best interests at heart."

"That is not your judgment to make."

"You think not?"

"Enough." Shona had pulled on her shift and a wrapper, the one Lady Abigail had offered the day before.

Audrey had been surprised Shona had decided to dress the night before instead of using it. Though maybe she had not seen it?

"I have already told Caelis he can accompany us as guard, Audrey. I will expect Thomas to as well. You know that had I a choice these past sennights, I would not have left my children's protection to our small band."

Audrey could not deny it and guilt assailed her. "I know it."

Caelis waved at Audrey imperiously. "Wait in the hall for us to join you."

"I will not." He may have compromised the other woman's virtue beyond redemption, but no further damage would be done to Shona's reputation or innocence this morn.

"Do not speak to her that way," Shona said sharply before either Audrey or Caelis could talk further. "She is my friend, not my servant and if you expect to be in our company you will treat Audrey with the respect due her."

Shock upon shock, the grouchy warrior inclined his head toward Audrey. "Pardon my offense. Will you please wait in the hall?"

"No."

He glared.

She crossed her arms and frowned right back.

"I am not going to ravish her . . . again." The devilment in his eyes said more was coming. "At least, not at this moment."

The loud sound of a hard smack against flesh came only a second before his wince of pain. He looked over his shoulder at Shona. "What was that for?"

Her dear sweet Shona, who had not a violent bone in her delicate human body, or so Audrey had always thought— her one dire threat to the dead baron aside—hauled back and punched Caelis right in the jaw. "I am no doxy to be spoken about thus. If your words were true last night, then I am something of far greater import to you. Don't you ever make light of the privileges I've given you against my better judgment. You've done that once and near destroyed my life and that of our son in the bargain. I'll not stand for it again. Do you hear me?"

"I believe Sir Percival has heard you clear back in England," Thomas said from the doorway, Marjory and Eadan standing by his side watching the exchange with wide-eyed startlement.

"Mama, you hit the nice man. It's not nice to hit. You said so," Marjory censured her mother.

Another time, Audrey would have found the exchange diverting. At present, she worried for what Shona might say in response.

Shona, clearly beyond reason or caution gave such a venomous glare to the warrior, Caelis should be very glad there were no such thing as snake shifters. "He is *not* a nice man. He is an arrogant, tell-all, *useless* MacLeod soldier!"

Marjory and Eadan stared at their mother as if she had grown enough heads to become the Hydra of mythology. Audrey did not blame them. They had never seen their mother upset like this.

Not even when she was burying her father and terrified for the very life of her son.

Caelis had been slightly amused through it all, including the surprisingly well placed hit to his jaw, but when Shona called him *useless*, he winced, his expression turning so bleak Audrey almost pitied him.

"Mama!" Marjory remonstrated, regaining her sense and showing none of her usual timidity.

Though admittedly that side of her nature rarely ruled between Marjory and her mother, the child knowing without doubt how very much the former Scotswoman adored her.

Shona spun to face Marjory. "Why do you think he's so nice?" she asked with undisguised bewilderment.

Marjory shrugged. She pulled away from Thomas to cross the room and stand near Caelis, who sat on the bed, the lower half of his body covered by the bedding.

The child took the big warrior's hand with her tiny one.

"I don't know, Mama. But I know it. *He's nice.* Not like Percy. You should not hit him."

Shona's eyes shown with wetness, but she conjured a smile for her daughter. "I am glad you find him so. Perhaps one day your mama will as well."

"You have to, Mum." The desperation in Eadan's tone was hard to hear. "Or we can't be a family."

The hopeless expression that crossed Shona's features said she wasn't as certain of that fact as her son was. For her part, Audrey wasn't either.

If Caelis pressed the matter, Shona would have little to say about it. Particularly after she had allowed him into her bed again.

Audrey shook her head at her friend's predicament. She knew not how to fix it. "Come, we will all bathe in the loch."

"Do we have to?" Eadan and Thomas both asked at the same time.

Audrey felt a much-welcomed laugh bubble up inside of her. Her brother was still such a youth at times.

Shona answered for her with a firm, "Yes."

Caelis went to stand and Shona moved with speed Audrey had not known humans capable. "What are you doing?" Shona demanded.

"Coming to the lake with you."

"You cannot rise naked from the bed in front of Audrey and the children." Presumably Shona left Thomas off the list because modesty between warriors was nearly nonexistent.

Particularly among the Highlanders, where those of a more barbaric disposition still went into battle with nothing more than the paints of war marking their faces and bodies.

"Why not? You did," he pointed out in a reasonable tone that Audrey did not believe for a second.

He was not daft, no matter how he might pretend.

"That is different."

"Aye, but when I asked her to leave, you became very angry with me."

"You didn't ask, you ordered."

He shrugged, showing that to him they were one and the same.

"I do not remember you being such an annoying man."

"That is to be expected. Six years ago, you did not consider me *useless*, either."

Chapter 8

Listen to your beast's instincts. It will not lead you astray like the words of a wily man.

—FAOL PROVERB

It was Shona's turn to wince, though Audrey was happy to see the baroness made no apology for her earlier words.

She simply grabbed his plaid from where it had been tossed on the floor and threw it at Caelis. "Cover yourself decently."

"Mum?"

"Yes, Eadan?" Shona responded, sounding harried.

"You do not believe Da is a nice man? Truly?"

Shona stopped her agitated picking up of clothing around the room. She'd managed to don her shift and the borrowed wrapper before the children and Thomas's arrival, but the rest of her dress, to be donned after they bathed, was in her arms.

Shona looked at her son, clearly wishing for a way out of answering his question honestly. "There was a time I thought he was very kind."

"But not now?" Eadan pressed.

"He has proven to be ruthless on an important occasion."

Which was no doubt how Shona had ended up pregnant and alone in England, Audrey thought.

"Sometimes a man has to be ruthless for the sake of his family," Eadan said, quoting his recently deceased grandfather.

Audrey knew that Shona was not overfond of that particular sentiment, though she rarely gainsaid her father on anything.

"In this case, it was for his own sake and not that of his family. We were left to fend for ourselves," Shona said with grudging honesty.

The honesty did not surprise Audrey. Despite protecting her children from the trials of the world surrounding them as much as she was able, Shona did not make it a habit to lie to either Eadan or Marjory.

Audrey could not understand the flash of triumph in Caelis eyes until he said, "So you admit you are my family," as he buckled the leather kirtle holding his kilt into place.

Instead of focusing on the fact that Shona so evidently did not trust him, he claimed victory in her wording. Audrey could see now that Shona would have to be most cautious in her dealings with this wily Faol.

Clearly chagrined, Shona deliberately turned away from Caelis, facing her son fully. "You've had many dreams about him, you said."

"Yes, Mum."

"And in your dreams, what kind of man was he?"

That was the Shona Audrey knew and admired so. A woman who respected her children even when others said the same should be rarely seen and never heard.

"He is a good man in my dreams, Mum. He watches over us and protects us from Percival and other bad men who would do us harm."

"I am glad to hear it."

Eadan nodded. "I think he's sorry, Mum. For whatever he did before."

Shona's features hardened. "Time will tell, Eadan."

"Grandda used to say that, too."

"Aye, he did." Grief washed over the baroness's features briefly. "He was a good man."

Eadan nodded, though he did not say anything more. He'd loved his grandfather, but even the young boy had noted how the old man had treated his grandchildren much differently than his only daughter.

Shona's father's love for her had been tempered by his disappointment in her the entire time Audrey knew the stubborn Scot.

"You didn't tell your mother about your dreams," Audrey said, to take both the boy and the woman's minds away from where they now dwelled.

Eadan shrugged. "She didn't believe in them."

"I am sorry." Shona cast a sidelong glance at the warrior who had come to stand much too close to her for propriety's sake. "I have come to realize there are many things I believed impossible that are, in fact, truth."

Had Caelis told Shona of his Faol nature? Audrey didn't think so, not the way Shona responded the same as ever to her and Thomas. Besides, wouldn't the wolf wait until he was sure of the human woman's allegiance before risking exposure?

Having grown up without a pack, there was much about the Chrechte way of life that Audrey and Thomas did not know, but one thing their mother had been most adamant about.

To tell their secret was to betray all their brethren as well as themselves.

On the way to the loch, Eadan yelled excitedly. "Look! An eagle."

Caelis's gaze flicked upward and a scowl came over his features. Then he did something entirely unexpected for such a serious warrior.

He yelled at the eagle as if scolding a naughty child. "Get you gone!"

Even more amazingly, the eagle screeched as if in defiant response. Then the bird swooped down from the sky, much to both Marjory's and Eadan's delight, the tip of one majestic wing brushing the top of Audrey's head before the noble bird soared back to its position high in the sky above them.

Shona's friend looked dazed. "What a beautiful bird."

"I'm sure he would be pleased to hear you say so," Caelis said with a snort.

Shona could not understand her warrior's attitude.

Neither, apparently, could Audrey, who shook her head. "Do not be daft. Even a regal bird like that one does not have the reason to appreciate my admiration."

"You would be surprised," Caelis replied cryptically.

The eagle followed them to the water, taking up a circular pattern in the sky above the loch.

"You'd best keep your eyes off my mate," Caelis said loudly.

And rather nonsensically, to Shona's way of thinking. "He's a bird. I'm far more concerned about you keeping *your* back turned."

Caelis opened his mouth and she just knew he was going to say something about having seen all there was to see already.

The warning look she gave him must have worked, because the shape-changer's mouth snapped shut and he turned his back so she and Audrey could ready the children and undress for bathing.

"I'm too old to bathe with the women," Eadan announced, stepping out of his mother's reach.

Shona was charmed. She could not help it. She was a mother and this sign of furthering independence from her son despite the upsets in his life brought a genuine smile to her lips.

"He's right," Caelis agreed, adding that Eadan was of an age to begin his training.

Shona *wasn't* so enamored of that particular claim, but her former beloved was being insistent. He pointed out that though Marjory was merely three years, she was already learning how to stitch.

Where he came by this knowledge, Shona could not help but wonder. Apparently the time she had spent sleeping the day before had been a productive one for him in his quest to get to know the children he was so adamant he wanted to claim.

"That is a ridiculous comparison," Shona argued.

Audrey added, "Thomas did not begin training until he was twelve."

"And I was never trained completely." Thomas's unhappiness with the haphazard way his father had handled his upbringing before ejecting him and Audrey from his home was in the young man's voice.

He looked at Caelis with admiration and some envy.

"You did right by my son, teaching him how to ride and to pay attention to the knowledge of the world his senses give him."

Thomas turned bright red and the admiration transformed to full-blown hero worship.

Between the way Thomas looked at Caelis and Eadan's attitude, there was no question that both Shona's son and young friend were completely beguiled by the tough warrior.

Since she found his attentiveness toward Eadan and gruff kindness toward Thomas a bit beguiling herself, she could hardly complain about that fact.

She gave in about the segregated bathing without another word, helping Marjory into the water and playing swimming games with her daughter to get her used to the cold temperatures.

Her gaze slid to the men as Audrey took Marjory, so she did not miss when Caelis took Eadan up onto his shoulders. Shona's heart squeezed in her chest.

The baron had not been a kind or demonstrative man and had no interest in helping Eadan, or Thomas for that matter, to learn anything.

Thinking about the great turns her life had taken in less

than a day, she did her best to wash the scent of lovemaking from her skin while Audrey washed Marjory's hair. Shona was no longer so certain she wanted to deny his claim on her, but she had no desire whatsoever to have their activities the night before announced to all and sundry.

Not by him, as he'd done with Audrey and not by her scent, no matter how much his wolf might want that.

"Here, use this." Audrey handed Shona the bar of lavender soap they'd brought with them from England.

Shona took the soap, wondering if Audrey had noticed the scent of lovemaking in the bedchamber that morning. "Thank you."

Nothing else was said while the two women washed each other's hair. Marjory played in the shallow water nearby with a small duck Thomas had carved for her.

At one point, the eagle swooped down again, this time touching Audrey's bare shoulder with the tip of his wing. She laughed and shooed the bird of prey as she might a rabbit in the carrot patch.

Caelis growled, the sound quite menacing, though he had not turned around. So, she could not understand how he'd known of the Eagle's brief visit. She put both from her mind as she and Audrey rinsed away the soap and sand from the bottom of the loch they'd used to get their hair clean.

"I was surprised to find Caelis in your bed this morn," Audrey said tentatively as she and Shona wrung the water from their hair. Her tone invited confidences without an ounce of judgment.

Nevertheless, a flush of shame warmed Shona's skin despite the chill of the loch's water. "He was standing guard outside my door when I woke and went searching for the children."

Which didn't begin to explain how the man had ended up in her bed. She couldn't explain that to herself, either, or the fact she'd wanted him to stay after they'd shared their bodies and their passions.

"I should have remained with you last night, but

Marjory wanted the comfort of my presence." Audrey's voice was laced with heavy regret and self-censure.

"My virtue is not your responsibility," Shona stated, finding it painful to acknowledge how very thoroughly she'd allowed her virtue to be imperiled.

"You *are* a virtuous woman." Audrey said, as if she knew exactly what Shona was thinking. "Whatever happened in the wee hours did not change that."

"You know 'tis not the way the rest of the world thinks."

"The rest of the world can go hang," Audrey said with more malice than Shona had ever heard in her young friend's voice. "You are the only one who treated Thomas and I like we mattered. You trust your children with us, but just as important, your hand has been open in friendship from the first day we came to the barony."

"I understood what it meant to be treated as less." Shona's pregnancy had made her less in her parents' eyes.

And despite how pleasing he found her feminine form, her deceased husband had believed himself superior by dint of English birth and the very basic difference that he was a man and she a woman. He also never allowed her to forget that she'd not come to his bed a virgin.

She'd once reminded him that she would not have come to his bed at all if she had been one. That had precipitated one of the few times he'd beaten her.

"Did you give into Caelis because you did not believe you had a choice?" Audrey asked in a quiet undertone with a quick glance at the warrior's imposing back.

Shona knew the sister of her heart was not asking about the true mate bond. How could she be? Audrey was still innocent to the strange world Shona had learned of only the night before.

No, Audrey wanted to know if Caelis had forced the issue. And Shona could understand why the other woman might ask such a thing.

Whatever he might be, the man who had rejected her and now proclaimed his desire to keep her was no rapist. "No."

"You are certain?" Audrey met Shona's gaze, her own blue one so very earnest.

"I am certain." Shona almost wished she could answer in the affirmative. It was so clear Audrey could conceive of no other reason for Shona's rash behavior. "He did not force himself on me."

Audrey sighed, the relief clear in her gaze, even if the confusion had not diminished. "I am glad."

Shona looked to where her daughter continued to play, oblivious to the adults' discussion.

Then Audrey's head snapped up and she looked over at the men standing with their backs to the bathing females. Shona's gaze followed her friend's and she saw that Caelis's stance had grown rigid, anger coming off him in waves.

Had Thomas said something to offend the giant warrior?

She'd thought her friend more intelligent than that. From the side of his face that she could see, Thomas on the other hand, appeared almost appalled by something.

Eadan was playing in the bushes, pretending to hunt and ignoring them all.

Or so Shona hoped. With the way her son heard things she'd thought it impossible for him to, she did not want him overlistening to *this* conversation.

Then it struck her. Caelis had heard Audrey's questions and was mortally offended. He should have heard Shona's answers as well then. So, why was he angry?

Was his manly pride that offended Audrey would even ask? Did he think Shona had not been strenuous enough in her denials?

Whatever his reasoning, the shape-changer would have to come to terms with the fact that both Audrey and Thomas were protective of Shona. As she was of them.

They were family, if not by birth.

Audrey looked away from Caelis and back to Shona. "I do not understand." Again, there was no censure in her voice, just bewilderment.

Unfortunately, Shona could not help her friend comprehend something she found so difficult to understand herself. "I cannot explain it."

Her friend probably found the truth no more palatable than Shona did.

"He hurt you grievously, left you with child."

"He did not know."

"How could that be?"

"It is not so difficult."

Audrey did not look convinced. "You gave him the gift of your innocence."

"You are so sure? Perhaps I was a strumpet, sharing my body here, there and everywhere," Shona replied bitterly, remembering some of her mother's more cruel words.

Audrey laughed, the sound carrying across the crisp still air above the lake. "You are no more strumpet than I."

"*You* are still innocent."

"So are you, of wrongdoing."

"Oh no; I gave myself to him. We were not even betrothed." Though she'd believed that was just a formality, had believed his promises of a future.

"You loved him."

"More than I ever want to love *any man* ever again."

Audrey nodded. "My mother loved my father and it brought her nothing but pain."

"Your father is a stupid and selfish man, entirely too vain." Anyone who would sell his own children into indenture merely to be rid of their presence didn't deserve the gift of fatherhood.

The man was a lesser baron, but a noble with extensive land holdings nonetheless. He'd had no need for the coin Henry had paid him for the privilege of bringing Audrey and Thomas into his household as higher-ranking servants.

Later, when laughter and splashing sounded across the lake as Caelis and Thomas played in the water with Eadan, Shona thought perhaps some men *should* get a second chance at fatherhood.

"He has not laughed like that since well before your

father passed," Audrey remarked as she plaited Marjory's hair.

"Eadan has always enjoyed the company of his Uncle Thomas." Henry had been very annoyed when Shona had bestowed the honorary titles of uncle and aunt on Thomas and Audrey.

His insistence they were mere servants had only spurred Shona on to continue with the practice.

Audrey just shook her head.

"Oh, fine. You wish me to admit that Eadan is clearly in alt being with his father?"

"Refusing to admit it would not make it any less true."

"I know." Shona sighed as she finished tying off her own loose braid, letting it rest over her left breast.

The braid would not tame her curls completely, but helped them remain manageable. Henry had always said her hair was her glory and insisted she wore it down with only a thin gold circlet on her head.

It had been fashionable, but not practical. Not that the old man had cared if Marjory's baby fists got tangled in the long red tresses, or flour from the kitchens inevitably ended up decorating the ends when she made bread.

He'd told her his cook could see to the needs of the keep, but the man had been a miser in areas not easily discerned by his knights or guests. He'd refused to provide enough kitchen help to feed the mouths living in his walls.

Of course Shona had stepped in to help. Particularly since her own mother had been cook until her death.

"You've got that look again."

"What look is that?" Shona asked Audrey.

"Sadness."

There was no point in denying the truth. "I was thinking of my mother."

"She was a good woman, but not half so kind as her daughter." It was a sweet sentiment, though not entirely true.

Before Shona's disgrace, her mother had shown her

daughter, and the others around them, a great deal of kindness.

Her husband losing his position as seneschal for the MacLeod, their move to England (a land her mother had hated) and then discovering her daughter carried a child out of wedlock had all taken a great toll on the older Scotswoman.

She said none of this to Audrey though, the topic of her life before England one Shona had always been loath to discuss. While the very reason for that habit now played in the water with their son, she found it difficult to break regardless.

The men left the water, taking Eadan behind a stand of bushes to preserve the women's modesty as they dressed.

Her son came out of the foliage dressed in a child-size kilt of the MacLeod colors. Shona did not know where Caelis had come by the small plaid, but it gave her no joy to see her son dressed thus. In truth, the silent claim by the big warrior sent a skirl of fear shivering down her spine.

In that moment, Eadan looked wholly like Caelis's child, with nothing to indicate an English baroness was his mother at all.

She opened her mouth to protest, but was interrupted by Marjory tugging at the skirt of Shona's heavy green velvet gown. "Mama?"

"Yes, love?"

"I don't want to ride a horse today."

Audrey and Shona shared a commiserating look.

In all truth, Shona knew not what the day would hold, but at the very least she thought the generosity of the Sinclair laird might extend to another night's lodging. "We will stay here for today."

"Promise?" Marjory asked with such hope Shona had to hide a wince.

Her poor daughter was tired of the adventure of travel. Eadan as well, no doubt. Neither child was used to spending so many hours confined from play, much less to a saddle.

And while sleeping on the ground under the stars had been an adventure the first couple of nights, it soon grew less charming, even for the wee ones. But Shona had had no choice other than to set the grueling pace she had done.

They had needed to put as much distance as possible between themselves and any soldiers Percival might have sent after them.

"Can we live here, do you think?" Marjory asked artlessly.

"I'm sorry sweeting, but our family is on Balmoral Island."

"You're still set on traveling there?" Caelis asked, reproof in his tone.

"My plans are not set." And that was all she would give the big warrior. "You are ready to return to the keep?"

Though clearly they were. Thomas was once again dressed in his English garb and Caelis had re-donned his plaid, his hair still dripping rivulets of water down his chest and back. Having done no better a job at drying, Eadan stood between the two men looking like a miniature version of the Chrechte warrior.

"I would not mind staying here for a bit," Thomas said, sounding every bit as hopeful as the children. "The Sinclair said I could train with his Chrechte, his elite soldiers."

Shona did not miss Thomas's attempt to explain the Chrechte away as elite soldiers. Just as others in her former clan had done when she'd lived among them, but after last night, Shona knew exactly what Chrechte were.

Elite soldiers they might be, but 'twas because they shared their nature with a beast.

She stared at Thomas, the young man who had come to live in her home when he was still a gangly boy of fourteen. She'd been only a few years older but felt decades wiser in the ways of the world.

This boy was to train with the Chrechte. That could only mean one thing.

"You have a wolf as well," she whispered, barely able to get the words past the tightness in her throat.

For if Thomas, honorary uncle to her children and close as a brother to Shona, was a shape-changer—that meant her dearest friend, the true sister of her heart, Audrey was as well.

And all these years, neither had said a thing.

Chapter 9

A mother, though of the softest feminine nature, will let her beast rule when protecting her child.

—SABRINE OF THE DONEGAL

"Wolf? I don't know what you mean." Thomas was such a poor liar, Shona had to wonder at his and Audrey's ability to keep their secret all these years.

"Stop your fabrications. Caelis told me. He *showed* me," she emphasized, so they would not think there was any room for doubt.

"You showed her?" Thomas asked, clearly shocked to the core. "But you are male and it is not the full moon."

"We gain control of our change once we have engaged in certain acts," Caelis said with a significant look at the children.

Shona had no idea what he meant, but Thomas seemed to understand just fine because he nodded and then turned bright red.

"You are a white wolf, are you not?" Caelis asked.

Thomas nodded his head doubtfully.

Caelis looked to Audrey, who gave a more confident affirmative. "Then you should have control of the change already. It is the way of your wolf. Others are not so lucky."

"I can prevent it at the full moon," Thomas said. "Mother taught us."

"If you can prevent the change, you can initiate it as well."

"I can?" Thomas asked, his eyes shining with delight at the thought.

"Aye."

"Will you show me how?"

Caelis gave a short nod of his head in affirmative.

Thomas's eyes glowed with such hero worship, in other circumstances it would have brought a smile to Shona's features. But numbness was taking over emotions battered by one too many blows.

"Did you know about Eadan?" Shona asked Audrey, her voice strained.

Though she felt distanced from the pain of yet another betrayal slicing at her heart and the way it manifested itself.

Audrey's face crumpled and Shona had her answer.

Not only were they both Chrechte, but they'd known her son was one as well.

For five years, Audrey and Thomas had known Shona's most shameful secret.

They had always been aware that her husband was not father to her son, and yet they'd kept their own mystery without a hint to the truth.

They'd kept *her* son's true nature from her. "How? How did you know?"

Was it something about the way her son smelled to them? He was always talking about being able to smell her sadness or a lie when she tried to protect him from the truth.

"Your father—"

"My father knew?" Shona cried, cut to the very quick of her being. "How? Why?"

She looked accusingly at Caelis. "You told him when you did not tell me?"

"No. I know not how your father came to know our secret, but 'twas not through me."

She did not understand the look of concern on Caelis's features. Though naught made much sense at the moment. The two people he had been certain would never knowingly deceive her had done nothing but for five years.

Revelation after revelation unfurled in her beleaguered brain. Her dearest and most trusted friends had proven beyond doubt that they did not trust *her*. Further, they were not so trustworthy. They had lied to her, hidden her son's nature from her.

'Twas that fact that was most difficult to accept. Well, almost.

The fact that her father had known was as devastating but not so hard to fathom. He had proven his lack of regard for her happiness too consistently for her to continue to pretend even in her deepest heart that he had loved her, despite his harsh judgment of her actions.

He'd known of Caelis's nature, though she did not know how. If she believed Caelis's claim he did not tell her father of the wolf nature, then her da must have found out some other way.

As former seneschal to the clan, however, her da would have been privy to secrets others were not. The how was far less important than the result though.

Her own father had known her son's lineage and what it meant, and he'd not thought her worthy of knowing as well.

Had thought she deserved the fate he arranged for her, marriage to a man of an age to be her own grandfather?

"He knew . . ." She could barely comprehend the level of betrayal pounding on her already beleaguered heart like the blacksmith's anvil. "If he knew of the Chrechte, then he knew what my pregnancy signified. He knew I was your true mate and yet he forced me into marriage with the baron."

Saying the words aloud made them no easier to believe or to bear.

"Your father forced you to marry?"

"You think I wanted another man's touch? You think I wanted any man to have a hold over my life after you used and discarded me?" The grief pouring off her made her tone shrill, her Gaelic slurred.

Her son made a sound of distress and guilt poured through Shona. She'd never pretended to be perfect to her children, but she had always, *always* tried to protect them from her distress.

It was a mark of how great the toll the last few sennights had been on her that she'd allowed them to see her upset to this degree. Her children had no fault in the pain besetting her and she would not let them pay the price for her own folly in once again trusting unwisely.

Using every ounce of her courage and will, she pushed back her feelings of betrayal and turned with a semblance of a smile to her son. "All is well, Eadan."

"Do you still love me, Mummy?"

"What? Of course I do." And five years old or not, she tugged her son into a fierce hug. "I love you more than my own life and I always will, I promise you."

"Someday, I am going to be a wolf," he whispered against her collar bone, his little boy arms wrapped tightly around her neck. "My dreams showed me. Like my da."

"I know." And deep inside, where truth resided, she did. "You will be an amazing wolf."

He pulled back, checking her face as if testing the veracity of her words.

"I'm telling the truth. Can't you smell it?" she managed to tease.

He nodded, his expression going from uncertain to a full-blown smile. "You aren't a wolf. Neither is Marjory, but that's okay. We'll protect you, Da, Thomas and me."

She could not look at the adult men without screaming, so she kept her focus entirely on her son. "Thank you, but until you are bigger, I will continue to protect you. All right?"

"I'll be bigger soon."

"Yes, I'm sure you will."

"Shona." That was Audrey's voice, pleading and worried.

Shona could not deal with the other woman's treachery, or what it implied right now.

"Shall we go back to the keep and see what Lady Sinclair has provided to break our fast?" Shona asked her children with a smile as bright as she could make it.

"I'm hungry," Marjory announced plaintively.

"Then we'll see you fed." Caelis leaned down to swoop the child into his arms. "Lady Sinclair's cooks make delicious, heavy brown bread."

"Do they have butter?" Marjory asked, patting Caelis's cheek. "I likes butter."

"Oh, aye."

"The laird provides well for his people," Thomas said, his voice falsely relaxed, tension ringing through his attempts to disguise it.

"He does. Surprisingly so. The Balmoral is the same."

Testimony to the goodness of the Balmoral laird did not give Shona the comfort it would have yesterday.

"And your clan?" Thomas asked.

"The current laird is more interested in building an army than feeding his people," Caelis said, disdain in his tone.

"Things have gotten worse then?" Shona asked, thinking it would do her no harm to dwell on something besides these new betrayals in her life.

Because make no mistake, if her father knew of the Chrechte, so had Shona's mother.

"Aye. It is much worse than when your family made MacLeod land their home. Few humans remain in the clan. Those who do struggle to keep the farms going, but Uven expects much for nothing."

"He always did."

"I did not see it."

"Just as you refused to see the way he treated his daughter. Does she still live?" There had been times Shona thought the other girl would not survive her father's foul temper.

"She does. She escaped and came here seeking refuge."

"Was she granted it?"

"Aye."

"Of course. She is Chrechte, is she not?"

"Nay. Uven's first wife, his true mate, was human."

"So am I."

"When a human and a Chrechte mate, the children of their union have as much chance of being born fully human as Chrechte."

"Regardless, if you knew this about Uven's first wife, how could you believe him that I was not your true mate?"

"I didn't know until later."

Did she believe him? Shona did not know. Too many lies had been spread over her like the honey of truth, leaving her exposed to the beasts drawn to their sweetness.

Shona took Eadan's hand and began the walk back to the keep. "I am glad Mairi found refuge. Perhaps she will even find joy here."

"She is mated, to a Chrechte healer. They are on Balmoral Island at present. She is training with an old seer of the clan."

"She has the sight?" Shona had always believed such gifts myths.

Now she knew some myths had more truth than what she had always taking as verity.

"She does," Caelis confirmed.

"As does Ciara," Thomas added with atypical timidity. "The Sinclair laird's daughter. You met her last night."

"I remember." Maintaining her civility with Thomas was no easy task.

"She believes Eadan has it as well."

Shona gripped her son's hand tightly, not willing to exhibit lack of belief in his dreams as she had in the past. "Then perhaps she will help him learn to use his gifts."

Eadan smiled brilliantly up at Shona, making her attempt at understanding worth the effort. "She told me the dreams are strongest when they are about something important."

"Like your true father."

"My lord would not have accepted my wolf," Eadan said with wisdom beyond his five years.

"I am sure you are right."

"Hiding your true nature from your parent is a painful thing," Thomas said in a subdued tone.

Shona cast him a sidelong glance. His shoulders were stooped in dejection.

She could no more help the words that came out of her mouth than the love she felt for friends who had found her as unworthy of truth as her parents. "I told your sister not thirty minutes past, your father is a stupid, vain man, not worthy of either of you."

Thomas jerked his head in acknowledgment but said nothing.

"We don't know what it means to be Chrechte other than to keep our wolves the most closely of guarded secrets," Audrey offered in a voice broken with emotion.

"Then it is a good thing you came to the Highlands where, apparently, others like you are abundant." Shona's tone sounded flat, even to her own ears.

With another oddly concerned glance at Shona, Caelis shrugged. "Not abundant, but there are packs in several of the clans."

"Uven's favored are many."

"The MacLeod clan is an exception. The lairds of that clan have been focused on increasing the Faol population for generations, since the first pack joined the clan. Uven has taken that dedication even more seriously than his predecessors."

"Why?" she asked, only vaguely interested in the reply.

They had reached the keep and the noise of the great hall prevented her hearing the reply, if indeed Caelis made one.

And Shona could not make herself care. Too many

thoughts and emotions warred for supremacy inside her head and heart, the cacophony so great inside her, the bustling great hall seemed peaceful by comparison.

Looking around at banquet tables filled with soldiers and other clan members breaking their fast, Shona had no hope of distinguishing which were Chrechte, and which like her, were human. She hadn't even known her son was one.

Was not even sure it mattered to her if any of the many seated here were humans who were something more. The ones who *had* mattered, the ones she might have expected to reveal this strange new world to her, had held back their knowledge.

Even her own son had known, through his dreams, what he was. He, at least, she understood fully holding back the knowledge. Shona had already unknowingly revealed her lack of belief in his dreams. And unlike his father, Eadan did not yet have the ability to prove the fantastical claims.

Part of her, that spark of mother love that never went out, was amazed by her son's belief not only in the dreams, but in himself. Eadan had faith the likes of which Shona had lost the day Caelis repudiated her.

She hadn't stopped believing in the goodness of others that day, but she'd stopped believing in herself. Shona could not trust her own judgment, nor could she be absolutely sure of her own value.

She wanted to believe she'd been worth more than to be used and discarded, but her own parents had made it clear she'd lessened herself in their eyes. And the one person she'd loved and trusted above all others had betrayed her completely.

Perhaps if theirs had been a new love affair, Shona would not have questioned her own worth so strongly. But she and Caelis had grown together in the same clan.

She'd fallen in love with him at such a young age, she could barely remember a time when just the sight of him did not make her heart take on a faster beat.

But he'd hidden this amazing side to himself from her

that whole time. And her father, who had known of the Chrechte, had as well.

To discover the two people she had let into her heart, who were not her own children, in the last six years had also hidden this secret from her hurt so deeply, the wound resided in her soul.

All the people in her life she would have thought would consider her worth the confidence had judged her lacking.

Except her son. Shona would never fault her son for hiding from her the nature that despite his dreams would have been more mystery than comprehensible to the five-year-old boy.

But her friends were adults, her parents had had the wisdom of age and Caelis had been her beloved. Young yes, but not a child.

Not even as young as Thomas was now.

All three of them—Caelis, Audrey and Thomas—kept casting her sidelong glances. Looking for what, she did not know. She had naught to give them.

No words of wisdom, or even condemnation. Surely they were not seeking some kind of absolution?

They'd all proven beyond doubt that her regard meant less to them than their other concerns, whatever those particular concerns might be.

Ignoring the glances and even first Audrey's and then Caelis's attempt to take her hand, Shona walked through the great hall in a fog of pain that dulled everything around her.

There were places saved for all of them at the laird's table and Caelis led them there through the noisy and boisterous soldiers.

"Is that the English lady?" someone called out. "She's too pretty to be Sassenach."

"Put her in clan colors and she'll be pretty enough," another said.

Normally such comments would cause her to blush hotly and mayhap even laugh. Today, they swirled around her with no more substance than the mist.

Laughter followed, until it was abruptly cut off and she looked to where Caelis stood, a low growl rumbling in his chest, his countenance like thunder. "Shona is *mine*," he snarled.

One soldier, close enough to Shona to touch—only because they had paused near the bench where he sat—paled and jumped back, nearly falling off the bench to put distance between himself and her.

"You're making a spectacle of yourself," she hissed. "Stop."

And suddenly that embarrassment she'd thought she was too preoccupied by emotional hurt to feel? It was right there, climbing up Shona's cheeks and making her eyes sting, it was so acute.

"I am making the truth known."

Did she truly need to spell it out for him? "You are embarrassing me."

"It shames you to be acknowledged as my mate?" he demanded, sounding thoroughly offended.

She wanted to shout at him, to demand by what right did *he* have to be offended, even if that had been the case. Which it was not.

But the only thing she could imagine making the current situation even more untenable would be to allow this exchange to degenerate into a public row.

"I'm *embarrassed* to be the center of attention." If that was not a good enough explanation for him, she feared she did not have the wherewithal to maintain civility. And 'twould not be Caelis bothered by that fact, she was sure.

She'd spent a little over five years as a baroness, having it drilled into her by her husband and parents that she must comport herself with decorum at all times.

The Scottish lass who grew up in the southernmost part of the Highlands would have laughed at the strictures she'd not only endured but embraced in the last five years. That lass had hidden deep in Shona's heart when shame was cast upon her by her well-loved parents at the realization that Shona carried Caelis's child.

Caelis glared at the soldiers closest to her and then turned that frown on Shona, though his features softened somewhat when his arresting blue eyes fell on her. "You are my mate."

"I have never once denied it." Which was more than he could say.

"Caelis!" the Sinclair laird bellowed. "Get you and yours over here. I'm hungry and Abigail has said I will wait to eat until my guests are seated."

Lady Sinclair frowned. "I did not know how much bellowing I missed when I was deaf. It almost makes me wish for the days gone by."

"You don't mean it." The laird lifted a now crying infant from her mother's arms and cuddled the wee babe close. "There now, sweet girl. All is well. Your father's voice isn't sufficient reason for all this fuss, now is it?"

"It is when he uses it at such volume," Lady Sinclair said with asperity.

But the infant quieted, gurgling up at her father.

Shona did not understand why Caelis did not sit immediately when they reached the head table, but then she noted the arrested expression on her former beloved's face.

He watched the laird and the babe with such a look of naked longing, Shona's heart was touched even through her fog of pain.

Whatever she might believe of the words he'd shared the night before, she could not doubt that Caelis would always treasure Eadan.

Shona allowed Caelis to tuck her into a seat across the table from Lady Sinclair and did not duck away when he leaned close. She felt sure whatever he meant to say, she did not want the others overhearing.

Sure enough, he whispered in an emotion laden voice, "I missed Eadan's and Marjory's babyhoods, but I will be there for the next one."

Chapter 10

Rejoice the gifts given through the sacred stones as blessings, not birthrights.

—CAHIR TRADITION

He took his own seat on the bench beside her, putting Eadan to his right and leaving the spot to her left open for Audrey and Marjory. Thomas rounded the table and took a seat across from Eadan beside the laird's sons.

In no mental condition to deal with Caelis's certainty that they would be a family, Shona simply ignored him. "Good morning, Lady Sinclair. Your daughter is beautiful."

"Thank you." The Sinclair lady looked fondly at the babe in her husband's arms and then let that gaze move to encompass all her children, including Ciara, who was seated to her left. "I am a very blessed woman."

"You are indeed."

Lady Sinclair's smile was near blinding in its happy intensity. "Did you sleep well, Lady Heronshire?"

Discovering a bit of that Scottish lass still dwelling in her deepest heart, Shona felt the stiffness of the address and didn't like it besides. "Please, call me Shona."

"And you must call me Abigail. To be honest, one of the

things I miss least about England is the stuffy habit of lord-and lady-ing everyone."

"Your clan calls you lady."

"It sounds different coming from them."

Shona was shocked that in her current state she could find the mundane amusing, but she heard herself laughing softly if briefly at Abigail's claim. It was all too easy to understand.

She used to compare life in England to Scotland all the time and in most cases, had drawn a similar conclusion: things done the same way did not carry the same impact. No matter how hard she had worked to change herself so that she had a place there, for the sake of her children and parents, Shona had never felt as if she belonged in that oh-so-civilized country to the south.

She had not been happy, though she'd found a measure of joy in motherhood. She had done her best to be content with her lot in life, even if her heart cried nightly for what it could not have.

But ultimately, Shona had never felt safe, or at home in England as she had returning to her homeland, even on the run from her former husband's evil son. "I do not think I will miss anything about England."

"You did not want to leave Scotland?"

Shona shrugged. "My desires had naught to do with my father's choices."

"I understand." The expression in Abigail's eyes said the other woman truly did, too.

"Becoming a mother made it more difficult, not easier to understand my father's lack of love toward me," Shona admitted.

Caelis made a sound of disagreement as did Shona's friends, but she disregarded them all.

Abigail's brown eyes glowed with saddened understanding. "It was the same for me."

"I doubt most sincerely you did something so grievous as to shatter your parents' illusions of your worth," Shona felt compelled to say.

"You are wrong. My mother and stepfather held me in no value at all because I could not hear."

"What do you mean? You hear just fine." At least it seemed so to Shona.

"I do now. I didn't then. I had a fever when I was a child. It took my hearing and with it my parents' regard."

"But that was not your fault!"

Abigail smiled, showing that the old pain might eventually let go of Shona as well. "No, it was not, but they were ashamed of me all the same."

"I am sorry." In that moment, Shona felt a kinship to Abigail that went deeper than place of birth or life circumstance.

"It brought me to Talorc and the family I share with him, so I cannot regret my past."

"You are a strong woman."

"She is at that," Talorc said with great pride in his tone.

Shona found herself smiling at him.

He returned the gesture, his grin growing when Caelis shifted beside her.

She looked up to her right and saw that the MacLeod soldier had a fierce frown on his face. She could not imagine what had him upset this time.

So, again, she opted to simply ignore him. She pointed out the obvious, but what still confused her. "You are no longer deaf."

"A miracle."

"Saints be praised."

"The One who made them, to be sure."

Shona nodded, satisfied at least that her own pain had not made her entirely oblivious to the feelings of others. "I am very glad you found your happiness."

"I am more suited to life here, though I never would have believed it before I was sent to marry a stranger."

Shona, who had some experience with that, shuddered. "Not all matrimony arranged by one's parents turns out congenial."

"A congenial marriage is a blessing all in its own right, no matter what led to it, love or politics."

Shona could not gainsay that piece of wisdom.

"And even less than joyful unions have their blessings." Abigail brushed her daughter's hair with her hand.

Marjory, who had been eating with single-minded determination, stopped mid-chew to smile engagingly up at her mother.

Shona smiled back, a measure of peace filling her heart that had nothing to do with the revelations of the past twenty-four hours.

And reminding Shona one lesson of great value she'd learned in the last six years. Life did not have to be perfect for moments of joy to color it with beauty.

Shona was taken further out of her own thoughts by the arrival of another warrior, this one wearing the colors of the Balmoral. The leather jerkin he wore with his kilt, however, gave him an appearance every bit as barbaric as Caelis with his bare chest (but for the swath of plaid that crossed it diagonally).

The Balmoral stood far too close to Audrey for propriety's sake, but then those in the Highlands were not as concerned with such *trivialities* as other clans or the English.

Usually, those same Highland clans kept to themselves. The fact that both a MacLeod and Balmoral soldier could be found among the Sinclairs was more than a little unexpected.

Shona honestly did not know what to make of it.

"Vegar, join us," Lady Abigail invited warmly. "I had thought you were hunting."

So the Balmoral soldier was welcome *and* an expected guest.

This spoke well for the relations between the Sinclairs and the Balmorals. Again, Shona could work up no excitement over what should have been good news to her ears. Surely she should be considering asking this Vegar to lead her to the Balmorals, at the very least.

Yet none of her previous plans were as real in her mind as the unbelievable turn of events her life had taken since she and her companions had been met by Niall and his warriors.

"Aye, I've been hunting. I found what I did not even ken I was looking for." Vegar's tone was laced with awed satisfaction and he gave Audrey a look of such heat, Shona felt herself blushing on behalf of her friend.

Whether or not Audrey could still be called by that title wasn't something Shona wanted to contemplate just then.

Audrey just stared up at the man, the most arrested expression on her lovely features.

Shona couldn't begin to fathom what was happening. This reaction was most unusual for the innocent Audrey, anyway.

Shona had no way of knowing if the Balmoral warrior made a habit of looking at women thus.

Abigail cleared her throat, amusement lurking in her lovely eyes. "Vegar, this is Audrey, friend to Lady Heronshire."

"Hello, sweeting." Vegar's low growl was at once both entirely inappropriate and filled with the most odd natural possessiveness.

Audrey colored then, her skin going a remarkable shade of pink. "It is a pleasure to make your acquaintance," she said in stilted Gaelic.

Audrey and Thomas had done their best to learn the language of Shona's homeland, but as Shona did with Gaelic, the pair reverted to English in times of stress.

Vegar recoiled, his expression going from interested, almost smitten and nearly awestruck, to stony in a heartbeat. "You are English."

"Oh, for Heaven's sake!" Abigail's frustrated exclamation was so loud, she surprised a cry from her babe. "Your tribe hasn't had dealings with the English in how many generations? Don't you have enough enemies in the Fearghall? Need you take an entire nation into dislike?"

"Who is making our beautiful Emma fuss now, wife?"

Talorc asked, his amusement more than Shona would have thought the situation warranted.

"You do not like the English?" Audrey asked Vegar. The Balmoral winced at the sound of her voice speaking English. She repeated the question in halting Gaelic, her expression crumbling even as the words left her mouth.

Vegar scowled. "The most treacherous among the Fearghall hail from England. 'Tis well known."

"That is interesting; none of your tribe has shared that tidbit with us," Talorc said.

Neither man's words made perfect sense to Shona, but Audrey didn't look confused in the least. Her ash gray eyes filled with deeper and deeper levels of hurt, while her mouth trembled though she bit her bottom lip to hide it.

"Why do you believe that?" the Sinclair laird asked, apparently oblivious to Audrey's distress or Vegar's anger.

"That is a discussion better saved for another time," Vegar responded with a look around the great hall.

So, not all the Sinclairs were aware of the Chrechte's true natures any more than Shona had been when she'd lived among the MacLeod.

"Talorc!" Abigail said with exasperation.

She was not deaf to the distress of her fellow English-woman.

Shona wasn't either, but nor did she understand it. Vegar was a stranger. While his low opinion of the English was not exactly pleasant for Audrey, or Thomas for that matter, to listen to, it could hardly be of great concern to them.

Or was Audrey worried Vegar's attitude would prevent them from finding refuge among his clan? Shona could not believe the younger woman was convinced of that notion— not after she'd warned Audrey about that very thing before they ever made the journey.

Vegar looked down at Audrey, shaking his head with clear disappointment. "English."

He didn't say anything else, but apparently that was enough for Audrey.

Her eyes darkened to storm clouds and moisture pooled

against the lower lids. "That is just too bloody perfect. I've lost the regard of my dearest friend in the world and my mate hates me because I was born in a country not his own."

Shona didn't know what was going on, but the distress in Audrey's voice moved her as nothing else could.

Before she could reach out a comforting hand though, Audrey had jumped from her seat. "Do not worry yourself, Vegar of the Highland. I no more want a dirty savage for a mate than you want an Englishwoman."

Audrey spun on her heel and rushed from the hall.

Shona had no idea what had happened, but she jumped to her own feet and glared at the newcomer. "Uncouth barbarian, how dare you upset my friend so?"

Vegar, who was looking after Audrey like a hunter deprived of his prey, jerked around to scowl down at Shona. "This does not concern you, *English*."

"I believe you have forgotten that *I* am English," Abigail said in chilling tones before Shona could open her mouth to respond.

Laird Sinclair inserted, "*Used* to be English." But then he turned a truly frightening gaze on Vegar. "Insult my wife and you insult me."

Vegar paled at that warning.

But then Caelis was standing behind Shona, his big body in a clearly protective stance. "Apologize."

"For what?" Vegar demanded.

"Raising your voice to my mate," Caelis replied in a deadly tone Shona did not like one little bit.

And then something struck Shona that she could not ignore. Everyone kept throwing that word around. *Mate*.

She knew what Caelis meant when he said it. He believed his wolf needed Shona's presence for contentment.

Audrey had called Vegar *mate*. Did she mean the same thing?

And if she did, how could she have known it so quickly. And if she knew in the instant of meeting, how could Shona believe Caelis's claim that he had not?

'Twas all most confusing.

She turned to face Caelis and discovered she liked the threatening look on his handsome face even less than she'd liked his tone that promised violence and mayhem.

"Do not take this so to heart. I am not so weak I cannot survive a few harsh words. Besides, *I* don't consider being called English an insult," she said as much for Abigail's benefit as because it was true.

She had learned in her six years living in the southern country that there were good and bad among the English, just like the Scots. Though this Vegar might well not realize it, that went for the Chrechte as well.

For all his faults, she would take her deceased husband as baron over Uven as laird.

"A woman with sense," Abigail said loudly.

Caelis ignored the laird's wife's words, just as he'd ignored Shona's. He was still too busy glowering at the other man. "Apologize," he demanded again.

"She would stand between me and my mate."

Caelis wasn't moved in the least by the other man's words. "If she does, than so will I."

"You are my friend, our bonds forged this past year as we trained to be Cahir."

"She is my true mate."

"As that Englishwoman is mine." There was slightly less disdain in his tone when he uttered the word *English* than there had been before.

But only slightly.

"You are Chrechte," Shona said. There was no longer in any doubt about what this man and Audrey meant when they used that word, *mate*.

The man did not bother to reply.

Caelis growled.

"I am," Vegar ground out between clenched teeth.

"And you believe on the strength of such a brief meeting that she is your mate."

"She is mine. English or Lowlander, Audrey belongs to me."

"Perhaps you should have come to that conclusion

before insulting the sweet woman to the point of tears," Abigail said scathingly.

"So you do remember her name," Shona added, making no effort to hide her own disgust at Vegar's reaction to meeting a woman he claimed to be his true mate.

And Shona was still uncertain what that meant in the face of Caelis's explanations the night before. If the rest of her morning was what to go by, it was nothing good.

Thomas stood then, his expression both fascinated and worried. A strange combination, Shona thought, considering that his sister was the subject of this particular debate. "Shona, would you still trust your children in my care?"

"Of course," she said before she thought about it and then frowned, but she would not take the words back.

Thomas and Audrey had not trusted Shona, had lacerated the small parts of her heart unwounded by life already with their lies, but did she trust him with her children? Yes.

She believed he would give his life to protect Eadan and Marjory, but that was something to contemplate on later.

"Do not change your mind now," Thomas said, as if reading Shona's thoughts. "Audrey and I have hurt you grievously. I only ask for the opportunity to explain."

Talorc barked, "Not here," showing he was not half as oblivious as he liked to pretend.

"Nay. And not now," Thomas agreed.

The laird nodded his acceptance of the promise, for promise it was, said in a tone far more serious than Shona usually heard from the young man. Even during their flight from England.

"You have a point, I assume, in asking if I trusted you with Eadan and Marjory."

Thomas nodded vigorously. "I did. Audrey needs you at present. Her mate has just rejected her."

"I did not reject her," Vegar growled.

"That's certainly what it sounded like to me," Abigail said with a frown for good measure.

Whatever favor she'd held the soldier in before, he'd

certainly slipped in the Sinclair lady's estimation with his behavior toward Audrey.

Vegar had gone from powerful, barbaric warrior to beleaguered man in the space of moments. His expression now was belligerent, but underneath Shona could see the worry in his color-changing eyes as they shifted from pale brown to green in his agitation.

"'Twas not my intent."

Thomas dismissed the bigger man with a shrug of one shoulder and met Shona's gaze, his own eyes, which were the same ash gray as his sister's, filled with worry. "She needs you and if you will go to her I would count it a great favor—not that I deserve one from you."

"It is not a favor to comfort a friend."

The look of relief on Thomas's features was hard to see. He was both so young and all adult protective male in that instant, it hurt Shona's heart in a good way.

She'd watched him grow from boy to man, and despite his deceptions about his true nature, she was pleased with the outcome.

"I will watch over Eadan and Marjory," he explained in case Shona had any doubts what his earlier question had been leading up to.

"I as well," Caelis said, his bad humor seeming to have taken another turn for the worse.

Though, once again, Shona had no idea why. The man's moods were as mercurial as spring weather.

Shona nodded to Thomas, including Caelis in with a short glance, and then turned to curtsy and take her leave from the laird and his lady.

"I will be up to check on you both after I have settled Emma." Abigail's clear concern relieved Shona more than it would have a day ago.

When she'd believed she knew Audrey better than any other. Now, Shona knew that Audrey's life was dictated by circumstances she still found fancifully hard to believe.

Presumably Abigail had more experience of this world

of mates and Chrechte, seeing as how she was married to one.

Before Shona could leave, however, Caelis's hand clamped onto her wrist like a manacle. He glared at Vegar. "Apologize."

Vegar sighed and dipped his head slightly. "I did not intend to upset you, Lady Heronshire."

Caelis growled again.

Shona sighed, vexed beyond reasoning at this point. *"What now?"*

"What would you have me call her? *Shona?*" Vegar demanded of Caelis.

"Aye."

Shona smacked Caelis's arm, wincing when it hurt her hand far more than she was sure it had his stonelike muscles. "That liberty is only mine to give."

"I'll not have you called by that bastard's name."

"I assure you, the baron was unquestionably legitimate."

"You did not belong to him."

Without any warning, bile rose in Shona's throat at the memory of how very much she had indeed belonged to the old man.

Abigail gasped as if she knew and Caelis reached for Shona, but she stepped away, turning to face Vegar.

She forced the sickness away to allow words to travel past her tight throat.

"I forgive you the small slight, but do not expect things to be so easy with Audrey. She's learned too well in her past how damaging a man's regard can be when he believes himself above the woman nature has ordained as his mate."

She didn't know the whole story of Audrey's and Thomas's lives, but she could assume their mother, not the baron, was the Chrechte. One thing Shona was certain of, if only in the possessive, superior way that drove Uven, no Chrechte man would willingly release his shifter children to serve a human master.

As their mother had been dead by the time they were sold into servitude, she had to have been the parent to share her nature with a wolf. The decision to do so had been entirely their father's.

A father who had no doubt been drawn to his mate as Shona was to Caelis, but who had treated the woman with little concern and even less respect as his *lehman*.

Thomas sucked in his breath as if Shona's understanding shocked him. Perhaps he *should* be surprised. He and his sister were nowhere near professional liars and they had managed to maintain their secret from Shona for five years.

They must consider her an idiot of the first order.

"How did my father realize you were shifters?"

"He said it was the way we moved," Thomas replied. "He knew the first time he saw us."

How strange to think of her father being so very adept at perceiving the animal-like grace of the Chrechte when he had been so blind to his own daughter's misery.

Chapter 11

The secrets of the Chrechte must be kept until the day comes when all peoples of humanity are considered one and equal in the sight of all others.

—THE WORDS OF THE *CELI DI*

Shona didn't bother to knock before pushing open the door to the room she'd found Audrey in with the children the night before.

Her friend stood silent and still, staring into space. Audrey's expression bleak; her eyes were wet and tracks for tears showed on her pale cheeks, but she was not crying. At least, not right now.

Shona sighed, her own anger and pain sliding into the background as she observed the younger woman. "He's an idiot."

Perhaps they were not the most politic words to speak, but verily, they were no lie.

Audrey started, as if she had not realized Shona had come into the room.

That was quite unusual and Shona now understood why. Her English friend shared her nature with a wolf and had the keener hearing of the beast because of it.

"Are you truly so distressed about the opinion of a man

you have barely made an acquaintance of?" Shona asked when Audrey remained silent, her head averted.

The younger woman turned abruptly, her long, pale blond hair flying around her. "He is not the only one whose regard I have lost this morning."

Shona sighed, not sure if she was ready to go into that particular imbroglio. "You did not lose his regard. He was simply surprised you are English is all. He's already lamenting his stupidity."

"And your regard?" Audrey's ash gray gaze implored her. "Shona . . . you are the sister my mother could not bear."

"So I have felt these five years past." She truly had, which made the betrayal at her friends' hands that much harder to bear.

"And now?" Audrey asked, her voice trembling with emotion.

"You hid the truth of yourself . . . the truth of my son's nature . . . from me for all of those years."

"We could not be certain he would shift. Mother told me that not all children born of a mixed mating would have a Chrechte nature. She was not even sure both Thomas and I would shift into a wolf. She died believing Thomas's nature was fully human."

"How can that be?"

"My first shift happened a full year before Thomas's."

"When was that?"

"With the coming of my menses. It started early and I shifted to a wolf the first full moon after. I was but twelve summers."

"Your mother died only a year later."

"Yes. She never saw Thomas shift." Audrey took a shuddering breath, old pain Shona understood all too well in the depths of her gaze. Her friends had both lost parents. "I always believed it was grief at her passing that brought on his first transformation to wolf."

"And your father did not know of your nature, of your mother's?"

"Thomas did not even know about me, or what Mother had been, not . . . until his first shift. I nearly lost him that night. He did not know what was happening." Remembered horror shone in Audrey's eyes.

"That is terrible. Why wouldn't your mother have told him the truth? Why didn't you?"

"It is against Chrechte law. We are taught that protecting our secret is the most important thing. Nothing else compares. Not family loyalty, not the loyalty of a friend." Audrey's expression begged Shona's understanding.

Shona did not know if she could give it. "But he was her son!" And Audrey's twin brother, though Shona did not point out that obvious fact.

"And I was her daughter. I knew nothing of what it meant to be a Chrechte, had never even heard the word before my wolf nature claimed me. My first shift was nothing I want to remember, believe me. I thought I was beset by demons."

Shona had no words. How could a mother hide something so elemental from her children and cause them such terrible distress? How could she teach those same children to do the very same thing? 'Twas wicked, to Shona's way of thinking.

"At least Mother knew to be looking for my first transformation. She made sure that she was nearby when the full moon came. I believed my brother would never shift and so was not watching out for him when it happened. It was horrible for him. He did not know what was happening any more than I had, but there was no one around him to reason with him, to tell him what was happening was natural. He believed he'd gone mad with grief, was terrified he would kill. Had he known how to accomplish it, he would have ended his own life that night."

"Protecting your secret is one thing, but that is monstrous. How could your mother think such a thing acceptable?" Shona wondered almost to herself.

"It was not Mother's responsibility. It was mine and I failed my brother that night."

"You were but thirteen summers."

"What has age to do with it?"

"Everything." By the saints, how was Shona to keep her anger at a woman whose fear of discovery had led to so much personal pain already?

Audrey let out an agonized breath. "I wanted to tell you so many times."

"Why didn't you?"

"Mother made me promise, over and over again . . . that I would never divulge the secret of our natures. By the time I met you, it was ingrained in me to hide the truth at all costs."

"The cost was nearly your brother's life. I cannot believe your mother wanted that."

"I do not think so, but she was most adamant. She left her pack to follow my father. The pack had disowned her, but she said they would come for her, and us, if we ever revealed the truth of the Chrechte. That they would kill us without a second thought if we betrayed them."

There was no doubt that Audrey's mother had believed her dire warnings because she'd passed that unshakable belief onto her daughter. It was in Audrey's tone and the way she held herself when repeating the threat.

"Do you still believe you are at risk from that pack?"

"I do not know. Mother told me so little. I look like her; what if someone from her former pack sees me and knows who I am? She thought they would rather kill me and Thomas than allow what they called *half breeds* to live. Her fear of them was great."

"Where is her pack?" The words were in Shona's head, but she hadn't spoken them.

They'd been uttered in that deep masculine voice she'd heard only recently in the great hall.

Vegar stood inside the door, his expression dark, Caelis behind him, his blue gaze seeking Shona's. Shona refused to lock eyes with the man set on claiming her. She wanted reassurances that he would not have acted as Audrey's mother had done, and feared she would not find them.

"I don't know." Audrey was also refusing to look at Vegar, her gaze fixed on the floor in a way that upset Shona very much. "My mother was from a holding on the border, in the northeast. She spoke very little of her past."

Vegar's expression darkened. "There is a pack made up entirely of the Fearghall and their females in that area."

"What are the Fearghall?" Shona asked even as she noted her friend's face paling.

Vegar answered, "They are a secret band of Chrechte intent on destroying all but the Faol."

Shona knew Faol as an ancient word for wolf. "You are saying other Chrechte are not wolves?"

"Some are birds. Eagles, ravens and hawks," Caelis said as he shut the door, closing the four of them into the room.

"We are called the Éan," Vegar added, his gaze never leaving Audrey's bowed head.

"You cannot be Éan," Audrey whispered. "The Éan want to destroy the Faol."

"Your mother was Fearghall." Vegar's tone was not accusing, not like it had been when he'd called her English downstairs. He spoke as if his words explained Audrey's.

Perhaps they did, but Shona was still confused. Hadn't Vegar said that the Fearghall wanted to destroy those not of wolf nature, not the other way around?

"Women are not Fearghall." Again Audrey spoke without looking at any of them. "If Mother had known Thomas would be a shifter, she would have sent him back to her people. She told me that once. *He* could have been made a Fearghall. Though she said the pack might kill him for having a human father regardless, even if he shifted. She still would have sent him and hoped," Audrey said as if admitting a shameful secret.

It was shameful, but not on Audrey's part. The mother she and Thomas had idolized was very different than the woman Shona had always been led to believe she was.

"Your mother did not know Thomas could shift?" Caelis asked.

"No."

"Apparently it did not happen until after her death," Shona added when her friend remained silent.

Caelis nodded, as if that made perfect sense to him.

"Your mother was upset you were the shifter and not him," Vegar guessed, sounding disgusted.

Audrey's head finally came up at that. "Yes."

"The Fearghall are twisted in their thinking."

"She loved me," Audrey claimed, but with not as much conviction as Shona had heard in her voice on previous occasions.

"I am sure she did, but she was taught from early years that her value was diminished because she was born female." Caelis sounded like he knew what he was talking about. "They would have shunned her for following her mate because he was human. The Fearghall are clearly strong among her pack and they consider it every wolf's responsibility to breed with other Faol, no one else."

That explained Uven's actions most clearly, and mayhap even Caelis's willingness to repudiate Shona. It did nothing, however, to comfort her still wounded heart.

Vegar rubbed his face, a sound of clear frustration mixed with disgust coming from him.

Caelis gave the other man a wry look. "You forget sometimes."

"What does he forget?" Audrey asked quietly.

"That I was once Fearghall, too."

"You were?" Shona asked, not happy with the confirmation despite her suspicions.

She did not know enough about this secret society to understand everything yet, but what she'd gleaned did not paint it in pretty light.

Caelis had said that those who called themselves by the name believed others of their kind did not deserve to live. Even at her most angry, she had never considered Caelis ignorant or prejudiced in such a deplorable way.

"You are disappointed in me," he said to Shona.

She nodded, seeing no reason to deny it. "Vegar said he knew of a pack made up entirely of Fearghall." And their females, but she did not see the need to repeat that distinction at that moment. "Which would imply that others are not."

"That is right."

"So you *chose* to align yourself with Uven's twisted thinking."

"'Twas not merely Uven. He believed what he had been taught, as did generations before him."

"But you are mistaken in believing Caelis was given the option of not following the Fearghall's ways," Vegar inserted. "Had he rejected their teachings, he would have been killed as other Chrechte were before and after him."

A cold chill settled in Shona's chest. "But you said—"

"The MacLeod are like that English pack. The men are Fearghall, the women Chrechte breeders, supporting the men at the risk of shunning and much worse. Audrey's mother was very lucky she was not killed by her former pack for deserting them."

Audrey gasped.

Shona nodded her understanding, if not her acceptance and turned to Caelis. "You broke away."

"I did." He did not sound proud, merely determined about that fact.

"I am glad."

Caelis nodded.

"It makes sense, though, knowing how easily you were convinced to send me away," Shona mused.

"I did *not* send you away."

"It amounted to the same thing."

"But that was not my intent."

"Oh, so you intended me to remain with the clan and marry another MacLeod?" she asked, finding that difficult to believe in the face of his possessiveness.

"No."

"You thought I should remain alone?"

"Why not? I have been." He sounded put out, like a cantankerous child.

"By your choice."

It was Caelis's turn to make that warrior's sound of frustration. "Yes, by *my* choice."

"Finally, you admit it."

"Is that what you need? Or will only the spilling of my blood do to assuage your anger at me?"

"I am no god to demand a blood sacrifice."

"I do not know what you want then."

That was easy enough. "Your admission that you chose the path you took."

"I already admitted to error."

And for Caelis, that had been hard. But for Shona, it wasn't enough.

"You weren't merely deceived. You were open to the deception because you believed yourself superior to me." His jaw clenched, Caelis nodded. There was no doubt he was no happier to make this admission than the previous one.

She could but hope that meant he no longer held such unacceptable views. "Your ability to transform into a wolf 'tis a magical thing to be sure, but it does not make you, or Uven for that matter, gods among men."

"I never said it did." Frustration-laced shame surrounded her big warrior like a cloud.

He had never said it, but he'd believed it. And mayhap Shona could forgive that, if he believed it no longer, but she would not pretend the blight on his thinking had never been there.

Audrey looked at Shona then, apology in her gray eyes. "My mother did. She thought herself above her mate just as he believed himself of greater value than her. Mother called his wife and the children of his legitimate marriage 'wretched.' When I was small, I believed it was her own jealousy and pain showing because she was only his *lehman*, but once I learned the truth of our natures, I realized she truly believed them beneath her."

Clearly, her mother's beliefs hurt Audrey.

"You never showed her prejudices," Shona soothed.

"You were too kind to be less than me. I loved my

half sister and half brothers and they cared for me and Thomas. I knew my mother had to be wrong. Her pack had rejected her for following her mate, but *you* accepted me as a cared-for friend when all others in your household looked on me as naught but a servant."

"I made few enough friends among the English," Shona joked, wanting to lighten Audrey's dark countenance.

It worked and the blond woman smiled.

"I have learned the wrongness of my thinking," Caelis ground out, a smile nowhere in evidence on *his* features. "Uven is unjust in his thinking. He does not respect the ancient ways though he claims to live by them." There was the pain of being deceived in Caelis's tone, his expression tight. Vegar watched him with a compassion that surprised Shona, and Audrey with a fascination that didn't.

"Uven is a blackguard in every sense," Shona said with all the conviction she felt.

Caelis nodded, no protectiveness toward their former laird like he used to have anywhere in evidence.

"But you are right. I allowed myself to believe and in so doing . . . I betrayed my true mate and broke sacred Chrechte law just as Thomas accused me of doing. Just as Uven has done."

She only vaguely remembered Thomas making such a claim upon his first realization of who Caelis was. She could see this admission was of great importance to Caelis, but it had little impact for her.

"You could have ceased your explanations at your acknowledgment of wrong thinking. At present, Chrechte law has little regard from me."

"But if I had—"

"No." Shona put her hand up. "Right now, I do not want to hear more of this world I was kept ignorant of for so long. I have more important considerations."

Later, they had much to discuss. No matter how much she might prefer to avoid doing so. But not at this moment.

Caelis frowned, his shock clear in the gentian blue of his eyes. "What?"

As if there could not be anything more important than Chrechte law. It took all of Shona's long-fought-for patience not to grind her teeth.

That same Chrechte law had caused the people she'd loved most in her life to deceive her. She could be forgiven for not perceiving it as the great source of wisdom and knowledge Caelis seemed to do.

"Friendship," she said with no shame. "My dear friend and I have words we need to speak and they do not require the presence of two arrogant warriors."

"You are expelling us from the room?" Vegar asked, his own surprise even more acute than Caelis's had been.

"I am." She nodded for good measure and stared pointedly at the door.

"But I must speak to my mate."

"I am not your mate. Yet," Audrey added when Vegar looked to argue. "Perhaps never."

"You canna—"

"What I can and cannot do is of no concern to you right now, barbarian."

Caelis grinned at that, getting some kind of amusement out of his friend being taken to task. Warriors. There was no understanding them.

Shona pointed to the door and gave both men equally hostile looks. "Leave."

"But—"

That was Vegar.

Audrey's arm came up, her strength reasserting itself as she straightened her spine. She pointed to the door as well. "Now. We would have our privacy."

Caelis crossed his arms and leaned against the door, "Be reasonable," he ordered, being anything but. "We have much to settle and not much time to do it in."

Shona crossed her own arms, the long velvet sleeves rustling as she did so. "That may be. I have only your word for the urgency of time, but this I tell you: I *will* speak with my dear friend before you and I have *our* discussion. She has been with me these past five years while you have *not*. The very least you can give us is a moment of privacy."

She thought Caelis would continue to argue, but he did not, his expression going from angry to sad to determined to stoic so quickly that each emotion passed almost before she could mark it.

Finally, the big wolf shifter grimaced and nodded, stepping away from the door without another word.

Vegar opened his mouth, as if to dispute the other man's decision.

But Caelis nudged the Balmoral soldier none too gently with his shoulder, his scowl and the firm shake of his head shutting the other warrior up.

Audrey added her own glare and Vegar relented. "Fine. We will go now. It is about time to practice our sparring anyway."

Shona and Audrey didn't respond to that bit of posturing. According to Abigail, the man's plans for the morning had included hunting, not sparring.

Honestly, Shona simply did not care in that moment. She just needed time away from both brooding warriors and their demands.

Caelis and Vegar turned in unison and left the bedchamber with no further argument. Though the look Caelis gave Shona as he walked out the door made her think he was hoping for her to change her mind and ask him to stay.

She didn't.

Chapter 12

The Faol were not created to exist alone. To share one's
nature with a wolf increases the need for companionship.
—FAOL ORAL TRADITIONS

*O*nce they were gone and the door had been shut
firmly, Shona turned to face Audrey.

The Englishwoman busied herself putting the room to
rights, folding Thomas's bedroll and tucking it under the
bed. "It is quiet surprising this Scottish laird has actual
beds in his guest rooms."

"'Tis not common," Shona agreed, no more eager than
Audrey to attack the subject at hand. "Mayhap it is the
influence of his English wife?"

"Perhaps. Though even in England, only the most
wealthy have multiple rooms reserved."

"They are not ornate," Shona observed.

Like the furniture in the great hall, the pieces in bed-
chambers were simple and functional. It was quite likely
that against all expectations, the laird and his lady had
guests far more frequently than the usual Highland keep.
Audrey's surprise, however, that there was furniture at all
was more than understandable.

"The keep itself is more formidable than I expected of the Highlands," Audrey added.

"I, as well."

Suddenly, Audrey's face crumpled and tears showed in her eyes. "Is this how it will be now? Stilted between us?"

"Saints above, I hope not."

Audrey laughed, the sound a bit watery. "I did not intend to hurt you. Or betray you."

"Would you have told me of my own son's nature?"

"In truth, I hoped to discover more Chrechte and seek the counsel of others. I did not like to think my mother's perspective the most enlightened."

"Why not seek out the counsel of your kind in England?" Though if the only Chrechte she had known of was her mother's pack, then mayhap it was just as well Audrey had not.

"The Chrechte live mostly in the Highlands, or so my mother said. Her small pack went south generations ago, though I do not know why. Perhaps because of the Fearghall among them."

"What do you mean?"

"I'm not sure." Again Audrey looked pained, but not, Shona thought, because of her this time. "I know so little of our kind. I did not realize that not all Chrechte think as my mother did until we came here."

"Your world has been as usurped as my own," Shona observed pensively.

"It has, but I am glad. I have always wanted to know others of my kind . . . find my mate." The tears spilled over.

Shona could stand it no longer and she pulled her dear friend into her arms. "Come, all is not lost. He clearly wishes to . . ." Her voice trailed off as she realized she did not have words.

"The term is *mate*, but I'll not take him to mate if he thinks I have no value because of the country of my birth." Audrey's expression turned mutinous. "That is no different than the Fearghall."

"You are right."

"And he cannot say any different." The militant gleam in Audrey's eyes was actually quite amusing.

Though Shona would never let her know so. "No, he cannot."

"He said he is Éan." Audrey sounded awed by that fact.

"What does that mean?"

"He shifts into a bird."

Shona remembered something like that being said. "What kind?"

"I don't know . . ." Audrey's voice trailed off and then her eyes lit with certainty. "The eagle this morn. It was him. His animal at least showed his approval for me."

"He saw you naked!" Shona exclaimed, not sure what she thought of a world where animals were not as simple as she'd always believed. She pulled the other woman so that they sat side by side on the edge of the bed. "Caelis said there are few Chrechte, but I feel as if they are all around me."

Audrey laughed. It was a small sound, but definitely an amused one. "That is very understandable. But only think, in your husband's keep and the others around us, there were none other of our kind."

"How do you know?"

"We would have smelled them."

"So you *can* tell?"

"Yes, the scent of animal is very subtle, but it is there. Mother claimed some of the strongest could mask their scent."

What an intriguing claim. "I wondered if you could identify each other."

Audrey nodded her expression turning confused. "You told Caelis you did not want to talk about the Chrechte."

"In truth, I wanted time away from looming and brooding warriors. And an opportunity to work out the issues between us."

"Yes?" the blonde asked hopefully.

"Yes. You are the sister of my heart. Besides, I do *not*

wish to discuss the laws he mentioned. He was quick enough to dismiss them."

"Doing so would have cost him a great deal . . . he must have been truly convinced you were not his sacred mate." The younger woman bit her lip, looking at Shona with a mixture of worry and earnestness.

"Our laird lied to him. Uven told Caelis that as his leader, *he* could tell if I was sacred mate to Caelis and that I was *not*."

"I would have believed my alpha had he claimed such a thing, I think." Audrey's brow furrowed. "I've never had an alpha, but I feel the instincts to submit that I do not feel so strongly in my human nature."

"Men believe all women have that instinct."

"Only foolish men believe such a thing."

"'Tis a teaching of the Church."

"Do not tell Father John, but I do not believe the Church always has the right of it."

Shona giggled, some of her despair lifting. "I do not believe that is a concern you need have. Father John is very unlikely to travel to the wild north of Scotland."

Besides being in his dotage, the jovial man of the cloth with a surprising tendency toward kindness was as round as a boulder and twice as heavy.

"You know, he used to let Thomas and I share in the Sacrament of Communion. Privately, of course."

"I never understood why you did not partake during Mass." But Shona found many ways of the English mysterious.

"We were born *natural* children and many, including the baron, considered us unfit to partake of the sacraments."

Shona shook her head, not even commenting on her deceased husband's stupidity. Audrey knew by now that Shona had disagreed with the man on so many things that it was impossible to innumerate them all.

"Are we *still* sisters?" Audrey asked, her voice small, the vulnerability there heartbreaking.

Shona could only answer one way. And despite her own

pain at Audrey and Thomas's deceptions, she realized there was only one way she would *want* to answer. "Aye."

"Thank you." Audrey squeezed her hand so tight Shona gasped, but she did not pull away.

"Family can hurt each other and still be family."

"Like your parents?"

"Yes. They did not disown me even though I hurt them gravely with my shameful behavior."

Audrey made a sound of dissent. "I wasn't talking about them still claiming you; I meant you continuing to claim them."

"But of course I would. They were my parents."

"They hurt you so much more than you hurt them."

"I am sure they did not see it that way."

"Then they would have been blind."

"Nay. I think they saw the real me and were disappointed. They tried to raise me better." Her mother had said so often enough.

And while Shona had been married to the baron, she'd thought maybe her mother had been wrong. That her behavior as a young woman had been an aberration.

She'd certainly never felt the drive to copulate with the baron that she had to receive Caelis into her body. But that in itself had led to its own guilt.

She'd been duty-bound to share her husband's bed but had hated every single moment of it.

"What do you mean?" Audrey asked. "You are a woman worth admiration from any direction."

Shona laughed, the sound as harsh as the pain in her heart.

"I allowed Caelis into my body when we were not even betrothed, and then last night . . ." She couldn't go on, her own disappointment in herself too great.

"He is your true mate."

"In the Chrechte way of things, that may count for much. But I am human."

"Yes, but, well . . ." Audrey gave Shona a questioning glance. "You felt compelled?"

"I did, but Audrey, I do not know if that was Caelis's wolf as I claimed to him, or if simply emotions I thought I'd been long quit of."

"Does it matter?"

"Only to me."

"I mean . . . you will marry him now, won't you?"

"I do not know."

"You have no choice . . . do you?" Audrey looked at Shona and then away, blushing. "I mean, you could be with child again."

"If Chrechte are as rare as Caelis has said they are, making a child cannot be that easy, even for mates." Eadan was truly a miracle.

"Oh, I am sure you are right, but still . . ."

"We did not do *that*. He insisted on holding back," Shona admitted, no more comfortable with this line of discussion than Audrey.

But unlike six years ago, at least she had another woman to talk to about it. Shona would never have confided in her mother.

"He is showing his respect for you?" Audrey said doubtfully.

"I am not so sure it was out of respect for me so much as his attempt to draw forth my agreement to marriage."

"How would withholding himself from you do that?" Audrey asked with all the innocence of a woman who had never been kissed.

Shona felt the heat crawling up her face. "I do not know what your mother told you about the act, but there is great pleasure to be found in it for a woman."

Too much pleasure for Shona, according to her mother.

"Truly?"

"Aye."

"Mother . . . she only spoke of it in terms of her wolf, how her beast could not live without its mate, no matter the cost to her pride."

"Oh. That sounds horrible."

Audrey shrugged. "She did not seem overly unhappy to

me, though I was but a fledgling woman when she died trying to give birth to another child by my father."

"Considering the life she must have had among her own people, leaving them for her mate may not have been the tragedy she implied it was."

"But she hated living without a pack. She told me so many times, saying she was sorry that I had no choice but to follow in her footsteps."

"I am sure there are benefits. I missed my clan when I left Scotland as well. There is safety in living among those who are family even when they are not related, but there are curses as well. Among the MacLeod, those were far worse than the blessings for a mere human like me."

At the time, she'd believed it was simply that she was not part of Uven's inner circle. Well, she hadn't been, but not because of any reasons she might have surmised.

"What do you think our future will hold?" Audrey asked with a look of longing at the door.

"I do not know, but whatever the future will hold, we will face it as family."

Audrey squeezed her hand. "Family."

"Your mate is formidable." Vegar thrust at Caelis with his sword.

Caelis swiveled in time to deflect the blow, directing the other man's sword into a downward arc with his own. "She has always been stubborn, but there is a hardness to her now."

"Among the Éan, a woman has never had the luxury of remaining too soft, no matter how tender her nature upon birth."

Caelis could not argue with that. Life in the forest, hiding from the Faol intent on destroying their kind had honed the Éan into a people of impressive strength and fortitude.

"It would be easier to plan for the future if she had the same forgiving nature she had before leaving the Highlands."

"Life changes us. You for the better," Vegar said without apology and a strong thrust with his sword.

Caelis fell back from the powerful movement. "Not soon enough."

"If you had come to your senses as a youth, you would just be another dead Chrechte who dared to challenge your laird's teachings. Now you will be the one to destroy his hold on the MacLeod."

"I do not think Shona cares if the MacLeod find relief from Uven's tyranny."

"Do you blame her?" Vegar asked.

"Aye. We were her clan."

"She left."

"Aye, to marry another."

"Again, I ask: Do you blame her?"

And Caelis understood his friend had intended his question to have deeper meaning. An inquiry he was not sure how to answer. It was not rational, or even right, but Caelis was jealous of the man who had called his true mate wife for five years and claimed Caelis's son as his own.

He knew his actions had led to the circumstances he found so distasteful, but that did not make them any easier to bear.

In truth, the knowledge that his rejection after claiming her body had led directly to Shona being forced into another man's bed gutted Caelis.

Worse, Shona had made it clear that marriage had not been an idyll for her.

Thinking of her enjoying another man's attention was disturbing enough. To acknowledge she'd had a duty to suffer that which *she* found objectionable troubled him much more.

The flat of Vegar's sword landed across Caelis's shoulders, knocking him out of his reverie. He tripped forward, regaining his footing and spinning to face his grinning friend.

"Lucky blow."

"Luck had nothing to do with it. Your inattention, on the other hand . . ." Vegar let his voice trail off mockingly.

"I have much on my mind."

They fell back to sparring.

"More to do with your mate than your upcoming challenge, I'll wager."

Caelis could not deny it, though he did his best to focus on their mock battle.

"My guilt is as great as my jealousy," Caelis admitted to his fellow Cahir with unexpected candor.

A sharp prick on his arm told him his friend had scored a hit. Both men jumped back, cursing.

Caelis swiped at the thin trickle of blood coming from the shallow cut. "It is a good thing we are not on the training field with others right now."

They were on the deserted secondary training ground separated from the keep and the other tract used by the Sinclair in preparing his soldiers for battle.

"We would not easily live this down," Vegar said with chagrin.

Caelis realized something only his great agitation had prevented from being immediately apparent. The injury would not have occurred if Vegar was not distracted by his own mate worries as well.

"*We* are distracted."

"You think?" Vegar mocked, making no effort to deny it.

"She's not going to forgive you easily."

Vegar shook his head with disgust. "Which one? Your mate, who is a mama bear with the Englishwoman, or mine, whom I have managed to offend beyond redemption?"

"Both, I'd say." Caelis lunged forward, knocking Vegar's sword from his hand so easily, it couldn't even be considered a victory.

This time, the other man's curse was more colorful and vicious.

Vegar rolled and grabbed his sword as he came up into a fighting stance again. "I am a trained protector among the Éan, now Cahir. I will prevail."

They had trained together in the secret, elite group of warriors begun centuries ago in response to the Fearghall. The last remaining Cahir lived among the Balmoral and were now busy training warriors from the clans determined to fight the Fearghall's despicable endeavors to rid the world of all Chrechte but the Faol.

"I do not think your warrior training will do you much good when wooing a woman," Caelis observed.

"It has taught me patience, persistence and the ability to take a wound and continue to fight."

Put that way . . . "Mayhap I will rely more on my warrior's training as well."

"You have already marked Shona with your scent. She will not deny you now."

"She is not Chrechte."

"Are the humans who lived among the Éan so different than those of the clans then?" Vegar asked.

The eagle had lived with his brethren deep in the forest until a year ago when their prince led them in joining the clans dedicated to restoring the brotherhood of the Chrechte and all its races. The humans who lived among them were considered part of their tribe in a way the packs had not embraced their own clans. All humans among the Éan knew of their Chrechte natures.

While only a trusted few in each clan were aware of the animal forms the Chrechte among them could take.

But he did not understand how that would make their human brethren different in this case. "What do you mean?"

"If a human woman allows a man to take what they call *liberties*, she is obliged to marry him. Are clanswomen not governed by the same obligation?"

"Not if the one in question is as stubborn as she is willful."

"Like your mate."

"Aye, exactly like my mate."

"The boy at the table . . . he smelled like you."

"He is my son." It gave Caelis great joy to say it, but the sorrow he felt at their time lost together immediately tempered his gratification.

"What happened?"

Caelis told Vegar the story as they continued their sparring, neither man showing the best side of their control or focus.

"Your alpha lied to you about your true mate?" Vegar's tone was laden with horror at such an atrocity.

"Aye." Caelis performed a running leap that ended in a forward somersault, which he leapt out of with his sword pointed at Vegar's femoral artery. "All Uven cares about is the pack increasing its numbers."

Vegar kicked Caelis's arm aside and spun out of reach of the sharpened sword. "You would not be able to get another woman with child once you'd consummated a true mating, no matter what your alpha dictated."

The fact that a Chrechte could not physically engage in sexual acts with others once a sacred mating had been consummated was one of the reasons true bonds were so revered and respected.

"I did not tell him that Shona and I had made love. Uven was particularly adamant about it and I did not want to disappoint him," Caelis admitted bitterly.

"He'd put himself in place of your father."

"To my detriment."

Vegar grunted an agreement as he narrowly avoided getting dumped on his ass by Caelis's sweeping foot. "You sent her away without knowing she carried your child."

"I did not send her away." Why he had to keep reminding people of that fact, he did not know.

It was Vegar's turn to come close to sending Caelis sprawling. "You thought your alpha would change his mind, given time."

"Exactly." See? The other Cahir understood what Shona refused to accept.

Mayhap one had to be a warrior to think with that kind of strategy.

"But he is Fearghall. He was never going to change his mind about you having a human mate." Vegar's words cut down Caelis's arrogant thinking like a sword going through the heart of a boar.

Shona did not believe Uven would have changed his mind either and clearly expected Caelis to have been equally as wise.

But he had not.

"I realized that too late." To his shame, Caelis had not opened to the awareness of Uven's treachery in regard to his mate until several other matters had forced his unquestioning faith in the laird to be shaken.

"She will not forgive you?"

"I dinna ken." He hoped, but he had no certainty.

"Does she know your plans?"

"I spoke of them, but not in detail. She knows I plan to return to the MacLeod."

Their swords clanged in rhythmic beats as they fell into a fighting pattern neither could easily break free of or win. It made them both sweat with exertion, but continued to show both their skills in a dull light.

"And?" Vegar prompted after a particularly loud clash.

"She never wants to return to the clan of our births."

"She plans to live among the Sinclairs?" Vegar's shock translated to a clumsy move on his part and it was his turn to weep blood from a small gash.

"Shona has family among the Balmoral."

This time, Caelis was able to compensate for Vegar's surprise-driven clumsiness and he did not draw blood.

"Are you going to let her go?"

"What choice have I?"

"The same options you had six years ago."

Caelis stopped moving completely, his sword falling to his side as his friend's words sank into his warrior's heart. "My clan or my mate?"

Vegar shook his head firmly, no pity in his expression, only a good dose of disgust. "Giving up or fighting for the woman Providence has decreed as yours."

Chapter 13

Chrechte nature runs true.

—Talorc of the Sinclairs

Caelis was no weak-willed coward unwilling to fight, but when he opened his mouth to say so, he could not get the words out. Because he *had* refused to fight for Shona six years ago.

He had left his sacred mate to fend for herself while carrying his child. Caelis had wanted Uven's approval so much that he had dismissed his feelings for Shona and done as the laird ordered, repudiating her completely.

Six years ago, Caelis had felt trapped between his duty to his pack and alpha and the woman he wanted to make his mate.

He was just as torn in two directions now. How could he fight for Shona when it meant either forcing her to return to a clan she so clearly despised or abdicating his own responsibilities and the promises he had made to the Cahir?

"What in damnation are you two doing?" the Sinclair bellowed as he approached them.

"Sparring," Vegar said, his tone just as surly.

The Éan recognized no alpha but their prince and were

still acclimating to the concept of living under a laird's authority within the clans.

The Éan had only recently joined the clans, having lived secretly in the forest under the reign of their royal family for the past centuries. The Faol had lost their royal family, or most of them, in MacAlpin's betrayal.

A pack alpha was not so different from a prince to Caelis's way of thinking though.

And they'd since learned that some of their own people yet carried the royal blood of the Faol. Himself included if the evidence of his son's gifts could be believed.

"When two *trained* warriors spar, they do not draw blood." Talorc glared with disapproval.

Caelis would have said something cutting in response, but the laird was right. There was no excuse for his and Vegar's carelessness.

Vegar scowled, his eyes fixed on a point in the distance. "This mating business is not so simple. No wonder my tribe encouraged bonding without seeking one's true mate."

"The Éan had little choice in your isolated home, but now that you live among the clans, God willing, many of your people will find their mates."

Vegar did not appear brightened by the prospect. Caelis could not blame him. He'd no desire to give Shona or their children up, but neither did he enjoy the difficulties their bond created in his life.

Talorc sighed, his expression tinged with unexpected understanding. "Abigail gave me a fair chase."

"She was ordered by her king to marry you." Caelis did not see how the laird could have had to chase the woman.

"But a Chrechte desires the heart of his true mate, not mere promises of fidelity."

"I would take the promises." He'd had Shona's heart once.

He had no doubts it was not on offer again. That organ now resided behind a prickly wall of impenetrable brambles.

"So you think."

"A warrior has no need of emotional entanglements." Vegar sounded very sure for a man so easily distracted by finding his mate.

"A warrior fights best when he has something of great value to fight for," Talorc said, quoting ancient Faol tradition.

"That refers to our tribe, or pack. A Chrechte is not suited to life alone."

"You quote more Chrechte teachings but do not understand them." Talorc unsheathed his own sword, dropping into a fighting stance. "Come spar with me and I will see if you can keep your blood in your veins."

Vegar and Caelis both moved to take opposing stances to Talorc. Soon the clang of clashing metal could be heard again, this time even more frequently and with more controlled rhythm.

"What do you mean, I do not understand our teachings?" Vegar demanded as he advanced on the laird.

Talorc maintained his defensive posture without losing ground to Vegar's attack. "A warrior's first concern is not his tribe or pack."

Vegar stopped moving, shock holding his body rigid. "You do not teach your warriors this."

"I do." Talorc's sword arced down, caught Vegar's and tossed the other blade across the ground like a twig. "Sacred matings supersede even our duty to pack."

"But . . ."

"A Chrechte can survive without a pack—but only in misery without his true bonded."

Caelis nodded his agreement before thinking about it. He felt the need to point out, however, that, "Love is not necessary between mates."

"Nay, but it makes life a joy when it is there."

"You sound like a woman," Caelis accused.

Then he spent the next fifteen minutes fighting a warrior that might well best him on the battlefield were they ever pitted in truth against each other, even with his new form gifted through the sacred stone. Because Talorc had been gifted as well and he was a formidable fighter.

Ciara's connection to the *Faolchú Chridhe* had turned out to be an amazing blessing for the Faol, particularly those committed to fighting the Fearghall.

Caelis was sitting on the steps leading to the keep and cleaning his sword while trying to decide if he wanted to return to the loch for a dip to rinse away the blood, sweat and dirt of sparring, when Eadan came running up.

Eyes shining with excitement, Eadan called, "Da!"

Caelis heart squeezed in his chest and he smiled at his son. "What are you about?"

"We're going searching for bugs." And then the small boy launched into a tale about what kind of insects could be found where.

The excited words tumbling from his lips ceased as Caelis's son's gaze fell on the cut on his arm. "You're hurt!"

Caelis shook his head. "'Tis naught."

Eadan turned back to his mother, who had been walking a pace behind with Audrey and little Marjory. "Mum, Da is *bleeding.*"

Shona's beautiful green eyes darkened with concern. "What happened?"

Maybe not all was lost. She'd responded to his touch with all the hunger she'd shown six years ago and had at least some consideration for his well-being.

"Sparring." Caelis would have preferred not to answer, but he was no child to pretend not to hear what he would rather not have been said.

Shona's confusion shone clearly on her lovely face. "I thought you were not supposed to draw blood during practice?"

"It happens."

"It's not supposed to." Eadan looked up, worry etched in his boyish features. "Thomas said so."

"Thomas has the right of it. Who were you sparring with that you came away marked?" Shona demanded.

"Vegar."

Shona's hands settled on her hips. "And you call this man a friend?"

"It was not on purpose."

"How could it not be on purpose? It was his hand on the blade, was it not?"

Despite his own embarrassment at their poor performance on the training field, Caelis fought a smile. "Aye."

"Well, then?" Shona's foot tapped against the packed dirt in front of the keep.

"Vegar has his own wounds," Caelis replied, figuring that would mitigate the little termagant's ire.

"Vegar? He is hurt?" Audrey asked, her pitch rising with each word. "Is it a grievous wound?"

"Not likely." Caelis snorted his disbelief. "He is fine; it is only a small cut like mine."

"Where is he?" Audrey demanded, not in the least appeased.

She turned and looked over the practice field, as if the warrior would magically appear.

Caelis wasn't sure he wanted to tell the agitated Englishwoman that Vegar had gone into the great hall to clean his sword and discuss plans for further Cahir training among the Sinclair.

"Where is who?" Vegar asked from behind Caelis. "Your brother is inside, speaking to the Sinclair."

Caelis looked back over his shoulder. "The woman is wondering about you."

Vegar smiled, smug. "Is she now?" Then his expression turned sour. "She's not looking to avoid me, is she?"

Ignoring their banter, Audrey spun around and rushed forward. "Let me see."

"What is it you wish to see?" Vegar asked, looking bemused for the first time in memory.

He made no move to block the blond woman's hands as

she pulled his arms this way and that until she discovered the small cut on his thigh.

She blushed crimson when she realized where her mate had been wounded, but did not back away. "This must be tended to."

Vegar replied, "I planned to wash in the loch."

"You'll be washing yourself there as well," Shona informed Caelis.

He shrugged. "If that will please you. It is not much to worry about." But he did like the fact that she was worried.

"We will still see it cleaned and treated with witch hazel."

"We?" he asked.

She rolled her eyes. "I'll not leave you to your own mercies. You did not show enough self-protection to avoid getting hurt in the first place. I'll not trust you to care for the results. It would upset the children."

Eadan was squatting on his haunches looking under a large rock he'd turned over and poking at the insects he'd found there with a twig. Little Marjory chased a butterfly. Caelis did not think the children were particularly worried about his small wound.

Nevertheless, he didn't argue. "We will go to the loch."

"I'll fetch the witch hazel," Audrey said decisively and then smiled down at the little girl who'd just fallen on her rump reaching for the fluttery insect. "Would you like to come with me, sweeting?"

Marjory shook her head and looked shyly at Caelis and lifted her arms. "Want up."

He reached for her, lifting her even as Shona argued he was too dirty.

"She's a child, not a silk gown. She'll wash."

Marjory giggled as he tickled her tummy. "Isn't that right, wee one?"

She nodded vehemently.

Eadan smiled, doing his best to hide the wistful expression on his face, but Caelis read it with easy accuracy. He reached down a hand for his son.

Eadan took it immediately and Caelis tossed his son up and around so he could sit on the warrior's broad shoulders. The boy's shout of glee pricked at the heart Caelis had told the Sinclair he didn't need engaged.

This wound would leave him bleeding longer than Vegar's sword tip, Caelis was sure.

How much had he allowed his own false thinking to cost him?

Shona finished treating Caelis's cut with the agrimony Abigail had sent back with Audrey along with the witch hazel she'd insisted on. "There, that should stop it swelling."

"'Tis barely an injury." Her nearness called to his wolf and his libido.

He wanted to take her into the forest and claim her fully. Then she would admit they were meant to be a family.

Only he could touch her for pleasure.

Her breath caught as if she knew his thoughts. Perhaps she did. His hardened sex pushed the kilt away from his body.

She inhaled as if she was the wolf and his scent drew her. "Even the tiniest lesion can sicken."

"I am Chrechte." He brushed his hand down the side of her face. "We rarely take ill."

She shivered but held herself back from leaning into his touch. "Need I remind you again? You are no god, Caelis. If Chrechte never sickened, all would still live since the first walked the earth."

"Our natures are violent." And sexual.

He wanted her until his teeth ached with it.

"Aye, no doubt. Your people surely have lost great numbers to war, but the fact remains . . ."

"None live forever, though we do tend to live longer. And our mates with us."

"Even human mates?"

"I do not know, but surely you have noted that Abigail does not show the aging of a woman with her years."

"She's hardly old."

"She is older than her appearance would suggest."

Shona looked thoughtful. "Why is that, I wonder?"

He shrugged. He was only glad that it was. Had the last six years not been difficult enough? He would not consider what old age might be like without his mate at his side.

Though he could not be sure now that she was not still intent on making him live without her. Last night notwithstanding.

She'd blamed that on his wolf and her response to the beast nature in Caelis.

Regardless, life was tenuous enough in the Highlands, even for the Chrechte. In that, Shona was well thought.

"There are some who live longer than others, by entire decades. Are they all Chrechte?"

"Aye, for the most part." He could not think of a single human who lived into his dotage among the MacLeod, but that could have more to do with Uven's attitude toward humans than anything else.

Shona sat back on the grass, her attention split between him and the children still searching for bugs near the shallow water with Vegar's and Audrey's oversight. The way Shona leaned on her arms put her lovely breasts on display and it was all Caelis could do not to take the unconscious invitation.

She straightened her skirts, the green velvet no doubt impressive by English standards but not what he wanted to see her wearing. He'd prefer her naked, but barring that, wearing a proper Scottish plaid.

She gave him a sidelong glance, her hands twisted in the heavy fabric of her skirt. "You said we did not have much time to discuss important matters."

Here it was, the moment of reckoning. "We do not."

"Why?"

"Caelis!" One of the Sinclair's younger soldiers came running. "Vegar! You must return to the keep."

Caelis jumped to his feet and then reached down to yank Shona up as well.

"What is happening?" she demanded as she fell against him, having not expected his move.

The feel of her body against his pushed against the urgency to follow Talorc's command and insisted on another urgency altogether. "You heard. The laird has ordered us back to the keep."

Shona was not similarly afflicted. "But why?"

"MacLeod soldiers have been spotted on Sinclair land," the young soldier answered helpfully with a smile for Shona that made Caelis want to smash his teeth in.

"What? Why?" Shona's body went rigid. "They are not welcome?"

"They are definitely not welcome." He tugged her along, sweeping Eadan up into his arms on the way. "I told you, the MacLeod's daughter sought refuge here last year."

Vegar carried Marjory already, his free hand fastened around Audrey's wrist as he pulled her toward the keep.

"But she is living with the Balmoral."

"And these MacLeod soldiers may well be on their way to Balmoral Island." Not that they would reach it regardless.

They had trespassed on Sinclair land without permission after their laird had declared enmity with the clan. The warriors would definitely be detained, but allowing Shona and her family to remain outside the keep's walls was not an option.

"Why are we rushing so?" Audrey asked breathlessly. "Would they not have been spotted a long ways off, as we were?"

"We do not know how far away the enemy is and we cannot be certain the Sinclair's watch accounted for all who crossed our borders." Vegar tucked Marjory more securely against his side and increased his pace.

Audrey tripped and nearly fell. Vegar did not slow down, but reached around her waist with his forearm, lifting her and carrying her as he did the child. Only he kept the woman's front away from him, her backside pressed against his hip.

Audrey's outraged cry cut off with an *oomph* as Vegar shifted her into a more secure position as well.

Caelis looked down at Shona and she glared back. "Do not even consider it."

He bit back his grin, but made no move to lift her from her feet.

Audrey was busy complaining, but from what Caelis could see, his eagle friend completely ignored the Faol's furious demands to be let down.

"Vegar is a strong warrior," Eadan said, admiration in the boy's tone. "Audrey is bigger 'n me."

"Aye, she is at that. And louder," Caelis answered after the woman in question let out a frustrated shriek.

Shona harrumphed. "You don't know how loud she can get, but your barbarian friend will discover it soon enough if he doesn't have a care."

Caelis's laughter at her warning should have annoyed Shona, but she found herself wanting to smile instead.

The man was too arrogant by half. So why did she find it so difficult to remain irritated with him?

Mayhap it was the way her son joined in his father's amusement.

Without warning, Vegar dropped Audrey and Marjory to the ground, pulling his sword from its scabbard in almost the same motion.

Caelis let go of Shona's wrist and withdrew his own sword from the scabbard on his back. "Get between us."

"What's happening?" Shona demanded even as she moved to obey his urgent instruction.

"Trouble."

She'd figured that much out when he'd drawn his weapon. She resisted the urge to say so though.

She and Audrey instinctively placed the children between them, turning with small daggers in their hands to face whatever trouble was approaching. It never occurred to her to doubt that something dangerous was indeed coming. If the man who shared his nature with a wolf said it was so, and his friend who could take to the skies as an eagle agreed, there could be no doubt in her own mind.

The Sinclair soldier stopped and turned back. "What are you doing? We must heed the laird's orders."

"We've a wee bit of trouble to take care of first," Caelis answered, his keen gaze fixed on the treeline to their left.

The soldier's eyes widened and he looked around as if expecting the bogeyman to jump out from behind a rock. He too seemed more than willing to take the warrior's word for it.

Audrey whimpered and Shona's craned her neck to see what had her friend so upset.

It was *not* the bogeyman. Rather, it was six enormous wolves coming at them from all directions, each one giving a low-throated growl.

"These are more of your brethren, I take it?" Shona asked, proud when her voice did not waver with the fear she felt.

"They are no brothers of mine," Caelis barked. "Not now."

Vegar spit on the ground. "Nor mine."

The young soldier started praying, his eyes going wild, his muscles tensed for flight. Or mayhap he intended to fight alongside the Chrechte warriors. He'd drawn his own dagger, but his fear was much more pronounced than Shona's.

"Get you between us," Caelis ordered the young man. "You will protect the women in case one of these rogue wolves gets past Vegar or me."

Shona didn't think the clearly untried soldier would be much defense, but she said nothing. Caelis was giving the man a way to relative safety that would spare his pride.

Somewhat.

"Can't he run for help?" Audrey asked, her own voice trembling, the terror there turning Shona's own trepidation to fury.

The past months had been difficult enough on the young Englishwoman, Faol or no.

"He would never make it before they tore him to pieces," Vegar growled.

Caelis nodded without looking away from the wolves. "He is not Chrechte."

That must have been for Shona's sake as he would know Audrey would already be aware of that fact. Her friend must be truly frightened out of her mind to have made the suggestion, knowing, as she did, the wolf abilities better than most.

The Sinclair soldier visibly shook at the idea of being torn to pieces by wolves as he rapidly made his way to stand with the women. Shona did not blame him.

And she held even greater respect for him when he helped her and Audrey create a triangle barrier around the children, his dagger to the ready, further supplications to "On High!" falling from his lips.

She was surprised the children were being so quiet. She spared a glance down and her heart swelled with pride.

Eadan was comforting Marjory, his arms around his sister. "All will be well, Margie. Da will protect us."

Then he started singing to her and his sweet little boy voice about broke Shona's heart. How incredibly blessed was she to have such amazing children?

She looked up and around, noting that the wolves . . . all six of them . . . had gotten closer.

No matter how intimidating they appeared in both size and number, she refused to believe Caelis and Vegar would not win in the coming confrontation.

When they were but a few yards away, the biggest of the wolves shifted to his human form. Right before their very eyes. The snarling expression on his face was just as malevolent as it had been on his beast. "For your sins against the Fearghall, you will die this day, Caelis the Betrayer, and everyone with you."

Caelis stood firm, no sign of fear or even anger at the insult showing on his features or sounding in his voice. "The Fearghall are wrong, Maon. Chrechte are meant to be brothers, no matter the race."

Maon snarled, "Only the Faol are strong enough to survive."

"Explain then, my people living all these generations despite the Fearghall's most despicable efforts." Vegar was clearly angry, but like with Caelis, no sign of intimidation showed in him.

"Dirty Éan!" the big—and *naked*—warrior spat.

"I am a Chrechte warrior with true honor. Something your laird has no knowledge of. He withheld Caelis from his true mate."

The MacLeod Chrechte sneered. "So you say."

"So I say." Shona spoke up, all the anger she felt at how these miscreants were frightening her children and Audrey in her tone. "I am his true mate and my son is proof of that."

"You told a human about us?" Maon asked with disgust. "She will have to die."

"You already said that," Shona pointed out, her own tone scathing.

Audrey elbowed her. "Do not antognize them."

"Why not? They're bent on attacking us, aren't they?"

"I don't know why they would be," Audrey said and looked at Maon. "Your laird's daughter is not with us."

Either Audrey had forgotten the denouncement of Caelis made only seconds before in her agitation, or she was deliberately ignoring it.

"We're not here for the *female*. She had no wolf, no value to the pack. Not like you. We'll take *you* back with us and you can breed for the pack."

Vegar let out a sound that sent chills down Shona's spine.

Maon acted as if he had not heard. "Uven received word that two of his soldiers who had been sent here live but are no longer loyal."

"I still wear clan colors." Caelis stood proud, in no way intimidated by the other man's indictment.

"You have no right to them!"

"I have more right than Uven, and soon enough, you'll know it."

"When you are dead, I'll shred the plaid you wear and burn it on top of your corpse."

Now that sounded like a man who had been trained by Uven. Shona didn't say so though, since Caelis had been as well, initially.

The sound of her son humming loudly gave Shona the comfort of the hope that her daughter at least could not hear the awful words spoken. With his enhanced hearing, Eadan was bound to have.

And still he remained strong and brave.

Motherly love and pride burned in her chest.

"Am *I* so valuable that Uven sent six of his strongest warriors to wreak his twisted justice?" Caelis mocked.

"A warrior does not have to possess honor to be a formidable foe."

"He has more honor in him than you," Shona spat. "He does not threaten innocents and children."

"He has cast you in the shadow of his guilt. Blame the betrayer for your fate."

"You sound like Uven, taking no responsibility for the evil you commit."

Maon's eyes darkened with something that might have been doubt, but he shifted back to his wolf before Shona could be sure.

Suddenly, with no signal she could see, all six wolves leapt to attack.

Chapter 14

No good will come from Chrechte fighting Chrechte,
but human nature must be appeased.
—Ancient saying attributed to first *CELI DI*

The battle was bloody, but Vegar and Caelis were
amazing warriors, tossing the giant wolves away with one
hand each and slashing at them with swords in the other.
They drew blood but made no deep wounds. It was clear
Caelis and Vegar were actually trying not to kill the wolves,
but the MacLeods had no such compunction.

One managed a deep claw strike to Caelis's chest as
another three attacked Vegar at once, bowling him down
under them.

Audrey screamed, the horror she felt testament to the
mate bond already forming between her and the eagle shifter.

One of the wolves scratched at Vegar's thigh, drawing
blood.

Audrey broke away from their defensive triangle and
ran toward the pile of wolves and warrior. She stabbed with
her dagger at one of the wolves. He turned on her with a
snarl and took a swipe at her, sending her stumbling back
with blood soaking her dress from gashes in her shoulder
and arm.

An inch over and the wolf would have cut her artery. Shona's dearest friend would have bled out, Chrechte or not.

Fury-tinged horror washed through her, but unlike Audrey, Shona would not move from her position of protector to her children. She could not.

One swipe of any of the wolves' lethal claws and her children would be dead.

That would happen over her own dead and bloodied body, and not one second before.

Audrey shifted into her wolf, a beautiful white creature about half the size of the ones trying to kill them.

Her dress fell away from her and despite the difference in their sizes, she attacked the wolf again, this time with teeth and claws.

Vegar erupted from the pile of wolves, a battle cry resounding in the air around them. One went flying. The other rolled in the opposite direction. His sword came down and straight into the heart of the wolf still fighting with Audrey. So much bigger, and obviously with greater experience, the now dead MacLeod wolf could have killed her in a moment, but hadn't.

Shona could not make sense of it.

Despite the chaos of the battle around them, Vegar pushed Audrey gently away. "Return to your heart-sister. I thank you for your help."

The uncouth man rose just slightly in Shona's estimation in that moment.

Audrey the wolf obediently trotted back, the blood on her fur attesting to the fact that shifting had not immediately healed her wounds. That was a question Shona would have to save for another day. It was clear, however, that her injuries were not bleeding near as profusely.

Still in wolf form, Audrey again took up her position as protector to Shona's children.

Vegar had returned to battle already, the glint of death in his eyes for those who might go near his mate again. The two wolves he had tossed away now fought for their lives, rather than trying to take his.

Caelis had been fighting with the other three, but his obvious desire not to kill them was doing him no favors. There were small nicks all over his body from fang and claw, but nothing grievous. Shona's heart rejoiced and she did her best to convince herself 'twas because he stood between her children and the wolves that would harm them.

While two kept him occupied, the other came running toward Shona, its sharp, drooling fangs bared.

The young Sinclair soldier moved in front of her just as the wolf reached them, taking the first bite to his forearm. He grappled with the wolf valiantly, but Shona knew he would not hold the beast off for long.

She readied her dagger. She could not send her children running, though the temptation was great.

There was no way little legs could outrun those intent on doing them harm. Eadan and Marjory had grown quiet. Their eyes round with shock, they clung to each other and huddled near Audrey.

They should have been terrified, but they seemed more dazed and clearly held no fear of the woman who had become a wolf.

Though Shona's son had been seeing such things in his dreams, for goodness knew how long.

Audrey moved closer to the children, standing over them protectively. Her own teeth bared, growls sounded from her throat that were suspiciously similar to those Audrey used to make when she was angry with the baron.

It put a new light on claims she had made that she was angry enough to scratch the man's eyes out.

Shona shifted her stance, prepared to enter the fray between the wolf and the soldier trying so valiantly to protect her.

An unholy roar sounded, and a second later the wolf fighting the young soldier went flying, landing in a broken heap nearly fifty feet away. The great beast had snapped its neck and tossed the giant wolf as if he weighed no more than a ball of yarn sniffed toward Shona, his eyes the same gentian blue as Caelis.

And she realized this, this . . . *man-wolf* was her former beloved.

She could hardly believe what her eyes told her to be true. This creature was nothing like the wolf Caelis had shown her and yet there could be no doubt in her heart they were one in the same.

Shock coursed through her, leaving her lungs empty of breath and her heart racing.

Standing over seven feet tall and twice as wide as even the biggest warrior . . . like Caelis as a man, hair covered his face and body, his features that of a cross between wolf and man. His hands had five fingers, like a man's, but each digit ended in a daggerlike claw. His feet were the same: five toes tipped with sharp-pointed nails that would gouge a hole in man or beast with brutal efficiency.

He stood upright, like a man, his torso, arms and legs shaped much as they were when in his human form but bigger. A lot bigger.

The long canines that showed when he growled toward one of the wolves inching forward on its belly were like his canine counterpart, but his snout was only slightly protruding, the man behind the beast there to see if one was looking.

And Shona was looking.

She wanted to reach out and touch him. Badly.

This wondrous beast was the father of her child. *Children*, if she believed his intention to claim Marjory.

The young soldier beside her crossed himself with his good arm before cradling the other close to his chest and starting to mutter fervent Hail Marys.

The wolves had stopped their attack, three of the four surviving Chrechte approaching Caelis on their bellies. The last one—she thought mayhap it was Maon—stood off at a distance, his hackles raised, his low growl at once fear-filled and menacing.

Caelis ignored them all as he moved within a breath of Shona. He did not touch her, but she could sense his desire to do so.

She reached out and took one of his great hands into

hers and brought it to her face, laying the claw-tipped fingers against her cheek.

The huge body stilled completely, air barely moving his chest in and out. "Mate?"

The guttural voice was not quite human, but the word was understandable. What he was asking was not.

She did not know what he needed, so she gave him what she wanted. She stood on her toes and reached up to touch the light hair covering his face. It was soft to her touch, his jaw beneath strong and firm.

She trailed her fingers down his neck to his enormous, muscular chest, covered in the same soft short brown hair. "'Tis a wondrous monster you are."

"Monster?" he asked in that growly voice.

"Wondrous."

"You do not fear."

"I have naught to fear."

The sound of vicious snarling made Caelis tense.

"He challenges you," Vegar said.

Caelis nodded, though his attention remained on Shona. She stepped back. "You have things to attend."

His gaze finally moved from hers, but not to where Maon was making his continued anger clear. No, Caelis looked down at Marjory and Eadan.

Their son was looking up at him with awe and a deep happiness Shona was not sure she understood. Marjory didn't look any more worried than Shona felt.

'Twas as if her small daughter sensed that the great beast was their ally and seemed comforted by it.

Caelis dropped to one knee and Shona had to stifle the urge to laugh. Did he think that made him less intimidating? He still towered over her, much less the children.

Marjory didn't seem to care. She let go of her brother and approached Caelis with no sign of trepidation.

The Sinclair soldier made as if to grab her back, but a growl from Caelis had him scurrying away. His courage showed, however, in the fact that he did not keep going but remained nearby.

"He doesn't know you are nice," Marjory declared with a frown for the soldier.

"I am not always nice, little princess." The words came out a little garbled in Caelis's guttural tones, but Marjory didn't seem to have any difficulty understanding.

"You are nice to me."

"Always," he vowed.

She nodded, popping her thumb in her mouth and reaching for one of his pinkies. He let her wrap her hand around it, giving Shona a bemused look.

It was a strange expression on such a fearsome countenance to be sure.

Eadan approached. "I will be like you one day, Da."

Shona whipped her head around to stare at Caelis. "Is that true?"

"I dinna ken."

"I do," Eadan said as he sidled right up to his father and climbed onto the bent knee. "My dreams said so."

"Then it will come to pass."

"I have to save the Paindeal *celi di*," Eadan said matter-of-factly.

"What?" Shona asked, her voice going faint.

Eadan smiled reassuringly at her from his perch that made him almost of a height with his grown mother. "Not for a long time yet, Mum. Do not worry."

She nodded, inexplicably glad her son was only five years old. Whatever destiny called to him, she had years yet to love and live with him as her own dear boy.

The snarls had not stopped the entire time Caelis interacted with the children and now they grew louder, the challenge in them obvious even to Shona.

Caelis lifted both children into his great arms and turned to face the one remaining defiant wolf.

"Submit," he barked in unmistakable command.

Maon shook his wolf's head, hackles raised, his fangs bared in threat.

The stupid Chrechte stared Caelis in the eye until Shona's man-wolf let out a bone-chilling growl. The other wolves, including Audrey, whimpered, but the big one just turned and ran away.

Caelis lowered the children to the ground and ordered Vegar, "Watch over them."

"Aye." The Éan did not appear offended at the other man's imperious tone.

Caelis turned to the three cowering wolves and pointed to the ground. "Stay."

None so much as raised a head in inquiry, but all dropped to their bellies completely and . . . *stayed*.

Caelis gave chase after the retreating Chrechte, running faster than she'd ever seen man or beast. Even after the head start Caelis putting the children down had given Maon, he easily caught up with the big wolf. Caelis grabbed the ginger wolf by the scruff of its neck and shook the animal.

Maon went limp and Caelis carried him back to the group, where the other three wolves had not moved the breadth of a single canine hair from their position of submission.

Caelis threw Maon to the ground and then barked, "Shift!"

All four wolves transformed to their human forms. The transition was no less magical for her having seen it before.

Shona recognized two of the warriors, one of an age to her and the other younger. Maon, the self-proclaimed leader, was three or four years younger. She had not immediately recognized the youth she had known six years ago in the angry man he had become.

A fearsome warrior to be sure, he stood leader over men both older and younger than him. Only one man appeared a complete stranger to her.

He looked younger, too, but Shona knew from Caelis that could be deceiving.

All stared at Caelis with varying degrees of respect—even Maon, though his was tempered by that unbanked fury he'd displayed from the moment of his arrival in the clearing in his wolf form.

"You are *conriocht*. It is not possible," Maon snarled, his defiance barely tempered.

Vegar's brow rose mockingly. "And yet here he stands."

"There is no sacred stone for the Faol anymore. The Éan stole our *Faolchú Chridhe*." Maon looked at Vegar with loathing, his disgust with the situation clear. "And you are this one's friend."

Caelis backhanded the man, knocking him back several paces. "He is my friend and you'd do well to remember that."

"Wait until Uven hears about this. He'll find a way to stop you. I could have, if these fools had not submitted." Maon glared at his fellow Chrechte.

"He's *conriocht*, guardian of the Faol chosen by the *Faolchú Chridhe*, our own sacred stone, to be our protector and leader," said the older man Shona had recognized. She thought his name was Sean.

"If he was chosen, it was with a purpose to do the Fearghall's bidding, but he's living here among the Sinclairs and the Éan. He's a disgrace."

This time, Caelis kicked the stupidly stubborn man, his roar of fury even giving Shona pause. Not that she feared him, but he was an impressive beast. And he was definitely angry.

"What is a *conriocht*?" Audrey asked, her voice uneven.

Shona had not even noticed her friend had shifted back to her human form.

"It is an ancient term for werewolf . . . man and wolf combined," Vegar said, his big body blocking Audrey's naked one from anyone else's view.

Interesting. Considering both Caelis's reaction earlier that day and Audrey's response to being seen naked in the loch by Vegar in his eagle form, Shona assumed the Chrechte were less concerned with nudity than their human counterparts.

Audrey pulled her shift back on and spoke with the sheer white fabric over her head. She looked equally skittish and fascinated by Caelis's savage form. "I have never heard of such a thing."

"Before yesterday, I had never heard of . . ." What had Caelis called himself? Oh yes. "Shape-changers."

Audrey replied, "But none have three forms."

"That is not true," Vegar said. "Chrechte with parents of two races can sometimes shift into two animals, both wolf and bird. It is rare, but it does happen."

"Truly?" Shona's blond friend had managed to get the shift settled into place.

But honestly, it did little for her modesty as see-through as it was.

Vegar didn't seem impressed with its covering properties, either, glaring at one of the MacLeod Chrechte whose gaze had strayed from Caelis to Audrey.

Vegar nodded in response to Audrey's question, doing his best to bind her wounds even as he helped Audrey cover herself with her dress.

Caelis stood to his full seven feet and spare inches tall, towering over them all. "I am *conriocht* and I claim my right as alpha to the MacLeod. Follow me."

Sean and the other two MacLeod soldiers who had submitted in wolf form immediately dropped to one knee with right fists pressed to their hearts and heads bowed toward Caelis.

Maon remained standing, his stance defiant, though he kept his distance from Caelis.

"Or what?" Maon asked with only a marginally less antagonistic tone.

"Or you die. My *conriocht* nature will be revealed at my choosing and no other's."

Shona wanted to protest. Not the killing of the odious man. Maon would have killed Caelis without a qualm, and Shona as well. Worse, he would have killed or stolen her children. Either was not a fate she would ever wish on them.

Nay, she wanted to protest the opportunity to live. "How

can you trust his vow of fidelity? Or any of theirs, for that matter?"

What was the submission of a wolf worth when he had the deceitful heart of a man?

Caelis looked at her, his gentian blue eyes the one familiar thing in his *conriocht* face. "I can smell a lie."

"You did not smell them approaching. They masked their scent," Audrey pointed out, awe for the feat lacing her tone.

"In my human form, I may not smell the masked scent. In my wolf form, that almost never happens. As a *conriocht*, they *cannot* lie to me, or mask their scents at all."

"Impossible!" Maon looked impressed despite his denial. "None can smell our passing when we do not will it."

Caelis ignored him and looked at Shona. "You will have to trust me."

He wanted her to believe in him when she'd learned six years ago to do so was to set herself up for untold pain. "My children's lives are in your hands."

"Our children." The ferocity of his tone brooked no denial.

She did not give him one.

"Do not risk them then."

"You would have me kill them without mercy?"

She spun away before words that would condemn her more than the MacLeod wolves could pass her lips. But when had anyone shown her mercy?

Caelis hadn't. Her parents hadn't. Certainly the baron had not, using her body when he saw fit despite knowing how little she wanted it. And the current baron would take what he wanted without remorse if she allowed herself to be within his grasp.

"You are stronger than all of us." The words were in Caelis voice, but they had not been spoken aloud.

She heard them in her head.

Fear that had not taken hold during or after all the strange revelations of the past days rose now over her like a spectre. She could withstand much, but what would happen to her children if she lost her reason?

A hairy, oversized hand landed on her shoulder. "'Tis the mate bond."

"What, what's the mate bond?" Audrey asked.

"He . . . I . . . no . . ." She shook her head beyond the ability to accept one more unbelievable thing, particularly one so very intimate and invasive.

If Caelis had access to her mind, he had known exactly how much he had hurt her six years ago. And still he had repudiated her.

He had known her desperation, her hopes, her fears and he had rejected her despite them all.

"No," he barked, the giant beast's expression pained in a way she could not comprehend. "I do not read your thoughts."

"You are reading them now!" she accused.

He shook his head, a sound that was no human word she'd ever heard coming out of his mouth.

She looked around her, wondering for one terrible moment if any of it was real. Or was she living in some twisted dream?

The impossible did not happen. She had believed because she had seen. But what if all she had seen were fevered imaginings of a mind lost to reality? She *must* be mad. Mayhap that explained all of it, this new world that was too wondrous for the mundane life she led.

She had never thought to see Caelis again. He hadn't wanted her. How could she believe he was really here, laying claim to her, Eadan and another man's child?

'Twas beyond imagination.

But she had imagined it. She must have.

"I am dreaming. You are not here at all." She could not help that her words came out more accusation than statement.

Her fantastical warrior had made her believe.

"Och, lass, stop this. I am here. You are here. 'Tis no dream."

"But . . ."

He shook his great head, tenderness she had not seen in those gentian blue depths for more than six years. "You are not dreaming."

"You—"

A claw pressed against her lips with the softness of a butterfly. "Shh . . ."

Chapter 15

A sacred mate's ability to share words through a mental bond is one of the greatest gifts of mating.

—ABIGAIL OF THE SINCLAIR

Tears sprang to Shona's eyes, though she knew not from where. Surely she was past crying her stress away.

Caelis's hand moved to cup her cheek, the palm so big it covered part of her temple and neck. "You are mine. I will not allow you to be harmed."

Vegar snorted. "Aye, you're his mate right enough. Under no other circumstances would he have revealed his *conriocht* so quickly."

"But . . ." She looked up into mesmerizing blue eyes. "I heard your voice. Inside my mind. You know I did."

"Aye."

"That is not normal."

"I stand before you a *conriocht*. 'Normal' does not define your life now, if it ever did."

"But . . ."

"You are mine." He said it again. Inside her mind.

She pulled away from him, his touch too much in that moment when she feared a connection of such magnitude she could well lose herself in it. "Can you hear my thoughts?"

"Only when you direct them to me."

"But I didn't . . . what I was thinking. You knew."

He shrugged. "I do not understand it, but it was as if each thought was an accusation from you to me."

"I wanted to say it, but stopped myself."

He nodded, as if that explained it. She didn't know if it did, but if this mindspeak between true mates was real, then Shona would have to be far more careful what she thought loudly around him.

"What will we do with them, then?" Vegar asked.

"Take them back to the keep."

"And then?" Audrey asked as Shona wanted to.

"Then we extend mercy and the opportunity for submission, as Chrechte ancient law dictates."

"They had no mercy toward us." And if Chrechte law was so merciful, then how had so many of his kind died to war as he'd claimed?

Of course, two wolves lay dead in the clearing. Men who would never return to their families or homes. Men, Shona suddenly realized, she'd probably known at one time.

The thought made her queasy even as she worried that allowing the others to live put her children at risk.

"Mum, Da will make it all right," Eadan said.

Shona looked down at her son and tried for a smile. Her son's worried look indicated her attempt was less than successful.

"These men have been taught to disregard the honorable ways." Caelis looked with regret down at their son. "As was I. I learned a new way. Perhaps they can, too."

Audrey didn't reply and Shona had nothing to add. Caelis claimed she was stronger than the need to withdraw mercy.

Mayhap he was right.

But in that moment, she could be glad the decision was not hers to make.

"We will go into the forest. Vegar, you go to the keep and fetch more of the Sinclair's soldiers."

"And some coverings for the men. They are naked," Audrey pointed out as if no one else had realized yet.

So, she still had the modesty Shona had always thought such a deep part of the younger woman. She'd simply . . . what? Accepted Vegar seeing her naked because they were mates?

This mating business had a lot to answer for.

"Take the children with you," Shona implored Vegar. "Please."

"No, Mummy. We need to stay with you and Da," Eadan immediately denied, reaching for his father with the first sign of true fear Shona had seen in her son this whole time.

Caelis lifted the boy without hesitation, saying something in a low voice that brought a relieved smile to Eadan's features and a nod of agreement.

Marjory latched onto the *conriocht*'s leg, her thumb tucked into her mouth. Caelis's giant hand rested carefully on her head, the gesture both gentle and clearly protective. Neither child showed signs of being overly upset by what they had witnessed, though both very obviously did not want to be separated from their savior.

Considering her son had barely survived his stepbrother's machinations and Marjory had spent two sennights on the run with her mother and friends, they might well consider this day less upsetting than Shona did.

"The big dog keep us safe," Marjory said around her thumb.

Shona found herself laughing and was glad to see that Caelis did as well. It was a strange, more guttural sound coming from his *conriocht* throat, but amusement glittered in his eyes. He was clearly not offended by being referred to as a dog.

Eadan frowned. "He's not a dog, Margie. He's our da."

Marjory did not look overly concerned by her brother's chastisement.

There was no joviality in Caelis's expression when he fixed his gaze on the MacLeod Chrechte. "We will go into the forest and await the other soldiers."

"Why? You're just going to kill us anyway." It was Maon, of course.

Incredibly, Caelis laughed again. "Do not presume to speak for your fellow Faol. They have already kneeled to me. All that is left is for them to speak their vows. You are no longer their leader and you were never their alpha. They were taught lies like you but recognize the truth when they see it."

Maon shut up then.

At Vegar's insistence, Audrey agreed to leave with him. He would see her wounds tended to immediately. The young Sinclair soldier also took his departure, his fervent praying finally ceasing, an expression of pain twisting his untried features.

Caelis laid his hand on the soldier's shoulder and the Sinclair man earned even more of Shona's respect when he barely winced at the contact. "Tell the Sinclair I owe a debt of gratitude and honor to this man."

The soldier looked up at the massive *conriocht* with shock.

Caelis met his gaze. "You put yourself between my mate and danger. 'Tis not a debt that will ever be fully repaid."

"Teach me to fight the wolves," the young soldier said.

"Why?"

"To better defend my laird and our clan."

"In time, you will train with the Chrechte, just as all his soldiers do."

"'Tis not the same. We don't know their true natures when training."

"You believe you can learn to best a Chrechte warrior in his beast form in battle?"

"If you teach me, I do."

"You have the heart for it. I will train you."

"You cannot do that!" Maon exclaimed.

Caelis spun around and glared at the man, his hand clenched at his side. "Do not challenge me. My patience with you is at its limit."

Maon fell silent, his expression mutinous.

Shona could not help admiring the stubborn determination of the other man, even if he was more wrongheaded than her stepson, Percival, and his father combined.

Shona took Audrey's hand and led her toward the forest, surprised and yet not when the others followed her, Caelis at the rear with Eadan still perched on his arm.

Despite the men's apparent submission, Shona kept Marjory well away from the MacLeods who had been willing to kill them.

Her head was too filled with her own thoughts to listen to Caelis as he spoke in that strange guttural voice to the men he used to call friends. She was peripherally aware that he talked about things like sacred Chrechte law, the Fearghall and something he referred to as the Cahir.

The three who had already shown Caelis submission in their wolf forms listened with a great deal more attention than Shona. Maon argued and insulted and yet, Shona began to realize he *wanted* to believe.

And that is when she put her own worries aside and started listening, too.

"A time is coming—'twill not be in our lifetime, but that of our children's children—when a great blight is coming up on the people of our nations. An illness so great it will wipe out entire packs as though they'd never been. Without our sacred stone and the help of healers, the Chrechte will cease to be."

Maon frowned. "We have healers among the Faol."

"Not enough. We will need the Éan and the Paindeal."

"The Paindeal," Maon scoffed. "They are legend and nothing else."

"That is what most of the clans believed about the Éan before they learned the truth," Caelis said.

"What do you mean?" Shona couldn't help asking.

"Until a year ago, the Éan lived like ghosts in the remote forest."

"Why?"

"Because of the Fearghall," Maon answered, though he did not sound as proud of that fact as she would have expected.

"Aren't they safe, now that they are among the clans?"

"The Éan are only safe when the Fearghall cease to exist."

"That will never happen," Maon scoffed.

"You think not?" Caelis challenged.

"He is right." Shona moved cautiously around the Chrechte men so she and Marjory could sit on the other side of Caelis. "As long as there is hatred among men, people like the Fearghall will exist."

Caelis gave an unhappy rumble of agreement. "But we will do our best to expose them among the Chrechte and help those who have been taught the lies to know the truth."

It was a laudable goal, but she did not think every Fearghall was just misguided. Uven was a prime example.

That man got entirely too much joy out of believing himself superior to others. He would have been a terrible laird even if he'd been entirely human.

"The Paindeal disappeared before the Éan stole our sacred stone and the Fearghall was created to find it and return it to the Faol."

"The Fearghall spend too much time hunting Éan to be hunting the *Faolchú Chridhe*."

"The Éan destroyed it." But even Maon did not sound convinced by his own argument.

Of course, according to the man, Caelis could not be *conriocht* without it. So, his very existence was proof this sacred stone still existed and was indeed accessible to the Faol.

"Both the Paindeal and the *Faolchú Chridhe* exist." There could be no doubt that Caelis believed what he was saying. "Just like the Éan."

"But we have always known the Éan exist."

"And the Éan have never forgotten the Paindeal, nor have some of the Faol."

"So, what? We are to chase after a myth?" Maon demanded.

"Aye, and find them if we hope to save our children's children."

"You say Uven held you back from your true mate?" Sean asked.

Maon glared at the forest floor. "He says you were just too stubborn to do your duty by our people."

"How can I, a Chrechte man, do this duty once I have mated and forged the sacred bond?" Caelis asked.

"You could not," one of the other men said. "And Uven knew this."

Apparently, from the man's tone, this was a well-known fact among the Chrechte.

This proof that Caelis had not lied to her about his last six years of celibacy was something she set aside to contemplate later.

"'Tis why he ordered me not to couple with Shona, but it was already too late." Caelis huge arm settled across her shoulder.

"You lied to him," Sean said in a tone that Shona did not understand.

It was almost as if he admired Caelis for doing so.

"Aye. And he never knew my deceit."

"That is impossible," Maon asserted. "Our alpha could smell your deceit no matter how you tried to mask it."

"He is no longer your alpha."

And Shona began to understand Caelis's intentions and his need to return to the MacLeod clan. He was not going back to merely exact vengeance on a laird who had lied and put his people's needs last. Caelis wanted to save others from the same fate. He wanted to lead the MacLeod people with the strength and courage and selflessness that Uven *should have* shown.

"So you claim." Maon's words were defiant, but his conviction lessened with every utterance.

Shona could almost find it in her heart to feel sorry for him. Until she remembered he'd threatened to kill her children.

"Do you really think he will survive my challenge?" Caelis asked with more humor than Shona felt.

"According to your words, you will allow *us* to live."

"Uven is more treacherous. He has earned his death, when it comes." There was no mercy in Caelis's tone now.

Apparently the Chrechte law of mercy did not extend to despot alphas.

"Because he withheld your mate from you?" Maon asked.

"Because he has killed mates, not just withheld them. Because he has murdered Éan, humans and Faol indiscriminately whenever they have gotten in his way. My own parents were victims of his treachery and he dared put himself in my life as substitute father. Because he lies and teaches lies as truth, knowing they are lies."

She did not think the others heard the pain in the *conriocht*'s gravelly tones, but it reached out to the heart she'd tried so hard to protect these past six years. She did not want to feel compassion for him, did not want to feel his pain.

But she could no more help herself than when Eadan scraped his knee and her own ached in sympathy.

"Uven believes what he teaches," Sean claimed.

Maon paled and looked ready to lose whatever he'd eaten to break his fast that day.

"Nay. He knows the truth. We are only as strong as our weakest link. And without our sacred stone, the Faol were the weakest link in the family of Chrechte for centuries."

Maon shook his head. "No."

"Aye."

Maon did not argue again. He shut up, his expression turning thoughtful. In a thoroughly surly way. If he was acknowledging his wrongheadedness, even if only in his own mind, he certainly wasn't happy about it.

Was that required response for Chrechte men, she wondered. To be cranky and out of sorts most of the time? Shona found herself laughing at the not-so-absurd notion.

Caelis looked down at her with concern and a yearning she did not understand. "What has you amused?"

"The nature of the Chrechte."

"You mean our wolves?" Sean asked, sounding puzzled.

"I mean the fact you all seem overly surly, or at least the men do." Audrey was not so cantankerous.

Caelis shrugged, his massive shoulders making even that small movement impressive and nearly knocking her sideways in the process. "We share our natures with a wolf."

"You share yours with more." And he had not told her. Again.

Again he seemed to read her thoughts. "You are not afraid of me like this."

"No. You are still Caelis."

"I thought you would be."

So he had not shown her the wondrous monster. Out of fear? She could not imagine this magical being having such concerns.

Or mayhap, he simply could not show her as he had the wolf. "Can you shift to *conriocht* at will?"

"Aye, though shifting back cannot happen as quickly."

"Why?"

"I dinna ken. It could be that when our race was created, a *conriocht* was meant to spend his time in this form, to better protect our people."

"Can you shift back now?" she wanted to know.

"Not while threat still exists."

"We've submitted to you," Sean said. "We would not harm your mate or child."

"Both Eadan and Marjory are mine," Caelis growled.

Sean nodded quickly. "As it should be."

Maon made a scoffing sound.

"You do not agree?" Shona asked, ready to defend her children against even a man who shifted into a wolf.

His beast was nothing compared to the beast who claimed loyalty to her. And as with his wolf, Shona found it all too easy to trust Caelis's *conriocht*, even if she could not yet bring herself to trust the man.

"The Fearghall are taught that there is no value in humanity," Maon said. "A human child would not be claimed by a Chrechte warrior under his authority."

"Uven's own daughter was human," Caelis said.

"Was?" Sean asked.

Caelis gave the other Chrechte a measureing look. "She shifts now, thanks to her Éan mate and our sacred stone."

"How could her mate have drawn on the power of our stone?" the warrior Shona did not know asked.

"He did not."

"Then why say thanks to him?" Maon asked, for once sounding more curious than antagonistic.

"He saved her life after her father and Ualraig, the blackguard her father meant her to mate, beat her and left her for dead."

Shona noted that not one of the men looked surprised by the news, but neither did they look particularly comfortable with it.

"Is he the one who killed Ualraig?" Maon asked.

"You are so sure Ualraig is dead and not a deserter like me?"

"There was naught but ashes left of our warriors, but we know the difference between human ash and dirt."

"Aye, Laith killed him."

"Ualraig was the most powerful of Uven soldiers."

"Nay, he was not."

"You bested him many times in training but Uven never promoted you to his second," Maon observed, again without the overt anger.

"Aye. I would not mate with another Chrechte, much less the man's poor daughter."

"You couldn't."

"He did not know that."

"He would have killed you if he had." There was no doubt in Maon's voice, or the faces of the other three.

Shona shivered. This world was new to her and there were many things about it she still did not understand, but she was struck with the certain knowledge that Uven would have killed her *mate* if the laird had known of the bonding between Caelis and Shona.

"He could no kill my da," Eadan said resolutely.

"Nay, he cannot now and the past does not matter," Caelis agreed.

Maon nodded, shocking Shona.

"Are you Uven's new second?" Caelis asked of Maon.

"No."

"Why not?" Shona could not help herself asking. Curiosity often drove her when she should leave well enough alone.

"I refused the assignment to go after his daughter."

"What?" Even in his not-quite-human voice, Caelis's shock was palpable.

"He was not a good father to his human daughter."

"Yet you would have killed my children," Shona said with more confusion than anger.

She was doubting her own words even as she spoke them.

"Chrechte do not kill children."

"You said—"

"What I believed would undermine my opponent with emotion."

"Oh."

"Jon did not kill the woman."

"Audrey."

"He could have." Shona had thought so at the time.

"Aye."

"Vegar would not take the risk he might."

"A man protects his mate." Maon's shrug should have been casual, but there was an air of grief about him.

And Shona remembered something from her old clan. "Jon was your younger brother."

"Too young to come on this quest."

"But Uven sent him anyway. And you defend the man." Shona could not understand it.

"He was my alpha. It was not my place to question him."

"You said *was*."

Maon looked at Caelis and then away.

"A Chrechte of honor values all life. An alpha worthy of loyalty extends both his protection and his consideration to those who swear fealty to him." Caelis spoke gutterly, but never had Shona heard him say words more *humane*.

"Members of our clan starve while Uven fills his belly with prey."

Caelis growled, but made no other reply to that claim.

Maon looked at him. "To be *conriocht*, the stone had to find you worthy."

"Maker of the stone, aye. The stone is but a way for us to connect to our Creator."

"You used to be Fearghall."

"I accepted truth when I heard it."

Maon nodded. "Taking over the clan will not be easy. Some must die."

"Fewer than if the clan stays in the hands of an unscrupulous man."

"This is what you were talking about earlier, isn't it?" Shona asked Caelis, certain in her heart she was right.

"Aye."

"Da is alpha," Eadan said.

"You're sure of that, are you, boy?" Sean asked with a smile.

Caelis growled, though Shona did not understand why.

Sean flinched but smiled. "I wasn't questioning your alpha status, *conriocht*."

Suddenly, Shona found herself sitting alone with both children, her snarling mate towering over them all. "I warned you: I can smell a lie."

Sean jumped up, shifting into wolf form between one blink of her eyes and the next. He didn't attack Caelis, but ran in the other direction.

Caelis looked after him; she could see his entire body tense with the need to follow.

"Go after him," she instructed.

"Nay." The fury in his tone made the word more a bark than anything recognizable.

He would not leave her and the children unprotected.

"Sinclair's soldiers will be here soon enough. I will go after him then."

Suddenly another wolf streaked past, which she recognized as Maon. She'd thought he was coming around, but then she'd thought Sean was completely won over already.

The sound of a loud bark came through the brush, then breaking branches, snarls and yelps, followed by a howl cut off mid-vocalization.

Maon came trotting back a moment later, his muzzle covered in blood, his hackles still raised.

Caelis dropped to a crouch and met the wolf with pats from his oversized beast's hands, growls and croons that could be nothing but praise and thanks. Though Shona did not pretend to speak *wolf*.

Caelis stood. "There is a stream that way. Go wash the blood of battle away."

The wolf obeyed and Shona clamped down her desire to point out that he still hadn't sworn fealty. Sean had as good as, but without conviction.

Caelis turned to the remaining two wolves. "Chrechte law states my mate and family are paramount. Speak your intentions to follow or defy me now."

The man Shona had never met stood. "I am not of the MacLeod clan."

"And yet you do the laird's bidding."

"I was ordered by my alpha to accompany the others on this quest."

"To destroy me."

"And the other Uven considers a deserter."

"We were to bring you back," the other MacLeod Chrechte said.

"To what purpose?" Shona had to wonder.

"To make an example of your mate and the other one."

She frowned. "Why do you not name him?"

Did this man think he was too good to speak the name of another he considered a deserter?

"We do not know which of the warriors lives."

"Oh."

Caelis did not offer the name of his fellow soldier. He glared down at the two men. "Choose now."

"I cannot swear fealty," the non-MacLeod said, but raised his hand in supplication at Caelis's growl. "I have been raised Fearghall from birth. You demand I abandon my brethren. My father."

"He is pack alpha," Shona guessed.

The man looked startled at her perception.

She rolled her eyes. "I'm a human woman, not an idiot."

"I give my word that no harm will come to you, your mate or your family by my hand or instigation." The man put his fist over his heart and bowed his head again. "You are *conriocht*, blessed by all that we hold sacred."

Caelis nodded. "I accept, but you will not go free."

The man did not look surprised at all by Caelis's pronouncement.

"And you?" Caelis demanded of the other soldiers.

Both men dropped to their knees and bowed their heads, speaking vows in what her father had once told her was the ancient language. She'd thought it was ancient Gaelic. Now she knew differently.

'Twas no doubt the original language of their people.

Caelis relaxed marginally and barked something back at them she did not understand.

He turned to her. "There is no more danger."

She did not ask if he was certain—not after the way he'd known Sean's heart even when the man presented the face of a friend.

"What happens to them now?" she asked.

"They'll be trained by me."

*C*aelis watched, unsurprised, as the Sinclair approached, his countenance grim. Though Shona and even the other wolves had seemed oblivious, Caelis had heard the other soldiers moving quickly through the forest for the past several minutes.

His *conriocht* had sensed the approach of the alpha as well, though Talorc moved with absolute stealth.

Caelis turned to the laird. "You heard it all?"

"Aye." Talorc's frown was fierce. "You are *conriocht*."

"You make that sound an accusation." If Shona's own glare were directed at him, it would have made even Caelis cringe. "He saved our lives."

"He revealed his third form to humans and to Faol who are unaware of the return of our race's protectors."

Maon returned from washing himself in the stream, having transformed back to man. "I shifted first."

Caelis wasn't worried about the Sinclair's anger, though he respected Maon for his honesty and willingness to have that ire directed at him. But nothing would have kept Caelis from shifting to his fiercest form when his mate and children were in danger; Talorc should have been well aware of that fact.

Dismissing the other alpha's wrath from his mind, Caelis focused on regaining his human form now that his family was no longer in imminent danger. Heat suffused his body and the air compressed around him in a way it did not when he shifted back and forth from his wolf.

A moment later, he swayed on his feet, his perspective that of a man again. Shona rushed over and offered her arm.

He did not make the mistake of smiling at the gesture or refusing her help. The woman was half his width—even as a man—and more than a head shorter, but he leaned slightly on her shoulder regardless. The force of her spirit more than made up for what she might lack in stature. Had she been born Éan, Caelis had no doubt Shona would have become one of their guardians as the princess, Sabrine, had been before her marriage to the laird of the Donegal.

Shona directed him toward a tree. "Lean here."

He stumbled forward, grateful when his back was against the solid trunk.

He was always dizzy after shifting from his *conriocht* . . . and hungry. He could eat a boar.

Talorc gave him a sympathetic look he was sure no one else saw—and if they did, would not understand.

But Talorc and the Balmoral pack alpha had also been chosen through the sacred stone as protectors of their people.

Not all on the Chrechte council were aware of this fact, which only went to prove that despite their efforts to live as a single people, trust between them all was not assured.

Thus far, there was only complete disclosure between the lairds of the Sinclair, Balmoral and Donegal clans. The others on the council only knew the barest facts about the Éan's return to the clans.

None of them knew about Prince Eirik's dragon form or about the return of the *Faolchú Chridhe* to the Faol.

Ciara, the newly appointed *celi di* of the Faol, followed advice given to her through visions by an ancient *celi di*. She was insistent the time had not yet come to reveal the sacred stone's return.

Unlike the Éan who only had one protector in a generation, the Faol could have many.

Right now, they had three.

The Éan's prince was a fearsome beast in his dragon form, more than capable of taking on an entire pack of *conriocht*, though.

It was a good thing they were all allies.

And if Caelis had his way, the MacLeod clan would join that group, its pack submitting to the authority of the Chrechte council as the others did.

As much as any Highlander submitted to another.

Most important, the MacLeod Faol would begin training in the true ancient ways of the Chrechte. His brethren would learn, as he had, that there was no honor in killing Éan simply because they shifted into birds.

Many would resist the truth that they were *not* superior to other Chrechte or humanity, but Caelis had faith in his fellow wolves.

Some would be like Sean, but more would shift their thinking just as they shifted forms.

"Are you well?" Shona asked, her tone filled with worry.

Caelis allowed himself to secretly enjoy the concern in

her demeanor and leaned more heavily against the tree. "Aye."

"He'll be hungry," the Sinclair informed her, with a look of knowing for Caelis.

"Because of your transformation?" she asked.

"Aye." His stomach gave an angry rumble. "It's always worse after I shift back from *conriocht*."

"Then let us get back to the keep." She looked expectantly at Talorc.

The laird shook his head with a smile. "I've a feeling you're going to be every bit as managing as Abigail."

"Your wife seems all that is amiable to me."

"Oh, aye. When she's of a mind to be, there is no more charming or pleasant." The pride in Talorc's voice was unmistakable.

"Women have to be strong in this world if we do not wish to be crushed under the plans of men."

The laird grunted surprising agreement, though Caelis couldn't deny Shona's words, either. She'd paid the price for Uven's machinations and then her own father's plans. Whether the man thought his arrangements for her were for Shona's benefit, they had caused her a great deal of pain.

They retrieved his sword and kilt on the way back to the keep, as well as the dead wolves. The Sinclair soldiers wrapped the bodies in MacLeod colors for transport, as was proper. There would be a joint funeral pyre lit that night on moonrise.

Sean's carcass was left in the forest for the animals and carrion birds, his treachery bringing its own reward.

Audrey watched the man Laird Sinclair had just declared her husband before he would allow Vegar to accompany her abovestairs. Things had happened so fast, but then, they could between wolves.

The Faol understood the base drives in nature and didn't fight those that were paramount, like that of mating.

Besides, Audrey preferred "wife" over *lehman* any day.

Vegar turned back from having dropped the bar on the door. Abigail had left some time ago, but she'd sent Ciara up with a healing tea, which Vegar had insisted on tasting before passing onto Audrey.

Thankfully, the laird's adopted daughter, not to mention *celi di* to the Faol, had not appeared offended by Vegar's precautions.

"She was not trying to poison me."

Vegar's brows drew together in confusion. "I did not say she was."

"You insisted on tasting the tea before allowing me to drink it."

"I wanted to make sure it was not too hot."

"Oh." That was . . . actually incredibly sweet.

And sweet was not a word she thought of in association with her mate.

"You are not as I expected from our first meeting."

He grimaced. "I believe that is a good thing."

She found herself smiling. "Yes, I do believe it is."

"I am not a bad man," he said, clearly offended.

Men could be so touchy. Her brother was more easily offended than either Shona or Audrey.

Deciding words were best left at present, Audrey took a sip of the honey-sweetened beverage made from what tasted like a combination of valerian root and chamomile. She would be asleep soon.

She wondered if Vegar realized what the tea was intended to do.

It would seem not.

He watched her, his hazel eyes dark with emotion she had never before welcomed in a man. Lust. She could not welcome it now, either. Audrey gripped the cup of hot drink with both her hands. She was not at all sure how he would respond to that knowledge.

Chapter 16

There is no greater gift than to be accepted by one's mate.

—NIALL OF THE SINCLAIR

"You nearly challenged the pack alpha," Audrey remarked, trying to understand Vegar's irrational behavior and avoid her own contemplations.

His insistence on caring for her had led to a near challenge and a *very* hasty marriage.

"You are *my* mate. Mine to protect. Mine to care for."

She could not deny his words. Despite the fact that Lady Sinclair had followed them to Vegar's room and insisted on treating Audrey's injuries, he had done most of the actual tending.

"Is that the way it is among the Éan?"

"Mates take care of one another, no matter their race of Chrechte."

"My father never played nursemaid to my mother."

Vegar shrugged. "He is English and human."

"He was still her mate." And though it was uncommon enough for a human to mate a Chrechte, when it happened, the bond was every bit as irresistible as it was between two of the Faol.

"Not a good one, by the sounds of it."

"He had a wife," Audrey admitted with shame even as she revised some of her own perceptions about the mating bond.

It inspired lust and an overwhelming need to procreate, but the tender touches and acts of kindness she'd witnessed between the laird and his lady were not a result of it. Emotion caused that behavior and attitude.

Would she experience that same emotion with Vegar?

"Not your mother."

"Not my dam, no."

Vegar shook his head. *"English."*

"That is not a curse word, any more than Éan is one that should be spoken in that tone. Whatever you may wish otherwise, your mate and now wife is English."

Vegar sighed. "I apologize."

"What?"

"You heard."

"You do not seem like a man who admits regret easily."

"I am not."

"So, I should feel privileged?"

"You are my mate."

"And that gives me special privileges?"

"Aye."

"I am still English."

"You are Chrechte."

"And a bastard."

"Your father is the bastard, not you."

"His parents were married."

"His behavior toward your mother and the woman who carries his name decrees him such."

"I always thought so," Audrey admitted. "His wife was not an unkind woman. She treated Thomas and me better than our father did."

"She is a woman of great character."

"My mother did not think so."

"That is to be expected."

Audrey found herself smiling at something that had

always before caused her pain. "Perhaps it is. Even if she had been his wife, I do not think my father would have known the first thing about tending another's ailments, least of all my mother's."

The shrug was in his voice this time. "Warriors are trained to treat wounds as well as inflict them."

"Are they?" She'd never heard of such a thing among the baron's knights.

Though that was not a definitive circumstance. Their father had taken Thomas's training very lightly. It had stopped almost completely when they were sent to serve in the Heronshire household.

Shona's baron had made sure Thomas knew enough to protect his wife and the children only in a very rudimentary way.

"Aye."

"Is it a Highlander tradition, do you think?"

He lifted one negligent shoulder, as if whether anyone outside the men he trained did as they did was of no importance. Probably, it wasn't.

Unlike her, Vegar did not appear to be a man who would care overmuch for the opinions or accepted practices of others.

Vegar pulled his tunic off and she gasped as his torso was revealed. To be sure, his body was all that a woman could desire in both husband and mate.

Strong and well formed, but it was the evidence of the battle he'd so recently fought that drew forth her reaction. "You were so intent on treating my cuts, you have neglected your own."

"You can treat them for me now." He removed his kilt and approached the bed, his tumescent sex worrisome.

She nodded, his health more important than her worry or embarrassment. Holidng close with one hand the fur covering her nakedness, she sat up and reached for the wet cloth floating in a bowl of witch hazel–infused water Abigail had left behind.

Audrey now realized the lady had done so not so her

own injuries could be treated again later, but so that Vegar's wounds could be cleansed.

He sat beside her on the bedding in a way that made it easy for her to reach the majority of the small cuts and abrasions he'd sustained. "You are very tenderhearted."

"Because I want to treat your wounds? You treated mine as well," she reminded him. And had in fact, ignored his own to do so.

Again she was touched by the heart revealed in his actions despite his sometimes off-putting attitude and words.

"Because you allowed the laird to proclaim us man and wife rather than allow me to challenge him."

"You were not being reasonable."

"There is no *reason* when it comes to protecting one's mate."

"If you say so." She reached out and touched him with the cloth, swiping at dried blood around one of his larger gashes. "None of these will need sewing."

"I am Chrechte. I will heal quickly."

"I know that, but I am still glad."

"Are you?"

"Yes, of course."

"Why?"

She did not understand the question. "I do not wish you to be in pain."

"You see? Tenderhearted."

"It is quite normal for a person to have compassion for others." Did he not see it so?

"You are Faol. I am Éan."

"You are my mate. Besides, I am not my mother. Whatever she believed, I cannot accept that others are less simply because they shift into a different animal, or do not shift at all."

"You and Caelis's lady are like sisters though you share no blood."

"We are."

"'Tis unusual among the Faol to be so close to a human."

"Perhaps I would have believed that before coming here, but now I am certain the Fearghall are exceptions among our kind."

"For the most part, but dinna be deceived, my beautiful mate, there are many Chrechte among the Éan and the Faol who believe themselves superior to humans. It is not only the Fearghall who believe the Faol are the strongest of the Chrechte and therefore superior. Do not be deceived about my people, either. Many believe we should remain apart and that we are better for the gifts we have been given through our own sacred stone beyond the ability to shift."

"What gifts? What do you mean?"

"Each Éan is gifted with mystical talents during the ceremony of their first shift."

"We do not have a ceremony for our first shift?" she asked, rather than said, because she was not sure.

"The Faol gave up many of their ceremonies over the centuries, but the Éan have always been the race with more mystical abilities."

"Which makes some of you believe you are better than the Faol?"

"Aye."

"And many of the English believe themselves better than the Scots." This false sense of superiority seemed to be a universal problem among all of humanity.

His hazel eyes doubted her words. "You do not?"

"There is enough to occupy my mind and time without spending any of it worrying if I am in some way better than others."

"Even a barbarian?"

Heat suffused her face. "I said that in anger."

He nodded.

"You believe me?"

"We are Chrechte. I could smell a lie."

Oh. Yes. It would take effort to grow accustomed to being around others of her kind besides her brother.

Which meant if he lied, she would smell it on him.

"You are no longer disappointed to be mated to an Englishwoman?"

"No." Only truth and sincerity infused his scent and his tone.

Inexplicable tears burned her eyes. She blinked them away. "That is good."

He smiled, his handsome face even more compelling.

"You are very appealing in your looks." Had she really said that?

Perhaps there had been something besides valerian root and chamomile in her tea.

His smile turned to a feral grin. "I'm glad you think so."

"Do not be arrogant."

"According to you, I have reason to be."

"Annoying warrior."

She went to rinse the cloth and wring it out, but it was an awkward task with only one hand.

He took the cloth from her and did it, handing it back to her when he was done. "Your touch, even in such an inno-cent fashion, evokes a strong reaction in me."

Her gaze flitted to his very large manhood. "I noticed."

He chuckled. "You are careful to look everywhere but there."

"We are married, but we are not mated."

He stilled, his expression turning almost frightening. "This is true."

"I would prefer not to engage in certain . . . activities until after we are mated," she said, her words speeding up until the final ones ran together.

"Why?" Had he even understood them?

"Neither my brother nor my dearest friend was there to witness our promises." They'd barely spoken any. "I would have both by my side when I speak my Chrechte vows of mating."

He didn't reply and she kept herself occupied finishing what she had started.

"Look at me," he ordered in an almost gentle tone when she was finished tending him and had dropped the cloth back in the bowl. He was back to looking and sounding dangerous. "Do you question the validity of our marriage because it did not happen before a priest?"

"No, though I will expect a priest's blessing in the future." It was not something she was willing to compromise on.

"Aye."

She nodded.

Surprisingly, he relaxed. "Why, then, do you wish to wait on consummation?"

She shook her head. She did not want to see his anger at her request.

"Audrey."

She bit her lip at the command in his tone, but did not obey it. "Surely you can understand my desire."

He barked out a laugh. "I think, sweet mate, it is you who does not *understand* desire."

He was not far off. Audrey was wholly innocent, Shona's claim earlier that there was great pleasure to be found in the act of copulation for a woman, the closest thing she had received to instruction on the matter.

"I wish to wait," she repeated.

"Mate." There was no doubt that this time, Vegar fully expected her compliance.

He would learn that using that tone would not always benefit him. Another time.

She found herself lifting her head so their eyes met.

His were devoid of the anger, frustration or even disappointment she expected. "You are healing, mate. I would not choose this moment to consummate our marriage regardless."

"Oh." That was . . . it was really rather considerate of him. "Thank you."

"Dinna thank me for doing right by you. No matter our differences, you can always expect that, at the very least."

"Oh." His words were not as comforting as the unexpectedly kind expression on his masculine features. "Can I expect anything else?"

"What do you mean?" The question as much as the perplexed drawing together of his brows made it quite clear Vegar truly had no inkling what she was talking about.

It was a bit disheartening, but she forged on anyway. "Do you believe in love between mates?"

"I believe it happens, yes." He did not sound any further enlightened.

She had no choice but to bluntly ask, "Will you love me, do you think?"

"Will you love *me*?" he asked, instead of answering.

She frowned at him, wanting to lie, but after his consideration felt obligated to reply with the truth. He'd smell the lie anyway. Arrogant, uncooperative, decidedly not forthcoming warrior.

He waited with eyes narrowed, a tension about him she could not understand.

She blew out a breath and spoke the truth. "Yes, I think I will."

"You do not sound happy about that."

"Truly? I am not." She'd seen the pain a woman lived with loving a mate who had not discernible deeper emotions for her.

"Is it because I am Éan?"

"It is because you are a hard man. I do not think love will come easily to you." If at all.

"This very morn, I would have agreed with you."

"Something has changed your opinion in such a short time?"

"Aye, you could say that."

"What?" she asked, perplexed.

"Seeing you fight with another wolf to protect me."

"How could that be?" In no way had she been at her best.

"You could have died."

That was true enough.

"I do not know how to fight." In fact, she'd done very little damage. Thinking back on those fraught minutes, it was a wonder she'd survived them at all.

"You fought with your heart. That, sometimes, is more important than training."

"You killed him." She would never regret the killing blow had come from him and not her.

Audrey did not think she would like knowing she had killed a man, be he in his beast form or not when he died.

"Aye." The word had a weary, unhappy undertone.

She would have expected him to be pleased, or at the very least proud of his feat. It was clear, however, that he regretted the other Chrechte's death.

"You didn't want to."

"Too many Chrechte have died from bloodshed."

"It is in our nature."

"Our *human* nature, mayhap."

Her lips curved in a small smile at the joke she knew he meant half seriously. "It will be no easy thing to fight the Fearghall."

"You are right, but the Éan and Cahir have been doing it for centuries."

"It is different now, is it not?" This joining of the clans by the Éan, it changed things.

The MacLeod laird's machinations were worrisome as well.

"It must be done."

"Yes."

"Your brother will join the Cahir."

"How can you be sure?" An awful thought formed. "You will not force him?"

"Nay. He has your heart. He seeks justice and truth. The Cahir will do well to have him join our ranks. And Thomas will find the destiny he seeks."

"You don't know him."

The firm set of Vegar's jaw and mouth said he did not agree.

But how could he claim otherwise? "You truly are *very* arrogant, aren't you?"

"I am a warrior of the Cahir."

"And that makes you always right?"

"It makes me more aware than even others of our kind."

"You would have me believe that with your training, you can tell a man's character after a single meeting?"

"We are Cahir."

"You already said that."

He smiled at her jibe rather than getting annoyed. "Chrechte have many gifts, which, when honed to a knife point, can slice through deception and illusions."

"Hmm."

"You do not sound convinced."

"And you sound much too certain."

"I am not claiming all Cahir, much less all Chrechte, can read a man's nature upon meeting him, but *I* can."

"How?"

"Our sacred stones bestow many gifts."

"So?" Would she spend the rest of her life trying to understand this maddening man's riddles?

"So, one of my gifts is to read a man's heart."

"What does that mean?"

"Even his most deeply hidden tendencies are as transparent as a loch in the still morning air."

"You can read thoughts?"

"Nay. Character."

It was all so very confusing.

"That explains it then," she said, her intention to tease as she felt nothing had really been explained at all.

"Aye."

"You don't know my meaning."

"What is it then?"

"You were so quick to judge me lacking when you learned of my country of birth."

"That was a mistake."

"Yes, but an understandable one."

"I am glad you think so."

She nodded. "If I had been a man, you could have read my heart. But since I am a woman, you had to spend time with me first."

She giggled at his outraged expression, her laughter ending on a yawn as the tea took its effect.

"You will lead me a merry chase, I think, Audrey of England."

"I do not think I am of England any longer. I have no home to return to." Not if she wanted to keep Shona safe.

"I am your home now."

That sounded nice.

She yawned again, trying to smile. "After the Chrechte ceremony, you will be."

He did not argue and she counted that a victory with the overconfident Éan warrior.

Vegar helped her to get comfortable in the furs, laying down beside her in a most comforting manner as she slipped into tea-induced sleep despite the hour of day.

When they returned to the keep, Maon and the two others who had promised fidelity were taken for intensive retraining with those assigned to the task by the Sinclair. They would learn the ways of true Chrechte honor that Caelis himself had undertaken before going to Balmoral Island to train with the Cahir.

The warrior who was not MacLeod was taken to the prisoner's tower. He had yet to reveal his clan and the Sinclair had declared him prisoner until such time as his loyalty could be ascertained.

Unlike a year ago, Caelis was no longer shocked by the fact the Sinclair did not simply kill the offenders. Talorc had not ordered Caelis's death, either.

He was far more impressed by the laird's wisdom and strength of character now, though. As Talorc had taught him, and later the Balmoral had reiterated, it was easy to kill. Not so easy to convince a man to change his path.

Shona insisted on Caelis and the children eating, though she did not even pretend to pick at the food Abigail had placed before them.

"How is Audrey?" she asked Abigail as soon as Marjory and Eadan were tucking into their food.

There could be no doubt that Shona wished she could be with her friend, checking on her well-being in person. She put her children's needs ahead of everything, however.

The fact that included staying with Caelis was to his benefit.

"Audrey will be fine. She'll heal fast, you'll see," Abigail promised. "She is resting with Vegar in his room."

"But . . ." Shona stopped, clearly unsure how to go on. After a guilty look at Caelis, she simply bit her lip and nodded. What was that about?

And then it hit him. Shona was upset her friend was in a compromising situation with the Éan warrior, but did not feel she had the right to say anything after the way Audrey had caught her with Caelis that morning.

"When is the ceremony?" Caelis asked Abigail, no doubts at all that one was planned.

"This evening."

"What ceremony?" Shona demanded. "You aren't telling me that Audrey and Vegar are getting married, *this evening*? Are you?" Shona's emerald gaze implored Abigail. "They've only just met."

Abigail bit her lip and looked at Caelis as if asking him a question.

He had no guess as to what that question might be.

After a couple of tense seconds, Abigail blew out a clearly frustrated breath and frowned at Caelis before smiling tentatively at Shona. "Talorc heard their vows before he would let Vegar take her upstairs."

"But . . ." Looking lost, Shona seemed to sink in on herself. "What is the ceremony you two are speaking of then?"

Caelis reached over and brushed her cheek. He wanted to touch her all the time. It was only more acute in his *conriocht* form.

This time, though, he was seeking to give comfort. "It is for their mating."

"She is my dearest friend and she was married without

me." Shona gave Caelis a very unfriendly look. "I do not believe I like this world of the Chrechte."

"Things are not done the same in the Highlands, Chrechte or not," Abigail offered in a clear attempt to smooth things over.

The gaze Shona leveled at the Sinclair lady was not exactly warm either. "Even in the Highlands, weddings do not happen in such an unplanned fashion."

"You would be surprised." Abigail's tone was wry, her expression knowing.

Shona crossed her arms and went back to glaring at Caelis as if the circumstances were entirely of his making. "I won't have it."

"She will be there for ours," he promised, hoping that reminder would improve Shona's rapidly deteriorating mood.

Her eyes snapped green fire. "Our *what*, Caelis who would be laird to Clan MacLeod?"

"Our wedding." He had made his intentions clear. Did she doubt them now?

"I am no Chrechte to be dictated to by my animal nature. And none can deny that I have earned the right to choose my own future. There will be no second marriage *dictated* to me."

Chapter 17

A Chrechte's senses are superior to a human's, but he does not always interpret what they tell him aright.

—GUAIRE OF THE SINCLAIR

"You would deny me?" Caelis asked, his dizziness after shifting nothing compared to the swirling in his head now.

Was she intent on denying his claim on her and their children? "Is it because you have seen my *conriocht* and now find marriage to me too frightening a prospect?"

"It is not your *conriocht* I find objectionable."

Meaning what? It was his wolf she found unpleasing? No. She'd claimed to trust him in animal form and had behaved near entranced by his beast when Caelis had shared the wolf with her.

His man, then?

He had never heard of such a thing. How could she find the form most like her humanity unacceptable?

"Because it was the man who betrayed me and who seeks to run roughshod over my feelings and rights as an independent widow now."

What rights as a widow?

"Those recognized by the law; while not near the

freedoms granted a man, they are far superior to those of a never-married woman."

She was right. Having questions he had not uttered aloud answered would take some getting used to. He had thought the question, though. Mindspeak seemed limited to directed thoughts and he would have to guard his own if he did not want to share them with his mate.

Chrechte were taught that though mindspeak was a benefit of a true bond, it did not always happen immediately upon bonding with one's sacred mate. It was like other gifts of the Chrechte, bestowed in its own time and growing stronger with use. Just as his ability to shift had been.

"What have these legal boons granted to your status to do with my claims to our children, or you, my mate?" he demanded, more confused than he'd ever been.

Talorc had once given the opinion that women were more different from men than the Chrechte from their human brethren. The man obviously knew what he was talking about.

"Everything!"

"Mama?" Marjory asked around a mouthful of berries. "You mad at our new daddy?"

Expecting Shona to deny it to protect her daughter from upset, he was shocked when she nodded her head without hesitation.

"I am, sweeting. Very angry."

"Oh." Marjory went back to eating, taking a bite of her bread and cheese, apparently unworried.

Why this was different than her mother's upset before, he did not know.

Shona turned her glacial green gaze back on Caelis. "Well?"

He had no idea what it was she was expecting. "You can invite anyone you like to our wedding," he promised, hoping she didn't have anyone in England she'd want brought north to witness their vows.

They needed to marry quickly, as he had to return to the

MacLeod lands and wrest the pack and clan from Uven's control.

"There. Isn't. Going. To. Be. Any. Wedding." Each word came out with precise enunciation, her voice as cold as the look in her eyes.

Unexpected pain lanced through Caelis. "You are denying me my mate and my children?"

There was no softening in her expression, but she shook her head with firm decision. "No."

"You said—"

"There will be no wedding or mating ritual, or any permanent bonds acknowledged between us until you have done what needs doing."

"What needs doing?" he asked with genuine confusion.

The way she reacted, it was clear she believed he was being sarcastic. Shona's eyes narrowed, her body going rigid as a distinct string of words came across the mating bond.

She'd called him a *half-witted son of a mange-ridden dog* inside his head.

The expression on her face said she was proud of herself, too.

Unamused, he opened his mouth to let her know just how little he liked being called names by his mate when he spied the way Eadan watched them with wide-eyed interest. Caelis snapped his mouth shut.

"I *will* have a proper proposal, Caelis, as I should have six years ago after you convinced me to give you what only my husband had a right to."

He had no answer to that. He should have married her six years ago and the young man he'd been had had every intention of dropping to one knee and asking her properly. Of course, he'd also been sure of her positive response.

He'd no desire to drop to one knee before her now. She was as likely to kick him in the teeth as she was to agree to marry him.

"If you believe that, there is a great deal to be learned between us before you ask such an important question."

"Stop reading my thoughts," he ordered.

And then felt the futility of the demand. Their mate bond only strengthened each moment they were together.

"Furthermore, you will go to my relatives and state your intentions before asking for anything further from me." She got up from the table, her movements precise and deliberate, her expression and thoughts closed to him. "Make sure the children both take a nap. They have been through an ordeal."

And with a whirl of velvet skirts and flying auburn braid, Shona flounced out of the great hall.

"Uh-oh . . ." Eadan looked worried.

"Aye?" Caelis asked his son, hoping the five-year-old understood what had just happened.

Because Caelis did not.

"You've gone and made her cross now."

That Caelis knew. "She becomes irate easily these days, I think."

Eadan shook his head and Marjory stared at Caelis mournfully. "You's in trouble. No pudding for you after supper tonight."

Caelis would have laughed, but he was beginning to suspect his situation was far from amusing.

"Mum only gets scrunchy-faced angry and all quiet when you do something very bad. What did you do, Da?" Eadan asked.

"I wish I knew."

"Men!" Abigail exclaimed, reminding Caelis she was still there.

"You know why my mate has just abandoned me with our children?"

"Of course I do. The wonder is that you do not," Abigail retorted, frustration with him turned to pity in the blink of an eye. "As to leaving the children, it's the one aspect to this situation that can give you hope."

"Aye?"

"Oh, yes. A woman of Shona's caliber does not leave her children with someone she does not trust."

Put that way, but no. 'Twas small compensation in the face of her clear refusal to marry him. "She's furious I want to wed."

"No, you idiot, Shona is angry you didn't ask her properly. She said so. She's also terribly disappointed she wasn't here to witness the vows between Vegar and Audrey. Your mate is upset and overwhelmed by all that has happened. It is your privilege and duty to make that better."

That was a simple pronouncement for the Sinclair to make. She obviously did not understand how impractical Shona's demands were. "She wants me to travel to Balmoral Island and approach relatives she has never even met to state my intentions toward her."

"That is not an unreasonable request."

"Mayhap not on the face of it, but every day I put off returning to my clan, Uven does more to destroy it from within."

Abigail's brows rose and then her eyes narrowed. "You have spent the last year training and did not resent the time taken to do so."

"That is different." She was a laird and pack alpha's mate; she should understand that without Caelis having to point it out.

"How?"

"It was necessary."

"Oh!" Abigail's expression turned every bit as outraged as Shona's had been. "You truly are an imbecile. Good fortune on winning your mate with that attitude. You will need it. Desperately."

And then the laird's wife was gone, leaving Caelis in a rarely empty great hall.

"Did you make the lady angry, too, Da?" Eadan asked with something like awe.

Caelis rubbed his hand over his face. "Aye, son, I believe I did."

"I think Margie is right. You aren't getting any pudding tonight."

"We don't serve pudding with supper every evening," Caelis pointed out reasonably.

Only this apparently was not something small Marjory wanted to hear, because she immediately started crying. "I wants pudding."

Caelis had no idea what to do.

"You'd better pick her up," Eadan pointed out as if speaking to a simpleton.

Mayhap that was exactly what Caelis was because he had no idea how he'd managed to upset three females in as many minutes.

Calming Marjory only required a trip to the kitchen for a honey stick, but he worried it would not be so easy to appease Shona's upset.

Dressed in clothes dusty and stained with blood from the battle in the forest, Audrey crept on silent feet toward the door of Vegar's room.

Shona had not come to see her all afternoon and Audrey needed to know how her friend fared. Was she angry about Audrey's wedding, such as it was?

Had she been too traumatized by the sight of Caelis in his *conriocht* form? Was she still angry at Audrey for hiding her own Faol nature for the years of their acquaintance? Had Audrey revealing her own wolf given Shona a disgust of her?

The door swung inward just as Audrey reached it, Vegar carrying a tray of food on the other side.

She jumped back, blushing at being caught even though she should be allowed to leave the room if she wanted to. "Vegar."

"Mate." He frowned. "You are dressed."

"I could hardly wander about the keep in my altogether."

"You are not supposed to be wandering anywhere. You are to be resting."

"I *was* resting." She bit her lip and tugged at her sleeves, noting a tear she had not noticed when donning her dress. "Now, I am going to my bedchamber."

"This is my room, therefore it is your room."

"That is hardly an acceptable living arrangement. I could not help noticing that this bedchamber is prepared for multiple soldiers to live in it. I cannot make my home with a gaggle of strange men."

"You are not making your home with anyone but me."

She looked significantly at the neatly stored belongings on the other side of the room. The yellow-and-black plaid with narrow red stripes in the pile was the same color as the one Caelis wore. She thought Vegar must share the room with Shona's mate, but it was quite apparent the small room was meant to house a group of soldiers. Each of the four walls had a small chest against it, which a single soldier might use or share with another. There was room for multiple bedrolls on the floor, though the soldiers would be crowded.

Vegar set the tray down beside his sleeping furs. "Caelis will be staying with Shona."

"They are not wed."

"They were not wed last night, but he still marked her with his scent."

Audrey huffed in consternation. "I thought we had washed away his marking scent."

"A human would not know."

"But you are not human."

"Nor are a good number of the Sinclair's soldiers."

"The Chrechte are more plentiful than my mother led me to believe."

Vegar shrugged. "I dinna know about that, but our numbers are not near what the stories claim they once were."

"I have never heard the stories."

"I will tell them to you."

"Thank you."

He shook his head. "Do not thank your mate for doing so little."

"It is not little to me."

"Our children will be able to take such a small thing for granted," he promised.

Their mother never would.

"Get back in bed, Audrey."

"I . . ." Thinking better of telling him she wanted to see Shona, Audrey said instead, "I thought you were attending to important matters."

"I was: getting you your even meal."

"You are not at all as I first thought."

He frowned. "You think there is aught odd about me seeing to the needs of my mate?"

"No, of course not. Well, maybe a little. My father never cared for my mother's needs and honestly, I do not recall her watching out for his comfort, either."

"That is not the type of mating I hope to have."

"It is the only one I have ever seen."

"Then you must take my word that even where tender feeling does not exist, a mating can be a great blessing for those connected by the bond."

And for a mating where tender feeling *did* exist? Because Audrey grew more certain by the minute in her barbaric mate's company that love would grow on her side very quickly.

His rough manners aside, Vegar was all that Audrey could have dreamed of in a mate . . . had she allowed herself to dream.

"Not all matings enjoy the sacred bond." That much she knew.

"Nay, but ours will."

She agreed with him, but did not understand how either of them could be so certain. Nodding her agreement, she looked toward the door, wondering if she just walked out if he would follow.

And what he might do about it.

"I will pick you up and carry you back in here, where I will undress you before tossing your clothing out that window there." He pointed to the small opening high in the wall through which the waning sun cast its dim light.

"You cannot throw away my clothes."

A single light brown brow rose, but he did not bother with a verbal reply.

"I need to see Shona."

"Why?"

"I am worried about her."

"What has you concerned?"

"She has just discovered the true nature of the Chrechte, then she and her children's lives are threatened, and she has not come to check on me."

The last was the thing that worried Audrey the most.

"Do you think the baroness will convince the Sinclair to nullify our marriage?"

"What?" She stared at him, unable to comprehend where the question had come from. "No! I told you, I accepted our mating."

"But you do not wish to consummate it."

"You said you would not do so regardless because I need to heal."

"It is not my motives that are under question."

"Mine are?"

"I did not say that."

"I think you did."

He moved the things on the food tray around, but to little effect in her eyes. "I offended you upon meeting."

"I thought it was I who offended you by being English."

He turned back to her, his rugged features creased in a familiar frown. "I told you that I regretted that."

She nodded.

"You are beautiful."

She started, not having expected those words at all. "I am still English."

He shook his head. "You will not throw that up between us for the rest of our lives."

"I might, actually." She smiled at him, letting him know it would not be in anger.

"You have a teasing nature." He did not appear upset by that realization.

"My brother has accused me of that, yes."

He tugged her toward the furs on the floor. "You need more rest."

"It will not tax me too greatly to see Shona."

"You will see her tomorrow night at our mating."

"I wish to see her now."

Vegar paused, looking down at her. "This is important to you."

"Yes."

"And you will not implore her to have our marriage annulled before we consummate?"

"No." She let him see he was not the only one who could frown. "But if I did have that intention, what would you do? Attempt to lock me in this room until we had consummated the mating?"

She could not believe she was speaking so freely, but he was her mate. She found that gave her a freedom in her speech she had never before experienced. She felt no hesitation to share her thoughts, regardless of what they might be.

"There is no benefit to speculation on that which is not a reality."

"You *would*," she breathed, shocked.

Hazel eyes met hers, no apology in them. "You are my mate. You spoke your vows without duress."

Vegar's definition of "without duress" might not match hers exactly, but for the most part, she agreed with his assessment. "And I do not go back on my word."

"'Tis good to know."

"You are ruthless."

"Aye."

"I am not certain *that* is good to know."

"I will be as ruthless protecting you and our family when it comes in time as I am in protecting our mating."

"That is something to be grateful for at least, I suppose."

"I will accompany you to Shona's chamber after you eat your latemeal."

"Why is she in her room?" Audrey would have thought Shona was eating in the great hall.

Unless the world of the Chrechte had become too much for her. Audrey's anxiety on behalf of her dear friend increased.

Vegar shrugged, clearly not worried about why his friend's mate was not sharing latemeal with the clan. "You can ask her. After you have eaten."

"You are very focused on me eating my dinner."

"You have injuries. A Chrechte needs rest and food to aid in quick recovery."

"Humans do as well."

"Aye, but I am mated to a Faol."

"You are very singleminded."

"You will grow accustomed to my ways."

"Will I?"

"Aye, 'tis the way of mates."

"Will you also learn *my* ways and to accept them?"

"Aye." The furrow between his brows showed confusion at her question.

A unique man indeed.

Vegar proved his intent focus when he actually helped her eat the mutton stew on the tray, then feeding her bits of the dark bread he'd brought with it. He cajoled and encouraged until she'd finished all the food.

And only then did he accompany her to Shona's room.

Stubborn, unique man.

Audrey knocked on the guest bedchamber's door, listening for sounds from within. She couldn't hear any voices, only muted movement as someone approached the door. Part of her was glad that Shona was obviously alone, but another part of Audrey worried at that fact.

"Where are the children?"

"With your brother and Caelis."

"Oh."

Again Audrey could not decide if that was something to

be grateful for, or should add to her worries about the baroness.

The door opened, the handle clutched in Shona's hand.

Her amazingly clear green eyes widened in surprised recognition. "Audrey! Are you well? Look at you, your dress is ripped. Is that blood? Oh, my dear Audrey, I can hardly believe today was more than a dream."

"It was real enough," Vegar said prosaically from behind Audrey.

Shona glared at him. "I am not speaking to you."

Audrey gasped with shock at her dear friend's rudeness. It was so unlike the woman she'd come to know over the past five years.

Shona blushed and looked beseechingly at Audrey. "He spirited you away and . . . and . . . I am very angry with him right now."

"Be as angry as you need to be, my lady, but what's done is done and there will be no undoing it." Warning chilled Vegar's tone, his frown very much in evidence.

Audrey rolled her eyes before giving Vegar her own glare. "We have had this discussion. I have given my word."

"You're doubting her integrity?" Shona asked, annoyance sparking in her gaze.

"Nay." Vegar laid his hand on Audrey's shoulder. "You are in good hands. I will be back to collect you in an hour."

"You are timing our visits?" Shona demanded in outrage.

"Audrey is still healing. She needs her rest."

Audrey rolled her eyes again, but both of them ignored her.

Shona was too busy nodding a grudging agreement and Vegar was simply walking away.

Audrey sighed. She supposed she should expect nothing more, not after such a short time and the inauspicious beginning to their mating.

Besides, she had refused intimacy with the man. Whatever his own plans, he'd taken that personally and so she'd finally realized.

She made to step inside Shona's bedchamber, but a strong hand on her shoulder stayed her. She looked up and briefly caught an intent expression on Vegar's face before his head lowered.

His mouth covered hers briefly. "Dinna tire yourself."

She shook her head and then nodded, her lips tingling from the kiss.

His dour face creased in a barely-there-and-gone-again smile. "You are a sweet one, my mate."

"Thank you," she whispered.

He turned and walked away again, this time disappearing around the corner that led to the stairs.

Chapter 18

The duty to pack is only overshadowed by sacred duty to
a true mate, but even then one's duty to his Chrechte
brethren cannot be dismissed entirely.

—FAOL TRADITIONS

"He's gotten over his aversion to England then,"
Shona said with asperity.

Audrey turned back to her friend but was given no
opportunity to reply before she was yanked into Shona's
arms for a bone-crushing hug.

"I was so worried. You cannot allow strange men to
spirit you away like that, even if he is your mate. Abigail
said you were well but with Vegar. You are married?"
Shona pulled back and met Audrey's gaze. "How did that
happen?"

But again, Audrey had no opportunity to say because
Shona squeezed her tight. "I wanted to find you and check
on you myself, but Caelis said you and Vegar would be
otherwise occupied. It worried me, I can tell you. I know
we have not discussed these things and you were entirely
innocent. Did he hurt you?"

Audrey choked out a laugh as her skin heated with
another blush. "No."

Relief covered Shona's features.

"I am still innocent," Audrey admitted.

Shona's eyes went wide again and she pulled Audrey into the bedchamber before slamming the door. "Why?"

"I wanted to wait." Feeling the pain of her healing injuries, Audrey moved to sit on the edge of the bed. "I do not *feel* married. You were not there to witness my vows, nor was Thomas. Vegar and I were married standing on the stairs for the sake of Heaven."

Shona sat beside Audrey and took her hand. "How did that come about?"

"Vegar wanted to see to my wounds. He takes being mates very seriously."

"That is good."

"Yes, but I have a feeling it is also going to be annoying at times."

Shona nodded, a great deal of understanding in her eyes.

"Laird Sinclair would not allow Vegar to accompany me upstairs, much less take me to his room because I am . . . I mean, was . . . an unmarried woman under his protection. Vegar refused to promise not to compromise me. He just kept saying I was his mate to see to as he saw fit."

"He's a very stubborn man."

"Yes, but I am quite accustomed to dealing with stubborn." Audrey gave Shona a significant look.

The baroness laughed as Audrey had meant her to. "You are, at that."

"At any rate, I was sure the two men would come to blows and that was upsetting enough, but then Laird Sinclair ordered Vegar to stand down. Vegar refused, point blank. He was going to challenge the laird. I just knew it."

"I still do not understand how you ended up married."

"That was Vegar's idea. He told the laird he could proclaim us man and wife if it would satisfy his *civilized* rules of propriety. I never knew civilized could be considered a dirty word, but the way Vegar said it . . ." Audrey shook her head. "So, the laird asked if I was willing to be made Vegar's wife."

"And you were because you didn't want him to challenge the Sinclair."

"Exactly."

"Men!"

"They are very demanding, are they not?"

"Still, I think you will enjoy Vegar's demands more than I did those of the baron."

Audrey shuddered, remembering the haunted look in her friend's eyes too many evenings when she said her good nights to Audrey and the children. "I am sure you are right. I enjoy his kisses very much."

"I noticed."

Audrey giggled, but sobered quickly enough. "I should still very much appreciate that talk you mentioned on the marriage acts."

"After I see to my own satisfaction that your injuries have been treated and we get you into clothing that is not torn or stained with your blood." Shona's eyes shone with tears. "I cannot stand the evidence of your actions."

"You have taken an abhorrence of me," Audrey said with sinking heart.

"Nay. How dare you judge me so weak." Shona's frown would have melted rock. "You are my family, no matter what blood runs through our veins. Seeing you risk your life and fight with that wolf while standing back in order to protect my children was the hardest thing I have ever had to do."

Audrey's own eyes burned with tears. "I left you and the little ones unprotected."

"You did what your instincts dictated, just as I had to. Neither of us could do all that we wanted."

They hugged again before Shona helped Audrey change her clothes and checked on her bruises and abrasions. "It is a good thing you did not enter into conjugal relations this afternoon. You are hardly in a fit state."

"That is what Vegar said when I told him I wanted to wait until after speaking my mating vows before witnesses who mattered to me."

"He is not all bad."

"I think he is not bad at all."

"He is surly."

"Yes, but under that, he is kind, I think."

"Caelis respects him."

"Vegar returns that respect."

Shona nodded, looking quite annoyed.

"What is it?" Audrey asked.

"Caelis announced we are getting married."

"And?" Audrey wasn't sure why that would have angered her friend so. "Don't you want to marry the father of your son?"

"He insists that he is both their father now."

"That is good."

"He's arrogant."

"Yes." Of that there was no doubt.

"He didn't even bother to propose."

"He does not seem like the type of man to get down on one knee."

"I would settle for the question without any pomp or circumstance."

"Would you?"

"I would."

"Would you say yes?"

"Of course."

"Does he know that?" Caelis did not strike Audrey as the type of man to risk rejection.

"Mayhap not, but he will ask or he will not receive."

Audrey smiled. "Stubborn, I told you."

"Aye, but I fear Caelis had no inkling just how intransigent I can be."

Nor how long the woman slow to anger held fury once it kindled, but Audrey did not say so. Her heart-sister and Caelis would have to find their own way to their relationship.

"You said there were things you wished to tell me before I went to my marriage bed?" she asked, embarrassed but determined to learn what she could.

"Aye." Shona frowned, a shadow of the despair Audrey

used to see in her gaze. "It can be both wonderful and terrible."

"I do not believe Vegar is like the baron."

"Nay, and you will not loathe his touch as I did the baron's. That in itself will make things easier."

"You said there was great joy in the act for a woman."

"I found so with Caelis."

"Not the baron though."

"Nay, but there are ways to endure."

"I do not believe I will need to endure with Vegar."

"I am more grateful than I can say to agree with you." The sincerity in Shona's tone could not be questioned.

Audrey had known her dearest friend had found her marital duties onerous, but she saw now they had wounded Shona deep in her soul. "Does Caelis know?"

"What?"

"How awful it was for you to be married to the baron?"

"It does not matter."

"I think it does."

Shona just shook her head and then proceeded to tell Audrey the most improbable things about the pleasure between a man and woman. Or at least Audrey would have seen them as so before meeting Vegar.

"It was not like that with the baron."

"Nay."

"What was it like?"

Shona just shook her head. "God willing, you will never know and I'll not give you thoughts to feed your nightmares or wedding-night jitters."

"Percival would have been worse," Audrey guessed.

"Aye. Submitting to him might well have broken me."

Audrey privately agreed. Even the strongest woman could only bow so far before she snapped in half, never to be whole again.

Hours after Vegar had come to collect Audrey, Shona paced her bedchamber, unable to sleep. Caelis most likely knew, too. He could probably hear her every footfall. Infernal Chrechte senses.

She wasn't a fool, no matter what her past with him might lead the man to believe. She had no questions about where he was spending his night, either.

Outside her door.

In the hall . . . with no bedding, or comforts.

Not that she was concerned about that. No. It was no concern of hers if a grown man chose to spend his night sleeping on a stone floor instead of using the perfectly good quarters provided by Laird Sinclair for his soldiers.

Really, it was not.

She glared at the door, still furious with him for his assumption she would marry him without so much as even the most rude request. Much less an actual proposal.

Did he not believe she deserved even such minimal consideration?

Mayhap he thought he had reason to make assumptions, but she'd maintained her uncertainty of her future from the beginning. Even after the folly of allowing him into her bed the night before.

Did he believe his willingness to kill for her, or shift into his *conriocht* put the onus of acceptance on her? According to him and everyone else, there could be no question she was his sacred mate.

That may well be, but that did not mean she would fall at his feet. Even if she could not seem to stop herself from falling into his bed.

Yes, he was father to her child, but Caelis had been that very thing when he had rejected her in favor of his alpha's dictates six years before. Even if he had not known it.

No, she could not start thinking that way.

But neither could she make herself ignore certain truths.

The most important being: he would keep her children safe.

She stopped her pacing and took a deep breath. More than any other consideration, that one swayed her.

The world was an even more danger-filled place than she'd known on her escape from the barony, which had been her home for all of her children's lives.

Caelis, as *conriocht* and eventual laird of his own clan—because she was certain he would wrest control of the MacLeod from Uven—was in a better position to protect Eadan and Marjory than most.

Marrying him, however, meant returning to the clan that had been only too willing to see the back of her and her parents. Because they were human. Though she hadn't known that was the reason at the time.

She would still be a human in a clan with too many who had been taught to see her as inferior for her humanity as well as her gender.

It was untenable.

She hadn't suddenly sprouted angel's wings, nor would she. *She* had no great magical ability to shift into another form and that was not about to change. Or would it?

Caelis had told Maon that Mairi could now shift into wolf form. Apparently, she hadn't been able to do so before. That's why Uven had treated her so badly.

He had not been pleased to have a daughter who was not fully Chrechte.

Could she shift now only because her father had been a wolf? Or was it some inevitable response to being mated to a Chrechte?

Though hadn't Caelis said her mate was an Éan? That would make her husband a man who shifted into a bird.

And Mairi now transformed into a wolf. Wasn't that what Caelis had said?

Had Caelis destined her to become like him without telling her? Was he hiding something of great magnitude from her?

Again?

She stormed to the door and pulled the heavy bar up so she could fling it open.

"Why are you out here?" she demanded of the man who was exactly where she'd known he would be.

"Where else would I be?" he asked, sounding far too reasonable.

"In your own bed."

"I do not sleep in a bed. Vegar and I prefer furs."

"You sleep with Vegar?"

He rolled his eyes at the nonsensical notion. "We share a room. As Cahir, it is preferable to the soldier's quarters."

"Why? Do you hide secrets from even your fellow soldiers?"

"You know I do." Caelis looked confused by her question. "Not all the soldiers in the keep are Chrechte."

"Even the Chrechte don't know everything about the Cahir."

"That's so like you."

"What do you mean?"

She glared at the fur on the floor.

"And you sleep on the floor like a barbarian?"

"Soldiers are not afforded the luxury of a bed."

She knew that, but she didn't say so. It felt like giving him ground. And she could not afford to do that.

"Where did you sleep all the years you lived in our clan?" he asked, as if making a point.

In a pile of blankets near the fire in the main room of her family's small hut. The laird before Uven had been willing to have a human as his seneschal, but that had not extended to Shona's family being invited to live within the keep. Only now did she realize why that was.

Not only had the man been Fearghall and therefore of the mind that Chrechte were superior to those without an animal nature, but he had a secret to protect.

The Sinclair had human soldiers and servants living in his keep, but the MacLeod's home was nothing like the Sinclair's. Not in size and not in security.

And if she was not mistaken, Caelis expected her to return and live in that very keep.

"That is entirely beside the point."

"If you say so."

"Do not patronize me!"

"I would not."

"Hah."

"You are upset."

She crossed her arms over her chest and glared up at him. "And you still haven't figured out why, have you?"

His blue gaze turned wary and she noted he did not answer immediately.

Dolt.

"I dinna care for you insulting me across our mating bond."

"I'm sorry." She hadn't meant him to hear that, which only made her angrier. "Even my mind is not my own."

"Stop yelling at me inside your head and I'm sure it will be." He sounded so reasonable, she wanted to smack him.

Sucking in air, she pushed the urge away. "Don't tell me what to do in my own mind."

This man brought out a side to her nature she had not even realized was there.

He sighed and rubbed his hand over his face. "I will try not to."

"Just tell me one thing, *oh great Chrechte male.*"

His jaw went hard and the gentian blue of his eyes turned dark. He hadn't liked her sarcasm and she didn't blame him, even if she was too angry to guard her tongue.

"Aye?" he bit out.

"Have you made me into shape-changer without telling me?"

He seemed to be counting off something in his head because his lips moved silently, forming numbers in sequence. "You believe I would do that?"

"You did not tell me the truth six years ago. You did not tell me about your *conriocht* until you had to show me."

Caelis's entire demeanor went from barely contained annoyance to tired frustration in the blink of an eye. "Let us discuss this in your chamber."

"I don't think so." Letting him into the room where the

bed was didn't seem to be the most intelligent move she could make this night.

"Then we will not discuss it." He turned away from her and sank back to the fur he had placed on the floor, letting his head rest against the wall and his eyes close. "Go back to bed, Shona."

"I wasn't sleeping and you are well aware of that fact."

"I cannot help that." The weary defeat in his tone confused her.

"You will not just dismiss me."

"We cannot have this conversation in a hallway."

He was right, of course. What had she been thinking to speak so openly about his secret in a passageway anyone might walk down? "I apologize."

She had no doubts, however, that he would have been aware if anyone were near enough to hear their words. She might lose sight of where they were, but she did not believe he ever did.

He nodded, though his eyes remained shut, his head turned away.

"You will not look at me?" she asked, bothered much more deeply than she wanted to be by the slight.

He must have heard the quaver in her voice she'd done her best to suppress because his eyes snapped open, their blue depths fixed on her. "You are my mate."

"And that makes it all right to ignore me?" If so, that was an aspect to mating that would not endear the practice to her at all.

"I am not ignoring you."

"Really?" she asked mockingly.

He flipped back his kilt, revealing his sex, dark and swollen with need. "I want to be in that room with you under me, our bodies joined."

"We need to talk, not copulate," she said from a suddenly dry throat.

He wasn't the only one affected by the strong pull between them. She wanted to touch and be touched, which was exactly why she'd refused to retire to her borrowed room to talk.

"You need to go back into the bedchamber and bar the door. *Now.*" His hands were curled into fists at his sides, a fine sheen of sweat gracing his upper lip and temple.

His hardness lay heavy against his thigh, the kilt outlining it lewdly. But she was not horrified as a proper lady should be.

No, she wanted to touch it, taste the clear drop of fluid pearled on the tip.

Whatever else he was feeling, there could be no doubt that Caelis wanted her with a need so fierce it was all she could do to deny him.

"I can smell your feminine desire, *mo toilichte.* Get you gone before I do something you will rant at me for tomorrow."

Before she could promise she would not, she hurried back into her room and slammed the door, leaning against it as she heaved deep, near-sobbing breaths. How could she go from anger to hungry desire so quickly?

"Bar it," he instructed in her mind.

She nodded. Yes, that was what she needed to do. But she did not move.

She could not.

The sound of his head thumping the wall made her jump, even though it was hardly loud.

"I want you," he said in a barely understandable tone inside her mind.

The very intimacy of the mindspeak making her ache all the more for the man she was on the brink of admitting would always be her beloved. Even that knowledge was not enough to cool her ardor.

"I am touching myself and thinking of your hand on me as I do it."

She moaned, the image in her mind near impossible to resist.

Were the sounds of pleasure he made in her mind or was

she hearing them through the door? Fevered desire burned through her, making her thighs clench together, the moisture there so great she could not ignore it.

Could he smell her need through the barriers of stone and wood even? She turned to face the door, but made no move to drop the bar into place.

Shona leaned forward, her hands pressed into the wood. *"Tell me. Am I like you now?"*

The sigh that came across their mental link filled with vexation, but was it because he was angry with her or frustrated by his sexual need? *"Nay."*

"You are telling the truth?" She was not one of them; she could not smell a lie.

Oh. *"I cannot smell a lie."*

"Nay."

"I am still as human as I ever was."

"Aye."

Relief poured through her—not that she was not Chrechte, but that he had not hidden anything else from her.

Or at least she thought he hadn't. How would she know? So much had been withheld from her to this point.

"Are there any more secrets?"

He said something in her mind that sounded like a curse, but she did not know. It had been in that ancient language he spoke with the other Chrechte.

"What?" she asked.

"Every word you speak increases my arousal."

"But that's not possible."

The sound of his groan definitely came through the door. *"I assure you, it is."*

"You are still touching yourself."

"Aye. But I would rather be touching you."

There was something wrong with her. She should be scandalized, but the knowledge excited her.

"You should stop."

"You should keep talking to me so intimately."

"I am not saying anything of an intimate nature."

"Every word inside my head is confirmation of our bond." His voice was replete with satisfaction and sexual urgency.

He was going to climax from the stimulation of their mental bond. Again, she should be appalled, but she could feel nothing but gratified by the possibility.

"Secrets," she said in a desperate bid to turn the tide of her own thoughts and desires. *"Are there any further secrets?"*

She could feel the pain of unfulfilled desire so strongly, it felt like her own, but she knew it was his. Was this another effect of the true mate bond?

"You have worked out for yourself that I plan to return to the MacLeod and take over the clan, have you not?"

She nodded against the door, her heart contracting at the thought of Caelis fighting Uven for the right to lead the clan. Even in a marginally fair fight, there was no way that Uven could come out victorious.

But the man was a weasel and no fight with him would be without treachery.

"Shona?" Caelis asked in her head, his voice strained.

She knew the source of that strain and did her best to ignore it.

"I am here," she said aloud, knowing he would hear her through the door.

"I must do this thing."

"I know." And she did.

Uven had to be stopped, for the sake of their clan, but also for the good of all Chrechte. He was an evil man who would do untold damage if he was left to continue his current path. She was not sure how she knew that to be true, but it was a certainty inside her she could not shake.

"You have not dropped the bar."

"No."

"If you wish me to remain out here, do so." His desire reached out to her through the thick wood and found a corresponding need in her heart.

She could not admit to it, but neither could she make herself drop the thick plank of wood that would keep Caelis on the other side. She didn't want him touching himself. She wanted to be the one giving him pleasure.

The door began to move inward and Shona stepped back, her heart in her throat.

Chapter 19

The Faol do well not to underestimate the cunning and resourcefulness of humans.

—EMILY OF THE BALMORAL

Caelis stepped inside, his big warrior's body vibrating with the desire darkening his gentian gaze and the fur he'd been resting on dangling from one big fist. "You should have barred the door, mate."

"You should have asked me to marry you six years ago." It was not what she'd intended to say, but she would not take the words back if she could.

They were true and he had to know it.

Tension she did not think had anything to do with his sexual need emanated off of him now. "Aye."

"I would have said yes then."

He winced. "I ken."

Saints above, where was she going with this? Why was she saying these things? Her physical craving for him had not diminished in the least and yet her mouth spewed forth with things completely unrelated.

Or were they?

"I am leaving for Balmoral Island tomorrow." She made the decision as the words left her mouth.

"You are rejecting me now as I did you then?" he asked, the ever present hunger warring with anger in his blue gaze.

Shona shook her head decisively. "You may come with us and make your intentions known to my family."

"You know I have other commitments."

She shrugged. Yes, she knew. Just like six years ago, Caelis had duties and intentions that superseded his promises to her.

"You will not be moved on this?"

"No." She'd compromised for this man before, and her life had been all the more unhappy for it.

Once again, his jaw appeared hewn from rock. "You know I must return to the MacLeod."

"And *you* are fully aware that is the last thing I want to do." Part of her knew that she might well end up living among her former clan again, but she would not do so on a whim. Nor would she return there as anything less than his fully legal wife.

"I cannot refuse my destiny. I am *conriocht*. That means I am protector for my people."

"And you believe protecting the Chrechte requires you to take over as laird of Clan MacLeod."

"I know it does. It has been foreseen."

Was she supposed to be impressed? She was. A little. Mayhap even a great deal more than a little, but that did not mean she would dismiss what she knew needed to happen to give a mating between them a foundation she could believe in.

"Do you know if too much or too little sand and loose rock is mixed into the soil of a motte, over time it will sink and the keep along with it?" she asked him.

He stared at her as if she'd gone mad, but she could not allow that to bother her.

"I know this because the baron told me once, rather gleefully, as he recounted the collapse of another baron's keep. The entire structure, which had taken four entire years to build, was utterly destroyed."

"Your marriage to the old man is something we would both do well to forget."

"That is not possible."

"Aye, it is."

"No."

He frowned down at her, clearly wanting to argue further.

She forestalled him.

"I hated every moment the baron touched me, but I love my daughter. I can no more forget her origins than I could Eadan's."

And if Caelis could not tolerate that, then there was truly no hope of a future between them. No matter what his Chrechte law said about sacred mates.

"She is mine," Caelis claimed fiercely. "Just as you are, if you were not too stubborn to admit it."

"You cannot undo her parentage just by willing it to be so." Any more than he could simply will Shona to be his mated wife.

"He is dead. I am alive. I am her father, now and forever." Utter conviction rang in his voice.

She shook her head in disbelief. "You're a very possessive man."

"I was not possessive enough six years ago, but I cannot regret that fact now."

"You can't?" Shona asked, shocked and more than a little dismayed.

"Marjory is meant to be ours, however she came to be. Can you regret your daughter?"

He'd asked her this once before.

She understood his motive better for doing so now. "Never."

"Aye."

"Making a family takes more than just claiming everyone belongs together." It required more than mere legal documentation as well.

"Aye, it takes some cooperation on your part."

And his, if he would but acknowledge it. "When a motte

sinks, the wall joints loosen and eventually, the entire keep will come down."

"We are back to mottes again?"

"Listen to me, Caelis. I will not be the keep that crashes under the burden of my sinking foundation."

"You are not a building," he said, exasperation thickly lacing each word.

"No, but our mating is like the keep that seeks to protect those who live within it."

"You admit we are mates."

"I have never denied it." Not once.

He spun away, slamming his open palm against the thick stone wall. "How can our mating protect our family like this fabled keep you go on about when you live on Balmoral Island and I live with the MacLeod? Keeps do not straddle two holdings, much less an entire sea."

"Six years ago, you denied me before my family, withdrawing your courtship formally to my father."

"To my shame." His proud head dropped, his shoulders sagging.

It was not her intention to make him ashamed. "That is not my point."

"What is your point?" he asked with barely suppressed impatience as he spun to face her again.

"That our mating now needs you to recognize me before my family once again." She put her hand on his forearm, imploring him with everything in her to understand. "If I have value in your eyes, then you will acknowledge that before others."

"Is not a mating and wedding enough for that?"

Talk about fabled entities. He kept talking about theirs as if it were already planned, but she'd not yet even agreed to marry him.

Not that he'd asked.

Because he *had not*.

"Thus far, your Chrechte ways have been naught but annoying to me, if you want the truth. *I* can put little faith in a mating; even less can I trust in a marriage after what I experienced with the baron. Standing before man and God, speaking vows of fidelity and honor in no way ensures a man will value his wife." Or that he, she and their children would live together as a family in harmony.

"He was a poor husband."

"There are much worse." Audrey's father and the current Baron of Heronshire, to name a couple.

"Not all mates are exemplary, either," Caelis offered as if doing so pained him.

"Knowing what I do now about the Chrechte, I am well aware of that. Uven's first wife must have been his true mate for him to have begot a child from her." They had been both married and mated, but that had not turned out well for the poor woman.

"Aye."

"My father always considered the circumstances of her death suspect, though I wasn't supposed to know." She'd overheard her parents talking.

"After learning how easy he found it to murder my own parents for disagreeing with him, I have no difficulty believing he would kill his human mate."

"The old laird was still alive when it happened, but my father never voiced his concerns. Now, I understand the old laird would probably not have criticized or even disapproved if he'd known his son killed his mate. Because she was human and they were Fearghall."

Caelis nodded, his expression grim.

"Believe it, or not, I do understand that the clan needs you."

"Good."

"But that does not mean I will disregard my own concerns."

"I am not trying to do that, either."

It was her turn to nod and say, "Good. You want me to have faith in institutions when *I* need to be able to trust you."

"You do not trust me?" he asked with every evidence of not actually knowing the answer.

Did he think the past twenty-four hours had changed everything?

From the wounded expression on his handsome features, she thought he may very well have done.

"Am I to snap my fingers and all is forgotten? How am I to trust you?"

"I revealed my Chrechte nature to you."

She thought that must mean a great deal more to his race than it possibly could to her, particularly when he had waited so long to do it. "After hiding it our entire lives, including when you were convincing me to share your furs without marriage."

The knowledge others had held it from her as well still hurt, but she was doing her best not to hold him accountable for her parents' actions, or Thomas's and Audrey's.

"I could not help myself. *I* believed you would be mine as well. It was no lie when I promised you marriage."

"Your wolf wanted its mate."

And the beast's needs would have made the younger Caelis convinced of his future plans. Shona could understand that a little better, especially considering how very much those same needs influenced her and she was not even Chrechte.

"Aye. And I was younger; I didna have the control. We had already waited so long."

She nodded, understanding and mayhap even accepting. "But what is there in that for me to trust?"

He opened his mouth and then closed it again, no words coming forth and the most interesting expressions coming over his face.

First shock, then consternation and finally enlightenment.

"Last night, I didna put my sex inside you."

She'd wanted him to. He'd known it, too, probably as intimately as she had. "You did not risk pregnancy and I thank you, but you did not leave my bed, either, and allowed Audrey to find us together. You cannot tell me you did not hear her stirring in the next room."

"Stone walls are thick. I did not hear her until she was outside your chamber."

"And then it was too late."

So he had not compromised her on purpose. Another mark in his favor.

"Aye. Do you want me to apologize for staying with my mate?" The frown he gave her said he'd do it, but wouldn't like it.

Clearly he thought that title gave him all sorts of rights and privileges. She wasn't sure it didn't, not with how strongly she felt the pull as well.

"No."

He stared at her expectantly. She simply looked back, waiting. Either he would come up with better arguments and convince her she *could* trust him, or realize how little he'd actually done to bring that about.

"I shifted into *conriocht* in front of you," he said after several seconds of silence, with the air of a man who should not have had to draw attention to an obvious fact.

"You shifted in front of others as well."

"I did it *for* you, to protect you and our children."

If he but knew it, every time he referred to both Marjory and Eadan as his own, Caelis added to the sturdiness of the foundation for their mating-marriage she was so concerned about.

And this was a point she found easy to concede. "I am convinced our physical safety is paramount to you now."

"But it wasn't before. That is what you are thinking." He turned away again, his body now rigid with tension.

"Is it?" she asked, not so sure that was the way she thought any longer.

"It never even occurred to me that you and your parents would leave our clan. It was your home."

"But not one where we were welcome, and you knew that better than I."

His jaw taut, he jerked his head in acknowledgment.

"And yet you believed we would stay, that I would remain with the clan. Unmarried."

Again that single jerk of his head.

He had said so before; now she believed him. Couldn't help herself, really. It explained too many of his actions and attitudes that could only otherwise be justified by believing him the monster she'd imagined for six years. Whatever Caelis was, *conriocht* or human, he was no monster. His assumptions six years ago had been arrogant, poorly thought out and bordering on the idiotic, but he *had* believed them.

"You thought you could watch over me, but by leaving with my parents, I took that option away from you." She was now absolutely certain that was how he'd seen it.

But he shook his head. "You would not have left if I had done right by you." His hands fisted at his sides. "I could have gone with you. I *should* have left the clan with your family."

And now he wanted her to return. Could he not see the irony in that?

She could, just as she could see the irony in what she was about to say. "I love you."

"What?" He turned back to her so fast it was a blur of movement in the glow cast by the single candle burning beside her bed. Absolute shock written over his features and in the very way he held his big body. "What did you say?"

"I love you. I never stopped." She'd wanted to, saints above had she wanted to, but she'd never been able to turn off her emotions.

She'd tried so hard, to protect herself, to protect her children, but the love and desire burned brighter inside her now than it had six years ago. Which was why she would not, simply *could not*, marry or ceremonially mate with this man if she did not trust him to do right by her.

She had more to lose than he did, though he would never understand that. His wolf had named her mate before she'd even known what desire was. They had waited for her, Caelis and his wolf, but he had not loved her.

If he *had* loved her, he would not have repudiated her.

Whatever he felt for her, it was tempered by his duty to the Chrechte and always would be.

She could accept that because she had no other choice to do otherwise, but she would not accept that she would *always* come last.

Oh, Shona had no doubt that he needed her, but he would survive losing her. He'd more than survived these past six years; he'd thrived and found a destiny he could never have dreamed of.

She, on the other hand, had come close to losing her mind and only the love and determination to protect and raise her children had saved her.

He had spent six years celibate. And while she was sure that had been a trial for him, she had spent those same years submitting to the touch of a man who killed a little bit of her soul every time he used her body to slake his lust. She had spent every one of those days until their individual deaths reviled by parents she loved with her whole heart. Each day, she'd stoically suffered slights big and small for being the Scottish upstart married to a man three times her age.

And none of it had compared to the ragged-edged wound in her soul that bled daily from Caelis's rejection and absence.

Terrible love had terrible power.

"You love me, but you do not trust me?"

"I cannot," she replied starkly.

Caelis swallowed convulsively, his hands fisting and releasing at his sides like he wanted to reach for her but would not let himself. "You do not believe I love you."

"I know you do not and I accept that." Need was not love, nor was the mating pull.

As he'd pointed out, not all mates loved one another. Uven could not have loved the mate he'd killed; he certainly had not loved the daughter they made together.

"Am I meant to be grateful for that?"

"I do not know." Was gratitude better than mere duty and lust?

"I am." He sighed, the expression in his blue eyes unreadable. "Very grateful."

Tears she did not expect burned at her eyes. She blinked, trying to dispel them, but the moisture continued to build.

He said another one of those Chrechte curses and closed the distance between them. Gently cupping her cheeks with his big warrior's hands, he brushed at the drops spilling over. "Dinna cry *mo toilichte*. Please."

"I do not mean to."

He bent forward and sipped at the moisture, pressing small, infinitely gentle kisses over her face. "Let me take the pain away."

"I can't." She would not risk another pregnancy and having her choices taken away from her now that she had acknowledged her love for him.

It made her far too vulnerable and he needed no further advantages between them.

He nodded, as if expecting no other response. "There are many ways for me to bring you pleasure to shatter the pain without copulation."

She did not know what he meant. Her experiences of joy in a man and woman's joining had all happened with him and other than the night before, she had never known the ultimate pleasure without him ending up inside her. "I . . ."

"In this, at least, will you trust me?" he asked.

He was giving them both an opportunity to move forward. She didn't know how to build her trust in him except through time and him showing the willingness to rectify the past as far as he was able.

But he was offering her another opportunity to build trust in him. If she let him do this and he kept his implied promise not to breach her body, that would be more solid rock in the foundation for their relationship. Wouldn't it?

The instincts that had been screaming at her to keep him out of her room earlier, were now telling her that sharing intimacy with him would help in ways little else could do.

"Please," he said again.

And she could not deny him. Did not want to deny him. She needed this opportunity to build trust as much as he did.

"Yes."

His huge body gave a violent shudder and a low growl of approval rumbled in his chest.

Caelis bent and lifted her into his arms, high against his chest, her shift flowing down his near-naked body. "I will overshadow every memory of the touch you did not want with pleasure. I alone will ever again caress your body."

"Promise?" she demanded though his words had sounded as much like a vow as anything she'd ever heard.

He looked down, a pain in his own gaze matching the wounds in her heart if she could let herself believe it. "I do."

"Never again." She would never submit to the unwelcome touch of another.

His mouth set in a grim line. "Only me."

"Only you."

"This is my vow to you."

She nodded, accepting his words as much as her damaged heart would let her.

"Never again will my promise to you be set aside because of my loyalty to another."

Her breath stilled in her chest. "You do not mean that. Do not say that if you do not mean it."

From the look on his chiseled features, there could be no mistaking the seriousness with which he took their words.

He laid her on the bed, making no move to remove her shift, and then stepped back. He placed his right fist over his heart. "I vow it."

"On your honor as a warrior?" she asked, unable to help the frisson of doubt prompting the words.

"On my honor as a Chrechte and *conriocht.*"

And he had promised her that no other man would ever touch her intimately. Fear that had been such a heavy burden, she hadn't even acknowledged it anymore, lifted off her, lightening her heart in a way she did not know was possible any longer.

"Percival cannot have me," she said, joy ebullient in her heart and tone.

Caelis fell to his knees beside the bed, his hands grabbing her own tightly. "No one. I will protect you with my life."

"Not just your son."

"I could not have my son or daughter without the gift of their mother. Never doubt it, you are of primary importance to me."

She wanted to believe his words. So much.

And she realized the choice was hers to make. Just as his had been six years ago.

Was she any less responsible for her own decisions now?

In that moment, she chose to believe.

She believed Caelis would not reject her again, that he would protect her with his life. Not by giving it away on her behalf, but by giving it *to* her.

"Thank you."

His face contorted with some great emotion. "You unman me, Shona. Dinna thank me for what I cannot help any more than I can stop my own lungs from breathing."

She brushed her hand down his face, loving the feel of his masculine stubble against her skin. "I will love you forever."

That was her vow to him.

And she considered it well worth making when his smile took over his features as he stood. "Thank you."

"Dinna thank me for what I can no more help than my own breathing," she said in imitation of his voice.

"I'll ever be grateful for it all the same." The smile warmed his voice, reaching out to touch and heal her heart.

"You look like a bride."

She wanted to be his, more than he could possibly understand. "Tonight I am only a woman in love."

"You are never *only* anything."

"Am I not?" She could not help her own grin at his claim.

He shook his head. "You dinna understand, but one day, you will."

She put her hand out to him in invitation. "Caelis . . ."

"You are *everything*, mate." He yanked off his kilt and weapons, laying them within easy reach of the bed.

Chapter 20

Intimacy between mates will not always result in babes,
but it should always result in a stronger mating bond.

—Ancient *celi di*

*T*he wounds from earlier were nothing more than
pink lines on Caelis's flesh.

Shona stared at him in wonder. "You are healed."

"It is the *conriocht*. When I shift into or out of that
form, my body heals."

"But not when you shift into your wolf?"

"Nay. 'Tis part of the gifts for the protectors of our
people."

"I am glad." She worried less, knowing he had this
amazing ability to heal from injuries. "Does it work even
for grievous damage?"

"I dinna ken." He prowled toward the bed, his wolf's
grace very much in evidence.

"Eadan said he will be *conriocht* one day."

"'Tis a gift to look forward to."

She nodded, the wonders of his Chrechte life paling in
the face of the desire that had been burning between them
all this time. Through every emotion laden word of their

conversation, the physical need between them had not waned.

"I want you," she told him with no shame.

"You will have me, now and forever," he promised.

In light of what he had said, his vow took on deeper significance. And put her own strictures in question.

What had she wanted from him? To be able to trust. Somehow, in the past minutes as he'd made promises she needed to hear but had not asked for, he'd given her that.

Or perhaps it had been that terrible power of an incredible love at work, but she no longer doubted her place in her mate's life.

He might not love her as she loved him, but he cared and he needed and he would protect her with his very life.

He would put the secrets of his people at risk for her and that was more significant than any mundane quest she assigned him to prove what he had already established.

His attention never straying from her, Caelis grabbed the fur he'd dropped earlier and laid it out on the bed, shifting her so she was on top of it.

Soft against her skin and thick, it gave additional cushion under her, but she got the feeling that his actions were not about comfort. There was special significance to this fur for him.

She did not ask. There were issues of greater import to address.

"I will marry you," she told him. "I would like Audrey and Vegar's marriage to receive the priest's blessing along with ours."

He stilled in his movements, his expression arrested. "I thought—"

"I did too . . . that you coming with me to Balmoral Island was necessary. It is not."

"It isn't?" Caelis sounded punch-drunk.

She shook her head. "I thought I needed you to prove something to me, to make reparations for the past."

"But you do not feel that way any longer?"

"No. Your actions may have precipitated my parents' loss of affection for me, but so did my own. Mostly, though, their actions were *their* responsibility. We cannot undo the past, nor would I. One thing I have learned is the capacity of my own strength, and that is a good thing."

"Aye."

"I love you, Caelis, Chrechte protector. My protector."

"Mate. *Mo toilichte.* Mine." His mouth came down on hers with a hunger that overshadowed anything that had come before.

She returned the kiss, pouring her love into and releasing the pain of the past through it.

Their tongues dueled while lips ate at each other and his naked body pressed against hers, the heat passing between them as if the fine lawn of her shift was not even there.

He pulled back, moving to kiss her all over her face, along her temple and down her neck. The entire time, he whispered words against her skin.

It was only as he caressed the sensitive skin behind her ear with his lips that she understood the words he was saying. "Thank you. Always mine. My gift. Thank you."

The words and the fervent feeling behind them brought moisture to her eyes and a lump of deep emotion to clog her throat. She blinked away the incipient tears and swallowed her emotion, too happy with his response to let anything mar the moment.

Even her own ecstatic feelings.

Caelis brushed Shona's shift up her legs, baring her alabaster skin to his gaze. The curve of her legs invited his touch, and the shadow at the apex of her thighs barely covered by the thin material drew his gaze and his hunger.

Hunger built to rapacious need by her words. She had promised to wed him, given him the gift of her love when he'd been sure that would never be on offer again.

The fact that she was so certain his own feelings did not match hers was not a conclusion he could gainsay. His actions had spoken too loudly for mere words to convince her otherwise.

"You are so beautiful," he breathed.

She laughed softly, shaking her head in denial. "I am but a woman with all the marks to my body giving birth twice has left behind."

He knew what she meant. The fine lines where her body had stretched to accommodate her womb swollen with child, the way her heavy breasts hung more like tantalizing pendulums than ripe apples.

No, she no longer had the body of an untouched girl with only eighteen summers, but that did not detract from her beauty to him. In fact, the marks time and circumstance had left behind only intrigued him and reminded him that he made love to a woman, not a girl.

A woman who should be proud of the loveliness gifted her, in all its forms. "They are the scars of battle you should wear with the same pride I wear my own."

She laughed, the sound dark. "That is a unique take on my imperfections. The baron could not stand to see them."

"Idiot." He'd hated the thought of her being happy with someone else, but had discovered that he despised the truth she'd been unhappy even more.

Caelis would help rid her of those memories, starting now.

He laid his hands over her thighs, brushing his thumbs along the inside and upward toward the red curls peeking from where he'd pushed up the hem of her shift.

Shona shivered, goose bumps of pleasure forming on the skin beneath his touch. "How can such a simple touch evoke so deep a pleasure in me?"

"We are meant for each other."

"The mating bond."

"'Tis not the only thing between us." She had to at least believe that.

She might well deny his love, but she must believe he had feelings for her beyond his wolf being inexorably connected to her.

She did not gainsay him and the soft expression in her beautiful emerald eyes gave no indication she wanted to, either.

He would show her that while the bond drew them together, it was only the beginning, not the boundaries of their joining.

He pushed her shift farther up, uncovering glistening silky curls. "So pretty."

"Pretty is not a word I think of when I see *your* nakedness," she teased.

"Naturally not. I am a warrior, not a maid."

The grin of mischief should have warned him what was coming.

"Now that I think on it, one part of your anatomy is very prettily shaped." She looked toward the hard sex jutting from his body.

Laughter and the joy only she could bring bubbled up inside him. "You think my cock is *pretty*?" he asked with a shake of his head.

"Oh, yes."

He spread his thighs wider so she had an unobstructed view. "It does not feel *pretty* right now. It aches."

"Does it?"

"Aye." And well she knew it, for all her sexy mockery.

"Mayhap I can help with that."

He wanted her to, but he had plans and they did not include his sex being within touching distance of her small, feminine hands at the moment. "Later."

"Caelis?"

"Let me have my way with you, Shona. 'Tis what I crave most right now." And despite his voracious hunger to bury himself inside her, the words were nothing but truth.

And meant he was sure in a different way than she would take them, but she would see.

She leaned up on one arm and tugged her shift all the way off before falling back to her elbows, the pose pressing her generous breasts forward, the invitation unmistakable. "Yes."

He could feel the smile curving his mouth and made no effort to stop it. "Your beauty is breathtaking."

She blushed, her embarrassment a spicy scent between them, making him laugh.

"You will reveal your nakedness to me, but you turn berry-red at a compliment?" he mocked gently.

"You are the only one who has ever considered me beautiful."

"Nay." He was sure she was wrong. "But I am the one intelligent enough to tell you."

She shook her head, long red silken strands rippling over her shoulders and against the mating fur he'd tanned and prepared six years ago for a mating ceremony that had never taken place. "Stubborn man."

Though the ceremony had not happened, they *had* used the fur. Not that he expected her to remember.

"I have been called worse." He ruffled the pretty triangle of hair at the apex of her thighs. "Are you blushing in other places, I wonder?"

She let her thighs fall wide with such trust that he wanted to shout his victory. Shona had said she did not trust him, but then she had agreed to marry him. He could infer her trust from that, but the truth of her heart showed in her actions. Whatever reservations she might still hold, she trusted him completely with her body. Six years ago, her doing so cost her dearly. That she would offer him this gift again made his wolf howl with delight.

He carefully pressed her legs up and apart, to give himself an unhindered view of the flushed and swollen folds of her sex. Slick with moisture, her body begged silently for his possession.

It was a sight unparalled. "You are beautiful, even here."

"You should not say such things."

"Why not? If they are true." He leaned down and pressed a tender kiss to her feminine nether lips.

Soft flesh gave against his own, the scent of her arousal such a strong aphrodisiac to him and his beast that a measure of ejaculate spurted from his aching cock. If he let himself even brush against the fur, he would come like an untried boy. Needing to taste, he flicked his tongue out and lapped at the fragrant juices. Sweet with the pungent flavor of her desire, the taste called to both his man and wolf on a primal level.

He moaned his pleasure against the swollen flesh and continued to taste, licking, laving and sucking with no thought but to share with her the pleasure he received at her submission to him.

She grabbed his hair, her fingers curled tightly around his warrior's braids. "That is . . . what are you . . . you must . . . *Oh, Caelis.*"

His name ended on a wail as his tongue flicked her clitoris. Satisfaction burned through him. He would show her that she was safe with him now, in every way.

He knew the importance of his mate.

She writhed on the furs, her body pressing against his mouth, sounds of ecstasy falling from her lips with the steady cadence of spring rain. He drank every one in with the thirst only a man who had gone six years in the desert could feel.

Sliding a single finger inside her, his sense of victory increased as her body clung to the digit, her inner muscles gripping him with surprising strength. She wanted him inside her mayhap even as much as he craved being there.

Soon they would consummate their mating and marriage, but only when he had proven himself worthy of the honor. Not like six years before, when he'd taken prematurely that which he'd then proven he had no right to because he had *not* honored her gift, as was right.

Moving in and out of her with his finger, he licked and suckled at her nether lips and clitoris until she was rigid with the need to come. She babbled her need while her body jerked against his mouth with both demand and supplication. It would take so little to bring her to that point of ecstasy she so clearly wanted, but that would not be enough.

Not enough to erase old memories. Not enough to supplant them firmly and irrevocably with new ones. Not enough to show her how very much he esteemed the gift of her body.

He backed off, sitting back on his heels as he mentally planned her further ravishment.

"No," she cried out, reaching for him.

"Shh," he soothed, his hand caressing her thigh and his wolf crooning in his chest. "I will give you what you desire, in time."

"Now," she demanded.

He grinned loving this show of confidence. "Soon."

He returned to her body, tracing those slim silver lines she had been so worried about with his tongue. She squirmed, making soft whimpering noises. He would show her just how enticing he found these marks of womanhood. He caressed her breasts as well, showing with his touch and mouth how much he enjoyed their curves and the hard berry-sweet tips.

She writhed against him, but he did not give into the urge to finish what he had begun.

He would bring her to the brink of climax, but she would only go over that precipice when he'd fed her a surfeit of pleasure. When he had created a new memory for her body that would supersede all others.

Shona responded to his every touch with a passion so beautiful, it took all of Caelis's self-control not to come himself while he took his beautiful mate right to the edge of the pinnacle time after time.

When he finally brought her to climax, she screamed out her pleasure and the convulsions around his fingers lasted minutes not seconds.

Her body finally collapsed back to the fur, boneless, her eyes half-mast, shallow panting breaths coming from between her parted lips.

"That was amazing," she gasped out between breaths. "How did you . . . Why did you . . ." She seemed unable to complete a thought.

That pleased him unutterably. "*You* are amazing." And he was so hard he hurt.

"No. You . . . you are the incredible one. You took nothing for yourself." The confusion in her tone and eyes was sweet to be sure.

"Giving you pleasure is a privilege I will never again take for granted."

Her eyes glistened again, but this time the sight did not hurt him. "I want you inside me."

"Soon." When vows had been spoken between them before witnesses.

She needed that, even if she no longer realized it. Mayhap, he did as well.

"I said I would marry you."

"Aye, and we will be married with a priest speaking his blessing over us."

"Why do you not join with me then?"

"Because it will come after."

She smiled at that, an expression deep in her emerald depths that said mayhap she was fully aware that waiting was what she needed.

"Will you . . ." She blushed again, her gaze dropping.

"What, *mo gra*? What do you want?"

"Not your heart," she slurred without near the conviction she'd shown earlier when claiming he did not love her. "I want you to do what you did last night."

He wanted that, too. So much. He moved up her body so he could rub his aching sex against her sensitized flesh.

She writhed, but did not push him away. "Yes, like that. Feels so close."

"Aye," he said across their mental bond.

"So intimate." She pushed up against him despite her evident lethargy.

He would have agreed but he was too busy coming against her body just that quickly, his seed marking her again and causing his wolf to howl with triumph. They had wanted her too much and for too long to last once her pleasure had been ensured.

He collapsed beside her, his hold on her tight despite his sense of relaxation.

She cuddled into him. "I am not going anywhere."

"Tomorrow, you leave for Balmoral Island."

She tensed. "What? You are refusing me now?" she asked, though sounded like even she could not believe that.

Good. "Dinna be daft, *mo toilichte*. We will leave after we break our fast. The day after tomorrow."

"We?" she asked, sounding both hopeful and still slightly worried. "Why the day after?" came out as a clear afterthought.

"How can you doubt it after what we just shared? And because your dearest friend is to be mated with the traditional Chrechte ceremony tomorrow evening."

"I'd forgotten." Shona's fingers worried against his chest. "How could I have forgotten?"

"It has been an eventful day."

"It has. And I don't doubt you."

"Good."

"When did you decide to come with me?"

"As soon as you announced your intentions of going."

She made a scoffing sound.

There had been no real decision to make. "I would trust your safety to no one else for the journey."

"Oh."

He surged up to lean over her, his warrior's heart catching at the expression on her lovely oval face. "You will make yourself known to your family. I will state my intentions toward you to them. But heed my words, mate, no one—not even you, my dearest Shona—will keep you from me ever again."

Her smile was like the sun coming through an unexpected break in a heavy gray sky.

Waking held tight in Caelis's arms was much more comforting and enjoyable than Shona would have admitted, even to herself, the day before. It seemed so normal to be cuddled together under a fur, their naked limbs entwined.

She didn't remember a fur being on top of them the night before, though. Hadn't it been one of the Sinclair plaids on her borrowed bed?

Caelis must have moved the one he'd brought with him from beneath them to cover them, but she could not remember him doing so. Though she'd been less than sensate when he finally declared the time for sleep had come.

In the morning light coming in through the high window, she could see more details of the fur and she realized she'd seen it before.

And not just the night before in the hallway.

She pulled the corner of the fur up to look at the soft leather underside; sure enough, there was an *S* and *C* burned into the leather with an intricate Celtic knot joining them.

It was the same fur they had made love on six years ago. Tracing her finger over the lines of the symbols, she tried to fathom what it meant that he had this fur with him at the Sinclair holding.

The tension in the body beside her told her that Caelis had woken up.

She looked up at his long-beloved face. "This is the same fur."

He did not ask the same as what; he simply inclined his head in agreement. "It is."

"How?"

"I use it as my bedroll, always."

"Even when you are going to another holding to bring back Uven's daughter?" Though the proof was covering her with delightful warmth.

"Even then."

"But why?"

"It is our mating fur."

"I don't understand."

"Chrechte tradition is that special furs are prepared for the joining of a Faol and his mate."

"But you did not make me your mate."

"Oh, I did. Our bond was formed when you gave your body to me."

"You *really* thought I would stay and that Uven would change his heart."

"Aye."

"You were stupid."

"Aye."

She smiled. "I love you."

"You said so last night."

"I thought you might like hearing it this morning, too."

"I do."

"Good." Even if he did not love her, so long as he did not take her love for granted, she could find contentment with him.

She was certain of it.

She had lived with worse and could feel only gratitude her past would never be her present.

Chapter 21

Raise a Chrechte child with knowledge of the sacred laws and he will grow into a man of honor.

—CHRECHTE SACRED LAW, FROM THE ANCIENT SCROLLS

*S*hona was delighted to find Audrey waiting in the great hall with Thomas, the children and Vegar when she and Caelis came down to break their fast.

The daughter who had been so shy when they left England was ensconced contentedly on Vegar's lap, talking to the rag doll Shona had made her when Marjory was a baby. She lifted the doll to Vegar and said something that Shona could not hear.

But it caused Vegar to look uncomfortable, and that brought a bit of a smile to Shona's face. She was shocked beyond believing when the dour warrior kissed the doll on its raggedy mop of a head and pretended to feed it.

Audrey laughed lightly and Thomas said something, but Vegar did not seem annoyed.

Or as unirritated as the man had ever seemed in their brief acquaintance.

"I am glad to see our children and their Uncle Vegar getting along so well," Caelis said with a smile in his voice.

Shona stopped in their progress toward the main table and stared up at him. *"Uncle?"*

"He is mate to your heart-sister. That would make him uncle, but he is also the closest I have to a brother."

"What about Darren?" she asked, naming Caelis's younger brother.

Sadness and anger emanated off of Caelis. "He died much like Jon did, on an assignment for Uven for which Darren had neither the experience nor training."

"Is that when you began to question Uven's ways?"

"I began to doubt our laird's omniscience when you left our clan."

Shona accepted the claim without comment, starting forward again. She noted that the warriors they passed were careful not to brush against her.

"You marked me with your scent again, didn't you?" she asked across the mating bond.

A rich chuckle sounded in her head though his face remained impassive. *"Most of these soldiers are human and have no idea you wear my scent."*

"Why are they so careful not to touch me then?"

"Because I am a formidable warrior and anyone looking at us recognizes you are mine."

"I don't even wear the MacLeod colors, much less a sign proclaiming me yours." She still wore her English clothes, but Caelis walked so close, there could be no doubt they were connected in some way.

"I am all the sign these men need."

"Arrogant," she said aloud as they reached the table.

This time, his laughter was out loud and for some reason both the Sinclair and Vegar joined in. Thomas smiled, too, like he was holding back mirth.

She glared at them all, but turned a smile on Abigail and Audrey. "Good morning."

"Good morning." Abigail's smile was kind. "You look well rested."

"I am. Thank you." She looked Audrey over critically.

"You slept last night." Shona was glad. She'd been worried her friend might lay awake in nervous anticipation of the mating ceremony to come.

"I did." Audrey gave a look toward Vegar that was not difficult to interpret.

Audrey might well still be a virgin, but she was no longer wholly untouched. Shona was deeply grateful the experience had so obviously been a positive one.

She could almost look with favor upon the cantankerous Éan warrior because of it.

"Are you still angry with Da?" Eadan asked as Caelis helped Shona to sit before joining her on the long bench.

"No, sweeting. I am not."

"Daddy says no puddings every night," Marjory announced unhappily.

"You are sweet enough to do just fine without dessert every night."

Marjory sighed, but nodded. "I likes it here better than home, anyways."

"That is good, because this is our home now."

"Here?" Marjory asked with a dubious look around the great hall.

Caelis leaned across the table and tugged Marjory's braid. "Nay, *mo breagha*. Our home is to the south. Your mama meant Scotland."

"Isn't England in the south?" Eadan asked.

Marjory's eyes narrowed. "I do not want to ride horses for days and days and days anymore."

"The ride to the MacLeod holding is not so long as to England," Caelis promised.

It was long enough, and he would learn that children Marjory's age did not make a discernable distinction between a couple of days shy of a single sennight and two full weeks. Anything over a day was going to earn her disfavor.

"We are going to the island," Eadan said to his sister. "We'll have to ride horses for that."

"How did you know about that?" Shona asked.

Had her son had another of his dreams?

"You said so. Our family is on the island." Eadan looked at her as if he was worried she'd forgotten.

Shona found herself laughing. "I did say so. You are right."

"We will leave for Balmoral Island tomorrow morn," Caelis informed the Sinclair laird.

"We will go with you," a big, dangerous-looking man who sat beside the laird's daughter Ciara said.

Ciara looked at her husband with question. "I thought we were not making our monthly trip to the island until the new moon."

"I have a mind to get to know Vegar's English mate and the woman who would tame the MacLeod."

"He is not laird yet," Shona pointed out, but 'twas clear these fierce warriors saw Caelis's place in the clan as foreordained.

"You doubt he will be?" the dark-haired warrior asked.

"Nay."

The man nodded his approval of her agreement.

Ciara made a very unladylike sound of amusement. "Lady Heronshire, this is my husband, Eirik."

"He is prince of the Éan," Caelis said to Shona in her head.

Shona stood enough to give a half curtsy to the Chrechte royal. "It is an honor to meet you."

The prince's eyes narrowed. "There is no mockery in your scent."

"Nor should there be."

Eirik's gaze flicked to Caelis. "The mating link has formed already?"

"It began six years ago," Caelis affirmed.

Eirik's nod was both approving and thoughtful this time. "Ciara said your former laird kept you from your true mate."

"My own idiocy and misplaced loyalty did that."

Shona had wanted nothing more than for the man to admit his culpability, but she did not enjoy the self-recrimination in his tone in the least little bit.

Patting his thigh, she said, "We have found our way back to each other and that is what matters."

"I think certain members of the MacLeod will see things differently."

Confusion washed over Shona. Was the prince warning of the opposition she would face returning to her former clan as the mate of a Faol?

"He is speaking of the Chrechte among the clan. A true mate is sacred and the fact that Uven withheld you from me gives me unquestionable right to challenge him as pack leader and laird."

Casting a sidelong glance at the man she'd promised to marry, Shona considered his words. "My return to the Highlands was fortuitous, it would seem."

"Aye, fortuitous indeed," Prince Eirik agreed.

Ciara nodded, her expression the peaceful one Shona identified with spiritual counselors who truly sought to bring those who followed them closer to their Creator. "It is imperative that Uven be deposed as laird over the MacLeod and we thought we had found the answer in Caelis."

"But?" Shona prompted, having heard the hesitation in the *celi di*'s voice.

"While the Scottish king will not involve himself in a clan matter so long as the one challenging for right to lead is a MacLeod, garnering the support of the clan is another thing entirely. Uven's betrayal of Caelis and the proof of that betrayal found in both you and your children will be enough to sway most."

"Both children?" Shona asked Caelis.

"The very fact that *mo breagha* does not carry my blood is an affront to our bond that can be laid squarely at Uven's door."

"What did you say, Da?" Marjory asked in her child's mixture of English and Gaelic.

"I said you are *my* daughter."

Marjory beamed up at the big warrior. "You are *my* da."

"Aye."

"My da, too," Eadan claimed firmly.

"Absolutely," Shona answered at the same time as Caelis said, "Aye," in his deep warrior's voice.

Happy with their agreement, Eadan went back to his food. Marjory, who ate small bites provided by Vegar, continued to play with her doll, once again content to ignore the adults around her.

Audrey had turned pensive as they talked and Shona grew worried.

"Is aught wrong, dear friend?" she asked in a side whisper.

Audrey looked at Shona and then Vegar and back to Shona. "What will become of us?"

Shona did not understand the question. Did Audrey mean her and Thomas? The Sinclair had promised to train Thomas in the ways of the Chrechte and Audrey was now married to Vegar.

Sudden melancholy overcame Shona as what these realities actually meant to her. Was she to lose the rest of her family as she had lost first her mother and then more recently her father?

"Caelis," Shona said through their mating link, not sure what she expected her mate to do to help.

But the thought of losing both Audrey and Thomas was untenable.

"We will travel to Balmoral Island with them," Vegar said to Audrey. "Afterward, I will go with Caelis to challenge Uven. I am to be his second."

Audrey's expression showed as much relief as Shona felt. They were not to be separated.

Despite her earlier words on the subject, Marjory was surprisingly content to get on a horse with Caelis so they could make the journey to the sacred caves for Audrey and Vegar's mating ceremony. Her daughter resisted riding with Shona at all, however, and made something of a production of switching between Caelis's and Vegar's mounts.

Both warriors were infinitely patient, making sure that

Eadan felt as welcome as his younger sister. The five-year-old spent as much time with the warriors on their mounts as on his own horse. And somehow, both men remained vigilant to surrounding dangers, even though the contingent riding toward the caves was large.

Thomas accompanied them, of course, as did the laird and his entire family, even the new babe. A full company of Chrechte soldiers surrounded them, including four wearing the MacLeod colors, ensuring that Audrey's mating ceremony would be better attended than any wedding she might have had back in England.

Pleased for her friend, Shona was nevertheless confused.

She understood Prince Eirik and Ciara coming. Apparently as Vegar's prince and *celi di* of the Faol, both would play part in the ceremony.

Neither Vegar, nor Audrey, however, was a member of the Sinclair clan. While Vegar was clearly welcome in the Sinclair keep, he had not sworn fealty to its laird.

So why had the man and his family come? For the Sinclair to take his small children—Chrechte or not—from the keep, even on his own land, was to put them at risk.

Shona would have asked Audrey if she knew the reasoning behind such unexpected witnesses to her mating ceremony, but the younger woman was clearly lost in her own muddle of nerves and bemusement.

"You have worn a most perplexed expression the past hour," Ciara noted as her mare drew alongside Shona's.

"I have lived the past six years in England, I know, but still I cannot make sense in my mind of your family's attendance to this mating ceremony."

"We will also be performing a welcome-to-life ceremony for my baby sister. In ancient times, they were done for all children born of Chrechte blood, but we have lost many of our old ways. We are seeking to renew them now that our sacred stone has been returned to us."

"Oh." That made a great deal more sense to Shona. "Would it not be better to wait until the babe was older?"

"Possibly, but my dreams have told me that the stone must be returned to the sacred caves on MacLeod lands. Father prefers to have the ceremony before we take the stone off his lands."

Shona did not understand the whole import of the sacred stones, but she knew they had special meaning to both the Éan and the Faol.

"Did you not just bring the Faol's sacred stone back to these caves?" Shona asked, more confused than ever.

"Yes, but now both sacred stones, the *Clach Gealach Gra* and the *Faolchú Chridhe* must be united in the chamber of the *celi di*."

"The Éan's stone is to be moved as well?"

"Aye. Anya-Gra will send her successor to live among the MacLeod and serve as *celi di* for the Éan from there."

"Who is Anya-Gra?"

"Eirik's grandmother."

"That would make her queen of the Éan?" Shona asked.

"No," Ciara answered, adding to Shona's muddied thoughts. "She gave up her claim to rule in order to serve as *celi di*, just as Eirik's sister, Sabrine, gave up hers in order to become a protector of the clan."

"Isn't she married to the laird of the Donegal now?" Shona tried to remember the things Caelis had revealed to her about his world thus far.

"She is, but before that she was a warrior."

The thought of a female warrior was surprisingly pleasant to Shona. "Why doesn't Eirik live with *her* clan?"

"As prince of his people, he does not officially belong to any clan, though he wears the Sinclair colors on occasion."

Shona had noticed that the man wore a leather kilt rather than a plaid. "As your mate, he chooses to live with your family?"

"He chose the Sinclair clan before we met. It was destiny." Ciara smiled. "He and my father have a rapport that makes it possible for a prince to live in the same keep as a very stubborn laird."

"That is good." Privately, Shona could not imagine it.

The Sinclair did not strike her as an easy man to live in the vicinity of, even if you were willing to swear fealty *and* submission.

"We spend a great deal of time traveling to the other clans where Éan have made their homes," Ciara said as if reading Shona's mind. "It helps."

"Ah."

Ciara smiled. "Yes, *ah*."

"You do not mind traveling so much?"

"I miss my family, naturally, but we do not have children, so it is not a great difficulty. I enjoy the relationships I have built in each of the clans over the last year. And I have as much a responsibility to them as *celi di* to the Faol as Eirik has as prince of the Éan."

There had been a shadow in Ciara's voice when she mentioned children. "You have not conceived, but you and Prince Eirik are sacred mates, are you not?"

"We are." Ciara grimaced. "I do not know if I will ever have the good fortune to bear a child. The *celi di* who mentors me in my visions does not think so."

"But why?"

"There is a cost to the calling I have been given." Ciara put on a bright smile Shona did not quite believe. "Sabrine has already provided the next generation for the Éan's royal line."

"But you crave motherhood."

Ciara looked startled at Shona's perception. "I thought I did a fair job of hiding that fact."

"You do not wear your desire on your sleeve, but I am a mother and I know the sparkle of that dream."

"Not all dreams may come to pass."

"This one will." Shona was certain of it. "You may never give birth, but you will be a mother."

Ciara's stared at her for a long moment before her entire face transformed with a stupefied kind of wonder. "*That* is what she meant. When the time is right, Eirik and I will adopt. Just as my parents claimed me for their own when I was without family."

Shona did not ask who Ciara referred to as *she*. Even a fully human woman could put two and two together to reach four. The *celi di* was talking about the ancient Chrechte woman she saw in her visions.

"Thank you for revealing the nature of my mentor's words. She is sometimes obscure."

"My mother could be that way." Memories of her mother before and after Shona's unexpected pregnancy assailed her.

Circumstances had changed so much for both of them. Shona was the first to admit that it had not been easy on her mother to make a new life in England, where she was cook in the house her daughter had been named baroness.

She had loved being a grandmother, no matter what she had thought of her daughter for catching pregnant with no husband in sight.

Ciara's face was filled with compassion. "She hurt you very much with her disapproval."

"I am sure Mother thought she was doing right, protecting me from myself and tendencies she thought were damaging."

"She was wrong."

Shona almost smiled. Even Audrey had never stated it so baldly before. "Mother wanted what was best for me."

"Her love was best for you. Withholding it could not alter your course or the woman you had become."

"With that attitude, you will make a fine mother yourself one day." It was one Shona shared.

God willing, her children would never doubt her great love for them.

"Thank you." Ciara beamed. "For your insight and your affirmation."

The *celi di* left then, to rejoin her husband. The blinding grin that overtook the man's intimidating features moments later would imply that Ciara had shared Shona's belief that they would indeed one day parent children they would call their own.

"You are a very special woman," Caelis said from beside her as his great warhorse nuzzled her mare.

She turned and smiled at him and Eadan, who was riding for this part of the journey in his da's lap. "I am pleased you think so."

Eadan grinned back proudly, clearly thrilled to be where he was.

"I am not the only one. Thomas and Audrey sing your praises; even the Lady Abigail is as protective of you as one of her own."

The words were gratifying, but they brought up another worry Shona had been doing her best to ignore.

"Will Thomas stay with the Sinclairs when we leave?" she asked, her heart twinging at the idea.

Caelis shook his head, the depths of his gentian gaze telling her without words he understood her feelings. "I offered to complete his training and he has accepted. He will wear MacLeod colors."

Emotion clogged Shona's throat, but she forced out a heartfelt, "Thank you."

Caelis had made no secret of the fact he did not like Shona's closeness to the young Chrechte, but he had still taken care that she would not lose Thomas from her life.

His next words confirmed Caelis's understanding of the matter. "He is important to you."

"As if he were my own brother."

"You have a big heart, Shona."

"For a long time, I tried very hard not to acknowledge my heart at all."

"I do not think you were ever successful."

Looking back at the way she'd accepted Audrey and Thomas into her affections as well as the love she had for her children, which grew daily, Shona thought he might be right.

But she *had* tried.

"I never loved the baron."

"How could you? Your heart was full of me. Besides, he was a bastard."

The baron had been neither kind nor considerate, but he could have been much worse and so both her parents took pains to remind her on any occasion they deemed it necessary.

"I refused to even speak your name aloud."

"But you never forgot me, just as I never forgot you."

"Even when Uven had convinced you of my death?"

"Even then. I did not try to make love to another woman even then. I would have known you lived if I had done."

She was sorry for the pain of loss he'd suffered, but couldn't regret he'd never been tempted by another woman. Even if he did not love her as she loved him—and she was not as certain of that fact as she'd once been—she was definitely his mate.

The only woman he wanted. The only woman he *needed* physically.

And that was pretty special, as he'd said, even if that was not exactly precisely what he had meant.

The mating ceremony was beautiful beyond imagination and yet more *natural* than any wedding Shona had ever attended.

It took place deep in the caves the Chrechte had named sacred, in a chamber redolent with the power of millennia's worth of spiritual ceremonies for the Chrechte. The chamber glowed with an inexplicable light emanating from the walls. The *Clach Gealach Gra* on the stone pedestal in the center burned brightly like it was lit from within by a flame so hot it burned white.

The light shimmered red as Prince Eirik led Vegar and Audrey to lay their hands on it and in speaking vows to one another in the ancient language of the Chrechte.

Shona did not understand, but Caelis translated the vows for her via their mating bond. The mutual promises of lifelong care, protection, respect, fidelity and honor brought tears to her eyes even as she imagined repeating them with Caelis.

They uttered their last vows and then a profound silence fell over the cave, the air so still Shona could hear her own heartbeat in her ears.

The stone glowed a deep, dark red like a blood ruby and both Vegar and Audrey released a simultaneous breath before looking at one another with a connection so strong, Shona could feel its power from where she stood.

"Your heart is pure," Vegar pronounced of his mate.

Audrey dipped her head. "It is yours."

It should have been too soon for such declarations, but Shona was certain she was not the only witness there who felt the absolute sincerity of their words.

"I will treasure that gift always," Vegar replied in a tone every bit as solemn.

Ciara stepped forward, another stone held aloft in her hands, this one glowing like a dark, translucent emerald. She invited Vegar and Audrey to lay hands on it as well before speaking a blessing over their union, which once again Caelis interpreted for Shona inside her head.

The blessing had the sound of a prophecy and Shona stored her joy for her friend in her heart.

The green light seemed to reach out and surround the mated couple and the Faol's *celi di*, swirling around all three of them like a glowing mist.

Shona felt drawn to the stone, the urge to touch it so strong, her hand lifted toward them before she forced it back to her side. With great effort, she held herself back, careful to keep thoughts of how much she wanted to touch it far from the forefront of her mind. She did not understand this need, but she would not give in and mar her friend's special moment.

Chapter 22

The gifts of the sacred stone require sacrifice on the part of the one blessed by them, but destiny cannot be denied.
—CIARA OF THE SINCLAIR

Prince Eirik pronounced Vegar and Audrey lifetime mates, responsible first and foremost to the sacred bond between them.

A great cheer went up, echoing off the stone walls of the cave, resounding with both triumph and happiness.

As a child, Shona had witnessed a wedding in her clan that received the same joyful response. She remembered thinking one day she would marry her warrior and the whole clan would rejoice. Even then, the only groom her mind could conjure was the young boy Caelis, only a few years older but a world ahead by a child's standards.

Laird Sinclair stepped forward, a black fur over his forearm, and offered it to Vegar. "For your mating."

Caelis moved away from Shona and only then did she realize he also had something in his hands. "That your mating may begin as it will continue, acknowledged by me and all Chrechte among the MacLeod." Her mate offered Vegar and Audrey plaids in the colors of the MacLeod.

The other soldiers wearing those colors came forward,

all dropping to a single knee and placing their right fists over their hearts.

"We will protect your mating and mate with our lives as is right among our kind," Caelis said in tones far more like his *conriocht* than the man.

"Aye," the kneeling soldiers said as one.

Emotion overwhelmed Shona, but she had her own gift to offer. She approached the newly mated couple and offered the silver hairbrush she'd brought among the few belongings she'd deemed absolutely necessary when she had fled the barony. "May you both find joy in your service to one another."

Vegar accepted the hairbrush, the tender glance he gave Audrey saying he knew exactly who was supposed to be offering the act of service. Then she handed Audrey a satchel filled with herbs and remedies. "May you care for your husband and children to come, healing scrapes as well as hearts."

Audrey's eyes overflowed with tears. "You prepared for this, even though you could not know . . ."

"I knew the sister of my heart would one day take a husband and that I would be prepared to show my good wishes for that joining."

Audrey embraced Shona, a soft sob sounding in her ear. They hugged for long moments before Shona stepped back and Thomas took her place. He offered his sister and the man by her side a butter-soft skin to cover their mating bed.

When she saw it, Audrey again started to weep, but Vegar simply muttered a heartfelt thank-you.

Afterward, everyone stayed in the chamber for the Sinclair's youngest child's welcome-to-life ceremony. The green stone glowed again, enveloping the child bringing forth gurgles and joy-filled baby laughter before fading.

Caelis and the other MacLeod soldiers accompanied the mated couple out of the cave. Minutes later, the howls of several wolves echoed along the underground passageways.

Caelis returned to Shona and the children shortly there-after, looking exactly as he had upon leaving. She'd no notion if he had shifted or not.

"Part of the mating ritual?" she asked.

"For the Faol, yes."

And Audrey was Faol, though her English friend had little true notion what that meant.

Shona merely nodded in acknowledgment, not certain she wanted details, as she would be facing her own mating ceremony at some point in the future.

The trip to Balmoral Island was uneventful, if Caelis could ignore the soppy looks passing between his fellow Cahir and the man's new mate.

Who knew Vegar even had that particular expression in his repertoire?

And the former Englishwoman spent as much time riding in Vegar's lap as she did in her own saddle.

For some reason, both Caelis's children found this vastly amusing and their giggles echoed through the forest as the horses galloped toward the sea.

Their party made it to shore where the boats were kept in a cave by the Sinclairs faster than he would have expected traveling with children and a newly mated pair. The sea crossing itself went quickly, with the four robust warriors to man the oars. The three women entertained and watched over Marjory and Eadan, making sure Cae-lis's son especially did not go tipping over the side of the boat into the waters.

Eadan had a sense of adventure untempered by caution that made Caelis both proud and terrified at the same time.

The boy showed no more fear of the sheer drop down the unprotected side of the switchback trail they had to climb to reach the Balmoral keep than he did riding a flat forest trail, either. Caelis breathed a strong sigh of relief when they reached the top and headed toward the imposing castle on the cliff overlooking the sea.

Shona laughed a little and he turned to her. "What amuses you?"

"When I first saw the Sinclair's keep, I had the wish but little hope that the Balmoral's would be as well fortified and imposing."

"It is near impenetrable."

"I can see that. My family here, if they had a mind to, could protect Eadan from Percival's evil intents with little effort."

"He has no need of their protection. He has mine." Was that still in doubt in her mind?

Shona smiled up at Caelis, her lovely green eyes sparkling with the love she'd admitted to. "I know, but surely you can see the irony?"

"I do." Though he did not like the fact she was still thinking of others protecting their son.

"I'm not," she said, exasperation twisting her smile.

"I said nothing."

"Did you not?" she asked, her eyes saying otherwise.

But he truly had not. He had not thought his feelings aloud, either. He was sure of it. He had never heard of mindspeak being so much like mind reading before. The latter being a myth parents told their children about in stories before bedtime.

Their traveling party was stopped and questioned at the gate, but let through because they were with Prince Eirik. Nevertheless, a small contingent of Chrechte soldiers accompanied them to the keep and did not leave them until dismissed by the Balmoral.

Caelis had no doubts the man would be able to point them in the direction of Shona's family. Lachlan knew his clan from the oldest Chrechte to the youngest human infant, by sight and by name. The laird not only participated in training all the soldiers, Chrechte and human alike, he spent time training with the Cahir each sennight as well.

His wife, the Lady Emily, took a personal interest in all the families of the clan, no matter their origins and encouraged friendships between her children and those of the kitchen staff as much as the highest-ranking warriors.

Moments after explaining their quest to find Shona's remaining blood relatives here on Balmoral Island Caelis was speechless from the knowledge imparted by Lachlan.

Shona was not so affected. "You are my cousin?" she asked the laird, her eyes shining with delighted interest. "How can this be?"

She was no doubt thrilled to discover her familial connection to the one of the most powerful Chrechte lairds in the Highlands.

"His mother was human," Emily, the laird's wife, offered. "It is not nearly as difficult as you might imagine."

The Balmoral smiled indulgently at his wife, but shook his head.

"Actually, my great-aunt who left our island to join her mate among the MacLeod was Chrechte. She was sister to my father's mother."

Lachlan looked at Shona expectantly. She stared back, uncomprehending.

"You are saying her grandmother was Faol?" Caelis asked his voice near faint with shock.

The Balmoral laird nodded. "Aye."

"But I'm human!"

"Those of mixed parentage are as likely to be born human as Chrechte," Lady Emily offered with an interesting look for her husband.

"But my father was human."

"He was," Caelis affirmed. *He* would have been able to tell otherwise; it would have been revealed in the man's scent.

Lachlan shrugged, apparently unconcerned by the fact his cousin had been human. "His mother was Faol."

But then, Lachlan's own brother had been human, with no wolf to share his nature. By all accounts, their father's reaction to his firstborn being unable to shift had caused resentment and eventually Ulf's death.

'Twas a sobering lesson not to be dismissed by a man with one Faol and one human child already.

"That explains Uven's predecessor appointing my da as seneschal." Shona sighed, the sound filled with weary pain. "My father never told me. Anything."

The fresh betrayal in her voice sliced at Caelis's heart.

Lachlan nodded as if he understood. "He was raised in a clan where the Fearghall had a deep stronghold. No doubt he believed he was protecting you."

"Perhaps he was taught, like we were, that to reveal the true nature of the Chrechte meant death?" Audrey offered, her concern for her friend apparent.

Clearly accepting neither explanation, Shona looked up at Caelis, her expression filled with pained helplessness. "Why?"

Ignoring the others around them, he turned to face her, cupping her cheeks, wishing he had an answer that could take away the pain. "I dinna ken, but this I know: it was not your doing. The lack was in your da, not you."

"I loved my parents. So much."

"They loved you, too." Neither had been effusive in their affections, but in their years among the clan, they'd shown the high esteem they held their only offspring in.

"It does not feel like it."

She had too many fresh memories to supplant the ones from her childhood, when she would have been certain of their love and care. And maybe that explained how sure she was that Caelis did not love her.

"They made mistakes, but they did not stop loving you."

"My father had to know how horrible my marriage would be for me and yet he pushed me into it."

Because her father would have known that Shona was true mated to Caelis or she could not have conceived his child. Caelis himself did not understand why the man had not returned to the clan to tell him of his child.

Shona's father must have known that Caelis would have claimed his true mate pregnant with his babe, no matter what his laird had dictated.

Instead, the former seneschal of his clan had forced his daughter into a marriage he had to know would be difficult, if not impossible, for her.

Only because she was more human than Chrechte had her body allowed penetration by the baron. Caelis could be grateful for that, because *had* her body responded like a Chrechte's, Shona would have been subjected to even more pain.

He was certain of it. The dead baron had been a lecher and a cur.

"He thought you were fully human," Caelis said to Shona now, knowing it would be little comfort.

"I'm not."

Caelis would not gainsay her on that claim. There was too much to support her supposition, though he'd never heard of a non-shifting Chrechte exhibiting other traits of their race.

It bothered him that he could not tell what Shona thought about the fact she was part Faol, but there could be no denying it either. Her reaction to her marriage to the baron was far more Chrechte than human and the strange way Caelis and Shona sometimes read each other's minds could well come from latent Chrechte gifts.

"You do not have a wolf." Of that he was certain.

Her eyes sparked with unexpected mischief. "I thought you said that you were mine as much as I am yours."

Relief flooded Caelis. If she could tease, she was not too devastated.

He would never again allow himself to be surprised by the depths of his mate's strength.

"He's your mate, then?" the Balmoral asked.

Caelis took a deep breath, surprised at the tension filling him that he had to force himself to ignore. The time had come to declare his intentions before her family.

Shona looked up at him, her emerald gaze questioning.

He leaned down and kissed her forehead before stepping back and facing Lachlan. "You are her closest kin, are you not?"

The Balmoral stood, clasping his hands behind his back. "Aye."

"Shona is mine."

The laird did not reply, but his expression challenged Caelis's claim without words.

"I *will* marry her."

Vegar made a snorting sound and turned away. Caelis glared at him, only to shift that scowl to Thomas when a sound very much like a laugh came out of his mouth as well.

"Will you?" the Balmoral asked, the challenge in his tone unmistakable.

Caelis opened his mouth to set the man straight when he caught sight of Shona in his periphery. He was doing this for her, to show her she had value in his sight.

"I am declaring my intent to you to make Shona both my mate and my wife."

The Balmoral inclined his head, but did not answer. Instead, he turned to Eadan. "Is this MacLeod soldier your father?"

"No."

Caelis felt that word with the power of a dragon's blow. He had to lock his legs in place, or he would have stumbled from the pain of it.

"He is not?" Lachlan asked, surprise in his tone.

"He is not a soldier. He is laird, and soon the whole clan will know it."

"Ah . . . and is this soon-to-be laird your da?"

"Yes." Eadan crossed his arms, his mouth set in a stubborn line. "He and Mum are mates."

Lachlan nodded, his own expression thoughtful. He focused his attention on Marjory. "What of you, little princess, do you call Caelis 'Da'?"

"I calls him Daddy," Marjory said in her high-pitched little girl's voice. "He's a big dog."

Caelis found himself smiling at her view of his *con-riocht*, though they would have to teach her discretion in how she referred to him.

Still ignoring Caelis, Lachlan turned to Shona. "You are my cousin, a Balmoral by blood if not by birth."

"Thank you," Shona said.

What did that mean? Why was she thanking him? Did she want to be a Balmoral? She'd said she would marry him. She would not go back on her word. Even if he had six years ago.

He would freely admit to himself, if no one else, that Shona was made of stronger stuff than even a Chrechte warrior could lay claim to.

"There is a story behind a Chrechte of honor who did not know he had a mate, or a son, much less a daughter to claim, the last time I saw him a month ago."

Shona nodded. "There is."

"That this same man I have considered both friend and courageous warrior somehow executed the bond between sacred mates and then allowed you to become separated is an unarguable truth."

Caelis would not deny it. "Aye."

"He intended to marry me," Shona offered, surprising Caelis. "Our laird denied Caelis's request for permission to do so, however."

"And rather than leave with you, he stayed with the Fearghall." Lachlan gave Caelis a look that made him feel like squirming.

But nothing compared to that moment he thought his son had denied him.

"Aye," Caelis answered, though the question was not for him. "By my own stupidity, I lost my true mate for six long years."

It got no easier to admit upon repeating.

"That would explain your celibacy. I wondered if you were not simply a more dedicated warrior than most," Lachlan mused.

Shona made a small sound of distress. He looked down at her. "What is the matter?"

"That time is over. We are to be wed *now*. This is the matter of importance, not the past."

"Is it?" Lachlan asked.

Shona nodded most earnestly at the Balmoral laird. "It is."

"You would accept his suit for your hand?"

"I already have."

"And yet he still brought his intentions before your family."

Shona looked up at Caelis, her eyes shining with gratified pleasure. "Aye."

Finally, he had done something right.

Lachlan nodded and met Caelis's gaze. "You have shifted from Fearghall to Cahir, embracing every sacrifice necessary, training with total dedication to protect all Chrechte. Your plans and destiny are to serve our people with your life, but none of that justifies dismissing the needs of your mate. Remember that."

Lady Emily nodded, giving her husband and true mate a loving look.

Caelis could not disagree with the sentiment, but questioned his true dedication to it. Shona had agreed to marry him, but she had also made it clear she had no desire to return to the MacLeod clan.

Could he turn away from one destiny for the sake of another?

The simple answer was that if he honestly intended to put Shona's needs foremost in his mind, if he were to honor the sacred mating he had been blessed with, Caelis did not have a choice.

"No!" Shona spun to face him. "Stop thinking in this manner, Caelis. I insist!"

"What are you talking about?" Audrey asked, looking askance at both Caelis and Shona.

Shona was wringing her hands and frowning. "He believes that in order to serve our mating best he must give up his destiny to take the MacLeod clan from Uven, but that is not true."

Caelis expected Lachlan to get angry that he would

even consider such a thing, but the older laird merely asked, "Why do you believe this?"

"Shona does not want to return to the MacLeod." And finally, he must stop ignoring that truth.

"That is not true," his mate immediately and vehemently disagreed.

Caelis turned to her in shock. He had never known her to lie, but she'd made no secret of her feelings. So, how could he believe her words now, no matter how his senses told him she spoke the truth?

"I did not wish to return to the clan *with Uven as laird*. Even in my own mind, I had not made that distinction until now, but Caelis, you must believe me. I loved our clan, I *love* our people and I would serve them with you, by your side."

"So, you would marry this man despite a past that left you alone with a child by him?" Lachlan pressed.

Caelis would knock the laird back on his ass, but for the fact he appreciated Shona's newly discovered family showing such protectiveness toward her.

Shona nodded, her small, feminine body held tight with sincerity. "I would."

"Our priest will bless your union before the evening meal," Lachlan announced.

Caelis expected Shona to balk. Tradition dictated marriage Masses be performed in the morning. She was one who liked to make her plans and she'd been appalled by the speed and lack of ceremony associated with Audrey and Vegar's wedding.

But she smiled wide. "That would be lovely. Will the priest speak a blessing over Vegar and Audrey's wedding as well, do you think?"

Audrey sucked in an excited breath. "Oh, would he?"

Lady Emily smiled, her brown eyes sparkling. "I am sure he would. He is quite accustomed to unorthodox weddings."

Both Shona and Audrey showed delight at this answer.

"Why do we need a blessing?" Vegar asked, looking bewildered.

Audrey crossed her arms and gave a glare that no doubt did Shona proud. "So we can tell our children about something other than a laird's words while you stood ready to come to blows on the stairway."

Shona stood before the Balmoral priest, ready to speak her vows with Caelis. Meeting Lachlan had been amazing and wonderful. To know she had family that cared, to know her children had had options for safety even before fate had brought Caelis back into her life gave her such a sense of peace.

But she did not want to stay on Balmoral Island, despite the beauty and obvious closeness of the clan, or the fact that their laird claimed her as family.

Her future and the future of their children lay with Caelis and his destiny to protect his people and the humans of the MacLeod clan from the false doctrines of the Fearghall. It was her destiny as well. She could feel the truth of that deep in her soul.

It would take those not of the Faol to turn the thinking of the Chrechte among the MacLeod clan from the misguided teachings of the Fearghall. Those wolf shifters would not come to see humans or the Éan as individuals worthy of life, much less respect if Uven succeeded in pushing all but the Faol from the clan.

She and her children would make the Faol stop and think about all they had been taught by that deceiving blackguard. Vegar's strength and honor as a warrior would challenge their beliefs that the Éan were the ones to be despised as lesser Chrechte.

But in this moment, her destiny was not paramount. The vows she would speak were. And everything within Shona longed to make these promises before God and man with her warrior, to bind them together with the ties of law and honor.

The priest said the wedding Mass with warm feeling, his attitude that of a friend though they'd never met before Lachlan had introduced them.

The homily he spoke about marriage was both moving and funny, but all laughter faded as he led Caelis to speak first his vows and then Shona to utter hers.

Caelis maintained eye contact through each word, reminding Shona that no matter who was there as witness, the ones who truly mattered were her and him.

The priest spoke his blessing over both newly married couples before the clan celebrated the marriage of their laird's newly discovered cousin.

Shona faced Caelis in the tower room Lady Emily had offered for their wedding night.

His big body glowed golden in the firelight, his muscles rippling with power and strength that both excited and soothed her.

This man, this *shape-changer*, was her mate, her husband. And she loved him.

Now and forever.

"You are my gift," he said quietly. "The blessing I never deserved but could not live without."

"You did live without me."

"I survived without happiness, without pleasure. Every day of the six years we were apart, I ached for you. The years I believed you lost to me through death, I was little more than a shell. My one purpose with any meaning was to serve my brethren, but I had no hope of anything for *me*, or for the future. *You* give me a future laced with joy, filled with pleasure, worth living not just for my people, but for my own life as well."

His words fell on her heart like rain on the parched summer ground. "Our future is what we make it. The past no longer has any bearing."

"Do you truly believe that?" he asked. "You have forgiven me?"

"Yes." She meant it with every fiber of her being, too.

He nodded and moved forward until he stood directly in front of her, his body heat reaching out to wrap around her like a touch. "This is the last time you will dress an English baroness."

"I am a laird's lady, but no baroness any longer." He could not know how much that pleased her.

Chapter 23

Ignore the sacred teaching and the lessons of the past at the peril of all Chrechte.

—ANCIENT *CELI DI*

"Exactly." Caelis set about undressing Shona with efficient movements, as if the sight of her in the English garb was too much for him to bear one moment longer. "'Tis a lovely dress, but I'll be happy to never see it again."

"I still have my MacLeod plaid." She'd kept it all these years and brought it with her from England, though she would never have admitted so before tonight.

He stopped, staring down at her, his expression arrested and lit with an inner joy she never wanted to see extinguished. "You knew."

"What?"

"That you were still mine." And he set about proving it by removing her clothes and touching her in ways only he had ever done.

This time, though, she was determined to do the same. Moments later, they both stood naked in the center of the room, his hardness jutting into the air between them, her body showing its own obvious signs of arousal, too.

Her nipples were pebble hard, tingling with the need for

his touch and his mouth. She ached deep in her womb and moisture had gathered between her legs, the scent of her need obvious even to her human . . . or mostly human senses.

He sniffed at the air, inhaling deeply and smiling with a feral light in his blue gaze. "You are ready for me and we have barely touched."

"I am not the only one." She jutted her chin toward his weeping purple erection.

He growled low. "No, you are not."

"That is a good thing." To be together in their desire more amazing than he could ever know.

"Tonight we consummate our marriage and our mating."

"Yes." She reached up to kiss him, needing the intimate connection.

He did not hesitate to give it to her, taking control of the joining of their lips with gentle but inexorable force. His tongue swept inside her mouth and an image of his sex invading her body in a similar fashion flashed through her head.

She knew that image had not come from her. It was too intense, too aggressive . . . too *male* in its perspective. *"Caelis?"* she asked across their mental bond.

"Hmmm . . ." he hummed against her mouth.

She lost the thought she meant to pursue as his big hands cupped her backside and lifted her firmly against him. The feel of their naked flesh touching for the first time with the knowledge that they were legally bound sent chills of pleasure throughout her body, leaving goosebumps behind.

"Mine," she heard in her head. *"Mo toilichte. Mo gra."*

The sense of possessiveness emanating off of him wrapped around her and filled her with inexpressible delight, adding to her excitement. More images of lovemaking between them, her body wrapped in his, his nestled in hers, played like the most precious of dreams across her mental landscape.

She did not know how he was giving her these mental pictures, nor did she care in that moment. Seeing what he wanted, what he dreamed about, made her realize this physical connection between them was every bit as important to him as it was to her. That it went beyond the physical to souls intertwining.

She spread her legs, wrapping them around his hips, allowing Caelis to fit her body to his so his hardened sex rubbed against her most intimate flesh.

She saw an image in her head of her body taking his inside while she leaned back, her breasts completely revealed to his gaze, their bodies moving together in perfect harmony. She shifted to make it happen, both of them groaning in deep pleasure as they connected in the most intimate way possible for the first time in six years.

The kiss broke; she knew not which of them made it happen, but she leaned back as she'd seen in her head, her breasts heaving as he made love to her standing.

'Twas the most incredible experience she could have imagined, his passion so honest and true, so tempered by emotion it could never be compared to the selfish, lustful groping she'd endured with the baron.

"You are mine!" Caelis shouted, his tone intense, his body straining hard and his eyes glowing as they did when he was *conriocht*.

He swelled inside her. Already large, he grew so that she could barely move on his sex, her swollen folds stretched taut around his *conriocht* cock.

"You are shifting."

Sweat beaded his brow, his face contorted with his effort to control his form. "Nay."

"Parts of you, surely." No matter how misted the memory, she would not have forgotten if he had been this large six years past.

He did not answer, simply moving her on his huge arousal, causing her pleasure that bordered on pain. But no pain came and the pleasure only grew until it exploded through her and she screamed her completion even as he came inside her, his seed hot and strong as it pulsed against her cervix.

"My mate, my wife," he said in the guttural tones of the *conriocht* as his body increased in size and she felt another climax build on the astonishing pleasure of the last one. There was no breath for her climax when it came this time.

Her body shuddered, convulsion after convulsion tightening her flesh as clawed hands held her with intense care. His face did not shift, he did not grow hair . . . it was Caelis, but with the body of a near giant and the sex to match it.

"You will carry my child again," he promised her. "And I will be there every day of your confinement."

She had no breath for words with which to reply, but she could say the only three that mattered across their mating bond. *"I love you."*

"And I you. One day you will believe it."

She might believe it now, but he gave her no opportunity to tell him as he began making love to her again, proving that a six-year wait was entirely too long for man or wolf to finally claim his mate.

They continued to make love into the early hours of the morning, falling asleep under their mating fur as the sky began to lighten.

Shona and Caelis did not join the Balmoral clan until the nooning meal the next day, and still Shona found herself stifling a yawn as they approached the head table.

Audrey smiled knowingly. "Good morning, sleepyheads."

Shona knew her young friend's transition from innocent to married woman would take some getting used to, but she smiled anyway. "Thank you for rising with the children this morn."

Audrey waved off her thanks. "Eadan and Marjory enjoyed getting to know their new family. Gail and Feth made them feel very welcome."

Shona had barely met the laird and lady's ten-year-old

daughter and eight-year-old son the day before, though both had attended her wedding.

She smiled at them now. "Thank you."

"They are very nice children," Gail said with the maturity of budding womanhood.

She had years yet of her own childhood, Providence willing, but the reflection of the woman she would become was there.

Feth shrugged. "I like Eadan all right. He listens better than Brian and Drost."

"Don't speak ill of your cousins," Emily admonished.

"I'm not." Feth frowned. "The truth is not speaking bad of someone is it, Da?"

Shona bit back a smile as she took her seat, glad she wasn't the parent having to answer difficult questions right that moment. She was too sleep-deprived to be as politic as that sort of parenting required.

"When are we going home?" Eadan asked. "We need to go soon. The bad man has to be stopped, Da."

"Home?" Shona asked, trying to make sense of the words her son had spoken.

"Our keep." Eadan turned to Lachlan. "Yours is very nice, laird, but we need to go home."

"The barony?" Shona asked, at a complete loss.

No doubt more to do with lack of sleep than her son not making sense. He was a very practical little boy.

"The barony is not our home, Mum. We are MacLeods."

"You, your sister and your dam will come to MacLeod land once I have confronted the laird and defeated him," Caelis answered, proving he was more cognizant than Shona about Eadan's meaning.

"Nay, Da. We have to come with you now. We should leave today." Eadan spoke with great earnestness.

And although she agreed their children needed to be kept safe, Shona also felt a nagging need to leave for MacLeod lands immediately.

"You canna come with me, son. 'Tis not safe," Caelis said firmly.

Eadan's features took on a stubborn cast Shona knew only too well.

"The dragon will protect us."

"Dragon?" Shona asked faintly, quite certain there was yet more of the Chrechte world she did not know.

"He is mate to the *celi di*, Mum."

"Eadan—" Caelis said warningly.

"The *celi di* must come, too. The *conriocht* in my dream said so."

Caelis frowned at their son. "Eadan, have a care what you say."

"No one who is not to hear will understand our words," Eadan said with such certainty that Shona felt a chill of affirmation climb up her spine.

She looked around them and noted that none but the laird, his wife and their small group paid any heed to their conversation at all. Not even the laird's second and his wife sitting at the same table.

How could this be?

"I'm doing it, I think," Audrey said, looking frightened and awed at the same time. "I felt something strange and wonderful when I touched the *Faolchú Chridhe*, but I did not know what it meant."

"How?" Shona asked.

"I'm not sure. There are stories about Chrechte gifts. Mother said they were myths, but now I've touched the sacred stone and I can *feel* it working in me."

"But how did you do it?" She still didn't understand.

"I was just sitting here wishing no one would hear Eadan's slips of the tongue."

"Why?" Shona asked.

Audrey shrugged, looking apologetic. "Mother ingrained in me the need for secrecy."

"So, no one but those privy to the discussion can hear it?" she asked, just to confirm.

Audrey looked hesitant to answer, but Eadan said with all the authority a five-year-old boy who was certain of his facts could muster, "Right."

"That is impossible."

"So is reading minds," Caelis said to her with a significant look.

"You said that was the mate bond."

"What we experience goes beyond the mating bond."

Unwilling to consider the implications of his words right then, Shona turned to her son.

"You saw a *conriocht* in your dreams?"

"Yes, Mum. He is from long ago, but said he would help me when I needed him."

"There is an ancient *celi di* who guides me," Ciara offered, the look she gave Eadan full of wonder. "I did not see her for the first time until last year."

"There is much to be done before I am of age," Eadan said as if quoting another and sounding much older than his five years.

"I . . ." Shona did not know if she wanted her son to be destined for such things, but then what choice had she?

She was mother, not Creator.

"You can all come to MacLeod lands once I have defeated Uven." There was no give in Caelis's tone.

"No," Eadan said with authority no child should have in his tone. "We must go with you."

"Why?"

"The *conriocht* said so." Now, at least, Eadan sounded like a child.

"You will be safer here, among the Balmoral."

"Nay. You must keep Mum with you or you will lose her."

Caelis blanched. "You cannot know that."

"You must protect Mum."

"The Balmoral will not let any near her. Here on the island . . ." For the first time in memory, Caelis sounded uncertain. "You are all safer here."

"Percival knows bad people." It was a child's way of putting things, but there was such certainty in Eadan's voice that Shona could not doubt his pronouncement.

"Percival would not come this far north, surely," Audrey opined with more hope than conviction.

Suddenly Eadan shrugged, looking exactly like the small boy he was. "We must go to the MacLeod holding together. Mum will be safe in the sacred caves."

"Besides, Shona must be with Caelis when he confronts Uven, or more will die because they will doubt their fellow Chrechte's claims." Ciara sounded no less certain than Eadan.

Shona felt the pressure of need pushing against her as well. "They are both right. I do not understand it, but I am sure the children and I must be with you to confront Uven."

"The Chrechte will be convinced by my *conriocht* that I am chosen as their leader."

"Nay," the Balmoral argued. "Some will assume you should submit the *conriocht* power to Uven. You must show the pack that Uven has disregarded sacred law."

Caelis did not look convinced, but he turned to Eadan, giving him a penetrating look. "Son?"

"Yes, da?"

"You are certain of this?"

"I think so." Eadan's confidence gave way to a child's uncertainty. "I only know my dreams."

"Your dreams are a gift we will never dismiss," Caelis promised.

Shona nodded her agreement. "We will all go."

Then she looked at Ciara and her husband, realizing she had no right to speak for them.

But the dragon—*Really, a dragon?* Her mind could not grasp it—agreed with a slight inclination of his head. "We will go and I will protect you and your family while your father fights to save the MacLeod clan from the wickedness of the Fearghall."

"Thank you," Eadan said formally.

Prince Eirik smiled and reached out to clasp Eadan's forearm in the way of warriors. "You will be a fine protector for our people one day."

"Yes. All Chrechte must be one." Once again, Eadan sounded more like a prophet than a child.

Shona's heart twinged, but there was naught she could

do about the life he was destined to lead except support and love him whatever it required of him.

"Men like Uven must be stopped. He has already done untold damage. Perhaps if I had gone before this, lives could have been saved." Ciara sighed, guilt in her posture. "The *celi di* has been telling me I need to return to the sacred caves, but I have resisted going."

"You cannot blame yourself for the actions of evil men," Shona assured Ciara.

The other woman shot her a grateful glance.

"Why have you hesitated to return?" her mate asked.

"You have unhappy memories of that place."

The Éan prince pulled his mate close and kissed her softly before releasing her. "I have no regrets from that day."

"You hate casting fire to kill."

"It is less bloody than my sword." The words were facetious, but Shona heard the weight that sat heavily on the dragon's soul.

A man might kill in battle, but to have the ability to rain destruction from the sky must be a terrible burden to bear.

They smiled at each other and Shona could not help wondering at the story behind that look. But right now, she had more pressing matters to attend to.

They were returning to the MacLeod holding and her children would be with her.

Shona survived her first sighting of a dragon, but was not at all sure she would live through riding one.

She looked up, and up, *and up* at the great flying beast Ciara's mate had shifted into under the moonlight. "Why must I and the children ride the dragon? Why can we not bring our mounts?"

Caelis cupped his warm hand round her nape, his focus entirely on her. "This way is safer for you and the children."

"It is safer, to *fly* above the earth where no person was meant to go than to ride our horses?" she scoffed.

He smiled indulgently and her heart caught. "The Éan take to the sky all the time."

"That is different."

"There is an urgency about this; we must move quickly. You yourself said you felt it."

"I did. I do." Though she did not begin to understand it. "But that does not mean I want to fly on a dragon's back."

"It is quite safe, not to mention enjoyable," Ciara chimed in. "My mate is a very adept mount."

Shona nearly choked on the laughter welling up at Ciara's unintended innuendo. The *celi di* seemed to realize at that same moment how her words could be taken and laughter trilled from her, breaking some of the tension closing in around their group.

She shook her finger at Shona. "You are a very naughty woman."

"I said nothing," Shona defended, but it felt good to smile.

The dragon snorted and Caelis shook his head, but his expression was warmed with something Shona could only name love. If she were going to name it.

Not yet ready to do so, she remained silent.

But the fact that the man had been willing to give up his destiny to keep her happy? That one telling gesture overcame doubts and certainties she'd thought ingrained for life on her heart.

"Mum, come on. We have to go." Eadan looked up at her with the typical impatience of a small boy.

And she was grateful for it.

"It's all right for you. You want to ride the dragon," she said with a mock frown.

Part of her envied both children their sanguinity about this adventure. Marjory was already seated on the dragon's back and ignoring her continued protests; Eadan was scrambling up now that he'd admonished his mother to hurry.

There was nothing for it. She had to go up on the mythical beast's back, to watch over her children, if nothing else.

Once she was in place, she checked to make sure the children were securely harnessed to the leather saddlelike contraption on Eirik's back.

Ciara took bundles from her mother and tied them to loops apparently for that very purpose. "I love you," she said to the Sinclair lady.

Both laird and lady repeated the words and then waved them off.

Shona looked down at Caelis as Eirik's dragon's body tensed in preparation of jumping into the air. "I love you, mate. Have a care on your journey."

"I love you," Caelis said for the first time in six years. "Watch over our children and enjoy your adventure!"

Eirik jumped into the air and Shona's reply was lost on the wind, but even she was not sure exactly what her words had been.

Caelis had said he loved her and she thought she might well believe him.

Taking to the sky was like nothing she'd ever experienced, shocking and frightening and exhilarating all at once. A scant quarter of an hour into the ride and she was very glad indeed that Caelis had insisted she and the children wrap up in furs.

Eirik flew with dizzying speed, causing a steady stream of cold wind to wash over his passengers.

Ciara appeared to love the flight, petting and talking to her dragon mate constantly as they flew.

Whenever she went silent, Shona was sure the other woman was using the mate bond to communicate with the Éan prince.

As the moon began to wane in the night sky, they landed in a valley Shona vaguely remembered from her childhood.

The clan had been discouraged from visiting the place though it was situated between a clear stream and hills, which blocked the high winds that often plagued the Highlands, even this far south. An idyllic location, but one she now realized Uven and the lairds before him had kept apurpose for the express use of the Chrechte.

Ciara dismounted first and then put her hands up for first Marjory and then Eadan. Shona waited until both her children were safe on the ground before she slid off the dragon's back.

Once she had dismounted, Shona turned away from the dragon to give Eirik privacy to shift back to a man. Her attention was immediately snagged by Ciara as the other woman pulled a dagger forth and pressed the stone from the handle into an impression on the rock wall.

While moonlight gave some illumination to the area, it was not bright enough to see the rock face in any detail. The sound of stone sliding against stone came and then the side of the hill opened to reveal the dark entrance to a cave.

Shona could not have stifled her gasp of surprise had she wanted to. The children made to rush forth in excited wonder, but she held their hands tightly.

"We follow Ciara," she admonished them.

Eadan frowned, but nodded. Marjory just yawned. The poor tyke had gotten no sleep this night and even the excitement would not keep her from somnolence much longer.

Ciara lifted a torch and fire *whoosh*ed past Shona to light it.

She jumped back and looked over her shoulder to see that Eirik had not yet shifted.

"He won't return to his warrior form until we are safely inside the cave," Ciara said to Shona.

That made perfect sense, but the fire trick had still been quite startling and so she said.

Ciara laughed and Shona got the feeling Eirik was amused as well.

"He finds it charming you referred to his gift as a trick. Others have been far more impressed," Ciara explained.

Shona smiled around a yawn. "Well, of course I am impressed. The man shifts into a mythical beast and breathes fire, after all, but in truth, my capacity for shock and awe is diminished of late."

Ciara nodded, looking very serious all of the sudden. "Yes, I imagine it has."

Ciara led them into the cave and down a long, narrow passageway, which opened into an underground cavern. The *celi di* immediately began lighting wall torches she must have known were there. But then, she'd been here before, hadn't she?

As each new torch was lit, it revealed more of the cavern in which they stood. The space was huge, bigger than any great hall Shona had ever been in, including that of the Balmoral's keep. Stone benches and seats were interspersed along the walls and a dais of marble graced the center of the room.

Other dark openings indicated passageways that led away from what had to have been a room of meeting sometime in the past.

Shona did not know if it was her imagination, or if the great cavern felt both welcoming and like it had waited for them. She only knew she felt safe here, with a sense of peace she'd never before experienced.

The tranquillity of the cave had affected her children as well. Both Eadan and Marjory looked ready to fall asleep on their feet.

Shona asked Ciara, "Is there a chamber I should prepare the furs for their sleep?"

"That way." Ciara pointed to her left. "There are several smaller chambers I'm positive were once used as sleeping rooms for the *celi di* who lived here."

"Did only *celi di* live here?" Shona wondered.

"I have always assumed so, though my mentor did not say that specifically."

"Hmm . . ." It was something to contemplate.

Later. Right now, she needed to get her children to a place of resting.

Shona found a likely room with what appeared to be a raised stone bed jutting out from the wall. A shallow basin, which had been carved out of the top, would make a good place to pile heather for comfort's sake. Shona had no heather, but she did have the furs. She laid that which had been wrapped around the children down and then helped Marjory and Eadan to get situated on top before covering them with her and Caelis's mating fur.

Despite the excitement of being in a strange and wondrous place, both her children were asleep before she'd reached the doorway of the chamber.

She retraced her steps to find Eirik and Ciara in the main chamber, now lit with numerous torches. He was still in his dragon form.

Shona looked questioningly at Ciara.

"I will sleep better if he remains dragon tonight."

"Oh."

"The others will most likely not arrive until after sunrise. You would be best served by getting some rest yourself," Ciara added with a smile.

Shona yawned again and thought the *celi di* had a very good idea. She returned to the chamber with her children and snuggled into the furs with them, that strange sense of peace making it easy to drop off to sleep.

Shona woke sometime later as she was lifted into strong arms.

"Mmm . . . hmm . . ." she mumbled against the thick column of Caelis's neck.

"Shhh, *mo toilichte*. I am just taking you to our bed."

She didn't ask him what he meant, but let him carry her a short distance to another pile of furs he'd arranged on the floor. He settled her into them before curling his big body around hers, providing both warmth and protection.

Shona did not wake fully again, but was aware when Caelis's warmth disappeared some hours later and then Marjory was placed into Shona's arms and another fur settled over both of them for added warmth.

Chapter 24

We cannot burn all our enemies to a crisp, no matter how great the desire or provocation.

—EIRIK, PRINCE OF THE ÉAN

While Eirik and his mate explored the sacred caves, Caelis and Vegar planned their challenge. The other four MacLeod soldiers had come with them as well as Thomas.

All were prepared to fight by Caelis's side for the right to rule the pack and the clan.

"Today is a Chrechte feast day," Maon offered. "The entire pack will be gathered at the keep with Uven tonight. The humans who remain in the clan know to stay away from his *special* gatherings."

Caelis knew this to be true. "Then that is when I must make my challenge."

"It will not be easy." Maon sighed. "Believing a lie is less work that fighting to follow the truth."

"Mayhap for some, but not all."

Thomas added, "And they will have the evidence of Shona and the children staring them in the face."

Caelis did not like that part of the plan and let his scowl say so.

"There is no other way," Vegar said firmly.

Maon nodded. "She must stand by your side—not only to prove Uven's lies, but to show that humans are not beneath the Chrechte and that her strength is greater than Uven's threats and machinations."

The statement was a huge change in thinking for the powerful Faol, and Caelis was glad he hadn't killed the man in their battle.

He could also grudgingly concede that Maon had a point, but he did not have to like it.

"Mum *is* strong," Eadan added, his little boy trust in his mother absolute. "She got us out of the barony when Percival wanted to kill me and keep her for his company. And she is *supposed* to be there."

The very thought of what kind of company Percival had in mind had Caelis growling. He pulled his son to him. "No one will harm either of you now."

"I know, Da."

Caelis knew there was no choice but to live up to the trust his son placed in him as well.

The sound and scents of multiple Chrechte came from within the keep, even from the distance Caelis and his followers stood in the forest.

He could not believe they had not been challenged as they approached the laird's home though. The MacLeod keep was not a fortress like the Sinclair or Balmoral holdings with high walls, towers and a bailey, but Uven had always maintained a posting of perimeter guards.

Usually paranoid, the Faol laird had grown so arrogantly complacent. According to Maon, the man had made it a practice in the last year to pull his perimeter guards into the feast. After the death of his second a year ago and the loss of the soldiers he sent north to fetch his daughter, Caelis would have thought Uven would want to increase security, not loosen it.

But apparently the laird believed showing disdain for his enemies was some kind of protection in itself.

He would learn differently this night.

There was only a single guard at the door and two who walked the grounds immediately outside the rough keep.

Vegar took out the two sentries with little effort, swooping in as an eagle and shifting to his human form to incapacitate without killing. He left each one unconscious and tied up behind the keep before returning to the others in the forest.

Uven was so confident the Éan lived in fear of the Faol, he had not trained his guards in defensive warfare against a foe who could fly. They didn't even watch the sky for the approach of a possible enemy.

"Good work." Caelis bumped shoulders with Vegar before turning to face Shona. "Remember the plan."

She nodded, a small smile forming on her too kissable lips. "Stay out of sight with Thomas and the MacLeod soldiers until you give the signal."

He bent down and kissed her. "Stay safe."

"I will." The dazed look in her eyes from the kiss was more comforting than her promise.

And Caelis took the memory of it with him as he approached the door sentry openly and alone.

Excluded from the revelry inside, the young Faol soldier had no doubt been assigned his position because Uven was angry with him. It was the way the laird ran his pack.

"Caelis?" the man standing guard at the foot of the steps leading up to the keep's entrance asked, recognition warring with surprise on his youthful features.

"Aye, it is me."

"Uven said the Sinclair had killed you."

"Nay."

"But . . ." The young soldier didn't seem to know what to say.

"I will speak to Uven."

The younger man nodded and then seemed to realize he should mayhap challenge Caelis's assertion. "Do you have permission to be here?"

"I am MacLeod. I am Chrechte. What more permission do I need? Will *you* challenge my right to be here?"

"I . . ." The youth swallowed convulsively. "Where were you? If the Sinclair did not kill you, why have you not returned to your pack until now?"

"I had much to learn. The Sinclair, a great Chrechte leader, did not kill me. He trained me to be a true Chrechte of honor."

"What does that mean?" the youth asked, sounding confused and strangely hopeful.

"It means that Uven has done naught but use this clan and pack for his own purposes. He has manipulated and twisted our sacred laws to serve his perverted goals," Maon said as he stepped forward.

The youth's eyes widened with shock. "Maon! You are on a special assignment for Uven."

"I was, until that task killed my brother and revealed to me the truth of Uven's twisted teachings."

"You are going to challenge our alpha?" the young soldier asked with clear disbelief.

"No," Caelis said, pushing the sentry aside inexorably but without anger. "I am."

He let out a short low whistle and moments later, his other supporters stepped forward. They surrounded Shona, putting themselves between her and danger.

The gate guard looked around himself, his tension increasing as no other guards stepped forward to back him up.

"You can stay here, or you can come and see Uven defeated as laird and pack alpha," Caelis told him before mounting the steps.

The others followed behind. He was not surprised when the scent of the gatekeeper joined theirs.

Caelis had a plan for how he intended to handle the challenge, but it would disappear faster than a challenging Chrechte under Eirik's dragon fire if the safety of his mate was threatened.

He threw the door to the keep open and stepped inside, his senses on alert in a way those within clearly were not.

Uven sat at the main table, eating with his hands, laughing in the loud baritone so familiar to Caelis.

Memories assailed him of this man who had been stand-in father, only for Caelis to learn that his true parent had died at the power-hungry alpha's hands.

"He stole much from you, but you are stronger than him. Even if you were not Chrechte, you would be stronger," Shona said to Caelis over their mating bond.

He allowed her words to fill his mind and his heart so he could do what needed doing. Uven, pack alpha and laird, had to die.

The corrupted laird and his inner circle all seemed to realize Caelis was there at the same time, their revelry dying with the speed of a candle blowing out.

Uven stood, dropping the leg of mutton he'd been chewing on. "So the prodigal son returns."

"I am no son of yours." Caelis did not raise his voice, knowing his fellow Faol could hear his every word even if he whispered.

He would not whisper, but he would not give the laird the satisfaction of thinking he'd driven Caelis to shouting either.

"You say that, when I raised you like my own?"

"After you murdered my parents, you took the place that did not belong to you. But that seems to be your specialty."

"You dare accuse me of murder?"

"You are guilty of it over and over."

The mutters around them grew in volume and Caelis was shocked to realize he heard criticisms of Uven from several directions. How blind had he been to both Uven's perfidy and the number of Chrechte already unhappy with the alpha's leadership?

Uven might be oblivious to the risks surrounding his clan, but he was aware of his pack's displeasure, as the there-and-then-gone-again grimace on his face showed.

"It is not murder when you kill the disloyal," he announced with an ugly superciliousness Caelis would never allow himself to be guilty of.

"Disagreement is not disloyalty. You are alpha, not a god."

"What are we but gods among humanity?" Uven countered.

Caelis did not answer, the scent of his mate coming nearer to distracting him. She would make a terrible warrior. She did not take orders well at all, but she made the perfect mate.

"You're an idiot," Shona said from behind Caelis. "A conceited liar who has no right to lead."

Caelis felt a smile take over the fury on his face. His mate was outspoken and fearless despite all she'd been through.

"You find this *human's* disrespect amusing?" Uven demanded, his own fury rising.

"My *sacred mate* only speaks the truth."

"She is human. She is *not* your true mate. I told you this."

"Oh, yes, you told me. You also told me she died, but both were lies."

"Anything I said, I said for your benefit," Uven claimed, sounding like he believed his own words.

But then, he'd always been adept at lying. Too adept.

"It is against Chrechte sacred law to withhold true mates from one another."

Uven slammed his fist down on the table, sending plates rattling to the rushes. "I make the laws for our pack."

"You are Chrechte subject to our ancient dictates, just as any other."

"She is not your true mate," Uven repeated.

A heavy *thump* sounded on the roof of the keep.

"What was that?"

The other Chrechte were staring at the ceiling, questions rising around them in a steadily increasing cacophony.

"Proof Shona is my true mate."

Uven's glare would have impacted Caelis at one time, but no longer.

A minute later, Eirik walked through the door to the great hall, Ciara and Audrey behind him, Eadan and Marjory each holding one of the women's hands.

"Who is this?" Uven demanded, but the way his nostrils flared said he knew.

"This is Eirik, Prince of the Éan and protector of his race." Caelis watched to see if Uven understood the implications of that statement.

The pack leader paled and said, "Impossible."

"Possible," Caelis disagreed.

"Kill him." Uven pointed to Eirik. "He is our enemy."

"He is my friend!" Caelis shouted now, not with a loss of control but with an absolute demand to be heard above the din. "The first to *try* to touch him will face *my* wrath."

Uven tried to look unimpressed, but he could not hide the lines of concern creasing his brow.

Good. It was time for the selfish leader to face the consequences of his egotism.

Once again, Caelis let his voice boom throughout the room. "I claim the right to challenge you for leadership of our pack and our clan."

"You are not MacLeod anymore." But even the youngest babe would be able to tell Uven was grasping at a threadbare rope to safety.

"I wear our colors. I am our clan, just as everyone here is."

And everyone in that room was Chrechte. Everyone could smell both Caelis's and Shona's scents mixed in Eadan, not to mention his marking scent on Shona. They could also hear and scent the truth because Uven in his conceit had done so little to hide it.

The man was so blinded by self-interest, he thought he was right.

"You assume you can dismiss our laws, murder all who oppose you and lie to any who will believe you without compunction or accountability." Caelis drew his sword and held the hilt in front of his heart. "I challenge you."

"You believe you can beat me, boy? You are a fool." Uven looked around him, but even his inner circle did not step up to deny the right of Caelis to challenge for the position of alpha.

The fact that he had strong warriors standing as a living wall at his back may well have impacted that.

"You would kill me over this little human slut?" Uven barked.

"I am no slut and I am not ashamed to be human," Shona enunciated, righteous indignation lacing her every word.

Caelis knew what Uven was trying to do.

He thought he would get under Caelis's emotions and cause him to act hastily, but Caelis didn't question his mate's strength or her ability to stand firm against Uven's stupidity.

She cared nothing for her former laird's opinion. His words could not hurt her even if they made Caelis burn with the need to feed them back down the laird's throat.

"You threatened him," Shona accused Uven, but Caelis did not know what she was talking about.

Thus far, the laird had done little but puff and posture. His assertion that Caelis was not strong enough to beat him hardly constituted a threat.

She turned to Caelis. "Uven threatened my father. He told him that if you and I mated, he would kill me to give you your freedom."

Fury washed through Caelis, but he did not understand how she knew.

"I can hear his thoughts," she said with awe. "I . . . I think it's my Chrechte gift."

"That's impossible. You are human," Uven disparaged.

Shona glared at him, loathing in her eyes. "You killed your own true mate because you believed Chrechte should never mate humans. You saw my father as an abomination because he was a human born of a Chrechte-human pairing. You raped my mother to teach both my parents some twisted lesson. *That* is when she changed."

Shona turned to Caelis, her eyes wet with tears. "It wasn't me. It was Uven and what he did to her. She didn't hate me; she wanted me away from him at any cost."

She loved me, but he broke her. The words came across their mate bond. *His actions nearly broke me, but they didn't.*

Even the fierce pride in his mate's voice could not control the the fierce rage gripping Caelis, but then his wife sent him an image that pulled him back from the brink of disregarding Chrechte law just as Uven had done.

It was a memory so beautiful it touched him to his very soul: the sight of his son drinking at his mother's breast for the first time.

Caelis pushed back his *conriocht* and reined in his wolf. "Accept my challenge, or concede and leave this holding never to return," he bit out to Uven.

Uven paled and flinched, but then rallied and boasted self-importantly, "You will die this night, upstart."

Caelis laughed and did not even bother to reply.

Uven shifted and attacked without warning or waiting for the formal challenge to begin.

Caelis did not bother to shift. He had been trained by the best to fight a Faol in his Chrechte form without shifting himself.

Avoiding the snapping jaws aimed at his jugular, he spun away and then turned back, landing in a fighting stance just as Talorc had taught him to do.

Uven snarled, saliva dripping from his fangs, his eyes yellow with madness Caelis used to mistake for Chrechte power. The beast lunged again, but this time Caelis was ready for him. He feinted and then lunged, taking hold of the huge wolf by its scruff and one foreleg.

Caelis twisted into a spin, waiting until he had built up enough momentum to release. Uven's beast sailed through the air to hit the wall so hard, the *crack* of a beam could be heard.

Clansmen shouted, but none came to the corrupt laird's aid.

The wolf slipped the first time it tried to stand. Caelis let Uven find his feet, though.

He would kill the old bastard with honor and take pride in his strength to do it.

Rallying, the beast growled, gnashing its teeth as it stalked toward Caelis, only veering at the last second to lunge at Shona.

Caelis roared and leapt, his warrior's hands closing around the neck of the beast before once again tossing it into the wall.

This time, Caelis gave the bastard no chance to regroup, but simply crossed the hall in a few long leaps to land against the wolf's chest with his knee.

He grabbed the wolf's head and looked into Uven's eyes. "For your sins against our people, you have been judged guilty and will die at the hands of the Cahir."

The spark of recognition in Uven's eyes lasted only as long as it took for Caelis to snap the wolf's neck.

He stood, one foot pressed against the neck of the dead Chrechte. "I am your laird. I am your alpha. Accept it, or leave."

"What if we want to challenge you?" one of Uven's inner circle asked.

Caelis laughed just as he had at Uven's overweening confidence. "Then challenge me."

Two did and two more Chrechte lost their lives. Caelis had given each the option to submit or die. Both had chosen death.

Three dead Faol lay on the floor of the great hall and Caelis turned to those remaining. "Are there any others who would challenge my right to lead?"

"You haven't even shifted into your wolf," the young sentry who had been guarding the door said.

"Humans are not weak like Uven always claimed."

"But you are not human."

"And yet as a *man*, I defeated three Chrechte wolves."

One man dropped to his knee, put his hand over his

heart and swore fealty to Caelis. Over the next few minutes, every male in the room followed the first Faol's example. But the women remained standing.

Shona came to stand beside Caelis and looked around them. "I am human. I am your lady. Do you swear fealty to me?"

It took a moment, but one by one, the men bowed their heads to Shona. All but one.

Uven's nephew glared at Shona. "I swear loyalty to no *woman*."

Caelis moved so fast that when he reached the man and smacked him to his face on the floor, the other Faol wore a shocked expression. "You will leave this holding if you do not both apologize to my wife, but also promise personal fealty to her."

He was unsurprised when the man refused. Caelis looked to Vegar. "See him off our land."

Vegar nodded, grabbing the man by the scruff of his neck.

"You're Éan," Uven's nephew spat.

Vegar grinned. "Good of you to notice, but I cannot claim to be impressed by how long it took you to realize that fact."

They left the great hall with the stupid Faol still sputtering about inferior Éan, even as Vegar yanked him along like a naughty pup.

Caelis looked around the room at the women and then to Shona. She smiled and nodded, understanding.

She addressed the female Chrechte. "Do you refuse to pledge allegiance to your new laird?"

"Women do not do that. Our pledges are given no value," an older Chrechte female claimed.

"But a woman's loyalty is every bit as powerful as a man's," Shona argued. "Why would you seek to have a weak clan?"

"We do not," Uven's own wife said.

"You don't," Shona affirmed, looking surprised and

then sickened for a moment. "I know what it is to be wed to a man not your mate. Uven is dead. The man who freed you asks for your fealty. Will you give it?"

The woman nodded and dropped to her knees, bowing her head and swearing a sincere oath of support for Caelis as pack alpha and laird and Shona as his lady. Soon the other women followed and the room echoed with the feminine voices.

"This clan will change. To survive and thrive, we must return to the true ways of the Chrechte. Uven has lied to all of us about what they are, but we will find our way back to honor, to a strong clan that respects and appreciates all of its members."

A cheer went up that turned into deafening roars as Caelis allowed his *conriocht* to take form.

He stood before his people and promised them that life would be different if they would let go of the deceptions of the past.

Filled with joy, Shona surveyed the room until her eyes rested on a man sneaking furtively toward the great hall's door to the great hall. He had an arrogance about him that she was much too familiar with. "Percy!"

"Where?" Caelis growled.

Shona's hand did not shake as she pointed to Percival, fear no longer plaguing her in the presence of the vile would-be child murderer.

"Stop and face your accuser, cur!" Caelis ordered.

Percival turned slowly, his expression filled with more disdain than terror. "I have no accuser."

"You tried to murder my son," Caelis ground out.

The baron opened his mouth to refute the statement, but Thomas was there, boxing his ears and knocking him to the ground before he could.

"He came here looking for her," Uven's wife said, pointing to Shona. "You used to be part of the clan. He believed you would seek refuge among us again. The English baron paid Uven handsomely to find you and bring you back to him."

"Why didn't you say anything at first?" Caelis demanded, fury lacing the *conriocht*'s tone.

"I did not know it was this woman he sought until she recognized him," Uven's wife said, pleading in her voice and demeanor.

Shona waited for her husband to prove he valued the women of his clan and pack enough to believe. She knew the truth from the thoughts in the woman's head, but he needed to believe Uven's wife without Shona's interference.

Caelis sniffed the air and then nodded. "Thank you for speaking up now."

The woman sagged, her relief at being believed visible. The clan had a long way to go to heal, but they would get there with her husband as alpha and laird.

Percival was standing again, showing he had a lot more pride than sense as he glared at them all. "I will leave you to live among these horrors," he spat at Shona. "I'll not have a woman who has lain with a dog in my bed."

Caelis stalked forward until he towered over the man, who only now showed enough intelligence to exhibit fear. "You tried to murder my son. You will die."

"No, you can't kill an English baron."

Suddenly a white wolf was there and Shona knew it was Thomas.

Caelis indicated the man with a single pointing claw. "Kill it."

Thomas attacked, tearing the man's throat out and ending his threat to her children once and for all.

Caelis called two of his soldiers forward. "Return the body to the barony. Death by animal misadventure."

The soldiers nodded and wrapped the body in a cloth before taking him outside. Ciara stepped forward, her expression gentle. "We have a mating ceremony to perform."

Shona opened her mouth, but no sound came out. A mating ceremony? Now?

"When better?" her mate asked, proving she'd been shouting her thoughts again.

"Four are dead."

"And because of that, many more will live."

Hope unfurled inside her. It was true. The reign of terror exercised by Uven was over. Percival's evil had ended this night as well.

But a mating ceremony?

Looking around at the hopeful faces of the clan, she realized they all needed this symbol of hope, but still Shona hesitated.

Caelis dropped to one knee before Shona, his big body still towering over her as a *conriocht*. "I love you, mate, with all that I am and can ever hope to be. Will you speak the ancient vows with me before the people who have promised us their fealty?"

"I believe you." She did. She believed he loved her. Believed he would never again leave her. Incandescent joy sparkled through her, lightening a heart that had seen too much grief. "You do love me. You have always loved me."

Finally, she understood. His mistakes had not been made out of a lack of love, but a lack of understanding of what the cost of his would be. He would never again ignore the potential cost to his mate for any decision he might make.

"I do. As wolf, as *conriocht*, as man, my heart and my life belong to you."

She nodded, her tears spilling over, her happiness the scent of spring flowers around them. "I will."

The mating ceremony was all Caelis had ever dreamed it would be, on the many nights he lay in a lonely pile of furs wishing for the mate he thought lost to him. She promised him everything in the language of his people, her emerald gaze fully cognizant of each word's meaning as he once again used their bond to remind her.

And they shared their joy with the MacLeod pack, accepting their brethren's oaths to support and protect their mating as was right and just.

They followed the ceremony, which took the pack from death to life in a few short hours, by rounding up all the human members of the clan and announcing Caelis's new position as their laird.

Each clan member was given the option of swearing loyalty or leaving with the option of being welcomed into either the Donegal, Sinclair or Balmoral clans. All chose to stay.

The heaviness of that trust weighed profoundly in the most joyous of ways on Caelis.

But nothing was more important than the new life Caelis began with Shona that night, as she accepted his love and reaffirmed her own, proving to the whole clan how important matters of the heart were to even the most powerful Chrechte warrior.

Epilogue

The same group that had traveled with them from the Sinclair all stood in the secret caves of the ancient Chrechte the next day. Caelis, Shona, their children, Audrey, Vegar, Thomas, Prince Eirik, Ciara, Maon and the other MacLeod soldiers who had first sworn fealty to a new alpha.

Ciara led them all down into the chamber of the *Faol-chú Chridhe* and now instructed Shona and Caelis to lay their hands on the sacred stone.

The mating ceremony the night before had been a public affirmation of their relationship, but today the *celi di* wanted to bless their union with the sacred stone.

The moment Shona's fingertips touched the giant glowing emerald, she felt the most amazing connection. The thoughts and feelings that bombarded her were not her own, and she realized from their content that they belonged to those around her.

"I can hear the thoughts of others," she said in awe. She'd heard Uven's contemplations in the great hall before the laird's death, but they had been muffled and disjointed.

Now, it was as if she could enter another's mind like walking into a room.

"It is the gift of your nature," Ciara said softly.

"But I am human."

"With Chrechte ancestry."

"You will help identify the Fearghall and aid the *celi di* for both the Éan and Faol to serve our people the way we are meant to."

"But I am no *celi di*."

Ciara smiled. "You are. You have been chosen."

"But . . ." Shona looked up at Caelis.

He returned the look with blue eyes filled with love. "Your destiny is yours to embrace or deny. I stand by you either way."

Happiness suffused her. "With your example, how can I do any less than embrace it?"

Then each one in the chamber laid his hand on the *Faol-chú Chridhe* to varying effect. When Maon touched it, though, a great light exploded around them and when Shona could see again, a *conriocht* who was not her mate stood among them.

It was Maon.

"You must find the Paindeal," Ciara intoned. "Your fate lies in reuniting our races."

Maon did not speak, his expression one of stupefied shock.

Caelis laid his human hand on the *conriocht*'s arm. "You do not feel worthy. You never will, but you have been chosen as protector of our people. What you do with that great gift is up to you."

Caelis turned back to Shona and reiterated, "Just as you must choose how much of yourself to give to our people."

"So long as you are by my side, I will serve the Chrechte of all clans and the humans of our own to the best of my abilities."

"I will always be with you. I love you more than my life, more than my duty."

And she believed him.

To the very smallest tendrils of her spirit.

GLOSSARY OF TERMS

bairn—baby

beguines—self-running nunnery without vows to the church, not supported by the official church as related to Rome (historically accurate term in the British Isles)

ben—hill

Ben Bristecrann—broken tree hill (a sacred spot to Ciara's family)

brae—hillside or slope

Cahir—warriors who fight the Fearghall

celi di—Scottish Highland priest practicing Catholicism with no official ties to the church in Rome (historically accurate term in relation to Scotland and Ireland)

Chrechte—shifters who share their souls with wolves, birds or cats of prey

Clach Gealach Gra—(moon's heart stone) the bird shifter's sacred stone

conriocht—werewolf (protector of the Faol, shifts into giant half wolf/half man–type creature)

Éan—bird shifters (ravens, eagles and hawks)

Faol—wolf shifters

faolán—little wolf (Gaelic term of endearment)

Faolchú Chridhe—(wolf's heart) the wolf shifter's sacred stone

Fearghall—secret supremacist society of the Faol intent on wiping out/subjugating other races of the Chrechte

femwolf—female wolf shifter

keeper of the stone—a Chrechte who has a special link to the sacred stone and can utilize its full potential for healing, gifting and bringing forth the protectors of the races (*conriocht*, dragon and griffin)

kelle—warrior priestess (mentioned in Celtic mythology)

Kyle Kirksonas—River of the Healing Church

loch—lake

mate—a Chrechte's chosen partner (if it is a mixed mating— Chrechte of different races, or a human mate—children can only result if the bond is a true/sacred one)

mate-link—the special mental bond between true/sacred mates

mindspeak—communicating via a mental link

mo breagha—my beauty

mo gra—my love

mo toilichte—my happiness

Paindeal—cat shifters (large cats of prey)

Paindeal Neart—(panther's strength) the panther shifters' sacred stone

sacred bond (true bond)—a mating bond that lasts unto death and will not physically allow the Chrechte involved to have intercourse with anyone but the Chrechte's mate

usquebagh—"water of life" (Scotch whiskey)

Read on for a special preview of

Ecstasy Under the Moon

A Children of the Moon novella
appearing in the anthology

Enthralled

by Lora Leigh, Alyssa Day,
Meljean Brook and Lucy Monroe

Available now from Berkley Sensation!

The Forests of the Éan, Highlands of Scotland
1144 AD, Reign of Dabíd mac Maíl Choluim,
King of Scots, and the Reign of Prince Eirik Taran
Gra Gealach, Ruler of the Éan

Una stood in shock, terror coursing through her like fire in her veins, burning away reason, destroying the façade of peace she had worked so hard to foster for the past five years.

Her eagle screamed to be released. She wanted to take to the skies and fly as far as her wings could carry her until the sun sank over the waters and the moon rose and set again in the sky.

The high priestess, Anya Gra, smiled on the assembled Éan like she had not just made a pronouncement that could well spell their doom.

Faol were coming here? To the forest of the Éan? To their homeland kept secret for generations? For very good reason.

Reason Una had learned to appreciate to the very marrow of her bones five years before.

"No," she whispered into air laden with smoke from the feast's cooking fires. "This cannot be."

Other noises of dissent sounded around her, but her mind could not take them in. It was too busy replaying images she'd tried to bury under years of proper and obedient behavior. Years of not taking chances and staying far away from the human clans that had once intrigued her so.

She'd even avoided Lais, one of the few other eagle shifters among her people. Because he'd come from the outside. From the clan of the Donegal, the clan that spawned devils who called themselves men.

She'd not spoken to him once in the three years he'd lived among their people.

The grumbling around Una grew to such a level, even her own tormented thoughts could not keep it out.

For the first time in her memory, the Éan of their tribe looked on their high priestess with disfavor. Many outright glared at the woman whose face might be lined with age, but who maintained a translucent beauty that proclaimed her both princess and spiritual leader.

Others were yelling their displeasure toward the prince of the people, but their monarch let no emotion show on his handsome, though young, features. He merely looked on, his expression stoic, his thoughts hidden behind his amber gaze.

The dissension grew more heated. This was unheard of. In any other circumstance, Una would have been appalled by the behavior of her fellow Chrechte, but not this day.

She hoped beyond hope that the anger and dissent would sway their leaders toward reason.

"Enough!" The prince's sudden bellow was loud and commanding despite the fact he was only a few summers older than Una.

Silence fell like the blacksmith's anvil.

Emotion showed now, his amber eyes glowing like the

sacred stone during a ceremony. "We have had the Faol among us on many occasions these past three years."

Those wolves had only come to visit. Una, and many like her—justifiably frightened by the race that had done so much to eradicate their own—had stayed away from the visitors. She'd avoided all contact and had not even stolen so much as a peek at any of them.

Not like when she was younger and had let her curiosity rule her common sense.

But Anya Gra said these ones, these *emissaries* from the Sinclair, Balmoral and Donegal clans, would live among the Éan for the foreseeable future.

Live. Among. Them. With no end in sight.

Una's breath grew shorter as panic clawed at her insides with the sharpness of her eagle's talons.

"It is time the Chrechte brethren are reunited." Prince Eirik's tone brooked no argument. "It has been foretold this is the only chance for our people to survive as a race. Do you suddenly doubt the visions of your high priestess?"

Many shook their heads, but not Una. Because, for the first time in her life, she *did* doubt the wisdom of the woman who had led their people spiritually since before Una was born.

"Emissaries are coming to live among us, to learn our ways and teach us the way of the Faol." This time it was another of the royal family who spoke, the head healer. "We will all benefit."

"We know the way of the Faol," one brave soul shouted out. "They kill, maim and destroy the Éan. That is the way of the Faol."

"Not these wolves. The Balmoral, the Sinclair and the Donegal lairds are as committed to keeping our people safe as I am." The prince's tone rang with sincerity.

The man believed his own words. That was clear.

But Una couldn't bring herself to do so. No wolf would ever care for the Éan as a true brother. It was not in their violent, often sadistic, and deceitful natures.

"It is only a few among the Faol today who would harm our people. Far more would see us joined with the clans for our safety and all our advantage."

Join with the clans? Who had conceived of that horrific notion? First they were talking about having wolves come to live among them and now their leaders were mentioning leaving the forest so the Éan could join the clans.

Una's eagle fought for control, the desperate need to get away growing with each of her rapid heartbeats.

"In the future, we will have no choice," Anya Gra said, as if reading Una's mind. "But for this moment in time, we must only make these few trustworthy wolves welcome among us."

Only? There was no *only* about it. This thing the royal family asked, it was monumental. Beyond terrifying.

It was impossible.

"You ask too much." The sound of Una's father's voice brought a mixture of emotions, as it always did.

Guilt. Grief. Relief. Safety.

Stooped from the grievous wound he had received at the hands of the Faol when rescuing Una from their clutches, he nevertheless made an imposing figure as he pushed his way toward the prince and priestess.

The leather patch covering the eye he'd lost in the same battle gave her father a sinister air she knew to be false. He was the best of men.

And forever marred by wounds that would never allow him to take to the skies again . . . because of her.

"You ask us to make welcome those who did this," he gestured toward himself in a way he would never usually do. He ignored his disfigurements and expected others to do the same.

"Nay." The prince's arrogant stance was far beyond his years, but entirely fitting his station as the leader of their people. "I *demand* you make welcome wolves who would die to protect you from anything like that happening again."

"Die, for the likes of me?" her father scoffed. "That

would be a fine day, indeed, would it not? When a wolf would die to protect a bird."

"Do you doubt *my* desire to protect you and all of my people?" the prince demanded, with a flicker of vulnerability quickly gone from his amber eyes.

"Nay. My prince, you love us as your father did before you, but this? This risk you would take with all our safety, it is foolishness."

Suddenly Anya Gra was standing right in front of Una's father, her expression livid, no desire for conciliation in evidence at all. "Fionn, son of Micael, you dare call *me* foolish?"

Oh, the woman was beyond angry. Even more furious than Una's father had a wont to get.

"Nay, Priestess. Your wisdom has guided our people for many long years."

"Then it is my visions you doubt," the *celi di* accused with no less fury in her tone.

Una's father shook his head vigorously. "Your visions have always been right and true."

"Then you, and all those who stand before me today," she said, including everyone at the feast with her sharp raven's stare. "All of my people will give these wolves a chance to prove that not every Faol would murder us in our sleep."

"And if you are wrong? If they turn on us?" her father dared to question.

Una's respect for her parent grew. It took great strength to stand up to Anya Gra, spiritual leader and one of the oldest among them.

"Then I will cast my fire and destroy their clans without mercy," the prince promised in a tone no one, not even her stalwart father, could deny.

Her father nodded, though he looked no happier at the assurance. "Aye, that's the right of it then."

Prince Eirik let his gaze encompass the whole of their community, his expression one of unequivocal certainty. "I will always protect my people to the best of my ability. Welcoming these honorable men is part of that."

Una noted how he continued to push forth the message that these wolves were good men, *trustworthy* and *honorable*.

He was her prince and she should believe him.

But she couldn't.

She knew the truth. Not that she hated all wolves. That would make her like the Faol who had taken her and done the horrible things they had done with every intention of killing her in the end, as they would kill any Éan they came across.

No, she would not share the unreasoning prejudices of her enemy and hate an entire race, making no distinctions between individuals.

But she could not trust them either.